Praise for the Novels of Don Callander . . .

"The sorcerer's animated kitchen is a delight, as is his brassy bronze owl . . . [illegible] es here."

[illegible] ny

"Amusing . . . deligh[illegible]

[illegible] us

"Readers who have followed the Fire Adept's progress . . . will welcome familiar characters and cozy settings in the latest entry in this light fantasy series for fans of all ages."

—*Booklist*

"Charming! A fantasy quest with aspects of a fairy tale . . . thoroughly engaging."

—*New York Times*

Don't miss any of the "*Mancer*" novels . . .

Pyromancer
Aquamancer
Geomancer
Aeromancer

Ace Books by Don Callander

DRAGON COMPANION
DRAGON RESCUE
PYROMANCER
AQUAMANCER
GEOMANCER
AEROMANCER
MARBLEHEART

MARBLEHEART

DON CALLANDER

ACE BOOKS, NEW YORK

This book is an Ace original edition,
and has never been previously published.

MARBLEHEART

An Ace Book / published by arrangement with
the author

PRINTING HISTORY
Ace edition / July 1998

The Penguin Putnam Inc. World Wide Web site address is
http://www.penguinputnam.com

Check out the Ace Science Fiction/Fantasy newsletter, and much more,
at Club PPI!

ISBN: 0-441-00538-1

ACE®
Ace Books are published by The Berkley Publishing Group,
a member of Penguin Putnam Inc.,
200 Madison Avenue, New York, NY 10016.
ACE and the "A" design are trademarks
belonging to Charter Communications, Inc.

PRINTED IN THE UNITED STATES OF AMERICA

10 9 8 7 6 5 4 3 2 1

I've still got a whole bunch of very nice people to whom I'd like to dedicate a book, but it's time to say thank you and farewell (for a while, at least) to my very favorite editor, Miss Laura Anne Gilman, formerly of Ace Science Fiction and Fantasy.
She always said Marbleheart was her most favorite character so this, his very own Adventure, is for Laura!
May our paths cross again and again!

Don Callander
Longwood, Florida

MARBLEHEART

Chapter One

Peaceable Valley

THE rushing, springtime-cold waters of Crooked Brook (long ago named, by the people of Faerie, *Koro-Khed*, which means "Enchanted Stream") closed over the Sea Otter's sleek form as he dove, strongly swimming, to the bottom just above Old Plank Bridge, scattering a school of startled troutlings before him.

Marbleheart's dark-furred body measured just under six feet long, from white-tipped whiskers to powerful tail. He was the largest son of a family of Sea Otters, born on far-distant Briny Deep in the cold, cloudy, windy, snowy northwest.

Once he'd been wild and completely free! Ranged down The Broad, along the desolate, sandy dunes of Old Kingdom's east coastline, then far south to the low bluffs of Choin, and up to busy Farango Water.

He'd led the exciting, independent life of a young Sea Otter.

Well, it hadn't been a boring life after he'd met Douglas Brightglade, either, the Otter admitted to himself, twisting and turning in the clear water.

He'd lived through a terrific volcanic eruption, enjoyed the excitement of howling gales in mid-Sea, flown magically eastward and westward, north and south. Even burrowed under the vast sheet of Perpetual Ice . . . and along the way had found his calling.

Douglas Brightglade, the younger Pyromancer of Wizards' High on the north bank of Crooked Brook, had asked him to be his Familiar!

His life had, for a while, been a matter of dashing off to rescue this fair maiden or assist that embattled Wizard. Fighting nasty witches at Coven. Setting a new Emperor on the Dragon Throne of Choin.

Those were the days!

An exciting life . . . but not so very exciting recently.

Now the furry Familiar's time was filled with serious study, with careful reading of ancient, musty, dusty books, of sneezing from fumes of bubbling retorts, peering through murky magnifying glasses, conjuring up columns of acrid smoke, and enduring endless discussions of wizardly Ways and Means.

"All *very* important and *very* useful and all that, I admit to you," Marbleheart said to a largemouth bass who came swimming by on his way to the reed beds below Augurian's Fountain.

"What's the matter with you?" snapped the startled bass, watching the Otter warily from a safe distance. "You eat regularly, don't you? No having to hunt for your supper in ice-cold water!"

Everyone in Crooked Brook knew of the Otter's appetite for fresh fish.

"Yes . . . and *that's* what's the matter!" snorted Marbleheart.

He pushed up with his hind feet and broke the surface under loose-planked Old Bridge, which connected Priceless's apple, peach, and pear orchards on the south bank with the wide, rolling, front lawn of Wizards' High on the north.

"I'm being *quite* unfair, of course," the Otter muttered unhappily to himself.

He dove again to examine the bed of freshwater oysters he'd planted in the cool, shaded water under the rickety bridge. His bivalve colony was doing extremely well. Promised a good feast or three, someday soon. Maybe some of those interesting shiny, pink, convoluted freshwater pearls Myrn had told him about.

He surfaced again, pulled himself up onto the sun-warmed planks of the bridge, and lay there on his tummy, fluffing his thick, dark brown fur. Drying Spells were all very well for emergencies, he considered, but sun was best for grooming his luxurious coat, after all.

"Peaceful!" he said aloud. "Nothing much doing, unless one is a Wizard with spells to cast and puzzles to solve in a dim workshop under a tall hill. I'll go check on Douglas. Maybe he needs some help. Or maybe not. There's always lunch!"

He glanced up at the sun in the cloudless sky, confirming the time nicely.

"Yes! Lunchtime!" He chuckled enthusiastically, forgetting his momentary gloom. "Wonder what old Blue Teakettle's whipped up for us this noontime?"

Blue Teakettle, who ran the Wizards' kitchen with easy and expert grace, with a pert tilt to her spout and a whistle of scalding steam, when necessary, was burbling crossly at the new Crystal Bowl, a wedding gift to Douglas and Myrn from Prince Bryarmote and his pretty Dwarf-wife, some years before.

"No, no, *no!*" Blue rumbled. "*Blue cheese* dressing! That's what the Masters like best with romaine, curly endive, and new cucumbers! You should remember that for yourself! Do I have to think of *everything*?"

Young Crystal Bowl groaned, rolled from side to side, and made a dull *clunking* sound to show how sorry she was she'd forgotten the dressing until so late.

"Well, there's still time to whip it up . . . just barely," clucked Blue Teakettle, relenting a bit. "I've got too much else to do to worry about dressing, young miss!"

She signaled Sugar Caster to begin setting the huge kitchen table. Toaster, who usually only worked hard at breakfast time, could be trusted to help Caster set things straight and place the polished Silverware correctly, Forks on the left, Knives and Spoons to the right, despite the boisterous antics of the troop of Soup Spoons on such a lovely, early spring day.

"Let me see," murmured Blue, counting the place settings. "Master Flarman, Mistress Myrn, Master Douglas, and the dear little twins, the Sea Otter, of course . . . and the cats. That's all for today, Master Caster! Augurian's off to his Warm Sea island and Mistress Lithold's returned to her Serecomba Desert for a month or two. Just the immediate family. Here! Otter!"

She'd caught sight of Marbleheart, who just then poked his nose and his curiosity through the open door from the courtyard between the kitchen and the Wizards' underhill workshop.

"Be a good sort and call the family to lunch, Sea Otter, my pet, please!" Teakettle bubbled.

Marbleheart was her very greatest personal favorite. Whatever the High's kitchen cooked, baked, fried, stewed, broiled, boiled, barbecued, sautéed, creamed, toasted, whipped, or otherwise prepared and served, cold or hot, Marbleheart consumed with invariable gusto and gratitude.

"Done!" Marbleheart grinned back at her. "Back in three minutes! Is that country ham with red-eye gravy I smell? *Ah!* Make that *two* minutes!"

Blue Teakettle had no sooner turned back to tell Oven to turn out three panfuls of hot, savory corn fritters into the pair of wicker Breadbaskets waiting patiently on the sideboard, when the Wizards' family and staff began to arrive from the washstand in the courtyard, laughing and licking their lips, and calling for those behind them to hurry or miss the best things to eat.

Lunch at the High was ever a pleasant time for reporting progress and reviewing everyone's activities and chores, through and in between courses from the spring salad at the beginning to the four-layer chocolate cake for dessert.

"Confusion is what it is, really," said Marbleheart happily to no one in particular.

"Confused? Not at all!" hooted Bronze Owl, who didn't eat, being entirely made of cast and highly polished purest bronze. He came to meals to enjoy the conversation. "Very clear! Don't you agree, my dear? All we birds, other than certain stay-near-home types, fly south to warmer climes in fall, and back north again . . ."

"Speaking of clear," interrupted Flarman Flowerstalk around a mouthful of peppery-garlicky sausage. As a Fire Adept, he was particularly fond of hot pastrami.

"Don't *slurp* your soup, please, Brand!" Myrn admonished her young son. "Why, what would Grandmama Brightglade say, could she hear it?"

"It's *hot*, Mama!" protested the little boy, waving his hand over the bowl, encouraging the steam to form fragrant swirls in the air.

"It'll cool shortly," his father told him, trying to sound very stern. "Be patient and don't play with your food, child!"

Marbleheart chuckled gleefully at the pretty pink-steam cloudlets, which didn't help parental authority much. Douglas gave his Familiar a reproving frown which insisted on becoming, at once, a fond grin.

"What were you saying about the weather?" Bronze Owl asked the elder Fire Wizard.

"Weather? Nothing that I recall," sputtered Flarman, finding the soup too hot, even for himself. "Weather?"

"You said . . ." Owl began to explain.

"Oh, about '*clear*'!" laughed Flarman, recalling the interruption that had been interrupted. "I said . . . '*Speaking of clear*'!"

He drew from his wide left sleeve a disk of clear, bluish glass . . . or what *seemed* to be glass . . . about three inches across and thicker in the middle than around the edges.

"A lens," Douglas said with a quick nod. "I've seen 'em in telescopes and such. Was it Lithold who had one? No, Cribblon it was who made a telescope . . . to see distant things."

"I use them at times, myself," agreed the older Pyromancer. "If you focus the sun's rays, you can start a fire quite handily, even without spelling."

"I know that!" cried seven-year-old Brenda brightly. "Marbleheart showed us!"

"I hope you're careful about fire-making, Marblehead, darling," cautioned Myrn, shaking her right index finger. "The children are a bit young, yet, to handle wild-fires."

"I am *always* careful of fire," Otter insisted.

"He made a campfire with a burning-glass and we cooked some mallmarshows," Myrn's daughter crowed. "Hot and brown and *very* sticky!"

"*Marshmallows*, silly girl!" her twin brother corrected. "*Yum!*"

Brenda made a face at him, but Brand pretended not to notice.

"Look more carefully," Flarman was saying to Douglas, ignoring the chatter.

He handed the lens to his young colleague.

Douglas squinted through the blue-tinted lens, moved it forward and backward a few times, bringing a slice of tomato clearly into focus.

Myrn leaned over to look.

"Perfectly ordinary convex lens," Douglas pronounced. "Useful for other things, too. I was thinking of building a telescope, myself. I'd like to study the stars this summertime on nights good for stargazing."

"Not my point at all!" snorted the older Wizard, reaching over to point a stubby forefinger at the lens in Douglas's hand. "Do you notice this?"

"An inscription, I guess," Douglas agreed. "But what does it say?"

"I was hoping you'd recognize the lettering," the older Fire Wizard told him. "Or Myrn? I can't figure them out, to tell you the truth."

Myrn and Douglas carefully studied the faint letters etched around the edge of the glass.

"Looks like Old Elvin Script," Myrn said, finally. "You read Elvin better than I do, Douglas."

"I thought *I* knew Old Elvin pretty well," Flarman told them, shaking his head, "but it might as well be Catscratch or Birdswarble or even Low Trollish, for all of me!"

"No, not any of those," Douglas insisted, handing the lens back to the older Wizard. "I'm sorry, Magister. Can't help you, off the top of my head. What is it?"

"Ah! At last you think to ask! It was sent to us by Chief Tet. One of his Highlandormers discovered it last year in a trash heap left by Eunicet's Army inside the Outer Ring of Highlandorm."

"Goodness! That was *years* back!" exclaimed Marbleheart.

"Ten years now, yes . . . but this thing, this lens, lay forgotten until last winter. The soldier brought it to Tet."

"Ah! Mystery!" cried Marbleheart, hitching forward eagerly. "Love a mystery!"

"There's more," Flarman declared. "The soldier tried to use it to start a fire one cold day while he was on duty. His sulfur matches had got wet, it seems. The glass focused the sunlight, as usual, but refused to raise even a single whiff of smoke, let alone start a flame!"

"I would think," Douglas said thoughtfully, "if the lens magnifies an image, it would also work as a burning-glass. The things go together. Usually!"

"*Usually!*" Flarman agreed. "But it's true! Take it out in the courtyard, m'boy. The sunlight focuses well enough, but it never gets hot enough to start a fire. Not a whiff of smoke!''

While the others finished their raspberries and cream, Douglas and Marbleheart went out into the courtyard. The early afternoon sun was bright and hot on the cobbles.

First Douglas and then his Familiar tried to burn a hole in a dried bit of oak leaf, but neither could manage to raise even a single, thin tendril of smoke.

''Something's not right here,'' muttered Marbleheart. ''It should work easily! I've done this sort of burning-glass thing dozens of times, myself, and seen others do it, hundreds.''

''As have I,'' agreed his young Master. ''Most strange!''

''Suppose we could read the inscription,'' the Sea Otter said, handing the lens back to Douglas. ''Might that tell us why it won't work?''

''Maybe. Give it a try this afternoon, shall we? See if we can figure out what it says.''

''I'll come along and help,'' Otter agreed. ''Nothing much else to do. A bit of mystery is always good to sink sharp Otter's teeth into, I says.''

They went back into the kitchen, where the noontime meal was over and the table was being cleared with a pleasant rattle-and-clink of Serving Dishes, Platters, Plates, Cups, Saucers, Glasses, Cutlery, Bowls, and assorted Pots, Pans, and Skillets, all lining up to get a hot, soapy splash and a thorough scrub in the sink.

Blue Teakettle supervised with a strict eye to good order and sanitation.

''Behind the ears! Behind the ears!'' she hissed to the rather thick ceramic Coffee Cups. ''Do it properly or do it over, you mugs!''

Myrn, on her way out with her children, stopped to give her husband a quick kiss.

''We're going up for quiet time.''

''Me, too!'' yawned Flarman. ''I was up and doing well before dawn!''

"Marbleheart and I'll look into your mysterious lens," Douglas told him, shooing his son and daughter after their mother.

"I'll look in on you later," Myrn promised as she followed their twins up the curving staircase.

"Me, too!" Flarman yawned again. "Sorry! I spent the whole morning trying to read that dratted inscription. Got nowhere at all."

"What did you try?" Douglas called after him.

"Fire, ice, hot water, cold water, and hot and cold airs, and was about to try a touchstone, actually. Start there, m'boy. Touchstone might work."

And he yawned himself right up to his bedroom.

A quiet afternoon at Wizards' High.

Outside, the earliest of warm summertime breezes escorted fluffy, white clouds gently from the west, bringing with them the odors of fast-sprouting corn and wheat and, as well, the rich smells of moist earth in new-tilled gardens and plowed fields.

Wildflowers in the meadows added their sweet scents. Bees hummed about, busy and happy, gathering spring nectar and distributing grains of pollen everywhere they went.

Across Crooked Brook, Priceless braced a ladder on a gnarled limb of an ancient crabapple, climbed stiffly to the fourth rung, and began sawing carefully at a winter-killed branch.

A family of saucy blue jays watched, coaching his work with considerable chuckling. Priceless ignored them.

On the uplands to the north a shepherd whistled, signaling to his collie. The dog shot off at full tilt to turn a trio of silly yearling ewes away from a steep-sided gully. In their new freedom on the hillsides, the foolish sheep might misstep and plunge into the hidden depression.

The Valley collie, luxurious tan-and-white coat glistening in the sun, flew after the straying ewes, easily and yet gently turning them away from unseen danger. Rolling their eyes in mock terror, the ewes, sleek and clean from having just been shorn of their winter coats, dashed off in the opposite direction into a clump of fuzzy-shooted yew.

"Ewes in the yews," barked the dog to her master.

She sat on her haunches, lolled her pink tongue, and panted with satisfaction. Another important job perfectly done!

Three small Trunketytown boys had found seats on the grassy north bank of Crooked Brook near Stone Bridge. They dropped baited fishlines, tied to springy sapling poles, into the water, speaking softly so as not to startle the trout just visible under the ripples.

Wily Mama Trout glanced up at the water-distorted images of the fisherboys, chuckled to herself and, flicking to her sprats with her tail, waved them off to quiet, cool safety under the opposite bank.

Master Brand Brightglade lay on his back on his cot, staring at the ceiling, half asleep. Across the room his sister Brenda breathed evenly and quietly. Their mother nodded over a book in a sunny window seat.

A few rooms away Flarman Flowerstalk slept soundly, snoring gently. Party and Pert, the High's lady cats, lolled at the foot of his great bed. Their consort, Black Flame, was sitting in a rear window, tail curled about his feet, staring down intently into the courtyard below.

Marbleheart Sea Otter, bored and restless again despite an hour of complicated incantations and meticulous experiments, of holding this or that piece of gear for his Master's investigations, emerged from the Workshop and slumped down in a patch of shade beside the kitchen well.

"I shouldn't be bored," he muttered to himself, half crossly. "I'm helping Douglas do fascinating, mysterious, unusual, unexpected, strange, dangerous, vital, wonderful, special, magical tasks!"

He sighed, blew moodily at a red ant wandering across the level slate near the well, making it roll over completely twice and scramble for safety under a loose paving stone.

"... and boring!" Marbleheart admitted wryly. "I'm ashamed of myself!"

An errant breeze stirred a dust devil just beyond his nose. Marbleheart sat up quickly to avoid a face full of fine silt.

The miniature whirlwind paused, coruscated brightly in the sunlight, and began to take on a shape.

"*Harrumph!*" coughed the Sea Otter in surprise. "What ... ?"

The glittering column of sparkling dust, brighter than the sun for a moment, suddenly solidified into the shape of a very small boy and settled to the ground.

"It worked!" cried the arrival. "Hello, Marbleheart! I wasn't sure, but it *did* work, you see!"

Marbleheart tilted his head to the right for a better glimpse of the tiny youngster. Then he grinned and nodded with pleasure.

"Prince Flowerbender!" he exclaimed. "Welcome to Wizards' High, Sir Prince!"

"Call me Ben," requested the son of the beautiful Marget, Queen of Faerie, and her consort Prince Aedh. "I've run away from home!"

"Run ... ?" choked the Otter, quite startled. "For goodness's sake! Won't your folks worry about you, flashing about in a whirlwind? Why ... ?"

"No matter! It's full time I undertook a Quest to Prove Myself Worthy. Come of Age!" said the small Princeling solemnly, seating himself on the old oaken bucket which someone had turned on its top to dry.

He was tall for a fairy, fully twelve inches, toe to top-knot, with luxurious brownish-gold hair cut in a neat pageboy bob, and wide-set violet eyes ... a handsome youth by anyone's standards. He was still quite young as fairies go, for that merry folk are Near Immortals and live for centuries and centuries.

"Flarman Flowerstalk's taking an afternoon nap, young sir," Marbleheart told him, rather formally, for one met few

Faerie royalty face to face in everyday life. "My Master, Douglas Brightglade, is within. . . ." He nodded toward the open Workshop door.

"Well, I'd just as soon leave them be, for the while at least," Prince Flowerbender . . . Ben, that is . . . laughed. "Actually, friend Sea Otter, I came seeking *you*."

"Me?" Marbleheart was flattered in spite of himself. "Why me?"

"Something told me you might be . . . well, that you might welcome . . . *er* . . . that I might persuade you to go Questing with me. I need a companion, you see, and you . . ."

"Impossible!" cried Otter, pretending shock at the very idea. "I've *much* too much very important work to do! Douglas needs me! Myrn and the twins need me! The Ice King's enchantments and everything! Why . . . !"

"Oh, *pooh*!" sighed the fairy in disappointment, drumming his heels against the side of the wooden bucket. "I hoped that you . . . and I heard what you just said to yourself. 'Bored,' you said. I heard you!"

Marbleheart drew himself up, gathering a suitably firm but polite and tactful refusal. But one that would, in effect, leave the door open for negotiation.

" 'Tis bad luck to lie to a fairy! Especially a Prince of Faerie like me," the tiny Prince warned.

"Well . . ." the Otter sighed after a further moment's pause, "I admit to being . . . sort of . . . bored and suffering itchy footpads and . . ."

"Fine! I hereby appoint thee, Sir Marbleheart of Briny Deep, to be my boon companion in adventuring!"

The Prince leapt from the bucket bottom and landed lightly on the slate paving.

"So . . . let's be off!" he said in a businesslike tone. "You'll be my courser, too, as well as advisor and councilor and picnicking companion! You love to eat. I imagine you're a pretty good campfire cook, too?"

Before Marbleheart could protest or disagree or even twitch a whisker, the young Prince of Faerie bounded onto his back, wrapped legs firmly around his chest, and grasped a handful of the Otter's glossy fur at the base of his neck.

Chapter Two

Considering an Adventure

MARBLEHEART twisted his head full about to look the Prince of Faerie in the eye, ignoring Ben's digging heels and pressing knees.

"Now, my dear young sir! A moment, if you please!"

"We must away!" cried Ben. "Before someone comes looking for me. I mean, for us!"

"If you want me for advisor and all that other stuff," Marblehead said, "I must advise you as best I can, Prince Flowerbender! . . . and you must agree to listen, at least!"

"Ben!" insisted the boy. "Plain Ben, please. And I'm all ears."

"Then listen to my very best advice, plain Ben! Late afternoon is *not* a good time to set off on a Quest, if one can possibly avoid it. Believe me! I know about such things."

Ben considered his words. "What, then? And, more importantly, *when*?"

"When? If my nose tells me aright, Blue Teakettle's roasting a tender crown of beef for supper, and there'll be

14

. . . let's see . . . I smell blueberry pie and sourdough bread
with strawberry jam, and . . .''

"Supper would be welcome," admitted plain Ben.
"What else?"

"Oh, cold milk from the Ladies of the Byre, of course,
and sweet butter, and cream for our coffee. And tangy,
yellow, nibbling cheeses, too. I can smell 'em from here!"

"Right! We'll stay for supping and start Questing on the
morrow, then," Ben decided at once. "That way we'll each
have *two* good meals under our belts when we set out."

"Where do we plan to go, then?"

He led the fairy boy into the Workshop, for the sun on
the courtyard cobbles was quite warm, even this early in
the summer.

"I've heard the fantastic, fabulous stories of Douglas and
Myrn . . . and you, too . . . adventuring in Nearer East," the
lad chattered away happily. "I want to see the great crater
lake and the remains of the ancient warriors known as San-
drones. And I'd really love to meet First Citizen Serenit
and see his New Land and Eternal Ice . . . or what's left of
it! Did you know there're no fairies nor even pixies nor
any nixies nor any wee folk in New Land at all? It was
under a thousand feet of solid ice until a few years ago!"

Marbleheart plunked himself on a stool at the work-
bench. Ben flew onto the edge of another and sat dangling
his feet.

"Now . . . if you want to visit those places, you've come
to the right guide, at least," the Familiar admitted modestly.
"Been to them all! Know my way around! You've got 'em
backward, however. We should go to New Land first, as a
stop on our way. Nearer East is a long, long way beyond
that and Sea is pretty wide east and west, north and south.
We'll have to give some thought as to *how* we'll travel."

At Ben's surprised frown, Marbleheart stopped. He
peered at the boy closely.

"Not thought of the great distances, eh?"

"Not really, Marbleheart. But between us . . ."

"Lacking magical means," Marbleheart lectured, "it'd take weeks to get to New Land from here! At the very least! And *months* more to reach Samarca. Those're just problems Number One and Number Two, m'boy."

"Problems?" sighed the Prince, as if he'd never heard the word before.

"Well, consider . . . how will we get to our destinations? We have a choice: magic . . . or walking . . . or swimming! Have you brought any useful Faerie spells?"

"Well . . . er, rather . . . well, you see . . ."

"Just what magics *did* you bring with you, Princeling?"

"Ah, well, you see . . . I didn't think much would be necessary, Marbleheart."

"How did you arrive here, then? That whirlwind of sparkles and dust?"

"Oh, that was a Well-Wishing! You have to have a genuine Wishing Well for that. There's one in my mother's flower garden, at home."

"And you gave no thought to how you'd get back home, *afterwards*?"

"Oh, Douglas or Myrn or Flarman or Augurian . . . they're all powerful Wizards and can send me home in a wink, I'd think."

Marblehead stood and stretched.

"My first bit of good advice you might not like. Come into the kitchen and we'll consider our plight over a mug of milk and a piece of chocolate layer cake, if any's left over from lunch."

"No problem there!" cried the lad, jumping to the floor.

"And we'll have to take one or more of our resident Wizards into our confidence, of course," added the Otter.

Ben pulled a long face.

"I . . . I'm not sure about that."

"But unless we tell one of them of our plans, how will we get there and home again? Walk? Swim? You might fly, but Otters don't have wings!"

"I thought *you* would know," Ben said plaintively.

Marbleheart considered the situation in silence for a long moment.

"First lesson, Knight Errant! Learn to take good advice. Come on!"

And he led the way across to Blue Teakettle's kitchen, dim after the bright sun of the courtyard but redolent of roasting meat, baking bread and pie crust, with all sorts of wonderful Kitchen Utensils stirring things up for supper.

"You've grown since your folks brought you to visit last Winter Holiday," cried Flarman. "How *are* your parents, son? Well, I hope?"

"Well, and busy at ruling Faerie, Sir," replied Ben, setting down his mug and licking a mustache of milk from his upper lip. "Very busy!"

"I see," murmured Flarman, reaching for his pipe . . . which he found, at last, after checking in all his wide, deep pockets and then up his left sleeve.

He touched the tobacco tamped in its bowl with his right forefinger and puffed twice. The tobacco sprang aglow, fragrant smoke curling about them lazily in the afternoon light coming through the kitchen's high windows.

"Prince Flowerbender informs me," began the Otter, eyeing the elder Pyromancer carefully, "that he's decided to go Questing. Part of his education. He wishes to visit New Land, and perhaps Nearer East."

"And your mother?" Flarman asked calmly, smiling at the boy. "What was her advice?"

"Well, Sir Wizard . . . you see, Flarman . . . Anyway . . ." Ben sputtered despite himself.

"Now, now, laddy—don't get all flustered," advised Bronze Owl, perched on the back of Flarman's chair. "Queen Marget's a sensible sort, to say the very least, and I'm sure . . ."

"Silence, metallic absurdity!" Flarman muttered to the bronze bird out of the side of his mouth. "Let *me* handle this!"

Bronze Owl tried to look as if he'd never uttered a word.

"Youngster," resumed Flarman, "tell me truly, please. You left home asking of your mother and father neither permission nor advice, did you not?"

"Yes sir! I'm sorry, but it's true."

"Did you fear they'd forbid your Questing, if you'd asked?"

"Well, I thought . . ." muttered Ben, blushing and fluttering his bluish gossamer wings in an agitated fashion.

"I suspect, if you *had* bothered to ask," clucked Flarman, relighting his pipe, which had already gone out, "knowing Marget quite well as I do, she'd have had not a single objection."

"Well . . . maybe not, Wizard . . ."

"Call me Flarman, m'boy," the Wizard insisted. "I'm not blaming you nor claiming you've done wrong. Not as thoughtful, shall we say, as you *might* have been. Did you leave home in anger, by the bye?"

"No! No, I just . . . decided it was high time to go a-Questing. I thought, well, 'You're not getting any younger, Flowerbender!' That's what I thought to myself, Flarman, sir."

"And you may be right at that!" Flarman nodded. "A Prince of Faerie needs plenty of experience in World against the day his Queen Mother decides he should rule in her stead."

"I read . . ." began Ben earnestly.

Just then Myrn and her twins came to see if afternoon tea was ready, and Douglas burst excitedly through the kitchen door, holding the mysterious lens wrapped in a soft cloth.

"We'll speak of this later," Flarman said quickly to the little Prince. "Let's have a spot of tea, first."

"Well, I've *sort of* figured out the legend on the lens, at any rate," Douglas told Flarman.

They sat around one end of the vast kitchen table, sipping fragrant, reviving, green tea shipped in chests from distant Choin, and nibbling coconut macaroons and powdered-sugar-dusted date bars.

"Tell us what we're talking about, my dear," Myrn demanded. "Now, young lady! Sit up straight and lay your napkin across your lap, please. See? Prince Flowerbender does it just right!"

"But, Mama!" the little girl objected, wide-eyed and innocently. "He's much *older* than me!"

"Older than *I*, you should say," Myrn corrected her, trying to be severe . . . but her ready smile rippled through. "Actually, Ben's just a *little* bit older than you, as I recall. Fairy children mature quicker than us humans."

"I used Lithold's touchstone, as you suggested, and it worked . . . after a fashion," Douglas was saying. "It's definitely connected with one of Frigeon's spells, I'm certain."

Years before, a battle-wracked Air Wizard named Frigeon had sought to conquer World following the terrible Last Battle in Old Kingdom, in which neither side really won nor lost, so both sides had gone into hiding.

Frigeon, the self-styled Ice King, an Aeromancer by training, had spun out dozens and dozens of obscure, highly complicated enchantments, enthralling helpless Men and innocent Near Immortals to further his selfish ends . . . or, Douglas had often thought, to ease his own terrible fears.

When Frigeon was finally defeated by the Companions of Light at the Battle of Sea and his selfish plans were finally foiled, his better nature, his conscience, had been restored. Flarman and Augurian of Waterand Isle, Douglas, and Myrn had set themselves the time-consuming task of rescuing the hapless victims of Frigeon's terror.

The newly discovered lens must be a clue to another of Frigeon's forgotten, foul deeds, Douglas guessed.

"What does it say then?" asked Marbleheart.

"Near as I can make out, it says something like this:

"Look closely from afar, over the left shoulder of the south wind, in the darkest part of full day, to find a Princess-daughter seeking her King-father's Crown."

"Congratulations, m'boy!" murmured the older Fire Wizard dryly. "You've managed to reduce an enigma to a riddle."

"It needs some work, I admit," Douglas sighed. "But it's a start!"

"And starts are very important. Our young guest from Faerie will agree. Starting must be made with care as well as dare." Flarman winked at Ben. "Best advice in both cases is to proceed with due thought."

"If you mean I went off Questing without giving it enough thought or plan, I have to agree with you, Flarman," said the lad from Faerie. "But . . . what's to be done?"

"First, relieve your good mother's worries and quiet your father's qualms," Flarman advised.

"I suppose so," Ben sighed.

"Having settled that, we'll send you Questing with at least a modicum of planning and some due thinking," continued the elder Pyromancer. "With a reliable guide."

"If you could and would, Magister!" cried Ben, adopting Douglas's favorite term of respect to the older Wizard.

"Give me your permission to discuss your Questing with your father and mother," Douglas suggested. "And I believe we can work out your first problem satisfactorily."

"But you're busy with this lens thing," protested the Prince. "You grown-ups . . . you're always *all* so importantly busy!"

"Never too busy to help a young man run away from home," declared Flarman, patting the tiny boy on the back. "But it must wait 'til after supper, I think."

"I should have word for you from home later tonight," Douglas promised.

"Another long evening of spell-casting and stirring up

secret fires," sighed Myrn. "Well, that's the lot of a Fire Wizard's wife, I suppose."

"You can help me greatly, sweetheart," Douglas said, leaning over to touch her hand. "It'll make the time fly faster, too."

"Was hoping you'd ask!" Myrn returned his smile. "But first, as Flarman says, there's dinner and before that there's baths for certain children . . . *and* for their parents. My husband looks like he's spent the afternoon rolling in coal dust! Come away, Brand! Brenda!"

"Can we sit at table tonight, then?" asked her daughter eagerly. "We're big enough now!"

The twins were fascinated by the Faerie Prince. They'd heard of and even met many such creatures many times before, but never had they met one so young, so perfectly small, nor up so close.

"I'll come along and we'll talk while you bathe and dress," Ben offered. "I can use a bath, myself, Mistress. If I may?"

"Of course!" cried Myrn. "In fact, I've a far better idea . . . let's all take a swim down at Augurian's Fountain! We'll be clean and cool, and sharpen our appetites for Blue Teakettle's roast."

Brenda jumped from her chair and ran to hug Marbleheart.

"You said you'd teach us the Otter Crawl!"

Marbleheart pretended to groan in protest.

"*Oh, me!* So be it! A promise is a promise! Both of you, and young Ben also, if he wishes. Handy stroke, the Crawl. Paw over paw, kicking straight back! Of course, it helps to have strong, webbed toes and a long, powerful tail to steer with."

The youngsters ran off to find their bathing suits while the two Pyromancers, the Familiars, and Bronze Owl sat and talked at the table a while longer.

"You think Marget will agree to the lad's going off on his own?" Douglas asked his Master.

"She must, eventually. The lad'll have an experienced Familiar with him, of course. Marbleheart's a clown at times, but he's nobody's fool. And Ben's a bright, intelligent youth . . . reminds me of an Apprentice I once knew," Flarman replied with a grin.

"Can't imagine who he's talking about," Marbleheart whispered to his good friend Black Flame.

Flarman's Familiar, who could never understand Otters' and people's perverse desire to completely and willingly submerge themselves in water, hot or cold, shook his head and went off to speak sternly to the Thatchmouse parents about their youngest male mouse-child, who was getting bolder and bolder at raiding the pantry.

Black Flame explained to Mama Thatchmouse that the High had plenty of food for all, but some of the things in the pantry would do the tiny child's tummy no good.

"I've sired simply basketfuls of kittens, myself," he told her earnestly, "so you can believe me when I say a parent must be watchful."

The Otter grinned when Black Flame returned.

"Well done, old Flame! You've helped avoid a tiny tummyache or three, I guess. As for your very good friend Sea Otter, I seem to have been temporarily adopted by this young Prince. I think I'll go see if he's yet learned to swim."

Chapter Three

Wayfarers

AFTER an hour's crystal-assisted conversation with Marget and Aedh in distant Faerie, Douglas went to find his Familiar. Otter was draped loosely on the stone wall at the lower end of the wide lawn, watching a company of Fireflies across the water weave intricate geometric patterns of greenish light under Priceless's apple trees.

"A word with you, old Marblehead?" Douglas asked.

Marbleheart waved a paw for him to be seated on the wall beside him, and for several minutes the friends silently watched the dance.

"You've spoken to Prince Aedh and his Queen-wife?" Otter asked at last.

"At some length, yes," Douglas said with a nod. "Aedh and Marget agree the boy should go Questing, even though the boy's yet quite young as fairies go. They're grateful to you for agreeing to be his companion."

"I never doubted it would be my pleasure, but it's a relief to hear they agree, anyway."

"There're a few points," Douglas added. "If you'd care to hear . . ."

"All ears," said the Sea Otter, flicking his left ear with a left afterclaw.

"You know how to call Deka the Wraith?"

"As well as I know my name . . . my name and a few other things," Otter assured him cheerily.

"Don't hesitate to call, if you two get into trouble too deep to handle. We depend on you for that."

"You have my most solemn assurance."

"You already know lots of useful little spells for making tents and blankets and campfires and things, I know."

"*Very* well, having learned 'em from an expert young Fire Wizard!"

"You recall Flarman's *First Rule of Traveling*?"

" 'Keep your socks dry!' . . . or, lacking socks, keep your feet clean and warm,' " the Otter recited. "I remember his very best, finest Warming Spell, too, although I haven't used it much these past two-three years."

"Good! My talk with Aedh and Marget? 'Twas most . . . well, *instructive*. Their Prince is the darling of the Faerie Court. Everyone absolutely dotes on little Ben! Wait on him hand, wing, and foot since he's been old enough to voice desire or make demand. His parents fear their little boy's rather self-centered. Precious little occasion to give serious thought for others."

"In the words of my own dear mother," Marbleheart observed dryly, "the kit's spoiled rotten, hey?"

"You've got it! I agreed to do without your tremendously valuable assistance for a while, Marbleheart, as I realize that an experienced Wizard's Familiar will be of greater use to the lad than if I or some other traveled with him on this first Questing. But you must be ever careful! He won't learn nor earn things if you do everything *for* him!"

"He needs," Marbleheart considered with a nod, "to learn the hard way . . . but not so much as to bring harm to himself . . . or to me."

"Or to his parents or anyone else. Marget reminds you

that a fairy child has tremendous potential for magic power.
He has to learn control!''

''I understand,'' said the Otter seriously, drawing himself
fully erect. ''Trust me!''

''Well, that I really do.'' Douglas laughed fondly, ruf-
fling the soft, thick fur between the Otter's shoulders.
''With all my heart!''

Marbleheart squirmed delightedly under his Master's
strong fingers and at his warm words, then rolled on his
back so Douglas could scratch his chest and tummy, too.

''Right now,'' continued Douglas, ''it's time we both got
to bed! You tell Ben of his parents' permission and their
trust. When will you leave?''

''Before the sun clears First Ridge tomorrow morning,''
cried Marbleheart at once. ''I'll say good-bye to you now,
for that matter.''

''Good-bye and best fortune, good old Familiar!'' murmured the Pyromancer. ''Now, get thee to bed!''

When the coming sun was just beginning to warm the
eastern sky from ebony to a soft slate-grey, Marbleheart
entered the Fairy Prince's room and tugged urgently at his
right ankle until the boy rolled over and opened his eyes,
blinking in the dim light of the Otter's candle.

''Time to go Questing, Knight Errant!'' whispered the
Sea Otter, softly. ''How soon can you be up and washed,
dressed for long, hard travel?''

''Ten minutes,'' Ben mumbled. ''What's for breakfast?''

''Not your problem, m'boy! Whatever 'tis, will get cold
as icicles if you take more than ten minutes.''

The Otter *gallumped* down the rear stair to the dimly
lighted kitchen where he found pancake batter ready and
waiting in Stoneware Bowl, and milk from the springhouse
already in Pitcher, still foaming from being poured.

''The lad'll be here in eight minutes,'' the Otter reported
to Blue Teakettle. ''You can start flapping those jacks any
time now.''

Blue dipped her spout in agreement and bustled about getting breakfast on the table with a minimum of rattle and fuss. In five and a half minutes the boy rumbled down the back stairs . . . no mean feat for a lad only a foot and a half tall . . . buttoning his tunic and yawning as widely as his mouth could gape.

"Promptness . . ." began Otter.

". . . is the Courtesy of Kings!" Ben finished, grinning broadly. "My father's favorite saying."

He hopped into his chair and, after waiting for the Otter to climb into his own place, began quite graciously to serve fluffy pancakes, offering his companion Syrup Pitcher and Butter Crock before he accepted generous servings of both for himself.

"Coffee, tea, or milk?" sang out a trio of Little Pitchers with big ears at his left elbow.

"Milk, if you please!" Ben replied. "Is that raspberry preserve? My very favorite! Marmalade, Marbleheart?"

With such polite small talk the two devoured a surprisingly large number of pancakes and drank nearly the full pitcher of milk between them, consuming several rashers of crisp bacon and a link or two of spicy breakfast sausage with sunny-side-up eggs.

The rest of the kitchen staff began stirring in the cupboards, drawers, bins, and cabinets, hopping or sliding or climbing or flying forth to find their places while the various Utensils prepared the family's breakfast with much good cheer and playful clatter.

"We won't wait for the others," Marbleheart said, forking the final bite of his fifteenth pancake into his mouth. He paused to lick the last of the maple syrup from his long whiskers and forepaws. "Good-byes take such a lot of time, you know."

"Let's be on our way!" agreed the Prince, carefully folding his napkin and waving his thanks to the busy kitchenware. Blue Teakettle stood by with a packet of rosy roast beef sandwiches with mustard and mayonnaise, two ripe, red tomatoes, and a paper spill of ginger snaps with tiny currants arranged on top to spell out sentiments such as 'Fare Well!' and 'Good Luck' and 'Watch Your Step!'

They walked down the silent center hallway and out the wide-open front door into the fresh summer morning. Bronze Owl seemed to be dozing . . . of course, he never *really* slept . . . on his usual nail.

"On your way, then?" he asked, snapping his eyes open with a metallic *click*. "Have a good Questioning, Sea Otter and Prince of Faerie!"

"*Questing*," the Prince corrected. "Thank you, Owl! Wish you could go with us!"

"Well, but I have my own work," sighed the metal bird. "You're in good company, as 'tis . . . if the sea mammal doesn't eat you out of everything the very first day."

The Otter and the Prince walked down the curving front walk, let themselves through the rusty iron gate in the low wall, crossed the brook by Old Plank Bridge . . . pausing while Marbleheart pointed out his freshwater oyster bed . . . and turned west toward Trunkety.

"I thought we were going north and east," Ben objected.

"We are! We are! But think for a moment, m'lad. We need camping equipment, and travel food, too. We can most easily get those at Dicksey's General Store in town. We'll need a sack of flour, a tin bucket of lard, a sugarloaf or two, salt for savoring, and a couple of new linen handkerchiefs . . . you didn't bring any of those with you, did you?"

"Never thought I'd need to blow my nose," Ben laughed aloud.

"Noses aside, we'll use handkerchiefs as tents."

"Ah. I see! I remember hearing of that Wizard's trick! Clever," exclaimed the boy. "Will you teach me how to do it?"

Talking thus they followed River Road west, side by side.

"Let me ask, if you won't be insulted," Marbleheart said before they had gone far. "Last time I met your folks, they were both as tall as Douglas—taller than Flarman. You're a fifth of that size, at best. What *is* your normal altitude?"

"Oh, just about any convenient size. Papa says he once made himself a giant, fifty feet tall! I'd like to've seen that."

"So would I! So, you can pick your favorite size, can you?" Marbleheart asked, truly interested.

"All fairies can do that! What size would *you* prefer?"

"We've a longish way to tramp, m'boy. Longer legs and more stomach-room'll get you further at regular boy-size, don't you think?"

"I was, actually," Ben said wistfully, "planning to ride Otter-back."

"*Ho!* Make your very best friend do all the walking and carrying . . . is that it? Let me tell you, young Flowerbender, Questing has to be a cooperative enterprise, each for the other, and one for all!"

As he told Ben of his first meeting with Douglas Brightglade on the reedy, sandy shore of Old Kingdom, the fairy boy grew to something just under five feet tall.

"We'll spend tonight most comfortably in Perthside with Douglas's mother and father. A gracious lady and a worthy craftsman. You'll love 'em!"

"And *then* we'll go east?"

Marbleheart nodded.

"By going southwest first and then east and *then* north. If we're lucky, there'll be a swift schooner or beamy brigantine ready to sail eastward from Farango Water, ready to take passengers to New Land, at least. If not . . . we must wait . . . or walk!"

"My dear Sea Otter," said Ben, half pretending to be haughty, "a Prince of Faerie *never* walks anywhere! Besides, I can fly! Why have pretty blue wings if you must *walk* everywhere?"

Marbleheart laughed and snorted together, then sneezed.

"We Sea Otters prefer to walk on dry land! Valley raises some of the best riding horses in World, and good old Squire Frenstil keeps a full stable of the very best. But, m'boy, horses are notoriously poor sailors, and we'll shortly be going across a great deal of salt water. All in all, an easier and quicker way is to walk, at least today and maybe tomorrow, and sail after that."

"We walk south and west to gain headway sailing east and north?"

"Exactly!" Marbleheart agreed. "*Lesson Number Two of Questing* for a Faerie Prince: Please note carefully. To go *one* way, it's sometimes necessary to go in the *opposite* direction, if for just a while."

Ben pondered this strange advice in silence until they came to Trunkety Stone Bridge and recrossed wide Crooked Brook into the outskirts of the largest . . . and only . . . town in all of Valley.

"How will we pay?" Ben asked the Otter in a loud whisper.

They'd picked out a waterproof packet of scratch-anywhere sulfur matches (handy to have, as Fire Spells are sometimes unreliable for fingerless Familiars, Marbleheart explained), a small sack of the best wheat flour, another of rolled oats, sugarloaves of a handy size for carrying, salted butter sealed in a tough stone crock, tins of evaporated milk (milk would be scarce once they passed beyond New Land, Marbleheart advised), salt and pepper in shakers with close-fitted tops against wetting or spilling, and various items of utility such as a cast-iron skillet and a smallish stew pot with a lid and three short legs, the better to stand firm over an open fire.

"You've no cash?" cried Marbleheart in surprise.

"A Prince never carries cash," Ben replied. "Never needs it! I ask, and whatever I ask for is given to me by someone."

"Well, *someone's* not around just now! We'll have to

trade for our grub. Those nice glass things on your shoe buckles, perhaps? They should bring us some useful change.''

"Glass? Those are genuine sapphires!'' Ben objected, looking in dismay at his shoes. "My mother had them cut just for me by the best gem-polishing Dwarfs!''

"Off with 'em, or go hungry! We'll get you a pair of good, tough, comfortable Valley-cobbled walking boots, instead. Diamonds and sapphires are pretty and sometimes even useful, but good boots are much more valuable when you need to go any distance afoot.''

Storekeeper Dicksey, who'd been hiding broad grins as he listened to the Sea Otter and his young protégé, gathered their purchases and piled them on the counter. He took a new piece of chalk and added the prices on the slate countertop beside the great red-and-gold coffee grinder.

"Will that be all, good sirs?'' he inquired solemnly.

"I can think of several dozen other things that would be *nice* to have,'' replied Marbleheart quickly, before the boy, who was eyeing a countertop jar of pink and white peppermint candies, could answer, "but as my young friend here . . . his name is Ben, by the way . . . will have to carry it all on his back, I think we shall have to get by with just these.''

"You'll need a good, sturdy backpack if you carry this much,'' Dicksey considered. He pointed. "There's my best . . . medium-weight Westongue sea-isle-cotton canvas, tough and tight as oak staves, with sturdy brass rivets that won't rust, ever, and good leather facings where wear or tear be most likely.''

"Just what the boy needs,'' agreed Marbleheart.

"Must *I* carry it all?'' whispered Ben to his friend as Dicksey went to fetch a pack from a shelf. "You're big as me and probably stronger, too!''

"Good point!'' said the Otter cheerfully. "If you can design a pack to stay on a Sea Otter's sleek shoulders, I'll be glad to carry half.''

Ben studied the backpack when it was brought but could see at once that it would not easily stay on the otter's back for very long.

"Now, if we move this strap and that buckle," he said to Dicksey, "it should stay very well on Marbleheart's back . . ."

"Need some reworking," the storekeeper agreed. "I see what you mean, of course. There's a very good cobbler Elf down the road a way. Name of Tappet. He can make the alterations to suit."

"Maybe that would be a good idea," Ben said to Marbleheart. "Buy a pack for you; get it altered. We've the cash to pay for it, now."

"Good idea, Princeling!" Marbleheart said. "Tell me, Dicksey . . . how long d'you think it'll take the Elf to re-stitch a pack to order?"

Dicksey estimated, "No more'n a day and then some."

"*That* long!" cried Ben, aghast at the slow pace of good craftsmanship.

"If not longer," added the storekeeper. "Old Tappet is very good, very careful, very busy . . . and won't be hurried, I'm afraid."

Ben thought about the matter while Marbleheart haggled with Dicksey over the value of the two large sapphires from the boy's silver shoe buckles.

"We'll throw in the pumps themselves," the Otter added. "Marvelously comfortable Elf-tanned mouse-hide leather, you'll notice. Fit any size."

Dicksey nodded in agreement and began counting out Dukedom silver *marks* and copper *pennies* in change.

"*I'll* carry the pack," Ben decided at last. "We want to be on our way today. You lead the way and watch out for dangers. I'll follow and tote."

"I knew you'd see reason . . . the reason why we should forgo an Otter backpack." Marbleheart chuckled. "But not to worry! In a day or so we'll be aboard a good, fast ship, traveling in total luxury!"

■   ■   ■

"Not many more ways to look," Douglas told Flarman later that morning.

"Surely the glass itself is rather unique, aside from any magic it may have been given," the older Fire Wizard clucked, shaking his head.

"Oh, the source of the glass is well known," Douglas admitted. "It was made from the fine silica sand of Far Southwest. Someone fired high-quality glass from it, and someone else ground the lens."

"And someone else, still, set a spell upon it? Any idea of what sort of spell it has, m'boy?"

"It has the marks of Frigeon's Aeromancy. But Air Spells are quite complicated, as you know. I wish Cribblon were here!"

Cribblon was a Journeyman Aeromancer, currently traveling in the Nearer East.

"Keep working on it," Flarman recommended. "I'd help you, but Augurian is asking for certain information he needs for his own researching. I may have to go to Water-and Island for a few days. Waterman needs my valuable assistance."

"And you need a change of scene, old Scorcher!" hooted Bronze Owl.

"You may be right," admitted the elder Pyromancer, joining in the laughter. "You have to admit Augurian's experiments will go faster with a second pair of hands to help and hold."

"Helping my Master is usually my job," said Myrn, who had just entered the Workshop, looking for a certain size of alembic she needed.

"No, no! The Water Adept needs a steady and strong hand on this . . . and you've your own hands full with babies and such," Flarman replied. "I'll go to aid old Waterspout. If we need you, we've but to call."

Myrn agreed. "I'll come at once, of course, if my Master

needs me. The children love Waterand and their Uncle Augurian loves to have them around, I know.''

''As I do, and I seem to have them to enjoy four times more often than my oldest friend, Augurian,'' Flarman sighed. ''Well, we'll see . . . shall we? Can I give you any help?''

''Not unless you can point me to our best two-liter alembic,'' answered the young lady Aquamancer. ''It's here, somewhere . . .''

On the wide, green, front lawn, well down toward the Brook, the Brightglade twins played with a family of nixies who lived beside the stream above Plank Bridge. The water fairies watched with fascination as Brenda shaped delicious-looking tarts of damp, white sand frosted with rich, red clay, and set them on a smooth stone to bake in the sun.

''Teatime, my dears!'' she sang out.

Brand turned from trying to catch a flashing trout sprat in his bare hands and scrambled up the bank.

''What flavors do you like best?'' one of the Brook Nixies asked, pausing with her hands poised over the tarts.

''Chocolate!'' called Brand, seating himself on the ground before the rock that served as their play table.

''No, strawberry!'' insisted his sister.

''How about lemon custard and a lightly toasted meringue?'' the nixie lass laughed. ''For that's all I know to do!''

''Lemon mer . . . mer . . . what you said,'' Brand nodded soberly.

The nixie, whose name was Coralbelle, screwed up her pretty, pointed, little face, clenched her fists tightly and brought them together with a soft *knock*, three times.

The sand-and-mud tarts quivered, shook, puffed up, turned golden brown and gave off a puff of sweet lemony aroma that floated off on the breeze.

''You be the Papa,'' Brenda directed her brother, seating

herself on the ground opposite. "Coralbelle and her brothers and sisters will be our children. Serve the tarts, Master Brightglade!"

"Done!" said the little boy gleefully, and in a moment he had handed out slices of lemon tart to the "children" while their play-mother reminded them to wait until all were served before beginning to eat.

"Delicious!" cried everyone, as required by the rules of playing "house" . . . not the least being Brand, who found he liked lemon custard almost as well as he liked chocolate.

Almost!

At the gate from the meadow into the kitchen courtyard Myrn stood, watching the children at play.

"Lemon custards," she laughed. "I can smell 'em, even way up here!"

"So do I," called her husband from the Workshop door.

"They can eat all they want," Flarman assured them from the shadows deep within the Workshop. "Nixie magic's lighter than river froth . . . and much more delicious, of course."

"I'm not worried," the Aquamancer said with a happy blend of laugh and sigh. "And the nixies' mother is nearby and watching them all, just in case."

"One of these days," Douglas began. "Well, they, too, will want to go Questing, like Ben."

"Not for a while yet!" Myrn declared firmly. "They've just mastered combing their hair and dressing themselves with their underwear right side out!"

She wondered why both Pyromancers thought this was so very funny.

"No! Not yet!" snarled the sour-faced Pirate Captain. "Believe me, these wicked, terrible, nasty, nefarious, black-handed Fire Wizards and their foul minions be doubly *dangerous*!"

The Captain slid down from the up-tilted rock he'd used

as a lookout, brushed his worn corduroys, and clapped his battered and rusty tricorn hat on his deeply sunburned, balding head.

"Tell *me* about them people," muttered his First Mate, a fat and sloppy man named Bladder. "In fact, Eunicet, I'd feel much better if we were a lot farther from that there Wizards' nest!"

"Don't be a sniveling nanny-goat! . . . any more than you can help," sneered Eunicet.

The men of his pirate crew exchanged glances but, through long association, knew better than to make comments. Eunicet, once Duke of Dukedom, had a fierce and sudden temper and was much too quick with his sharp tongue and dull cutlass.

"Now what?" Bladder groaned, seating himself on the ground and pulling a leaf-wrapped bit of dried meat of dubious pedigree from his coat pocket. He began to chew vigorously, for it was tough and gristly.

"We *watch*," Eunicet growled. "Make camp back of this ridge and post a lookout up top. Eventually Flarman and Douglas will leave, and then . . ."

He found a more-or-less comfortable rock on which to sit. He searched for a piece of *boucan* in his own pockets and began to gnaw. The dried meat was very salty and almost as hard as the teakwood it resembled.

"Here! *You!*" he snapped to the Bos'n. "Take a party and find a cave or overhanging ledge to sleep under, come night. Out of sight and out of weather."

"Aye, aye, Cap'n!" yelped the Senior Petty Officer.

He told off three of the nine crewmen, all looking very uncomfortable here in the dry, rocky vale high above Valley. They preferred rolling Sea waves for their daily scenery.

"Set the forenoon watch!" Bladder grunted to Eunicet. "I had the mid watch last night, I did!"

"I wouldn't trust any one of you to do the job at all, could I help it," Eunicet replied unpleasantly, levering himself off the rough rock, still chewing vigorously on his chunk of *boucan*.

"Good!" chuckled his second-in-command. "*You* do it, then! I'm for a soft patch of moss in the shade and a good long nap!"

He moved away down the slope, herding the remaining sailors before him.

The Captain of Pirates spat out the last, totally inedible bit of gristle, thumbed his nose after the withdrawing pirates and, removing his hat once more, crept again to the rim of Last (or First, depending on which direction you were facing) Ridge.

He shaded his eyes from the late afternoon sun and settled down to watch his old enemies' stronghold, Wizards' High, in the distance.

Even from that far away he could see two children playing on a patch of shady lawn in front of the cottage. Occasionally he caught glimpses of people moving between the house and the caves under the hill behind it. He recognized Flarman Flowerstalk's plump figure. The second man was a much-grown Douglas Brightglade, he surmised.

An hour later he saw the slim, graceful form of a young, dark-haired woman come from the house to fetch the children. Eunicet was too far away to hear what she said, but the grimy brats . . . a girl and a boy, he decided . . . came to her and the three waved at some unseen friends by the stream before disappearing through the big, double front doors of the cottage.

"Wish Bladder hadn't dropped my best spyglass overboard," Eunicet grumbled to himself.

For a long, hot time nobody appeared around the cottage. He did see an old man working among the apple trees across the stream from the cottage.

Eventually the Pirate Captain, self-styled Eunicet the Wickedest, the Bloody-Handed, the Foul-Mouthed (his men called him, out of his hearing, "Bad-Breath"), the former usurping Duke, the Exile (as he now sometimes styled himself), and Pirate Prince (as he would *like* to be called, someday) closed his weary, red-rimmed eyes . . . and immediately fell sound asleep.

Chapter Four

≈≈≈

The Peachpit Charter

SHIPWRIGHT Douglas of Perthside, a tall, sturdy, keen-eyed, middle-years man whose dark hair had just recently become salted, rather handsomely, with silver, straightened from his theodolite and waved his hands over his head.

"Perfect!" he shouted to his rodman, fifty yards away at the other end of a neat pile of newly sawn timbers. "Straight as a die, Napworth! Stake it up! Carefully, now. She'll sail crooked as an eel, if she's off by only a few hairs."

Napworth, a boy edging close to manhood, nodded understanding and set about driving a row of pinewood stakes and connecting them with clean white-cotton string.

The Shipwright shouldered the heavy theodolite and turned to walk up the strand to his wide, many-windowed office. A yard runner, the chubby, cheerful youngest son of one of his best ship's carpenters, puffed up to him, saluting.

"Wriggles? One seldom sees you winded by hurry," chuckled the Master Shipwright.

"Message from the Gatekeeper, sir," panted the lad.

"Trying to lose this baby fat, sir, you see. Duke Thornwood has published his latest manning requirements, sir! Overweight boys is definitely frowned upon, says he. From the gatehouse, Master Shipwright! The message, I mean."

He plunked down wearily on a newly sawn twenty-four-inch-square timber and mopped his brow with his cloth cap. The late afternoon sun was warm, and the nearness of Farango Water kept the slow-moving breeze humid . . . which was good for the great stacks of laths, boards, and timbers all about, covered with clean canvases, ready to hand when the wrights required them.

"Thank you, son," the Shipwright murmured. "Keep it up! You'll be midshipman in this very hull, once you show proper trim, I'm positive!"

"Thankee, sir! When the time comes!"

Douglas, the father of the famous Pyromancer Douglas Brightglade of Wizards' High, strode up the slope toward his office. Balancing the theodolite over his shoulder with one hand, he unfolded the note with the other and read it through once, then again.

"Important visitors!" he muttered aloud to himself. "Well, let's see . . . who can they be?"

He soon picked out two figures standing just inside the yard gate, chatting with the old sailor who acted as Gatekeeper, guide, and guard.

"*Ho!*" called the Shipwright, setting the instrument against the office wall. "Marbleheart, old crab-snatcher! Who's your young friend?"

Marbleheart stood on his after legs to hug his Master's father and be hugged warmly in return.

"Here's Crown Prince Flowerbender Aedhsson of Faerie, man-sized for a change," said the Otter, waving to his companion. "He and I are off Venturing! Questing, to use *his* word. Your Royal Highness, this is Master Douglas Shipwright, father of the Pyromancer Brightglade. He's also known as Douglas, but of Perthside, here. Shipbuilder . . . Prince!"

"My very great pleasure, Your Highness!" said the Shipwright, bowing solemnly. "Welcome to Perthside and Farango Water!"

"Call me Ben, please," replied the fairy, bobbing a return bow and holding out his hand to shake the builder's. "A pleasure for me, Shipwright! Your fame is only a little less than that of your son, the Fire Wizard."

"I take second rank to my son right gladly. He's earned his good repute by great and dangerous deeds."

"As to why we're here," continued the Prince of Faerie, grinning, "I decided it was time to find out all about World. One day I'll rule all of Faerie and I need to be ready!"

"No better way than Journeying in your Craft, just as all good apprentices must," agreed Douglas of Perthside. "Would you like to inspect my yard? I'll guide you myself."

The man and the boy, followed by the Otter, turned back down the slope.

"We're currently abuilding three great, fast, square-riggers, as you can easily see. Those two, for Thornwood Duke's growing merchant fleet, and this one for the new Emperor of Choin, who's planning to expand his country's trade over-Sea, Choin shipbuilding having fallen into sad state in recent times."

He led the Otter, who was always ready and eager for sightseeing, and the Prince, who had a Bump of Curiosity as large as anyone's, down among the noisy and busy ways, to see the ships being constructed, ranging from the keel laid just that morning, to the tall Choin-bespoken square-rigger, ready on its skids to be slipped into the fjord.

"We'll turn her over to the chandlers, sailmakers, and riggers come Monday," the Master Shipwright was saying. "With all three under construction at various stages, you can get a good idea how we wrights go about our crafting."

Ben delightedly devoured every detail, every method.

"Are there no fairy shipwrights, then?" he wondered aloud.

"Wonderful craftsmen, too, believe me! Wish I had a crew or two here. Nobody saws more beautiful cuts nor does smoother planing and sanding! Not that my people are any sort of slouches. Faerie-built ships, you must know, with their different requirements, are usually smaller and shallower of draft. Many of your tradespeople in recent years have entered World business in their own ships."

"Oh?" said Marbleheart. "I wasn't aware of that, Papa Douglas! What do the merchants of Faerie offer in trade?"

"I know that!" offered Ben, delighted to find a subject he knew better than his companion. "We're purveyors of finest furniture and splendid toys, of course, and intricately fashioned jewelry, and of specialty foods, candies, preserves . . . things like that. And Faerie merchants have found an eager market for our soaps and medicaments, too, I'm told."

"My goodwife," Douglas Shipwright nodded, "has a chestful of Faerie elixirs, salves, and pills, enough to cure just about anything. She's better than the best Dukedom physickers. They come to *her* for advice and prescriptions!"

"Just an excuse to see and talk with the beautiful Glorianna," Marbleheart insisted. "Were it *I* who knew fairy medicines, they'd never come to me at all!"

"Nonsense!" the Shipwright scoffed, but he was pleased by the Otter's kind flattery of his wife, nevertheless.

He sent the boy Wriggles puffing ahead of them to Overlook House, perched easily and gracefully atop the low bluff above the noise and smoke of the busy port and shipyard.

"My goodwife will want to meet and greet you both, prepared with all the necessary bonbons and bath towels and such," the Shipwright told his guests. "You'll stay with us until you must go looking for adventures, of course!"

"I wouldn't want to stay anywhere else," Marbleheart assured him. "I've already told the lad, here, all I remember of your house, table, gardens, and workshops.''

"If I weren't set on Questing," the boy said thought-fully, "I'd apprentice myself to you here and learn the ship-wright's art. Altogether fascinating! Filled with all sorts of arcane mysteries!''

"Even a King of Faerie should know a good, useful manual art or two, if just for his own amusement," Douglas agreed, quite seriously. "If nothing else, shipwrighting trains the mind to think carefully and plan ahead, to guard against all the possible mistakes one can make in a complex undertaking."

"Not too different, I should think, from statecraft," laughed the boy. "Perhaps I'll come, later on, and ask for a place in your yard, Master Douglas."

"Welcome . . . *if* you can pass the entrance examina-tion," replied the man, nodding his head.

"Examination!" exclaimed Marbleheart. "I didn't know there was a test for becoming an Apprentice!"

"We instituted it a few years back. When men and boys lost their livelihoods during the late War, during Dead Win-ter and the Dry Summers and all, shipbuilding was one of the first trades to recover, thanks to Duke Thornwood. We were swamped with farm lads looking for work."

"Did you turn them away?" Ben wondered.

"No, we took them on . . . most of 'em knew something of tools, and all knew a lot about hard work. The yards were then, as now, working at top speed. We trained 'em as they came. Then, when things settled a bit, most of them returned to the land . . . their first love, I think."

"But this examination thing?" the Otter prompted.

"As much to discourage youngsters from running away from home . . . without a bit of arithmetic, reading for blue-prints and instructions, and a taste for hard work. When they learned they had to know how to measure very exactly and add and subtract mixed numbers, they saw the impor-tance of schooling. To enter the ranks as Journeyman and maybe Master Shipwright you have to know your schoolwork. Now the Moots all over Dukedom offer the necessary basic schooling,'' Douglas the Shipwright explained.

Talking of this and that, ships and sails and even sealing wax, the three climbed the shore to the Shipwright's sunny, wide-gardened, hilltop house. They were met at the gate by a tall and handsome lady.

"Glorianna, my goodwife!" her husband introduced her proudly.

Glorianna smiled warmly, curtsied gracefully to the young prince, and ruffled the Otter's thick, smooth fur.

"All are welcome here, but a Prince of Faerie is most welcome of all, for your kind mother and father and the people of Faerie have been very good to us and to our son,'' she told the lad.

"I'm the one honored,'' insisted Ben graciously. "Douglas Brightglade has spoken of you many times and I feel I know you already, Lady Glorianna!"

"Well, let's see how you feel about me after you eat at our board and sleep in our house,'' laughed Glorianna. "Come! I've a sunny room ready for you on the second floor, overlooking the fjord. Your bath will be soon ready . . . just as soon as you can be ready to jump in. How about you, Marbleheart? Bath? Nap? Stroll in the gardens?''

"All three, if there's time before dinner. Bath first, I suppose, then a sniff or two of your wonderful herb garden. Skip the sleep, for now. What's for supper, Lady?''

"Golden-fried shrimp fritters, for starters,'' said the lady of the house, knowing the Otter well enough to speak precisely of food. "Chicken stew the way Farango Water goodwives make it . . . with a generous pinch of yellow saffron from upland crocus flowers. Buttered boiled potatoes, of course, and a salad of spring onions and early, tender, sweet greens. And a fat apple pie of the last of the winter keepers sent down Crooked Brook by wonderful old Priceless, with plenty of cinnamon and brown sugar. Yellow cheese, too.''

"Forget the bath and the flower-sniffing!" cried Marbleheart gleefully, throwing up his forepaws. "Let's eat!"

Down Farango Water from the bustling shipyard was a village known as Edgewater Bight where, the following morning, Ben and the Otter were directed to a new clapboard building with a large, ornate sign over the front door announcing "Shipping Agent."

"This's something new, I'm told," Marbleheart explained to the boy. "Used to be you scared up your own passage or cargo space for a Sea voyage. Learn of a ship about to sail where you wanted to go. The agentry idea's a great help, worth the fee, for it keeps track of all the incoming and outgoing vessels, from whence they come, and where they'll call. Saves a lot of weary footwork."

"You talk, then. I'm not sure I know what to ask."

"Leave it to the Sea Otter," chuckled Marbleheart.

They opened the agent's glass-paneled front door. A bell on a curled spring on the doorjamb jangled pleasantly.

A young man with red hair, starched linen cuff protectors on each wrist, and a rather harried look, glanced up from his desk and then rose.

"Welcome to Farrwell's Shipping Agency," he greeted them cordially. "How may we serve you, gentleman and gentle-beast? Vacation sail to Warm Sea? Perhaps cargo space on a ship headed for Old Kingdom? Lots of brand-new opportunities for young, ambitious merchants, over there."

"Good morning," answered Marbleheart, determined not to be rushed. "A very good day for a Sea voyage, or I miss my guess, sir!"

"The weather reports from our watchers down at Cape Smerm say the latest spring storm has now passed across middle Sea, sir. Weather is warm and balmy with steady southeast winds, except in the far west where there are still unsettled conditions."

"We're considering a voyage to the *other* end of Sea,

however. Our first stop might be Wayness Isles. We want to visit New Land.''

"No problems, either place," said the redhead. "Never been to New Land, myself, but I understand it's pleasant for visiting and profitable for business."

He showed them to seats before his desk, a tall rolltop incredibly stuffed with papers, books, and ledgers, set against the back wall. As a preliminary to discussing business, he offered the travelers coffee or tea.

"Yes, tea! Hot, with plenty of sugar, please!" answered Marbleheart. "Ben, m'boy?"

"Coffee with cream, if you please," said the Fairy Prince politely, "and two lumps of sugar."

The clerk disappeared for a moment into the back room and returned with a tray of dainty Choin cups on dragon-painted saucers, a fat sugarbowl, and a pitcher of thick, yellow cream.

"I apologize for not introducing myself," he said, seating himself once again. "I am called Dowalt of Craneswood . . ."

"Ah, Craneswood!" cried Marbleheart, sipping gingerly at his hot tea. "Know it well! Up toward Woodbine."

"You're right, Mr. . . . ?"

"Now *I'm* remiss! This is my friend . . . ah . . . Ben of Faerie, and I am . . ."

"Of course! You're Marbleheart Sea Otter, the younger Pyromancer's Familiar!" interrupted the clerk. "I know of you right well, Master Sea Otter! Very few like you in Dukedom, are there? It's a very great pleasure and an honor!"

He managed to treat the young Prince with deference and courtesy without asking his rank or stature. Fairies are best treated with respect. And this one was not your usual shy forest-dweller or mischievous sea sprite, he could see.

"We wish," Marbleheart said again, "to visit New Land. Our acquaintance Serenit, the First Citizen there, has done-wonderful work reclaiming the great, deep, wide glacial valley.''

"And we wish next to go on to Nearer East, to the Port of Samarca," added Ben. "I hear it's most unusual and quite fascinating."

"So I've ever heard our Seamen tell," Master Dowalt said with a cheery nod. "I've never visited there, of course . . ."

He admitted, when Marbleheart asked him point-blank, that he had never been anywhere further afield than Capital.

"I hope to travel, one day," the clerk sighed, looking more than a little wistful. "But I can suggest to you ways and means to reach your destinations. It's all here in our Journal, collected directly from Shipmasters and Seacaptains and such, daily."

"New Land, then?" Marbleheart prompted.

"Here's the current in-port list," said Dowalt, drawing out a piece of foolscap on which were neatly written several lines and a column of figures. "Prince Bryarmote's *Watersprite* just made port yesterday; she'll leave for Dwelmland Sea Gate at the end of the week, her Captain Flusster assured me just last eventide. Three or four passenger berths and working-deck space for four more. The first class asking price . . ."

"No; not if you have anything earlier," Marbleheart said quickly. "We wouldn't want to impose on our host here that long!"

"Well, then, young sirs," Dowalt said sadly, "I've little else to offer more immediate. Perhaps something will arrive today or tomorrow. If not, you'll have to wait until *Watersprite*'s off-loaded and laden with new cargo. I'm sorry . . ."

He was about to refile his sheet of paper when Marbleheart said suddenly. "What's *that* . . . on the back side?"

"*Ah!* 'Tis a ship-rigged schooner, registered in a place west of Choin known as Home Port. *Peachpit* is her name. A smallish, cramped sort of vessel, I'm afraid. Don't know much of her, either, for she's never called at Farango Water before. Never heard of Home Port, for that matter. Nor had several old sailors I've asked.''

"She's headed for New Land, however?" Marbleheart asked. "We might be able to abide her facilities for the five or six days of such a passage."

"I've visited her, of course. Neat enough looking. Captain is . . . ah . . . a young woman. Name of . . . let me see. Is it Lorimer? No, I remember . . . Lorianne! Pleasant enough young lady, I think, but quite young for full captaincy."

"A lady Seacaptain!" Ben exclaimed. "Rather unusual, isn't that?"

"Not so much, since the Ice King's War. So many poor lads were lost in that terrible war! Women stepped into their sea boots."

"But you don't know much about her ship, nor of this Seacaptain Lorianne, either, do you?" the Otter asked, sounding doubtful. "Why does she want to go to New Land, did she say? Mostly dressed stone and rough timber come out of Serenit's valley, so far. I would think . . . a smallish schooner could carry very little in the way of cargo of that bulk."

"I didn't, of course, ask her business," admitted the clerk. "Her asking rate is quite low, but cabin space is limited. I should imagine, for the right fee, this lady Captain would agree to move out of the cabin and let you have a Captain's bunk and comfort, such as they might be."

"I don't think it's a good choice," said Marbleheart reluctantly. "Ben, we may have to choose between walk or wait. Wait five or six days for Bryarmote's *Watersprite*. Much more reliable."

Ben frowned.

"Perhaps we could convince the Captain of Bryarmote's schooner to leave sooner," he said to Dowalt.

"Not likely, young sir. *Watersprite* is loaded to the gunnels with valuable cargo, mostly bulky minerals, ores, and ingots of purified metals. I know, for I arranged for its purchase. Her homeward cargo will be heavy machinery from Michael Wroughter's foundry, I'm told, and such must be laded with exacting care. Not much hope they would hurry that sort of thing, I'm afraid.''

''Unless we purchased her outright,'' suggested the prince.

Marbleheart jerked erect at his suggestion.

''Recall our limited resources, Ben, m'boy! I've no idea what such a ship would cost, even unladen, but surely much more than we have to hand.''

''I suppose you're right, Marbleheart. *Rats!* Money is something one should never travel without!''

''Money can be a terrible burden, too,'' said the Otter gruffly. ''If we can't wait, we'll walk!''

''Perhaps we should visit this lady Seacaptain's little ship . . . er, schooner? Her ship's name is rather unusual, isn't it? *Peachpit?*''

''Of course, I'll be pleased to take you to visit her,'' the redheaded clerk offered. ''Just as soon as my partner returns from his morning calls. Early this afternoon, shall we say?''

''We'll stroll down and have a look at her this morning, the sooner to make a decision,'' Ben decided. ''If that seems a good idea to you, Sea Otter.''

''Why not?'' Marbleheart shrugged. ''Point her out to us, Master Dowalt, please. We'll come back and book our passage through you, be sure, if we're pleased with *Peach-fuzz.*''

''*Peachpit!* All right, then,'' the clerk agreed, rising to point out their way through the front window. ''There's *Peachpit*, riding to anchor. Far end of the hard. You'll have to hire a waterman to take you out to her.''

''We'll go over and check her out,'' Marbleheart told him. ''And thank you! Enjoyed doing business with you. Be assured that your commission will be paid, if we decide to ship in any bottom here.''

"I'll lose not a wink of sleep over it," Dowalt laughed. "A pleasure doing business with *you*, Sea Otter and High . . . I mean, Master Ben."

"I misunderstand her name," said Ben as the waterman sculled them across the sunlit roadstead. "I'd have thought they'd call her *Peachblossom*, or *Peaches 'n' Creme*."

"No accounting for some Seacaptain's tastes," growled their boatman, shaking his head. "Especially when that Seacaptain's a lady."

"There are usually private and personal reasons for a ship's naming," Marbleheart observed.

He lay stretched full-length in the rowboat's prow, trailing a casual forepaw in the rushing bow wave. "Boats are fine," he was thinking, "but swimming's more natural for us Otters."

"Do you know this lady Captain?" Ben asked the waterman.

"No, sir! Never met her. Don't hold much with women captains, meself. Oh, I guesses they're just fine, taken all in all. I 'members when a woman's place was over a stove, between sheets, or piloting a cradle, but little else."

He rested on his oars, spat over the side for masculine emphasis, and raised his hoarse voice to hail the schooner, which, his passengers noticed, actually had peach-pink sails furled to her booms. And pots of geraniums and petunias on her counter, nodding in the mid-morning breeze.

"'Hoy! *Peachpit* schooner, there!" the boatman bawled. "Landsmen to visit ye! Permission to come alongside!"

"Landsmen, indeed!" Marbleheart objected. "I've been across more leagues of salt Sea than all the harbor boatmen on Farango Water!"

A girl, flaming red hair tied back with a strip of faded blue kerchief, popped up from below, looking quite surprised.

"Lay alongside, then," she called back after a moment

of looking. "Mind you! Don't scrape the paintwork. Wait!
We'll rig a coir-mat to ease the rub."

She called over her shoulder and shortly, as the rowboat
waited easily on the boatman's oars, the red-haired girl and
an older man with straggly beard and even shaggier pantaloons draped a mat of picked coconut fiber over the near
rail to cushion the contact between the waterman's boat and
the sloop's low scantling.

"Come aboard, then!" the girl invited the waiting passengers.

She'd taken a moment to whip off her kerchief, run a
comb through her mass of auburn hair, and stuff her apron
down a companionway into the ship's tiny cabin. "My
name is Lorianne. I am Captain and owner of *Peachpit*."

When the Otter and the fairy were on deck, she smiled
graciously and returned their polite bows.

"Captain Lorianne," Ben said seriously. "A very good
morning, Mistress!"

"Pleasantest welcome aboard *Peachpit*, sirs," returned
the young lady. "How may I help you? A moment,
please!"

She turned to the ragged and somewhat overly thin sailor
who'd helped her rig the coir over the rail.

"That will be all, Castorbean!"

The man gave her a sour nod, a rude sort of salute, and
shuffled off toward the forecastle, where two of his mates
sat on the deck, mending a pink sail . . . or pretending to
do so . . . while straining their ears to hear their lady Seacaptain speak to visitors on the quarterdeck.

"We seek passage to Nearer East, ma'am," Marbleheart
explained. "Will you be going that far? Or touching at New
Land? That would take us well on our way."

"Let's study the charts," said the girl, shaking her head.

She led them down into *Peachpit*'s tiny main cabin. They
all had to walk stooped low in order to move beneath the
low overhead. The space was lighted by three round port-
holes on each side, standing open to admit the breeze.

Lorianne knelt gracefully and, reaching under a bunk, rummaged for a box of charts and maps. Marbleheart and Ben glanced about.

Certainly the crew . . . three or perhaps four of them . . . slept on the open deck, or in one of the cargo holds below. A tiny galley just forward of the main cabin would just manage to provide hot meals. Two narrow bunks and a table, two benches. A two-shelf bookcase hanging on the after bulkhead was crammed to overflowing with leather-bound volumes that showed signs of having been well read.

Every major stick of furniture was bolted firmly to the deck to keep it from shifting as the deck tilted with Sea's rolling.

"Ah-ha! *Eastern Sea!*" exclaimed the girl from under the bunk.

She straightened up and unrolled a large chart with Dukedom to the left, and the northern countries beyond Dwelmland, marked *Highlandorm, Eternal Ice*. It showed the western coast of Nearer East on the far right margin, but not, Marbleheart noticed, as far south as Samarca.

At the bottom of the chart was a narrow strip of land marked *Choin Empire & Desolation* but little else.

"Rather an out-of-date chart," commented the Otter. "It doesn't even show New Land where Eternal Ice has melted."

"Oh?" asked the girl in surprise. "Word hasn't reached us of such a change. I must correct it. Eternal Ice gone, eh? Most interesting!"

She pointed to the long, narrow fjord of Farango Water and the spot of black ink newly labeled Edgewater Bight.

"Here we are. And you say you wish passage east and north to this New Land. It is here?"

She placed her finger on the wide, long, but entirely featureless white wilderness labeled *Eternal Ice Glacier*.

"The ice is melting back northward. It was maintained by the spells of the late Ice King. Frigeon was defeated some years ago," Marbleheart explained.

"Frigeon? Don't recall hearing that name, ever," said Seacaptain Lorianne.

"Maybe you've heard of Last Battle in Kingdom?" Ben asked.

"Oh . . . a bit. Legends, I always thought," Lorianne said, shaking her head. "Far removed from Home Port, I suppose."

Marbleheart looked at her in some surprise, then turned back to the chart.

"We'll visit an old friend here in New Land . . . First Citizen Serenit," he explained, tapping the spot where he thought Serenit's lodge at Flarmansport now lay.

"For a proper fare," said the girl, nodding, "we could easily put you on or very near that spot, sirs."

"What cargo will you carry?" asked the fairy.

"Well . . . little or nothing other than stones for ballast! Unless we find suitable cargo here for Wayness or New Land. What could we carry to New Land that would pay for carriage and yield a profit on our return?"

"Must be something," Marbleheart shrugged. "I'd ask our friend Dowalt the shipper's agent. He'll know what you can and will want to carry."

It struck the Otter as strange that she didn't know much about cargoes and rates of exchange, nor even be sure of the cost for their passage.

A fare was at last named, and Marbleheart gestured to the boy. They excused themselves to go on deck for a brief private conference. The *Peachpit* crewmen watched without expression from far forward.

"Obviously needs the business," Ben said urgently. "And the voyage is not far. I'm sure we could find her a profitable cargo at either Wayness or New Land, if not here. Help her out!"

"I don't know," muttered the Otter, shaking his head slowly. "Something about this doesn't quite ring well or true, if you know what I mean."

"Crew's a surly-looking lot," Ben nodded. "But look,

old water-weasel, if she's short of cash . . . maybe they haven't been paid. That would explain their being unhappy, wouldn't it?''

"Perhaps. Still . . ."

"*I* think we should charter *Peachpit*. We'll be both helping ourselves and assisting this young lady, too, at the same time."

Marbleheart finally nodded his head.

"We'll sail with the morning tide," Lorianne almost sang when she was told of their decision. "I know you're in a rush, sirs, so I'll not delay for a cargo here."

The first third of their passage money was paid in the silver Dukedom *ducats* from the sale of Ben's shoes. "First light tomorrow, sirs! Give you time to say your good-byes ashore and fetch your dunnage. And perhaps time for me to find a quick cargo of some sort."

They shook hands solemnly on the bargain, and one of *Peachpit*'s crewmen hailed the waterman to come alongside to take them ashore.

"I must purchase stores," Lorianne told her scruffy-looking crew after the passengers had climbed into the shore boat and shoved off. "Bottlebrush, come with me to row and help carry. Castorbean and Prude, clear the after-cabin of my duffel. I'll sleep in the main cabin."

"Aye, aye, missy," Castorbean said in a much more pleasant tone than before. "Do worse, by far, for a good meal!"

Lorianne frowned at him until he turned away to direct the lowering of *Peachpit*'s tiny jolly boat.

"Food and company and, with any luck, a profitable cargo to carry," she called to her crew. "Come on, Bottlebrush! *Pull*! Sooner we shop, sooner we get to eat!"

Two days' ride to the north, in the city that had been called Capital of Dukedom for more years than anyone could remember, young Duke Thornwood, former merchant

Seacaptain, victorious naval hero, and good friend to several powerful Wizards, listened to a long report from his naval station at Cape Smerm, the southernmost tip of Dukedom.

"Piracy, M'Lord Duke!" the officer was saying. "Captain Friddler reports six ships of various registrations—two of them streaming our own colors, Your Grace!—have gone mysteriously missing in the past six-month."

"Two of our own, Mother!" exclaimed Thornwood, turning to the salt-and-pepper-haired lady seated by a nearby window. She was listening while making careful, tiny stitches in an elaborate embroidery. "Very serious!"

Duchess-Mother Marigold nodded. "*Someone's* on a rampage! Six ships in a single half-year!"

"Go on," Thornwood ordered the naval officer. "What else does Friddler report on this matter?"

"He's moving as fast as he can. Has so moved, ever since the first ship went missing, last autumn, but our station is isolated and manpower limited, M'Lord! He asks for more men; more ships."

"Of course he does! He shall have them, and as quickly as we can get there!"

"'We?'" his mother asked, raising her eyes from her work.

"Yes, Mother. This is much too important to delegate to others. Commerce and safety at Sea are vital to Dukedom's interests. We can't allow pirates to go unswung . . . or at least chased far, far away!"

Marigold sighed but smiled, also, nodding to her handsome son.

"And you are best suited to lead the pirate-hunters, I agree. You're just like your father, I vow!"

"You'll be here in my stead, so I've no worries about leaving for a few weeks. I'll send a warning to all coastal Moots, first, and inform Flarman Flowerstalk, too. Valley has the best view of the long, empty Parch coast . . ."

"Flarman is busy with those very difficult disenchantments," his mother reminded him.

"We can handle pirates on our own," her son assured her, excited by the thought of going to Sea once again. Besides, these wicked raiders had dared to attack his own ships just off his very own shores!

"Tell Flarman and Douglas, anyway," Duchess Marigold agreed. "And take your umbrella and best sea boots, son! It's stormy at Sea at this time of the year, I'm told."

Chapter Five

On High Sea

THORNWOOD Duke reined in his destrier before the Oak 'n' Bucket in Trunkety two days later and swung easily from the saddle, nodding and smiling to the crowd of Valley farmers and townspeople who spilled out to greet him.

"Lord Duke!" they cheered, waving cloth caps and mugs of ale. "Step down and share a jack of Innkeeper's spring brewing with us loyal and contented Valleymen."

"My very intention!" chuckled the handsome young nobleman, tossing his reins to the inn's potboy. "Your very best, all round, Innkeeper! It's all too seldom I've the delight of riding down to Trunketytown and enjoying an early summer's evening with my Valley friends!"

"Here comes Frenstil, hisself," someone called from the edge of the crowd.

This elderly gentleman, former Squire in the household of the late Duke Thorowood, Thornwood's father, came across the green at an unaccustomed trot . . . he who seldom rushed anywhere, the onlookers chuckled . . . and first bowed to the young Duke, then threw his arms about him and saluted him with a strong squeeze of genuine affection.

"Too long since Valley last enjoyed your visiting, M'Lord Duke!" he greeted Thornwood. "Will you stay for a day or three? Your men-at-arms can quarter at my farm. With the Valley Patrol contract stalls there we've plenty of feed grain, bedding straw, clean stabling, and clean bunks."

"Frenstil, old campaigner!" laughed Thornwood, pounding on the older man's back, still sturdy if a bit thin with years. "We'll take your offer for my horse soldiers . . . for a day or two. I must consult with the Wizards a bit, and then we're off to Farango Water to take ship. *Pirates*, sir! Six ships've been snapped up or sunk this year, their crews slain or set adrift!"

The men . . . and women and children, also . . . of Trunkety and the Valley farmsteads gasped at the news. It was the first word they'd had of piracy so near to home.

"Anyone seen the Captain of the Valley Patrol? Seen good old Possumtail?" asked Thornwood, once they were all settled around the trestle tables or on the thick grass in the inn yard, sipping excellent new-beer, which for a few weeks each summer replaced Innkeeper's usual dark autumn ale as Valley's preferred thirst-quencher.

"He rides this way each evening, of course," replied Frenstil. "He should roll into sight across Trunkety Bridge any moment."

"I need to bespeak him. We'll wish to muster his troop for a while for our pirate-hunt. We'll want experienced men at Fort Smerm as backup, while we search for the pirates at Sea."

"Possumtail's ready any day for just such a lark," someone called. "He's been complaining loud and long, of late, about the peacefulness of Valley, Sir Duke!"

"Quiet and peace should be appreciated and enjoyed," Frenstil shot back. "Uproarious ways come all too frequent for my ancient bones! When you get *my* age, you young bucks . . . !"

"Well, I could stay to toss off this bracing new-beer for

another two hours, but I must ride up to the High," the Duke interrupted, for Frenstil would otherwise have gone on at great length. "When Possumtail comes, ask him to ride a bit further and wait on me, up to Flarman's cottage."

"I understand," said the storekeeper Dicksey, who had strolled across the green to join the party gathered outside the inn, "that Flarman left yesterday morning to visit Wizard Augurian on his Warm Sea island for a few days. But young Douglas is in residence, along with his goodwife, the pretty Myrn, according to my boy who delivered groceries there yestereven."

"Douglas'll do me!" Thornwood nodded. "One must expect at least *some* of our Wizards to be off whizzing about on their important business. I find it so, at least."

He arranged for the Valley Moot, through Squire Frenstil as Moot Speaker, to call up the Valley Militia.

"As usual," Frenstil confessed, "in good times the Militia tends to slack off and become a social club for the younger men."

"A few mornings of marching up a sweat and afternoons of shooting at butts should bring them back into fettle," Thornwood considered. "I'll go off to see the Wizard, or I should say the *Wizards*, now that Mistress Myrn is a full member of their Fellowship."

"We'll muster Militia for your inspection in the morning, then. At ten o'clock? Here on the green, M'Lord," promised Frenstil, who had been elected Militia Colonel over and over for years. "And the Farmers and Mechanics Reserve. Older, more experienced men can be useful, too."

"The ones who beat Eunicet at his starving games and helped us trounce Frigeon's Fleet at the Battle of Sea? None better in a pinch!" exclaimed the young Duke. "Drink up, gentlemen! Get to your beds early! We'll polish up your march-counter-marching, shooting skills, and crawling through bramble bushes before noon tomorrow. You'll need a clear head for that, I guarantee!"

■   ■   ■

"Will you really need the Militia, let alone the Reserve gaffers?" Myrn questioned Thornwood.

Blue Teakettle poured cups of steaming, fragrant, green Choin tea. They were sitting on rustic chairs by the ancient Fairy Well, under the bright, cool stars of early evening.

"Our countrymen . . . and their ladies, also . . . need to be included in the defense of their homes. Although these pirates will probably never come closer than Cape Smerm or perhaps raid ashore at Wayness, if they get even *that* bold," Thornwood answered. "When this is over, purring Party, I'll ask to carry two or three of your latest litter back to my Lady Mother! She was saying just a few days ago that our refurbished Capital has a phenomenal increase of mice and even some bold rats. A few of Black Flame's well-trained offspring will be kept busy and draw much-deserved praise in Capital."

Party rubbed her chin against the nobleman's hand, bumbling happily. A dozen kittens played in the grass or swarmed onto the Ducal lap to share his warmth with their mother . . . or aunt, for fully half of the kittens were sons and daughters of Pert.

"Well, just so they remember they've farm and field work to do," Douglas said, referring to the Militiamen, not the cats. "Men go dashing off on exciting excursions, given half a chance, rather than plowing and tilling and planting and such."

"Are Wizards any different?" Myrn sniffed.

"Papa," asked young Brand, leaning on his father's knee, "how old must *I* be to join the Militia, marching and shooting?"

"A few years yet, I'm afraid, soldier-boy," said Douglas. "Keep practicing with your new bow and arrows, however. Some of your farm friends are already quite good. You must keep apace in order to serve in the Valley Militia."

"I can hit a mark the size of my hand at ten paces," Brand announced to the Duke. "Three times of four!"

"I couldn't do *nearly* so well when I was your age," Thornwood confided, most seriously. "I preferred horse and lance, I'm afraid. I regret neglecting my archery, even today, young warrior!"

"I can ride, too," Brand claimed. He then added gallantly, "But Brenda's better!"

"A day or two organizing the Militia and sending Valley Guard to help man Smerm," Thornwood told Douglas and Myrn, "then I'll lead my regulars down to board ships at Perthside. Your father, Douglas, says there'll be good, fast bottoms waiting to carry a sizable armed force to chase these pirates."

"You'll strike fast and hard, then?" Douglas asked. "I'll come with you, Thornwood."

"You'll assist in other ways by staying here!" Thornwood said seriously. "I'll keep you informed of what we do and where. May I call on Deka to carry messages between us?"

"Deka knows you and will come when you call," Myrn assured him. "She's very interested in you, to tell the truth. She wondered recently if you'd yet chosen a Duchess. I told her . . . 'Give the poor man time! He's still rebuilding a whole country!' "

"Every female I know . . . and lots I've never met . . . is determined to get me married," the Duke chortled, throwing his head back and slapping his thighs in glee. "My choice for Duchess will come, one of these days. From out of the blue. I realize," he sobered and nodded to Myrn, "it's a serious, serious matter, choosing a wife who will also be my Lady Duchess."

"Nonsense!" Myrn objected, throwing up her hands. "It's up to Dukedom to suit your wife, Thornwood! Not the other way round."

"Do you think so? Well, in that you agree with my mother, I must say. She says to me, 'Wait! Somewhere and someday, your true love will appear. You'll know who you've been waiting for all this time, once you see her.' "

"That's the proper idea," Myrn agreed, equally serious. "Nevertheless, we women will be on the lookout for suitable candidates!"

"Those blam-damned, putty-headed, parboiled, cracked-pate, overstuffed, noisy, grog-swilling Valley farmers!" raved Eunicet, made angry and hungry by the wafted aromas carried by the gentle west wind up Valley toward First Ridge . . . broiling sausages, toasting cheeses, fresh-baked finger rolls, tangy spring onions, cucumber-and-onion pickles, tender cabbage slaw made with thick cream and aged-in-wood vinegar, and heady Oak 'n' Bucket new-beer.

"They eat such trash, with such offhand laughter, whilst I starve on this miserable rock, belching from tough, old mushrooms and nasty bits of sour bread without leavening or sweetening!" the former Duke raged on.

The High's green lawn was in clear sight, but too many miles away for anyone to hear his shouts.

"But you can never tell about Wizards!" The former Duke choked on his rage. "They've listening powers, I've been told. And long sight, too!"

"They'd have seen or heard us by now, in that case," groused his second-in-command, the former general of his army and tavern-brawler named Bladder, lying on his back below the rimrock. "*If* they was listening, that is."

Eunicet regarded his First Mate sourly.

"You sweaty, smelly, sour, useless old dog's breath! I told you to go with the work party down to the shore to gather clams and catch us some crabs. What if they should decide to run away?"

"No such luck," Bladder sniffed. "We'd be better off without 'em, the gutless swab-pushers!"

"Nonsense! Without *them*, whom would you and I order about, curse, and browbeat? And who'd carry our loot back to the ship, then?"

"Browbeat and bottom-beat, perhaps, but they're not much good at fighting on dry land. No decent pirate ever was. Well, if *you* won't go, I guess I'll have to, dear Captain! They're probably lost or have miscounted the number of ridges to cross to get back here.''

He stood, stretched, belched on the half-cooked mushrooms he'd just eaten, scratched his backside, which was stiff from lying on hard stone, and shambled down the hill to climb Middle Ridge (whose name never changed, no matter from which direction you approached it) and over and down and up again, over Last (or First . . . well, you get the idea!) Ridge to the shore of Sea.

Eunicet screwed his right eye to the second-best spyglass he'd borrowed from one of his petty officers.

By the light of the stars and hanging lanterns and the bonfire on the High lawn he saw Douglas Brightglade hoist two children on his shoulders and carry them inside the cottage.

''And that must be his goodwife, the one called Myrn. She don't look any bit of a Water Adept,'' the ex-Duke muttered to himself.

He recognized Duke Thornwood, of course, although he'd only once long ago met him in person. He particularly detested Thornwood. That young man with the fringe of golden beard had once had the gall to reclaim his rightful Ducal seat, which Eunicet had stolen from old Duke Thorowood by wicked tricks. And some help from King Frigeon.

''Why should *you* be in such a happy mood, foul adversary?'' the pirate snarled aloud. ''I'll teach *you* to be handsome and laughing with ladies and lolling about on the greensward! Enjoy your picnic, Dukeling! Vengeance will be mine!''

His stomach growled testily and he tasted sour bile rising in his throat. Sliding down the tilted rock face, he snapped his stolen spyglass closed and replaced it in his pocket.

''I'm hungry, by Rennit!'' he shouted. ''Bring me food!''

The rocky uplands answered with thin, mocking echoes.

■ ■ ■

Weathering Cape Smerm after many short, arduous tacks, *Peachpit* scooted before the strong westerly breeze along the rocky south coast of Dukedom. The charts, although old, rightly warned of rocks awash and sunken, with shifting sand banks further offshore.

"If this wind holds," said Seacaptain Lorianne, passing a basket of hot buttered biscuits to Ben, "we'll be just a night and a day to Wayness Isles . . . and perhaps additional cargo, if the shipping agent is correct."

"Wayness is a pleasant enough place," Marbleheart murmured. "But somewhat a backwater, these days, what with the growth of Westongue. They still build sturdy boats for fishing and pleasure, walk rope and twist cable, and weave excellent canvas, too. Yes, a pleasant place, I've heard. Never been there, of course."

Mate Castorbean, looking rather more pleasant (and less gaunt) than Marbleheart remembered him from three days before, came aft to bespeak his captain.

"Wind's freshening and swinging around to north a bit, Captain, ma'am," he reported. "Fair for this Wayness place yet a while, I judge."

He stood, easily swaying to the sloop's motion, while Lorianne turned to Marbleheart to ask her passenger's desire.

"We'd like to see Wayness, and you need the cargo," the Otter told her. "Go ahead! We can get a good meal or two there, anyway."

"Good meal decides it, then," laughed the girl. "I apologize again for never learning to cook!"

"The biscuits and the strawberry jam were delicious," Ben told her. "When Questing, Marbleheart says, one must expect to eat strange foods and have short commons, at times. Maybe we can get Fairy Waybread at Wayness. Do they know of it, do you think?"

"I've no idea at all," answered Lorianne. "All right, Mate! Go about and run close-reefed from this new wind."

"Aye! I'll do just that, ma'am!" the sailor answered, tugging at his forelock. He turned away and began to shout orders at the other three crewmen waiting patiently on the main deck.

"Your crew . . . ?" began Ben to Lorianne. "Well . . . they still seem unhappy, don't they?"

"*Seem?* Downright sullen ever since first we came aboard!" Marbleheart insisted.

"They never really wished to sign on for this voyage, and they don't relish serving under a woman," the lady Seacaptain confessed. "*Peachpit* is *mine* . . . but the needed sailing skills are theirs, I'm afraid. They're good Seamen. A full stomach and useful employment. They're much better off than they care to admit."

"I certainly hope so," muttered Marbleheart, standing on his hind legs to stretch and gaze out over the chop of the darkening Sea. "For I know a bit about Seamanship myself, having swum in and traveled on these waters for a number of years. The wind seems to be swinging further north since your mate reported, Captain!"

"So it is!" cried Lorianne.

She strode forward and called orders to the men, just resting from setting the new course. They glanced up, tested the wind for themselves, nodded, and began the sail-trimming process all over again.

"Maybe we should help?" Ben whispered to the Otter, a worried frown creasing his brow.

"I don't think we should . . . at least not yet," Marbleheart considered. "Sailors are a touchy bunch when it comes to working their ship. But I'll tell you one thing for sure, matey! "We'll find it impossible to make Wayness on this wind."

"Tell me how you know," the fairy lad urged when the Otter had flopped to the deck once again. "I want to learn this Seagoing business!"

"Can't swim yet! Is that it?" the Otter teased. "Not even after I so carefully taught you my famous Otter Crawl?"

"Lack of practice," the boy insisted. "Why do you say this wind will never take us to Wayness? It seems to be blowing fair that way, if my eyes aren't fooled."

Marbleheart explained earnestly, "The wind's switching to the north of west, and my instincts and experience say it'll not stop sliding sideways until it blows from the north or even northeast, almost dead against our course to Wayness. We're in for a nor'easter, m'boy! Might last two-three days, at best, if the winds blow true to usual. It's turning colder already."

"A nor'easter, say I," Thornwood told the officer waiting at the head of the gangplank. "Well, that's not so bad . . . a bit rough on the landsmen, perhaps. Carry us well out to Sea and give us the weather gage of the pirates in a day or two once it moves around to the southwest again. They're most likely hiding somewhere on the coast or behind one of the Skipstone Islands."

"Board the soldiers quickly then, M'Lord," advised Captain Friddler. "Take us two hours or a bit more, I judge, and getting colder and windier by the minute."

"Make sure they're snugged down fast."

"No fear!" replied the Captain. "At once, M'Lord!"

He shouted new orders against the rising wind to hustle the landsmen soldiers up the gangplank.

"One good thing," Thornwood said to nobody in particular. "This northerly wind'll keep the pirates in their secret harbor, wherever it lies! If they intend to continue to harass Dukedom's coast, that is. Or it might blow them all the way to Choin!"

"Choin'll hang 'em without blinkin' an eye or holding a trial," one of his younger officers snorted. "Pirates steer well clear of Choin, I hear!"

"Heave to under storms'l and ride 'er out!" advised Castorbean. "Wind'll blow us all the way to the coast of the Choin, given a chance!"

"As you say, then, Master Mate," Seacaptain Lorianne agreed. She had her doubts about the foul-weather courage of her crew, if not about her ship. "We'll heave to. You're the expert sailor!"

"So I be," grunted the Seaman, forgetting to salute.

As an afterthought he added, as he turned away, "Aye-aye, ma'am!"

Chapter Six

Gone With the Wind

MARBLEHEART, an old Sea hand, sniffed the strong wind now blowing from just east of north. Full, cloudy night had quickly fallen, filled with salty spume and the shrill yammering and clattering of rigging. The crew had furled all sail except a single storm sail on the fore to give the helmsman *some* steerage control.

"Can smell the flocks of upper Valley and the supper smokes of Trunkety, I should say," he reported to the Prince of Faerie.

"Even I can tell we're moving southwest, *away* from the coast, and fairly fast," Flowerbender said, looking up at the scudding clouds close overhead. "I've mastered the square knot. Go over the next one again. Half hitch, is it?"

"Never mind the half hitch for now," muttered his companion. "I'm not a professional Seaman, but I'm certain these crewmen aren't handling this ship with proper care."

He scrambled aft, ignoring the steep pitch of the deck, to the poop where Lorianne clung with white-knuckled effort to the wheel. As the Otter came up, a sudden twist of waves and wind all but jerked the girl off her feet to one side, then flung her back again.

Marbleheart threw his forelegs about her waist and clung to her until the ship settled once more.

"Too much to handle for just one," he shouted over the increasing scream of the wind. "Order someone up here to help!"

"I—I—I . . . you're right!" gasped the girl, chancing loss of control by dashing her soaking auburn hair from her eyes. "Fetch Castorbean! I can't make him hear my voice."

"Right! Hold fast, lass!"

Marbleheart slithered back down the slanting deck, passed Ben clinging to the port rail amidships, and crashed open the fo'c'sle door. The four crewmen were huddled in their bunks.

"First Mate!" roared Marbleheart from the doorway. "Hit the deck, old man! Lend a hand at the wheel!"

"No use! No blasted use!" howled Castorbean from the depths of his bunk, to which he clung fiercely with both hands and all available toes. "We're as good as lost! It's getting worse by the minute! No use!"

"Old man!" snarled the Otter in his ear, baring very sharp teeth. "If the helm's loose, all's lost! Come on! Up! *Up!*"

With urging by the Otter's strong legs and sharp teeth, the First Mate struggled to his feet and allowed himself to be prodded bodily out and down the slanting deck. A wave crashed over the bow and dashed around their knees. The Otter and the Seaman clung to the mainmast fife rail, sputtering from the salt spray.

"She can't take much more!" howled Castorbean. "She'll founder! She'll dis-mast! She'll split down the middle! *We'll die!*"

"Only if we let the tiller go wild! Must keep her head to the wind!" Marbleheart screamed back, nipping at the Seaman's bare legs to get him moving aft again. "The girl hasn't enough weight to hold her steady, nor the strength!''

The storm's fury had increased threefold by the time the two struggled onto the poop and grasped the wheel beside the bedraggled Lorianne. With firm grips on the spokes, they managed to steady the helm once more and keep the schooner's head pointed into the howling wind.

Douglas and Pert stood in the doorway of the underhill Workshop, watching the rain drum the cobbled courtyard, scrub the black stones, and stream off the cottage thatch.

''Pity poor Seamen on a night such as this,'' the Pyromancer said to the cat.

She wrapped her tail tightly about his right leg and blinked silently.

From the kitchen door Myrn called, ''Supper, my dears! This storm'll last the whole night; an Aquamancer can tell.''

Douglas spoke a small Dry Spell and walked easily between the pelting, fat raindrops, hopping lightly over puddles, not getting wet at all. Pert followed closely behind, keeping under his spell-umbrella to the open kitchen door.

''Hope old Marbleheart and Ben are still with my folks,'' Douglas said to his goodwife, once the kitchen door was closed and the storm's uproar muted.

''Marbleheart can take care of himself, comes stormy weather,'' Myrn assured him. ''And fairies have ways to hide from storms, too, I suppose. Here! Hang up your slicker, and I've brought your warm slippers. We'll sit by the fire after supper and tell tales to the children. 'Cozy' is the secret watchword for wet nights like this, my love.''

''Story! Story!'' cried the twins gleefully, swarming over their father.

''After supper's eaten,'' laughed Douglas. ''Blue Teakettle's made us hot and savory chicken stew and plump dumplings, just perfect for a chilly night, I see . . . and smell. She knew a storm was on its way!''

■　　■　　■

Eunicet shoved one of his sailor-pirates deeper into the shallow Middle Ridge cave, to make more room for himself by a tiny, smoky fire.

"Get some sleep!" he ordered his six remaining crewmen. "Storm won't last out the night, I'd say."

"Could last for days!" muttered one of his men.

"Take the first dog watch!" the former Duke snapped angrily at the speaker. "Now!"

"But, Captain . . . !" howled the complainer. "We've no oilskins against wet and chill!"

"Too bad for you, matey!" snarled Bladder from the other side of the fire. "Go on watch outside as ordered . . . or I'll twist me knife in your quaking liver and toss your bleeding body in the bottom of yonder ravine!"

Bladder looked fully capable of such a terrible deed, softly caressing his freshly whetted belt knife. The man shrugged and left the cave, to be immediately drenched by the pouring rain and buffeted by the northeast wind funneling between the steep ridges.

"Keep an eye on him," Eunicet growled softly. "He'll take leave of us for good and all!"

"No great loss," Bladder shrugged. "Let him run!"

"Pilot knows of a sheltered anchorage just ahead," Captain Friddler reported. "Should take advantage of it, m'Lord!"

"Worst luck!" sighed Thornwood, pounding the rail beside him to help him decide. "Fine, then! Carry on, Friddler! If we can't sail in this wrack, neither can pirate craft."

"Wise decision, sir," Friddler said. "I'll signal for the others to follow us in."

Groundswell, *Firedrake,* and *Hedgehog* read and repeated the lantern-flash signals at once. Friddler spoke to his Officer of the Deck, and the watch on duty dashed madly about in the driving rain for several minutes making the necessary change in sails.

"Spyglass Island's deep bay's good shelter from a

nor'easter," the Captain shouted in Thornwood's ear. "Be in a tall lee. Deep, quiet water, too."

"We'll ride 'er out there, then," agreed Thornwood.

He blew a trickle of rain from his nose but refused to go below until his squadron was safe under Spyglass and anchored in a small, unnamed bay over a hard sand bottom.

At midnight Marbleheart was aware the wind had again increased, but blew steadily still from the east-northeast, driving poor *Peachpit* Southwestward.

"We're making a fast way," he shouted to Ben.

The boy was not bothered by the cold nor the wind nor even the wild pitching of the deck. He seemed to enjoy it, in fact.

"Relieve the helm!" came a cry from aft.

"Aye! I'll pass the word," Marbleheart shouted back.

In a few minutes he'd rousted out the other crew members. Ben helped the lady Seacaptain to the main cabin, where she fell onto her bunk with a shuttering sigh.

"Change those soaking clothes, Seacaptain. I'll see if I can get something for your supper."

He disappeared, returning a few moments later with chicken sandwiches left from lunch, as well as a half-pitcher of warm ale and a chunk of soft cheese.

"I'm famished, I admit," sighed Lorianne, sitting up on her bunk. "Share this with me, friends! Last we'll get for hours and hours."

Marbleheart appeared from deck, puffing and blowing lustily. The companions ate without talking, not because there was nothing to say but because the shuttering, shivering, shattering, creaking, groaning, snapping, rasping of ropes and timbers, and the constant howl of wind and hiss of water, made conversation impossible.

Before she finished her sandwich, Lorianne had fallen asleep. The Otter and the lad tumbled her into her bunk and sat at the cabin table, clutching its edge to keep themselves from being flung about by the wild gyrations of the lightly laden schooner.

"They've let her fall off the wind!" Marbleheart gasped.

"Not very reliable Seamen, are they?" asked young Ben.

"Not very! Our only hope in a storm is hold her head into the wind and ride 'er out. If she's slued *across* the wind . . . probably roll on her back, dismast entirely. Sink or shatter!"

"Let me check, this time," Ben offered.

He went to the door and wrenched it open, admitting an almost solid wall of salt spray which threw him off his feet for a moment until *Peachpit* surged up and away.

On deck Ben clung to the weather rail to force his way aft.

"Nobody at the wheel!" he shouted. "Where's that blasted cowardly crew?"

Marbleheart, who'd followed him aft, heard his exclamation and plunged to his side.

"The poor fools! Jolly boat's gone! We've got to turn her back into the wind again . . . or take a long, cold swim, m'boy!"

"Waken the Seacaptain?"

"No time . . . and she's already exhausted. Follow me! We'll do whatever the Otter and the Fairy Prince can do!"

There came a tremendous *crack* of splitting timber, a sharp rattle-snapping of broken lines, and the aftermast whipped suddenly over the side, furled sails, trailing ropes, standing rigging, and all, to be carried off downwind, flying like a child's kite before the blast.

"Oh, *oh*!" Marbleheart shouted. "Now we're for it! No crew! No sails! No mast!"

Before Ben could answer, a second, louder ripping split the air.

A terrific gust plucked the sagging mainmast from its stepping and hurled it over the side like a spear. Without the balance of the lost masts, the ship rolled until its port rail—what was left of it—plunged deep under rushing water.

Turned on her beam-ends, the schooner struggled valiantly to right herself.

"*Hang on!*" shouted the Otter.

Ben wedged himself between a remaining bit of rail and the forward bulkhead of the aftercabin.

"Must be *something* I could *try*, at least," he shouted. "Hold a minute, Marbleheart!"

"Minute may be . . ."

A much vaster, more terrifying, greater, tumbling and swirling grey-green wave broke over *Peachpit*'s port afterquarter, making the poor schooner plunge, leap, shiver and shriek, and shudder like a forest hart pierced through the heart by a huntsman's arrow.

"We're in deep trouble!" Marbleheart thought to himself.

Tons of icy water crashed down on him, again and again, but the Sea Otter held on for dear life, breathing in the scant moments between waves.

Chapter Seven

Otter Overboard!

MORE at home in turbulent water than on any deck, the Sea Otter kept his head as poor *Peachpit* suddenly rolled over on her back and, judging by the muffled roaring, cracked in two.

Husbanding his last full breath before the final roll, Marbleheart struck out strongly, instinctively avoiding loose planks, pieces of broken masts, splintered yards, jagged ends of railing, and sodden masses of sailcloth rolling in the turbulence like pasta in a boiling pot.

The figure of the fairy boy appeared before him for a moment. He lunged out, grabbing Ben by the back of his jerkin, drawing him along with him as he struggled to free them both from the floating wreckage.

Like two corks they popped suddenly into the insanely screaming wind.

"I can swim . . . I think!" Marbleheart heard the fairy boy cough.

Taking him at his word, the Otter released his grip and concentrated on gasping great lungfuls of air and salty froth.

He caught another glimpse of the Prince of Faerie. Despite the hurly-burly of the Sea's surface, Ben was breathing evenly, moving his arms and legs to keep himself afloat and right side up.

"Way to go!" shouted Marbleheart.

Another upwelling surge of dark water crashed over them both, driving them deep under the surface. By then they had each taken on a fair lungful of air. Marbleheart fought valiantly to keep from coughing and losing it again . . . and after a long moment his head emerged from the waves.

"Arrrgh! Haff! *Haff!*" he choked.

"Are you . . ." came Ben's voice from behind him

Marbleheart whipped about, avoided a ragged chunk of beam careening by, and swam to Ben's side.

"Keep well away from the heavy stuff and keep your head out of the water," he advised, wheezing his words. "Don't struggle more than you have to, to stay afloat. Relax!"

"Good enough advice, I suppose," the boy coughed back.

There was a short respite between raging swells. The Otter reached out for a nearby timber and rested his legs by taking a firm grip with his foreclaws, letting the wood keep him afloat.

Ben followed suit.

"I could fly away," he gasped into the Otter's nearest ear, "but I don't think I could carry you with me. Wet . . . too heavy!"

"Fly without me! I'll be fine. This is puppy's play for us Sea Otters, m'boy!"

"No . . . I'll s-s-stick with you, M-M-Marbleheart! At least until we see some place to which to f-f-fly."

"You're absolutely right. Even grammatical!" the Otter decided.

It was black as the far inside of the Wizards' High cellars! And much colder and wetter.

■ ■ ■

Marbleheart pushed his foreclaws deeper into the hard oak-knee timber. Ben somehow managed to lash himself to the yard with his broad belt, losing his fancy dress scabbard in the process. His sword had disappeared long since. They clung fast to the timber and shouted encouragement to each other until at last the rain eased and the wind lashed less insanely.

Steep waves still shot them up and down but, toward dawn, even the waves became gentler . . . rollers rather than breakers . . . which made it easier to float along at some ease, if still extremely cold and wet.

"Storm's passed," Ben observed hoarsely.

"Wait for daylight," Marbleheart advised. "Watch for a landfall. Even a bit of reef barely awash would be very welcome."

"No sign of poor *Peachpit* . . . nor the crew," said the boy, mournfully.

"Lost, I'm afraid," agreed the Otter. "Remember the spelling you were about to try?"

"Not a word," sighed the young fairy. "I . . . I never committed it to firm memory, Marbleheart. I'm so very sorry!"

"No problem, I guess," the Otter grunted. "But next lesson, my dear young Prince . . . *pay attention!*"

The wan light of morning grew and clouds scudded overhead, shredding into grey rags and then into white streaks as the weak sunlight came and went. The wind died even further and the waves smoothed into long, easy swells. At last a blinding blaze of sunlight broke through a rift in the clouds, spotlighting them for a few minutes . . . but showing no land, nor even bare, lonely rocks, anywhere within the great circle of horizon.

A second timber floated close by, tangled in hempen ropes.

"*Peachpit*'s main boom, I think," cried Ben, who'd

spent his time aboard ship memorizing the various parts and pieces of the ill-fated sloop's rigging.

"Latch on! Bind the two pieces together. We'll make a sturdier raft!"

Following the Otter's directions and with considerable flopping about and flailing in the water, they managed to align the two timbers side by side and bind them as tightly together as possible with soaked line. They then clambered wearily out of the water and bestrode their two-log raft.

"*C-c-cold!*" shuddered the boy.

"Paddle!" Marbleheart ordered. "That will help keep us warm and maybe move our craft with some useful direction."

They lay atop the lashed timbers and stroked with hands and paws, first on one side and then on the other, pushing the crude raft slowly forward. The sun shone out again, and its rays gave some warmth, drying clothing and fur.

"Headed west and a bit south," Marbleheart estimated after an hour or more of paddling.

"Away from Dukedom?" asked the boy. "Away from our destination, too."

"Worry about destinations later. It's a big Sea, m'boy! Fairly filled with islands, as I recall, in these latitudes. Or is it *longitude*? Do you see anything?"

"Hold a minute!"

Ben carefully rose to a sitting position, then knelt with a knee on either timber, grasping a bit of metal cleat screwed to the spar.

He stood as tall as he could and gazed downwind . . . there was no use looking upwind, he realized. Marbleheart worked with all four legs, paddling furiously to keep the ungainly raft steady in the water.

"*Something* ahead," Ben called out. "Don't have any idea what it might be! Wood, at least, or so it seems. I could fly . . ."

"Paddle a bit more, rather. We'll catch it up . . . if just out of curiosity," decided Marbleheart.

■   ■   ■

It took the better part of an hour to reach the strange, squarish, narrow flatness floating low in the water.

"A bed!" Ben exclaimed in surprise.

"Now I see! Four posts . . . yes, definitely a bedstead," replied the Otter, standing to look and just catching himself before sliding into the water when he stretched up too high.

"Careful!" warned the Prince of Faerie. "Paddle! Almost there!"

Suddenly the tattered fore-end of their makeshift raft *clunked* against the floating bedstead. Managing somehow to keep from rolling into the water, both travelers reached out to grasp the bed's long side.

The mattress had miraculously stayed on its ropes, and even a wet tangle of blankets and sheets had remained aboard. They saw a movement under the blankets.

"Ahoy!" cried Marbleheart. "Ahoy! Are you all right?"

From the middle of the sodden bedclothes emerged a pale face framed in soaking red hair. The face at first stared at them blankly, then smiled wanly, wearily, and began to weep.

"I thought . . . thought . . . all was lost," wept Lorianne. "My poor, poor crewmen! My brave sailors! My *Peach-pit*! "

Marbleheart and the lad climbed into the bed, where both hugged and comforted the weeping Seacaptain, patting her and assuring her all was well, at last.

"B-b-but . . . my men!" Lorianne gasped. "I'm so glad you're safe, Marbleheart! Ben! But . . . my crew!"

"When last seen," the Otter said softly, "they took to the jolly boat and set off on their own."

"It's . . . it's . . . all my fault!" sobbed Lorianne, shaking her head. "They . . ."

"They brought it on themselves!" Ben insisted. "As my companion here says: In a storm, *don't give up the ship*!"

Lorianne, who had evidently heard this bit of wisdom

before, at last nodded sadly and tried to dry her tears on a damp and salty bit of bedsheet.

"I was sound asleep and suddenly there was a crash and . . . I was no longer in the cabin at all," Lorianne told them, when she'd recovered enough to speak.

"Remarkable!" the Otter cried, sniffing about the bed. "Just enough good solid wood to keep it afloat! Mattress made of tight-woven cloth, stuffed with some sort of fibers. That helped, too, I guess."

Lorianne smiled for the first time. "Better than two yards lashed together, at least."

"*Any port in a storm*, as old Casper Marlinspike often said." Marbleheart shrugged. "*I* say, Mistress Seacaptain, we're all three very lucky!"

"Be nice if things were less damp, however," commented the fairy. "It'll never be completely dry, I suppose. Did I say how pleased we are to find you . . . or have you find us . . . Lorianne? It was a close thing for us all for a while!"

"You haven't seen the jolly boat anywhere, have you?" the girl asked anxiously. She set about wringing her hair dry and combing it out of her eyes with her fingers.

"Neither sigh nor cry," Marbleheart told her sadly. "It just proves another thing Casper once told me: *Stick with your ship!* In this case, your bedstead."

"I had no choice!" the girl protested. She shook off her grief with a severe nod of her head. "We could make ourselves more comfortable if we wrung out some of these blankets."

"And use them to make a sail, perhaps?" Marbleheart said thoughtfully.

The sun was setting. They had seen not even one small islet all day long. Sea had moderated to the point where they could stay fairly dry aboard the bedstead . . . although the salt water evaporating from their bodies left an uncomfortable, itchy crust of salt.

It didn't bother the Sea Otter as much. He was used to it.

"A lot more to this Venturing than I ever thought," sighed Ben as they spread out blankets, quilts, pillows, and sheets to dry in the hot tropical sun.

"Sailing for New Land was a Venture," the Otter muttered. "*This* is an *Adventure*!"

Marbleheart and Ben struggled to raise, between the two head-end bedposts, the tiny, makeshift sail Lorianne had laboriously stitched and lashed together with pieces of light line and unraveled wool shreds.

"We're making a bit of headway, anyway," sighed the girl, slumping wearily beside the Otter. "I've no idea how fast. And no way to control direction, either. We're at the mercy of the winds."

"Wind's from the northeast, just now," Marbleheart estimated. "I could easily catch some fish, mates, if you'll eat 'em raw. Not a bad meal, if you get the right kind of fish."

"The thought's getting more and more attractive by the minute," Ben laughed.

"I thought you fairy types were Near Immortal and didn't need to eat as regularly as Men," wondered Lorianne. "Am I wrong?"

"We don't die easily . . . not as easily as Men," admitted the Prince. "But we can get powerfully hungry. Better try some of your raw fishes, Otter. I guess you two're less able to stand the bite of hunger."

Marbleheart went over the side, disappearing for several long minutes in the darkening Sea. The fairy and the girl huddled together, sharing a bit of almost-dry blanket and conserving their body heat.

"Oysters!" said Marbleheart when his head broke the surface. "Quite decent bivalves. Tasty and tender!"

"I'm hungry enough to eat even raw bar," sniffed Lorianne. "How do we get at 'em, I wonder?"

"Leave that to a Faerie Prince!" Ben said, drawing his sharp dagger from his belt. "Sword was lost, but it'd have been too awkward for this work, anyway."

He attacked the dozen or so oysters Marbleheart dumped into the bed, prying them open. As quickly as he had one oyster free of its shell, he handed it to Lorianne, who popped it into her mouth, chewed a moment, then swallowed.

"Not half bad!" she insisted. "Rather salty, but not too much. Take some for yourself, Ben, and our oyster fisher deserves a large share."

"I've already eaten," Marbleheart told her. "These will be enough? More where they came from, folks! Just say the word."

"No, I'd better not make a pig of myself," the girl began and then she cried out, "*Ouch!* Something . . ."

"I forgot to warn you of pearls," Marbleheart apologized. "One in a hundred will have a pearl of some sort . . ."

"Pearls?" asked Ben. "What are pearls?"

"Here, then," said Lorianne, spitting something into her hand. "*This* is a pearl!"

The boy took the tiny pinkish sphere in his hand and studied it closely. Marbleheart leaned over and nodded his head.

"Seen 'em in all sizes and colors, myself. Douglas had one *this* big . . ." He indicated at least three inches between his forepaws. "It was magical, however. Frigeon used it to hide his conscience."

"I never heard such a tale," cried the Lady Seacaptain.

"A way to pass the night's darkness, then," suggested Marbleheart. "It's getting cold. It'll be fine for me, being well furred, but you two should wrap up well."

The girl sighed wistfully. "A fire would be especially comforting."

"I've still got the matches," remembered Ben, digging

the waterproof tube from his trouser pocket. "But . . . what to burn, and where?"

Marbleheart, without a word, went over the side again and stayed beneath the waves for quite a long time. When he at last surfaced he lifted a large, flat, shallow shell over the side and braced it atop a pile of drying blankets.

It was more than two feet across, roughly circular, only two or three inches deep at its center. It was lined with gleaming, multihued mother-of-pearl, but its outside was a dull grey-brown and rough as distressed stone.

"If we can get some dry bits and pieces of cloth to burning," the Otter suggested, "enough to dry its own fuel . . ."

"And keep it small," suggested Lorianne, pleased with the prospect. "So as not to catch all the bedding afire!"

"No fear," Ben insisted. "The Otter, here, is Familiar to a famous Fire Wizard, you remember!"

They rummaged about in the bedclothes and managed to pile together a good-sized handful of shreds of wool stuffing and cotton sheeting which had fairly dried.

Ben prepared to strike a match. Marbleheart asked him to wait a moment and intoned the Drying Spell he had long ago learned from Douglas Brightglade.

"I usually use this on myself," he explained. "Dry my fur in a second or two. Watch!"

The tangle of shreds and threads sizzled, steamed, and popped a bit but very shortly fluffed out and became silent . . . and dry as the best tinder.

"Now, m'boy!" the Otter said. "Strike your match and set the stuff burning. I'll dry some chunks of driftwood. Plenty of it floating round us. There! Should burn quite well."

Sea had become flat calm in the wake of the storm, so the bed-boat rode easily without rocking, tipping, or shipping water. The small fire in the flat shell burned brightly gold and blue with only a little smoke.

The shipwrecked company crowded about, holding out

hands and paws to absorb the warmth and finish drying fur and skin.

"How wonderful!" Lorianne cried, her normally cheerful nature returning at last. "Something to eat and, now, light and warmth! We should tell our stories, I think, to get to know each other better. We may have to share this bed for a long time!"

"Ladies first," murmured the Otter politely.

Lorianne fanned out her skirt to dry. Ben sat cross-legged, elbows on knees. Marbleheart wriggled his long body into a fairly dry, fairly comfortable semicircle, belly toward the flames.

"Well, my name . . . as you already know . . . is Lorianne," began the girl. "I—I—I don't recall much of my earliest years, shipmates. My first memories are of a fisherman's comfortable cottage on the broad river running down to Sea, far to the west. I live there at Home Port with Uncle Braiser and Aunty Philadestra.

"I know they aren't my parents. I don't know *how* I know. Perhaps Uncle or Aunty told me. I've no idea who or where my father and mother could possibly be. I think they might have been fisherfolk, lost at Sea. Uncle Braiser has said *almost* as much, several times, but generally he and Aunty refuse to talk about where I came from. Perhaps they just don't know."

She paused to turn her skirt to dry the back side.

"I used to try to imagine it for myself, you know. I had plenty of time to myself. Aunty and Uncle have no children of their own, and the fisherfolk children are mostly older than me. They tend to stay away . . . I don't know why. Sometimes I think they fear me."

"You were badly treated?" Ben asked sympathetically. He reached out and patted her hand, to show he sympathized.

"No . . . not really. They just . . . stay away."

"What did you do, then? When you grew up, I mean," the fairy asked.

"Aunty was looking for a good, honest, hard-working young man for me to marry. She often talked about marriage, you see, but none of the older boys seemed to suit her. I was rather fond of them myself. They were so big, so rough, and loud . . . young men who knew and talked of little but boats and nets and lines and such."

"Young men're often like that," Marbleheart observed. "It doesn't mean they don't like you!"

Lorianne considered this for a while in silence.

"You may be right, Marbleheart. They aren't *unkind* to me. They are . . . polite . . . I guess. But none ever came calling.

"As I grew taller and handier with things, Uncle took me aboard his *Peachpit* schooner. It was the largest of our village fleet. He went farther and netted the biggest catches of all the Home Port fishermen . . ."

"Does your place have a name?" wondered Ben, who was trying his hand at broiling oysters on a stick over the fire.

"*Home Port*," repeated the girl. "That's what everybody calls it."

"Go on, then," urged the Otter. "You learned to navigate and sail from your uncle?"

"Yes! He taught me to read charts and Sea changes, and which lines to snub up tight, and which to cast loose. How to judge the winds and set the sails. That was a happy time . . . until one day, last spring, Uncle and Aunty called me to them and told me to take *Peachpit* and go on a trading voyage to the east. They never said, but I . . . *felt* . . . they were sending me away from some sort of danger. Of course, I went. The four older sailors who usually worked Uncle's schooner agreed to serve as crew."

"They were not happy to do so, were they?" asked the fairy, popping a sizzling oyster into his mouth and sucking in cool air when it proved too piping hot.

"No . . . oh, they are . . . were . . . *polite* enough and performed their duties well. But I never felt they served will-

ingly. Seamen have some sort of silly superstition about
women serving aboard a ship. I learned that when I was
still very young.''

''Poor sailors!'' sighed Marbleheart.

Lorianne looked as if she might cry again, but at the last
moment she straightened, blew her nose, and shook her
pretty red head.

''I really made a mess of it all, didn't I? Lost *Peachpit*.
Lost my poor crew . . . and they *were* good men, for all they
hated to serve a lady Seacaptain.''

''Conditions being what they were,'' Ben considered,
''you cannot blame yourself for their fate. We ourselves
were fortunate to survive!''

''I . . . I suppose you're right, Sir Prince!''

''Call me Ben,'' the lad insisted. ''Prince-ing is no use
at all when you're adrift at Sea without an oar!''

Marbleheart had been considering the girl's tale in silence.

''They . . . Uncle and Aunty . . . never said why they sent
you away?''

''Well, to tell you the truth, at the time I was so excited
and flattered to be sent off on my own, it never occurred
to me they had any sort of larger, more urgent reason. Later
I realized they were sending me away to safety. From what?
I have no idea at all, Sir Sea Otter!''

''Merely Marbleheart,'' clucked the animal.

He glanced long at the bright stars and sniffed the east
wind in great draughts. He dabbled his right forepaw in Sea
over the side, and examined the bits and strands of seaweed
and flotsam floating by on the surface.

''We're considerably further west than I'd have
guessed,'' he told his shipmates. ''Halfway to . . . whatever
is northwest of Choin and southwest of Old Kingdom. I
remember the maps, but there was never much written
down in that corner.''

''I've seen Flarman's great maps!'' cried Ben. ''Things

written there like '*Here Dwell Horrible Sea Serpents!*' and such.''

"What it means, I think, is we're being blown swiftly back along your outward course, Lorianne. We're likely to end up at Uncle Braiser's own dock, given a day or two, or five, or six. Hope you enjoy toasted sardines and oyster stew without the stew!"

"Oysters are really very good," the girl decided. "And Sea fish are very nutritious and tender, cooked on an open fire."

"Besides," sniffed the Fairy Prince, "what choice do we have?"

"I suppose between us we could call up a storm or a strong wind to blow us back to Dukedom," the Otter suggested.

"Well, it *might* be worth a try," agreed the boy without much enthusiasm. "Tomorrow morning, shall we try it? The lass here is about to fall over from weariness. And so are you, Marbleheart, if I miss not my guess. And even I, the mighty, powerful, splendidly trained, and fully educated Prince Flowerbender Aedhsson of Faerie, am hearing an urgent call to slumber, although these blankets still feel rather clammy!"

But when he looked about, he found his companions were already asleep, and the easterly wind had freshened again. *Bedstead*, as Lorianne had dubbed their awkward craft, was making fairly good leeway . . . toward the west.

Chapter Eight

Warning of Pirates

IN the absence of the elder Pyromancer, Douglas rose even earlier than usual the morning after the storm to perform both his own morning chores and those of his friend and mentor.

There were the Ladies of the Byre to milk and tend and let out into the rain-fresh meadow. He greeted the speckled hens and, as the rooster watched proudly, shooed them from their nests and gathered their new-laid eggs for the family's breakfast and for the light, frosted cakes Blue Teakettle would cause to appear at the supper table that evening.

He opened the wide doors and transoms of Wizards' Workshop to let the fresh, cool morning air circulate, which it did very well by some mysterious means built into the maze of workshops, laboratories, storage rooms, and passageways dug by the Dwarf Bryarmote long ago.

Meanwhile Blue Teakettle huffed and bustled happily about the big, good-smelling kitchen, preparing breakfast while old Sugar Caster directed Plates and Bowls, Knives and Forks and Spoons into their proper places.

Myrn came down the broad stairs with Brenda and

Brand, newly scrubbed, carefully combed, and dressed in sturdy outdoors clothing, ready to break fast and tackle their morning lessons. Then they'd play in the new summer sunshine and languid airs.

Douglas refilled Flarman's largest spirit lamp with scented alcohol and set it under a bulbous retort. He laid out the tools he'd be using that day as he pursued the riddle of the strange lens sent to the High by Chief Tet of Highlandorm.

He stuck his head in the kitchen door at this point to find breakfast was not quite ready. Blue, at home on the Range, was eyeing the poaching of eggs and reminding Frying Pan to turn out bacon strips before they burned.

To pass the meantime, Douglas directed the long-handled hazel-twig Broom to begin clearing washed-down soil, grass, and small pebbles carried off the High onto the cobbles by yesterday's storm.

Beside the courtyard well he found, seated in a row on the curbing, the entire Thatchmouse family and a guest.

"This is my distant cousin, name of Flittery Chipmunk." Papa Thatchmouse introduced the tiny, striped stranger. "He comes from upper Valley, a long ways off. With news."

"Welcome to Wizards' High, Master Flittery!" smiled the young Wizard, offering the tiny brown rodent his right forefinger to shake. "Always welcome a visit from a neighbor!"

"Thank you, thank you, *thank you*, M—M—Master Brightglade!" replied the Chipmunk. "I—I—I have come with n-n-news! Or perhaps it's not news to you Wizards? But I thought . . ."

"Come inside and meet my goodwife and family, first," Douglas interrupted, opening the kitchen door. "We can hear your news over breakfast."

"Honored, honored, *honored*!" chattered the small animal.

His chattering was playfully imitated by the five lively

Thatchmouse children, until Mistress Thatchmouse told them to *hush*!

"We're usually up and about long before you Great Folk, being mostly night critters," Mrs. Thatchmouse explained, shooing her children before her through the doorway. "It's a great, great honor, however . . ."

"We've been very remiss, I say, in not inviting you to dine more often," Douglas insisted.

He lifted the entire Thatchmouse delegation and their guest onto the kitchen table and introduced them solemnly to Myrn, to Blue Teakettle, to the twins, and to Bronze Owl, all in their places, waiting for the morning meal to begin.

"So very pleased to meet you!" cried the lady Aquamancer. "Here, sit on my left. No, Brand! Leave the baby mice to their mama. You can invite them to play *after* breakfast, if you like."

"We know them all very well," insisted her son. "We've played with them all, numbers of times, Mama."

"Time now to eat and talk, however," Bronze Owl reproved the lad. "Playtime'll come soon enough. Perhaps your little friends would like to join us in our lessons? Eat a good breakfast, first, students!"

"*You* never eat!" scolded Brenda, waving her fork.

"I make up for it by talking. Besides, remember . . . if I were an ordinary, flesh-and-blood kind of Owl, one of my most favorite snacks would be . . ."

"Tender little mice!" squealed the Thatchmouse children in horrified glee. "He'd eat us *alive*!"

"Now, children . . . !" began their mother.

"They're teasing me, ma'am," the Owl explained. "May I pass you some of these corn fritter crumbs? Most delicious with maple syrup and butter, I'm told!"

Breakfast went on with a great deal of pleasant chatter, more than a little laughter, and some gentle teasing. The Thatchmouse children were quite at home on the High Table, as they called it, and the Brightglade twins were, after resisting the first few temptations to show off, on their best company behavior.

Flittery Chipmunk turned out to be a pleasant, if rather too serious and very bashful, visitor He was, he said, a strict vegetarian and would have to refuse the scraps of pork sausage patties and the thinly sliced breakfast steak, but those date-cakes and that oat porridge smelled divinely wonderful to him. He had three small bowls of the last, with cream and sugar, and a dot of yellow butter.

"I *must* tell you my n-n-news, Sir Wizard!" he insisted at last, "before I fall over asleep and nap 'til l-l-lunch!"

"Tell us, then . . . if you've had enough to eat," Douglas agreed. "I'm prepared to listen all morning, if it takes that long."

"Not n-n-n-nearly that long, I assure you!" cried the Chipmunk, who had almost regained his usual perky self-confidence. "Sir Wizard, I was yesterday morning, just before the b-b-beginning of the storm, gathering early-ripening seeds on Near Ridge. Or Far Ridge, as my eastern cousins insist it should be called. They live on Seaside to the east."

Douglas said he'd not had the pleasure of meeting the eastern branch of the Chipmunk family.

"Well, I was n-n-nosing about quite happily, when I spotted a party of raggedy, dirty, noisy Menfolk huddled together in a shallow cave on the west slope of Middle Ridge."

"Anyone we know . . . or should know?" asked Myrn.

"If I wasn't a sensible 'munk, I'd swear they were *p-p-pirates*!" chirped the animal, "and, what's more, I swear I recognized their l-l-leader. He was dirty and unshaven and dressed in tattered canvas pantaloons and a dirty, torn shirt, you see, and he was shouting at his p-p-people most terribly, saying all manner of mean things . . . and at that moment a name popped up out of memory."

"Go on!" urged Douglas, leaning forward.

"Years ago that very man came to my grandfather's

home, up near Capital! Granddaddy lived on the estate of one of old Duke Thorowood's knights. I was reared there myself, you understand.''

"And?" Myrn prompted in her turn.

"A-a-and this pirate ch-ch-chief? He was either a perfect double or the very man himself! Old D-D-Duke-that-never-was Eunicet! In the flesh! I'd heard he'd been banished to a far distant island in a part of S-S-Sea called Warm.''

"That's my understanding," agreed Douglas gravely, "and yet you've seen him right here, on the edge of Valley? Evil tidings! Especially with Duke Thornwood and all his soldiers off chasing pirates at Sea. Well . . .''

"I *could* be wr-wr-wrong," chittered the 'munk earnestly. "Or, rather . . . no! I'm sure I'm right! It *was* bad old Eunicet, for sure! Turned pirate, too, I vow!''

"I'm not at all surprised," Myrn sniffed. "Just the sort of sneaky, nasty trickery Eunicet'd try, isn't it? Although how under blue sky he got off that lonely island, I'd be very interested to hear.''

"As I recall, Casper was marooned there, once. He escaped by building a boat from spare parts from ship-wrecks," Bronze Owl suggested. "But Eunicet . . . ?''

"He had that Bladder person with him. Rather clever, for all he's sluggish and tricky. . . . Well, I'll have to check this out," decided Douglas, looking rather worried. "They'd have been well advised to stay far clear of Duke-dom! Many Valley farmers'd as soon string Eunicet from a hay-hoist as blink twice. He'll be in considerable danger here, if he doesn't know it.''

"I'll get a bonnet and come along to help," began Myrn, but then she stopped. "No, someone must stay here with the children, what with Marbleheart and Flarman away. *Drat!* Who will you take with you, Douglas?''

"No one," decided her young husband, rising from the table after one last gulp of milk. "Frenstil's short-staffed here in Valley, what with the Militia and the Guard off with Thornwood. *Hmm!* Bronze Owl . . . ?''

"Yes, Douglas?"

"Fly and warn Thornwood. Goodness knows where *he* is . . ."

"Gull friends will know where to find him. Storm yesterday will have driven his fleet into shelter somewhere. I'll go at once!"

"Tell Thornwood what we've heard. Perhaps he should sail for home, if his quarry's here in Dukedom, no longer at Sea."

"Change your clothing, my dear," said the practical Myrn, "and I'll have Blue Teakettle pack you a hearty lunch with enough left over if you decide to stay past suppertime. Best go by way of the Feather Pin! The sooner we have firm information, the better for us all."

Douglas stooped to kiss his children, who had been watching and listening with wide eyes and open mouths.

"What's to become of us?" wailed little Brenda, frightened by the sudden flurry of events. Her world was usually quiet and peaceful, and everybody in it was friendly.

"Not to worry, my pretty girl!" Myrn soothed her fears, catching both children up into her arms. "Here's a powerful, quick, brave, and accomplished young mother Aquamancer close by to protect you. With Bronze Owl off for the day, you probably should play in the courtyard, this morning. The grass on the lawn is still wet. Keep within the meadow gate, please."

"We'd rather stay with you, Mama," said Brand, who was valiantly hiding his own disquiet. "We'll not be a bother, we promise!"

"Well, then, of course! But move with me and don't wander off. Go, Bronze Owl! Tell Thornwood what's going on. I'll send a message by Deka the Wraith to Flarman and my Master at Waterand Island."

The household scattered to their tasks, leaving the Thatchmouse family to finish up the breakfast crumbs, which they did quickly and neatly.

"I'll return home with the Fire Wizard," decided Flittery Chipmunk. "Thank you, neighbors!"

"Call on us another time, when we'll sample the cider in the ice house and nibble some ears in the corncrib," Papa Thatchmouse invited. "*Now!* Children, best we make ourselves scarce, as good mice should. Mother, you and I will take turns manning the lookout on the highest ridge-pole."

"We'll help you, Papa," said his youngest son earnestly. "Six pairs of mouse's eyes are better than just two!"

"Our son is growing up," murmured Mrs. Thatchmouse to her husband.

Douglas pulled on his boots and folded Flarman's tattered old Cloak of Invisibility—it is, of course, very difficult to mend an invisible cloak—into his pack to keep his lunch from being squashed, took the Chipmunk on his shoulder, and set off for the Ridges.

Although he used the Cloud Fairies' famous flying Feather Pin to transport himself and Flittery Chipmunk over Near (or Far, etc.) Ridge, it took them some hours to locate the shallow cave in which the pirates had sheltered during the storm.

"Rain's washed away most of the odors," complained the little 'munk, shaking his head in apology. "I *think* they were here, however, Wizard! Under that great, leaning-over rock, the one looking like it's ready to slip into the valley?"

"A rather skimpy shelter, however," Douglas thought to himself, but he didn't say it aloud. Flittery was trying his best under difficult circumstances.

They scrambled up a steep slope of scree, only to find the pirate's cave empty. Within were the ashes of a fire, still warm.

"They were here not long ago!" exclaimed Chipmunk after a few minutes of close inspection. "I can smell 'em quite too well, here inside. Nasty, dirty crowd! They slept here, you see, on this bed of dried salt grass. Ate a shore dinner, from the looks of the shells and things."

"We'll search further afield, then," the Pyromancer said with a nod. "Let me see . . ."

He stood in the shallow cave's mouth, turning slowly around from left to right, humming a useful Seeking Spell in a low voice. Flittery stood silently in the cave shadows, not wishing to interfere.

"They left shortly before noon," Douglas told him at last. "Most of them, that is. One or two stayed here a short while longer, then went east over Middle Ridge. *Ah!* It's clear to me now . . . their leader *is* old Eunicet!"

"What shall we do, then?" worried the 'munk, sighing anxiously. "We've lost them, do you think, Master Douglas?"

"No, not at all! I believe we'd be wisest to track down the smaller party, first. They . . . not more than three . . . can maybe be persuaded to tell us details of Eunicet's plans."

"Eunicet!" groaned the rodent. "Is he a Wizard, also? Or merely a Magician?"

"I don't think Eunicet would qualify even for Magician," Douglas told him cheerfully. "Come along! There're still many hours of light to see by."

Bronze Owl, flying swiftly and surprisingly quietly for all his brazen feathers, took the advice of a pair of gannets he'd encountered and arrived at the fleet anchorage just as the Dukedom captains were casting off their mooring lines and preparing to set sail.

"Must see Thornwood!" Bronze Owl told Seacaptain Friddler of the Ducal flagship *Donation*. "At once! Dukedom is threatened!"

Friddler turned pale at the metal bird's stark words.

"He left us early this morning . . . some four hours since, Bronze Owl!"

"Left? Where did he go on this rock?"

"I can't say, I'm sure. He went down along the shore after breakfast . . . for a stroll and a bit of a think, he said."

"Not unusual for Thornwood."

"About an hour ago he sent word for us to resume searching for the pirates, without him. Said he'd met an old friend and was going to the rescue of someone in danger. No more than that, Owl!"

"Well..." Owl sighed deeply, after a long quarter-minute of staring out to Sea toward the south and west. "Thornwood's no fool. The best you can do is follow his orders, I guess. But I can tell you the pirates may not be at Sea, now, but ashore in Dukedom ... somewhere east of Wizards' High!"

He related the chipmunk's news and, when he'd finished, the burly Seacaptain at once gave orders to the fleet to set all sail and head for Farango Water.

"We can't do any better than that," he said to the helmsman.

"A good place to be, Farango, if danger threatens at home. Lord Duke'll take good care of hisself, Cap'n! I've followed him all over this here Sea in past years, and he's done what's best, I'll swear, every time. Smart *and* lucky!"

Friddler and Bronze Owl nodded to each other, not quite as sure of things as the old quartermaster.

"Flags!" the Captain called to his signals yeoman. "Signal the fleet! Make 'Follow me home'!"

The night wind that drove good ship *Bedstead* westward became stronger and stronger again, steady from east of northeast, not so strong as to be dangerous but strong enough to push the ungainly vessel at surprising speed, pushing against the small sail, tall headboard, and low footboard.

Of a sudden the low-riding bed-boat struck something hard and unyielding, spun sideways and immediately crashed into a great, rounded, almost-submerged rock.

In the darkness all the three Seafarers could tell was they were suddenly in the midst of a boiling bit of shoal whose black rocks looked like nothing so much as huge, sharp teeth gnashing and lashing the waves to a white froth.

"Should have foreseen danger!" yelped the Otter. "Or smelled it!"

"Hang on, mates!" screamed Lorianne, suiting action to words by grabbing the nearest bedpost with both hands. "We're in for a rough ride!"

Chapter Nine

Deep Sea Deliverance

ON his morning walk Thornwood had chosen a path along the shore on wet, hard-packed sand.

There was something . . . had always been something . . . about the early morning Sea which raised his spirits and calmed his thoughts. As he strolled he stooped frequently to pick up an empty shell here or a bit of wave-smoothed driftwood there, occasionally slipping a particularly pretty specimen into his coat pocket for later study, perhaps to add to his growing collection at home of interesting marine mementos and specimens.

Nearing the point of land which he'd set as his strolling goal, he was attracted by a flat, colorfully marked, spiral shell half buried in the sand.

"*Chambered Nautilus*, it is!" he cried aloud, startling a long-legged bittern who'd trotted energetically beside him just at the edge of the water. "You don't see many of them on these beaches, do you?"

"Plenty of 'em on the western shore," chirped the bird, bobbing his head quickly.

"Never been there," the young Duke remarked thoughtfully.

"Strange things to see and eat, over to west," added the bittern, nodding several more times.

Thornwood examined the beautifully swirled shell for a moment. When he turned it over in his hand, it spilled a quantity of fine white sand and a half-pint of warm, salty water on his boot toes.

He laughed and strode into the surf to rinse sand from the specimens he'd gathered.

As he straightened, he found himself eye to eye with a huge square green face. Below the large, liquid, lazy-seeming, golden eyes was a wickedly curved beak.

"Sorry to startle you, M'Lord," said the face. "I was just lying here, letting the fresh storm waters carry away some of these pesky barnacles along my keel, you see. Didn't mean to startle . . ."

"No need to apologize!" cried Thornwood, smiling back at what he perceived to be friendly eyes. "I hope I didn't startle you, in fact."

"Not much startles a Great Sea Tortoise."

"Great Sea Tortoise . . . of course! I've heard of you . . . or one of your family. From one of my very best friends, Douglas Brightglade of Wizards' High?"

"Journeyman Douglas! Yes! I'm Oval, who was be-friended a few years back by that young Apprentice. I've seen you, now I think of it! Pleased to meet you, Lord Thornwood Duke! Yes, I remember you! At Battle of Sea."

Thornwood patted the enormous tortoise on her thick carapace in greeting.

"You're well these days, Mistress Oval? I thought you usually frequented Warm Sea, near the island of Augurian, the Water Adept."

"I stay closer to home, usually," replied the Tortoise, grinning broadly now. "I had, a few months ago, a sudden desire to see the lands and waters here in the west. Douglas and Myrn had told me of Choin and Old Kingdom."

"Choin . . . yes, it's south of here, across this widest part of Sea. However, I've been told the Choinese consider Sea Tortoise a great delicacy."

"I can be delicate when I want to," Oval admitted, "but a fisherman wanting to dine on Sea Tortoise would have no easy task. Size alone . . ."

"I see what you mean," Thornwood agreed soberly. "As for me, I'm here with my fleet, looking for pirates who've been attacking and sinking ships in the waters off Cape Smerm at the mouth of Farango Water. Have you run into them?"

"No, I can't say I've heard of nor seen pirates . . . but then, I haven't been looking or listening. I coasted along the Choinese shore for some weeks. A sort of holiday, you understand. I was just returning homeward and thought to stop and give greetings to my friends in your beautiful Valley."

Thornwood stood hip-deep in the rolling surf as they talked.

"Piracy's much too common, I'm afraid."

"Well, for what it's worth," said Oval, resting her chin on a soft mound of wet Seaweed, the easier to converse, "I heard rumors early this past autumn. The wicked Duke Eunicet has disappeared from his prison island. I suppose I should have carried the news to you or Douglas or at least to Augurian. But . . ."

"No, no one expected you to be jailer for the nasty usurper!"

"You're too kind," the tortoise murmured sadly. "I must make it up to you! What can I do to help you, now?"

"Well . . ." murmured Thornwood softly. "Now that the storm's died down, my sailors and soldiers, once we find these pirates, are capable of subduing them easily. It's the job of the Duke to see to public safety, even at Sea."

"Still, I'd feel better if I could help."

"You hear a lot of the news passed between fishes and other Sea creatures?"

Oval nodded ponderously.

"Could you ask around, then, and discover where these pirates are hiding just now, in view of the storm and all?"

"I can do it as quickly as anything," agreed the enormous Sea Tortoise, and with no further ado, she spun about, paddled swiftly across the rippled shallows, and disappeared into the blue depths of Sea a few yards beyond.

"I should've told her to bring news to me at the anchorage," the Duke muttered, slapping his thigh. "Oh, well . . . I can wait here. Hello! Where's that bittern got to?"

The tiny bird came to his call and in a moment had flown swiftly off in the direction of the fleet, bearing the Duke's orders.

Thornwood walked to the top of a tall dune. The wind was insistent but not strong, with a touch of northern chill in it. He removed his boots, stockings, shirt and trousers, wrung as much of the salty water from them as he could, and draped the clothing and boots to dry on a sturdy bush growing on the dune.

He gathered an armful of dried driftwood, bits of timber and twigs, and in a very short time had built a cozy fire in the lee of the dune.

Myrn popped her porcelain darning egg from a child's everyday stocking, dropped the newly mended item into her sewing basket, and stuck her darning needle into a ball of wool yarn, wrapping the leftover length of brown yarn about it, sailor-fashion.

She stood and glanced from the window of her private parlor off the bedroom she and Douglas shared just beyond the big, sunny nursery. The day was clear and somewhat windy, the sun sparkling brightly on Crooked Brook, and clouds scuttling from over First Ridge (or *Last*, etc., etc.) toward the southwest.

On the uplands there were tannish white puffs of several flocks of Valley sheep grazing the early summer grass. Otherwise there seemed to be nothing, nor anyone, in the entire peaceful landscape.

A slight stir among the willows along Crooked Brook, therefore, at once caught her eye. Looking more closely, she saw a group of ragged men making their way through the waterside thicket, heading toward the house under the High.

"Shepherds?" she wondered. "No, they look more like . . . sailors! Why are they here, I wonder?"

She walked quickly from her parlor, along the upstairs hall, and down the winding stair. The great, double front door stood ajar, as it usually did on pleasant days, inviting fresh breezes and friends within when they came by. Bronze Owl, still off on his errand to the fleet, was not hanging from his favorite nail.

As Myrn stepped out into the bright late morning, she halted in surprise.

Six men, armed with naked steel blades, heavy iron marlin-spikes, or wicked-looking belt knives, stood on the walkway, scowling at her fiercely.

"Ah, Mistress Brightglade!" said the scruffiest and dirtiest of the lot, waving a rusty, old cutlass at her in a threatening manner. "Stand and be ye silent, I command! Consider yourself my captive!"

"Eunicet, is it?" Myrn gasped, a surprised cough. "Why . . . what do you here, usurper? You must know . . ."

"I know when I've found myself a hostage, girl, a keep-safe from your husband's foul magicking! And I know he and that old dodderer Flarman are away, also!"

"You've caught me, then!" said the pretty Aquamancer, nodding calmly, her emotions under control once more. "Step within . . . uh . . . *gentlemen*! Lunch will be ready in a few minutes . . ."

"And we'll eat it readily," said a second man, heavy and huffing from the exertion of the walk from First Ridge. "I be Bladder, dearie. You'll have heard of me?"

"Yes, yes, yes!" snapped Eunicet, poking at his second-in-command with the pommel of his sword. "Speak when I tell you to, tavern-creeper!"

"*Poof* to you!" returned Bladder, indignantly. "You're not Duke of anywhere, not even a desert island, and all have equal say on a proper pirate crew!"

Eunicet seemed about to argue the point, but Myrn was ushering his bedraggled crew down the hall toward the kitchen.

"We'll talk this over at lunch, then," she said brightly. "Ah! Almost ready, Blue?"

The Teakettle nodded, obviously disconcerted by the rough appearance of the newcomers. She began directing the service of hot, fresh bread, and jampots, dishes of condiments, and of bread-and-butter pickles.

"Be seated, please," invited the Aquamancer. "Eunicet, suppose you and Master . . . Blabber, is it? . . . no, Bladder . . . sit on either side of me, here. You'll be hungry and hot, I 'spect, poor Seamen, after your long hike this morning. Iced tea, anyone?"

Suspiciously at first but with increasing enthusiasm the pirates began to gobble the fresh-baked bread with raspberry, grape, and strawberry jams, gulping down frosty tea or steaming cups of strong coffee.

"My husband is not at home, as you've noticed," said Myrn pleasantly, spreading her own slice of bread with a generous dollop of preserved strawberries. "Perhaps I can help you?"

"*Nonsense!*" snarled Eunicet, the effect spoiled somewhat by his own mouthful of bread and grape jam. "Nonsense! You are my prisoner, little lady! Be good enough to cower, snivel, weep, and beg for mercy!"

"Oh, as to that, I rather think you misjudge the situation, ragtags!" Myrn snapped testily. "You are, as long as *I* choose it, my *guests*. I'll not long endure boorish behavior in my own house! I would have thought your mother or somebody'd have taught you better manners!"

"Leave be! *Hey!*" Bladder whispered to his furious Captain. "Eat first. Make demands later!"

The six pirates forgot their cutlasses and wicked-looking marlin-spikes. They stuffed themselves with the first decent food they'd tasted in days . . . weeks, if truth be told. They filled themselves with crispy fried chicken and hot, buttery corn fritters, and asked for seconds on the mashed potatoes and the pickled beets.

Blue Teakettle ordered Great Skillet to fry more chicken . . . even she had not expected such voracious appetites this noontime.

While the pirates were ears-deep in the second batch of chicken, eyeing a molded salad with increasing interest, Blue Teakettle nodded to Myrn, then spoke quietly to old Sugar Caster, sending him sliding from the kitchen unnoticed by Eunicet or the rest of his crew.

"Some good brown Oak 'n' Bucket ale, sirs?" Myrn asked to draw their attention from the departure of Sugar Caster, just in case.

Ale Jacks, with thick heads of rich, tan foam, pranced across from the service sideboard and presented themselves to the delighted sailors.

"More bread? Or salty soda crackers go well with Innkeeper's premium ale, I hear," Myrn purred, watching Sugar Caster disappear up the rear stairs. "Plenty more of both, and dessert ready when you are, me hearties!"

"Now look *here*!" snapped Eunicet at last, pushing away his third jack of ale, untasted. "Tell me! Where has Douglas gone off to, eh? And old Flarman Fire Breath? We saw that blasted brass doorknocker clatter off early this morning, and then Douglas shot up and eastward . . ."

"More figgy pudding, then?" Myrn interrupted him, smiling politely. "You look in the need of some repair to clothing, sirs! Perhaps there we can assist you! What do you think of the Trunkety Inn ale, General? You're the expert on potables, I'm told."

Bladder had eaten seven large pieces of golden-brown chicken, six slices of bread heavy with butter and jam, two great helpings of mashed potatoes, a serving of molded salad with mayonnaise dressing, and was digging greedily into a deep dish of pudding. The whole kitchen staff stood transfixed with awe at his enormous capacity. They'd never seen such eating . . . nor such terrible table manners!

"Best I ever tasted!" Bladder replied to her question. "Oh, Eunie! Let it lie! Enjoy the lunch. Business can wait."

Eunicet howled in frustration and foul temper, so loud that everyone at table dropped fork and knife and snapped heads round to stare at him, aghast.

"Where in *tunket* is the *gorblimey* young Wizard? I ask you, young woman!" the former Duke exploded. "And when do you expect your menfolk back, pray?"

Myrn winced at his coarse language but maintained her dignity and her control.

"To tell you the truth, Douglas has gone off with a friend to find some pirates reported between the Ridges," she answered calmly. "As for Flarman . . . he'll be with my Master Augurian, off in Warm Sea. And you'll be interested to know that Duke Thornwood is, even now, at Sea looking for you and will return shortly, I suspect, for Bronze Owl went to tell him of your appearance!"

Her frankness startled Eunicet, who, in her place, would have lied and blustered.

"*Now!*" he bellowed. "I shall fortify this rickety old hovel, I say, and hold you and your children . . . I know of them, you see . . . until one of the Wizards . . . or both of them . . . return! I have accounts to settle with them, little missy!"

"You are, if not exactly welcome, at least to be treated as guests as long as you're here!" the Lady Aquamancer reminded him . . . and herself . . . sharply. "However, I suggest you behave yourself as well as are your men, Eunicet!"

The former Duke howled again in red fury and would have drawn his sword if one of the Bowls, full of pudding, had not at that moment maneuvered itself under his flailing left fist. Pudding flew all over the tabletop!

"Oh, dear!" cried Myrn. "Quick, Blue! A damp towel. And another bowl of pudding for our 'guest'!"

Eunicet achieved the unlikely feat of choking on a mouthful of chocolate pudding laced generously with thick, sweet cream. When he had been pounded firmly on the back by his grinning First Mate and wiped clear of the splashed mess by a half-dozen damp linen Napkins, the Pirate Captain seemed at last to recover himself.

"Well, you must admit that we have you captive. We'll hold you in fear and trembling until we've bargained with your husband and old Flowerstalk!"

"I expect Douglas'll be along later today, once he finds you're no longer hiding among the Ridges. As for Flarman, I believe it was his intent to remain on Waterand for several weeks. He and Augurian are looking for a solution to one of your former master's wicked spellings."

"*Arrrgh!*" Eunicet ground his teeth. "Bladder! Pull your rascally men from the hog trough! Set armed guards about this wretched place. Search the house from top to bottom and also the cave under the hill. Begin by binding this snippy girl tightly with ropes! And gag her insolent mouth, also, if she won't be silent and obey commands."

"You'll do no such thing!" cried Myrn, now thoroughly roused.

She rapped on the tabletop with her fork.

"I'll have my way, I assure you!" snapped the Pirate Captain. "Tying up is the *nicest* thing I can think to do to you! Find her brats, Bladder! We'll see how sweet little mother behaves when we're toasting their toes in the fire!"

Sugar Caster had hopped as silently as he could up the back stairs. At the top he'd turned right and hurried down the hall to its far end.

He pushed open the door to the twins' bedroom and found young Brand lolling on his bed, waiting for his sister to finish dressing for lunch. They'd expected a call, long since.

"Lunchtime!" cried Brand, rolling off his cot with a *thump*!

"I'm just now ready!" his sister said, hopping down from her mother's vanity where she'd been trying a new way to comb and braid her thick blonde hair.

"Hush! Hush!!" Sugar Caster whispered urgently. "Plans are changed! Your mother is ... entertaining ... some very *unpleasant* guests and she wishes you to go, instead, across to the orchardman's house. Quietly and quickly, dear Wizardlings! Your mother sends you this by me, I assure you."

Brand and Brenda exchanged glances, partly of surprise and partly of concern. But they were not the children of Wizards without having gained some sense of discipline ... when it was necessary.

"She doesn't want us to see these people below stairs?" Brenda asked Caster. "At all?"

"By no means!" coughed old Caster, glancing over what would have been his shoulder if he'd had a shoulder. "Quickly, quickly, my dears!"

"We mustn't go down either the back stairs or the main stairs, then," Brand considered. "Always wanted to try the west porch roof, Brenda!"

"Well, I *suppose* it'd be all right ..." considered Brenda. "They couldn't see us, that way."

"Decided!" said her brother with a quick nod.

He opened the small window overlooking the thatched roof of the wide porch at the west end of the cottage. Once through the window, the twins dropped softly onto the thatch and slid down to the edge.

"Wait! I'll go with you," whispered Sugar Caster, fearing the pirates might overhear. "You'll need someone older to help you!"

"Well, he *is* older, that's true," whispered Brenda to her twin with a low giggle. "Come along, Sugar Caster . . . but be quiet!"

In a minute the twins and Sugar Caster had swarmed down a pillar from the roof to the floor of the porch . . . a climb Brand had secretly contemplated for some time . . . and disappeared across the lawn, passing Fairy Well, heading for Old Plank Bridge.

Chapter Ten

Bodies in Motion

THE neat farmhouse, set among the straight lines of blooming apple trees, was quiet and peacefully empty.

Pinned to the front door was a slip of lined notebook paper on which Lilac, the orchardman's goodwife, had neatly printed in red crayon:

GONE TO TRUNKETY. BACK AFORE DUSK. IF THIS BE YOU, MISTRESS MYRN, YOUR APPLE BUTTER IS SET OUT ON THE KITCHEN TABLE.

YOUR LOVING FRIEND.
LILAC

"Well, we'll get no lunch here, then," sighed Brand after laboriously spelling out the goodwife's message. "Hello! Door's open!"

The twins and Caster entered the farmhouse, which smelled at all times of the year of apples and of cinnamon, of pungent herbs hung to dry, and of last summer's wild-flower sachets laid among washed and ironed pillowcases and sheets in the hall closet.

"I don't think they'd mind," murmured Sugar Caster, "if you helped yourselves to some apple butter and bread."

"Not mind at all," agreed Brand.

In the kitchen they indeed found the dozen stone jars of newly put up apple butter on the table, each jar covered with a square of red-and-white-flowered gingham bound in place with a twist of brown string.

"Bread!" called Brand, exploring the sideboard. "Is there a bread knife? I'll have to slice it myself."

"Let Sugar Caster do the slicing. He's an expert!" his sister said, lifting Caster onto the table. "There'll be morning's milk in the springhouse."

In a moment the two were seated on ladder-back chairs shaped to fit the old couple, spreading delicious tart-sweet condiment on crusty wheat bread.

Caster watched them eat and shared their conversation. It was strange, he said, to be in a kitchen in which the utensils, plates, pots, and pans were not magically animated.

"Somewhat disconcerting, actually," he thought aloud.

"Oh, I think it's rather nice to do things for ourselves, for a change," Brand mumbled around a large bite of bread. "Not that I don't love our Kitchen Crew at home. They're very good friends, all!"

Brenda nodded, remembering just in time it was impolite to speak with her mouth full.

When they were finished Brenda gathered the plates, knives, spoons, and milk glasses, washing them carefully in Lilac's wet-sink. Brand dried them all with a soft, old floursack dishtowel and climbed on the counter to replace the dishes in their proper cupboard.

"Now what?" he wondered.

Brenda stood at the kitchen door, gazing out across the garden, just now beginning to celebrate the coming of summer with early-blooming flowers and tender, new shoots of carrots, peas, beets, trellised vines of beans reaching up,

big-leafed rhubarb, and young green spikes of onion and
garlic . . . a most pleasant sight, even to a girl of seven.

"We must stay until Grandmother Lilac returns," Sugar
Caster suggested, but with just a hint of uncertainty in his
voice.

"Or we can walk down to meet 'em," Brand countered.
"Yes! Along Crooked Brook and across Stone Bridge,
maybe?"

It took very little persuasion to get his more cautious
sister to agree to the excursion. Sugar Caster, a servant of
a lifelong bachelor and unversed in the ways of children,
made no objection. They left the orchardman's house and
started down the road along the south bank of Crooked
Brook, walking easily, enjoying the sights, smells, and
sounds of water, of rustling grass, amid new-blooming
flowers and summer birds singing in newly leafed trees.

At Augurian's Fountain, a short way downstream, they
paused to take a drink and paddle their bare feet in the
shallows, watching Marbleheart's shy relatives, the Brook
Otters, darting back and forth in the clear water in pursuit
of the young trout.

Brand waded out a way until his sister recalled him to
continue their journey.

"You'll get all wet, and you might catch cold, Brandy,"
she insisted. "Think how bothersome to have sniffles when
the weather's so fine!"

The boy nodded at last and retraced his steps to the bank
slowly, struggled there to pull his knee-length stockings
over his wet toes, and put on his shoes, lacing and tying
them with little difficulty.

At seven he was already handy at most such important
tasks.

"I got my skirt a bit damp," complained his sister.

"It'll dry in a minute," Brand promised. "Come on! I
don't see Grandfather Precious nor Grandmother Lilac on
the path. They'll be still talking at the General Store, I

suppose. Or sharing pints and a bit of lunch at the Oak 'n' Bucket, this time of day."

They met no one on the path, not even at Trunkety Stone Bridge where, later on a warm day, they might have come upon some of the town children playing or even swimming, although the water was still quite winter-chilled.

The afternoon breeze was warm, slow, and soft.

"Everybody's to home, taking their naps," Sugar Caster yawned.

"May be!" agreed the little boy. "*I'm* not sleepy . . . much. We might stop here a bit. Sit in the shade where the grass is tall and soft. Watch for Precious and Lilac to come along."

They slipped off their shoes and stockings again and lay flat in the fragrant young grass in the deep shade of a very old great-grandsire willow that grew near the head of the town's one street.

The tree sighed sleepily over them. The grass murmured soothingly.

The travelers . . . even Sugar Caster . . . fell, almost at once, into deep sleep.

Less than a quarter-hour later, as they slept looking like lost angels in the grass, Precious and Lilac passed them, unseeing, heading for home.

"I must finish trimming them middle branches to our pears," Precious was saying to his goodwife.

"That old Dicksey!" murmured Lilac with a soft laugh, stooping to pick up a stick lying by the side of the road. She'd use it as a staff to ease her old legs. "You'd think he'd have black lisle in stock! Can you imagine . . . !"

"Don't blame old Dicksey, m'dear," her husband chuckled. "We'll stop and rest a bit by Augurian's Fountain, shall we?"

"I can make it all the way home! *I'm* not yet that decrepit!" sniffed his goodwife.

"Oh, but it would be so pleasant, on a summer's late

afternoon, to sit and hold hands, and watch how the drag-
onflies dart about, and say hello to the trouts and the ducks
that live there.''

''I'll agree, even if I don't really need the resting,'' Lilac
conceded at once, smiling fondly at her sturdy orchardman.

They walked across Stone Bridge and disappeared up the
streamside road, chatting softly of nothing very important
at all, just enjoying each other's company.

Douglas Brightglade had said thank-you and good-bye
to Flittery Chipmunk, urging him to call at Wizards' High
more often.

He turned his steps downslope and homeward, noticing
the telltale signs of passing pirates as he went, trying not
to let it worry him.

''Myrn is *quite* capable of taking care of herself, house,
and children,'' he said to himself. ''She is, after all, a full
Aquamancer!''

Still . . . he hurried his steps.

He could have used the Feather Pin to move more
swiftly, but he wanted to follow the traces the pirates had
left. When he and the 'munk had followed the smaller party
of pirates to the shore, nobody was about.

A saucy bittern, when asked, said two Seamen had
boarded the ketch anchored offshore since the day before,
hoisted anchor, and raised sails. They'd disappeared over
the horizon, some hours since.

''I wonder where Eunicet got the ship?'' Douglas asked
himself. ''Stole her, I imagine. Well, best to tackle Eunicet
now, before he can do something else wicked.''

At about the time Precious and Lilac crossed Stone
Bridge at Trunkety, Douglas stooped to study footprints in
wet sand beside Crooked Brook just upstream of the High
cottage.

''Six of 'em, yes,'' he counted.

He stood in the deep blue shade of the willows and studied the High cottage, its grounds, and what he could see of the barn, dovecote, and Workshop under the steep hill behind.

"Did you notice a band of Men coming along this way?" he stooped to ask a beaver cub who popped out of the stream just beside him.

"Yes! *Yes!* Mama says I should tell you. 'Twas old Eunicet . . . him what was Duke back before I was whelped, you know? Wicked-looking Men, they was, Wizard Douglas! Swords and long knives!"

"I'm sure they were fit to startle any brave young beaver! Did you see them go from here?"

"Swords and all! Straight up to the front door they went!" the young beaver puffed breathlessly. "Met Mistress Myrn at the doorstoop, they did, sir!"

"And did you hear what was said, I wonder?"

"No . . . much too far away! Mistress Myrn led them inside, we saw. Closed the door tight, she did. Terrible pack of starving wolves, *I* say! All tatters and torn breeches, and carrying shiny sharp knives!"

"Thank you, Master Beaver!" Douglas murmured soothingly, for the young animal was obviously highly excited about what he'd seen and had to tell. "I promise to go quickly but quietly! Thank you for your warning!"

The beaver cub nodded several times and stood, front paws clenched, on the bank-top to watch the young Wizard stroll away toward the cottage, openly for all to see.

"Braver nor me, I swears!" the beaver admitted aloud to himself.

Then he turned and plunged into the Brook, swimming strongly back toward his folks' lodge upstream.

Rather than enter the cottage by the closed front door, Douglas circled around the east side and climbed over the meadow gate, which creaked loudly if it was opened.

There he met Red Rooster scratching for bugs between the cobbles.

"Seen anything of a band of pirates?" .

"No, can't say's I have, Douglas," replied the fowl, whose name was Chanticleer, a name much bestowed by hens on rooster chicks everywhere. "You might ask them stupid doves, o' course. They stays close to home in the heat of day."

"I will, and thank you," replied Douglas, looking up at the dovecote. The doves were all within, cooing softly in their midday nap.

"No use stirring them up, however," Douglas decided.

He went to the kitchen door and glanced through the panes into the cool interior.

"Pirates, all right!" he exclaimed. "Myrn has things well in hand, I'd say."

Two pirates came from the Workshop, glancing uneasily behind them as they came. They were at once startled and frightened to see Douglas suddenly in front of them in the bright afternoon sunshine.

"W-W-W-Wizard!" one squeaked, dropping a loot-stuffed pillowcase to yank his cutlass from his belt. "Hold, then! *Stay!*"

"Not going anywhere, actually," said Douglas with a slight smile. "Part of old Eunicet's crew, are you? *Don't bother!*"

This last was to the second pirate, who'd managed to extract a long knife from his belt. The blade was apparently sharp enough to cut the pirate's braided leather belt quite in twain, and the man abandoned all thoughts of blade and burden to keep his breeches from dropping about his ankles.

"Oh, too bad!" Douglas laughed. "You've rope, there, I see. Better lash your pantaloons on high, sailor!"

He turned to the first pirate, who by then had gotten his own cutlass into a sort of guard position and was standing, unable to decide what to do with it.

"Eunicet's here, I take it?" Douglas asked him.

"Cap'n's within, sir!" the sailor gulped. "Come quietly and I'll take you to him."

"I'll lead the way, then. Once your mate's tied his new belt!"

He opened the kitchen door and walked within, blinking a bit in the sudden dimness.

"Here's my husband," came Myrn's voice from the gloom. "Eunicet's here, darling. He wants to take us captive and extract magic and ransom from us . . . if he can."

"I would expect that of him," Douglas said dryly. "Hello, Eunicet! I see my wife has made you and your men welcome."

Eunicet, looking sinister and wicked in the dimness of the kitchen, pointed his sword at the young Pyromancer's chest.

"*Hold right there!*" he snarled. "Bladder! Have him searched for weapons!"

The two men told to conduct the search stepped forward uneasily. They hastily decided that the Wizard carried no weapons, only a ragged old cloak in a shoulder sack containing odds and ends of strange things like mushrooms, bits of string, some smooth stones, and a packet of roast beef sandwiches.

He obviously posed no great threat to heavily armed opponents.

"Now, old enemy," the former Duke laughed nastily, "Stand before me and be careful of what you do with your hands. First sign of any spelling and your pretty little bed-partner gets . . . well, perhaps, a cut or two? Or a whipping with my mate's belt? *Stand to, Bladder, and be ready!*"

"I suppose it'd be foolish to demand 'What do you here, Eunicet?' " Douglas said calmly. "Obviously you're up to no good. Or have you come to ask forgiveness and a second chance?"

"Don't harass me," growled the pirate. "I wouldn't take Dukedom back if it were offered on a silver plate!"

"I don't believe it'll be offered! What *do* you do here,

then?'' Douglas asked. ''Do *you* know, sweetheart?''

This last was directed to Myrn and was followed by a warm hug and a kiss, despite Eunicet's brandished weapon.

''And I remember *you*,'' continued Douglas, ignoring the grumblings and rumblings from the pirate chieftain. ''Bladder, aren't you? Lost a bit of weight, I'd say, since we saw you off to . . . what *was* its name, that island? I forget!''

''We called it Banishment, no matter what it was called aforetimes,'' replied Bladder. ''Good to see you again, Douglas Brightglade! Pyromancer Brightglade, is it now? How's old Flarman Flowerstalk doing, these days?''

''*Bladder!*'' shrieked Eunicet.

''Sorry!'' grunted the former General of the Army of Dukedom. ''Sorry! Don't mess with a man when he's a sharp blade to hand, I advises,'' he whispered aside to the young Wizard.

''*Bladder!*'' Eunicet repeated, now growling deep in his throat.

''Now, I suppose you want us to bargain for our freedom,'' Douglas said to the former Duke. ''What is it, I ask again, that you desire?''

Eunicet, in the face of calm reasonableness . . . and after a black scowl at his First Mate . . . slid his sword into its scabbard and waved them all to seats at the kitchen table.

''We've eaten of your food and secured your persons,'' he began, striving for the same sort of calm Douglas was showing. ''First off, we must set a guard. Bladder, when you're done curtseying and groveling like a peasant, post your men!''

''Let's see,'' Bladder said, scratching his heavily bearded chin thoughtfully. We've four crewmen left to do the work. I will . . .''

''Do it!'' snapped the pirate captain. ''Just *do it*!''

Two of the men were sent to post watch outside the front door, to warn if anyone approached, and the other two were sent out to the courtyard between the house and the High.

Bladder stayed just inside the kitchen door, so he could hear and see everything that went on.

"I want to know," Eunicet said evenly to Douglas and Myrn, "where are your brats? You'll be more cooperative when I have them in hand."

"You're a wicked, cruel, foolish, mean-spirited, ugly-tempered, born loser," Myrn snorted derisively. "If you want them . . . you'll have to find them on your own!"

Douglas said nothing but glanced at his angry wife in approval.

"You'll be quicker to tell," decided the former Duke, "if I start slicing small pieces off your husband with my knife!"

"Perhaps," Myrn considered. "Why don't you try it? I believe Douglas can take care of himself, of me, and of our children."

"This is getting us nowhere," snorted Bladder, plumping his rather broad bottom into the chair at the head of the table. "I say we simply . . ."

The chair, which was the one normally occupied by the older Pyromancer, suddenly gave a sharp lurch and, tilting forward, dumped the First Mate to the floor, on the way rapping his chin sharply on the table edge.

A chorus of giggles, sniggles, soft guffaws, and hoots came from the cupboard. Blue Teakettle *shushed* at the plates and saucers, but had trouble smothering her own bubbling chuckle.

Bladder angrily leapt to his feet, hitting his head a fearsome *crack* on the edge of the heavy mantelpiece.

"Dad-blammer!" he choked. *"Friggety bibulousity!"*

"Mate," Eunicet laughed, despite himself, "even the furniture recognizes you as a clown!"

"I'll build up the fire in yon fireplace, is what I'll do, and use furniture for fuel," spluttered the angry pirate. He wiped at his tearing eyes but remained standing.

"Keep on wasting your time," advised Douglas before Bladder could regain his composure enough to begin being destructive. "Eventually, soon-or-late, someone is bound to come."

"Good advice." Eunicet nodded his head. "Bladder, stop trying to think and listen to your commander!"

"Aye, aye, Sir, gracious leader," snapped his First Mate with obvious ill-will.

"I've considered our situation carefully," continued the former Duke of Dukedom, "and have formed a plan. Leave off your bluster, man, and take two of the guards into the Wizards' workrooms across the way. Search for powerful magical tools."

"Fat lot of good that'll do," snarled Bladder. "I wouldn't know a retort from a love philter!"

Chapter Eleven

Missing in Action

EUNICET sighed mightily and rose gingerly from his chair . . . the one Marbleheart usually sat upon at meals.

"I'll have to do it, myself, then! It's *always* this way," he complained to Myrn. "It's why I lost Dukedom and was beaten by the lady-skirted Highlandormer dandies. I have to do *everything* for myself!"

"No good arguing *that* point with you, Eunicet," murmured Myrn sweetly.

"Damnation!" the pirate swore. "Mate Bladder, stay with the prisoners here and see they do no harm nor work any spells. Summon the front door guards. They and I and the good-for-nothing-much swab-jockeys out back will search under the hill. I, at least, will know what to steal when I see it!"

With which he stomped out angrily, yelling to the four crewmen to follow.

"Sorry I sort of lost my temper, Mistress," Bladder told Myrn. "I used to be famous for my nasty disposition. Dukedom's foulest mouth, they called me, but all those

119

years on an island with nobody to talk to but that . . . that
. . . *person* . . . dried up most of me bile!''

"Cup of tea while we wait?'' asked Myrn, gesturing to
Blue Teakettle on the front of Range. "It'll take Eunicet a
while to cover the whole of the Workshop, not to mention
the storage rooms behind and below.''

"Pleasure, ma'am!'' replied the pirate second-in-
command, reseating himself gingerly, this time halfway
down the long table. "Sugar, if you please. No cream!''

The three of them sat sipping tea and talking as the sun
dropped toward the western horizon. Once calmed and act-
ing sociably, the former General of Eunicet's Army became
rather pleasant.

"I . . . I've often thought of dumping old Eunicet and
finding a place to settle me quietly down,'' he admitted.

"What keeps you from it?'' Douglas inquired.

"Ah, well . . . I do have *some* loyalty, you know!''

"Loyalty? To Eunicet?'' snorted Myrn. "How far can a
little loyalty go, I ask you?''

"Well, ma'am . . . nobody else ever gave old Bladder
any bit of a chance, you know. Back there in Capital in the
bad old days, I mean. People mostly shunned me, or treated
me like horse-droppings. Smelly, but useful in the right
place. Eunicet sprang me from prison and made me an officer and *listened* to me . . . at first.''

"I can understand that, I think,'' Douglas said. "And
you stuck with him for that?''

"That, and the promises of power, loot, and riches beyond calculating, of course,'' admitted the pirate, sighing.
"Precious little of *them* have I gained. I really do wish I'd
jumped ship when we reached the mainland and gone off
somewhere. Somewhere nice and quiet . . . with a steady
job to earn me keep.''

"Not too late,'' Myrn murmured.

"No . . . don't suppose it is. Where'd I go? ''

The young Wizards exchanged glances, but for several
breaths nobody spoke.

From the courtyard Rooster sounded a loud crow, and a moment later a second, ending in what sounded very much like a gleeful chuckle.

"Well!" sighed Douglas, leaning back. "Nothing to prevent you from going just about anywhere, anytime you like. What would you do, Bladder?"

"I was once a pretty fair metalsmith," the pirate remembered. "I was probably happiest then, now I think back. Took over me old dad's smithy up in Capital, I did, when he died. I was only fourteen or so, in years.

"Then along came the war! Remember? Business went to the dogs. Taxes up the chimney! Nobody wanted to pay someone to shoe their horses or mules, with money so short. Iron was hard to get, what with the arming of Eunicet's soldiers. And, I admit, it was more exciting to join the Army than to sweat over a forge."

"Blacksmithing is an honorable trade," Douglas observed. "Pyromancers take special interest in smiths, too. Plenty of work, nowadays. Things've changed."

He gestured to several lamps about the kitchen which at once sprang alight, spreading a warm, golden glow over the whole big room. Blue Teakettle blew a soft, blue-steam whistle. Pots and Pans on their shelves began at once to stir and sort themselves out for the tasks of preparing supper.

"Chicken stew with savory dumplings!" Blue sputtered from the front of Range. "Everybody up! On your toes! Cups? Lend an ear! Supper in just over an hour, Master and Mistress!"

"Stay for supper, won't you?" Myrn asked the former General and lately pirate.

"Well, ah, you see . . . well, I'd be honored, ma'am. Chicken and dumplings! Haven't had a bite of such vittles since . . . well, since my best blacksmithing days!"

"We'll tend the animals, you and I, and then you'll want to wash up, I suspect," Douglas said, rising.

"Ah . . . er . . . what about . . . *you* know . . . old Eunicet and the others?" Bladder whispered.

"Let 'em go hungry for a while," Myrn said. "The cellars and back caves under the High are a huge labyrinth, Bryarmote tells me. They won't find their way out in time for supper, I'm afraid."

Bladder rose to follow Douglas into the early dusk, where the Ladies of the Byre waited at the meadow gate to be admitted, stalled, milked, and bedded for the night.

Myrn inspected the busy kitchen with lively green eyes, nodded to Blue Teakettle, then walked down the hall and out the front door. It would be an hour before full darkness settled over Valley.

"Time my angels came home to bath and supper," she said to an early firefly who darted up to flash hello.

She walked down the sloping lawn, crossed Old Plank Bridge, and in a moment was knocking at Lilac's kitchen door.

"Hello, Myrn, me dear child!" the orchardman's lady greeted her. "Came for your apple butter earlier, did you?"

"Apple butter? No. But for my children, yes."

"Children?" asked Lilac, raising her brows in surprise. "Haven't seen them all this day. Did you think . . . that they were *here*?"

"I sent them over to you at lunchtime," Myrn explained, a nagging tooth of fear beginning to gnaw. "They were told to stay with you 'til suppertime!"

"Never even seen 'em!" cried Lilac, catching Myrn's concern. "Now, *now*! Don't be afeared, just yet. Maybe they're out to the barn with Pa. Let's go see . . ."

The elderly orchardman appeared from the milkshed carrying two large buckets of creamy, white milk and humming contentedly to himself.

"Pa!" called his wife. "You got the twins? Myrn's here to collect 'em."

"No!" replied Precious. "Now, you mothers, both! No,

not a sight nor a sign of them all this day. Be they lost?''

"I . . . don't know," cried the Aquamancer, shaking her head. She explained how, when the pirates came, she'd sent her children across the stream to be safe.

"We was down to Trunkety," Lilac explained. "To get some black lisle thread from Dicksey, but he'd none, so we ate lunch at the Oak 'n' Bucket as a treat and walked slowly home in mid-afternoon. Never saw sign of the children, poor dears. Oh, Myrn! Where could they have gone when they found nobody to home here, I wonders? Oh, dear!''

Myrn swallowed her maternal panic with some difficulty.

"A moment, please!" she said, cutting short the goodwife's worried chatter.

She stood in the center of the barnyard, ignoring the lowing of the cattle and the nickering of Precious's plow horse, who'd sensed the trouble nearby. Turning slowly, full about, Myrn closed her eyes and murmured a Seeking Spell to herself.

"They *were* here," she said at last. "And ate a lunch of apple butter and fresh-baked bread.''

"I *wondered* who'd been into that new batch and who ate the dinner bread," Lilac cried in anguish. " 'Twas our young chicks, I'm sure of it now. Cleaned up after themselves, you see, nice as could be, so I thought no more on it. It could have been anyone come to call or, more'n likely, Pa taking a snack!''

"Not me!" insisted Precious. "But where could they have got to, not being able to return to the High, like you say?''

Myrn pointed down River Road toward Trunkety.

"That way, and not returned yet! I'll go after them.''

"Now, Mistress, don't worry yourself about them. I know you must have your hands full with them wicked men . . . pirates, you says? . . . up to the cottage . . .''

"Well, thank goodness, I don't sense them come to any harm," sighed the twins' mother.

"Pa'll ride down and fetch 'em home. Return them to

the High soon as you'd like," promised Lilac. "Pa, carry a lantern . . . and *hurry*! 'Twill soon be pitch black and no moon! Even Wizard-mothers worry about young ones out on a dark night!"

Myrn was torn between accompanying the orchardman and returning to help Douglas. What if Eunicet and his men found their way out of the amazement under Workshop? And Douglas should know of this development, at once.

"Fetch the little imps, then," she decided. "I'll go tell Douglas. *Oh, me!* I used to wonder how a mother could bear to spank a child . . . now I begin to understand."

"Nonsense!" puffed the childless Lilac, giving her a hug. "Perfectly safe for the bairns to wander down to town on a pleasant summer's day. With us old folks not to home . . ."

"I suppose so. Well, Lilac! Precious! Again Douglas and I are in your debt. Thank you . . . and bring them back but keep them here. We still have the matter of an armed pirate crew with us. I'll send word when 'tis safe for them to return home."

"Send someone down with their nightclothes, then," suggested the practical Lilac as her husband started off toward the barn. "And clean linen to wear tomorrow morning, if needs be."

"Soon as I get home," promised the lady Aquamancer. "Thank you, dear, sweet, Lilac! I'll send word of what happens up at the cottage, soon as I can! So you'll have no need to worry about us, too."

Lilac watched her husband ride off on their plow mare Jennifer, at a faster pace than usual, downstream, and then waved to Myrn as she crossed Plank Bridge.

"Likely been asked to dinner somewhere in town," Lilac comforted herself. "Who could resist them sweet chicks?"

Awakened by an empty rattle from Sugar Caster in the first cool of early evening, Brand sat bolt upright.

"Wake up! It's late!" cried Caster.

Brenda rubbed her eyes a moment, then scrambled to her feet also, looking lost and bewildered.

Brand took her by the hand and began walking toward the village green, where already there were lights aglow in many windows.

"Must be near suppertime," he said. "Nobody's about."

"We should go home!" insisted Caster.

"You told us Mama said to stay away until she sent for us."

"That's not *exactly* what she said . . ." it countered.

But the bright lights of the Oak 'n' Bucket Tavern were close before them, and the walk home long and likely to end in full darkness, so the children went to the inn, straight as arrows, and peeped in at the front door, which, as usual, stood wide and welcomingly open.

"Hey, 'tis the Wizards' yonkers!" laughed a bluff-mannered farmer just leaving for home and supper. "Greetings, young Brightglades, both! Come within! It'll grow dark and maybe chill in a few minutes, now the sun be set."

Innkeeper came from around the end of the bar and stooped to shake Brand by the hand and give Brenda a pat on the cheek.

"What do you here, lad, lassie, and pot?" he asked gently.

"It's Sugar Caster," Brenda corrected him.

"We're looking for Grandfather Precious and Grandmother Lilac," the boy explained. They'd known Innkeeper all their short lives, and knew they could trust him.

"Well . . . Precious and Lilac *were* here, some time back, 'tis true, but they've left. Said they were headed up home."

He led them by the hand through the noisy bar and the Ladies' Parlor beyond, into the bright, steamy, bustling kitchen where his goodwife, Clover, was supervising a half-dozen tasks at once. With her round, pink cheeks and sure movements, she reminded the twins of Blue Teakettle.

"Now, me sweet Clover!" said Innkeeper when he'd

captured her attention among the rattle of pots and clatter of pans. "Here be little Brenda and her brother Brand. And a Sugar Caster, whatever that might be! They came to find Lilac and Precious, but them two's already gone off home."

Clover sat down on a low stool and gave the children a warm, peppery hug and a sugary kiss each, saying, "Oh, so you've missed them, did you? Not to worry! Here, we'll send our boy Rolfe up to the High to tell your folks you're here, shall we?"

"Yes, please and thank you, Mistress Clover," said Brenda with a quick bob, relieved now that someone was about to do something to get them home.

"Off you go, then, sonny!" called Innkeeper to a lanky, towheaded, freckled boy of (perhaps) fourteen who was peeling potatoes at a sink nearby. "Ride up to Wizards' High and tell 'em their kids're here, safe and sound. Mamas and Papas, for all they be Wizards, worry just as much as any, I'm sure!"

"Meanwhile, little ducklings," his goodwife nodded, "here's two clean towels and a bit of Dicksey's best hand-and-face soap. Go you both to the bathhouse out back and wash the dust of the road from your hands and faces. When you come back, I'll have some good, crisp bacon fried, and eggs ascrambled, just for you, to stave off hunger until Papa Douglas comes down for you."

Rolfe, not at all displeased to leave his potato-peeling, slipped smiling from the rear door while the twins went to find the bathhouse across the Inn's stableyard.

"Why be they here, I wonders?" murmured Innkeeper to his plump wife. "Why did the orchardman leave without them, if they came with 'em?"

"Old folk be forgetful of things, you know," sighed Clover, going back to baste the evening's roast, slowly turning before the large kitchen fire. "No great harm done, however, I s'pose!"

■   ■   ■

Bedstead bumped loudly across a succession of huge, wave-wet rocks, rumbled over coarse pebbles, rocked steeply to port, then back to starboard, and finally settled, after several long moments of buffeting from breakers, stuck fast.

"*Whew!*" puffed Marbleheart in relief. "Thought for a moment we'd have to swim!"

"Ashore?" asked Ben, picking himself up from the bottom of the bed. "*Ah*, yes! The coast! Wonder what place this is?"

"Look it over as soon as the sun rises," puffed the Otter. "Are you in one full piece, Mistress?"

"Not a scratch!" answered the Seacaptain. "But I fear we've gone fast aground. Is this Home Port? No, I don't recognize it at all. Pretty forbidding place, I'd say!"

"Things could be far worse, I don't need to tell you," Marbleheart snorted. "Let's have something to eat, friends and fellow castaways, and go ashore as soon as daylight comes. Tide's ebbing, I judge, and won't rise to take 'er off again for some hours. If ever!"

By dawn the rain clouds had rolled away westward, leaving the air clear, warm, wet, and still.

Under a new sun the voyagers saw their situation in a better light. Just to the west, towering two hundred feet in the air as straight as tree trunks, was a black basalt cliff.

Its top was obscured by fleecy clouds and at its feet, between *Bedstead*'s resting place on a reef of jumbled rock and the high cliff, stretched a mile or more of calm, clear, green water, and then a narrow strand of wave-rounded stones and smooth, dark pebbles.

"I can fly us ashore," Ben offered. "Carry you, Otter, and the lady also. I've carried heavier loads many a time."

"Well, I don't favor a swim, this early in the morning," Lorianne said with a grin. "Why not fly?"

"You'll learn to love flying. As much fun as sailing, actually," Marbleheart chuckled. "How to do it, Flower-bender?"

"Easy enough," cried the lad.

He unfurled his gossamer wings and, making them hum, rose straight up, lifting the Seacaptain and the Otter off their feet. His wings made a blue blur in the still morning air, but they bore their burden well and, in a few minutes, the shipwrecked mariners stood together on the narrow shingle between two enormous stone sentinels carved some ages before from the cliff above.

"Mainland or island?" Lorianne wondered, gazing up at the forbidding cliffs. "How to tell?"

"Easy as gooseberry pie," replied Ben. "Fly up high and look down from above!"

"You two have a good look. Get our bearings. I'll see if I can find something worth eating here on this beach," Marbleheart suggested.

"We're off, then! Up and away, Prince of Faerie!"

They rose into the clear sky, straight up.

When the high-fliers returned, the Otter was busily grilling a mess of sardines and preparing to scramble a clutch of freshly laid eggs.

"What's up?" he called out to them even before they'd touched down on the smooth pebbles.

"*We* were, silly Otter!" Lorianne laughed, exhilarated by her very first flight.

Ben set her carefully down beside the fire and hastened to poke at the grilling fish, which gave off a tantalizing aroma.

"Ready to scramble the eggs, borrowed from a Chicken of the Sea I met," explained Marbleheart. "Like 'em cooked firm, lightly browned, or runny, Lorianne?"

"Firm, *not* browned," Lorianne decided. "I usually like my scrambled eggs with ketchup, the fisherman's friend, but I've lost my supply, I'm afraid."

"No ketchup trees nor catsup bushes around here," Ben said. "Plenty of salt, but no pepper! Well, 'tis an island you've shipwrecked us upon, Sea Otter."

"A volcanic island, from the looks of it," added the busy beast, flipping the fish onto a clean, flat rock, followed by the hot scrambled eggs. "Eat with our fingers, I guess. No need for salt here, nor even ketchup. Culinary science says the fish'll make the eggs salty enough!"

The three ate in relative silence for several minutes before the Seacaptain wiped her lips with the hem of her skirt ... effective, if not particularly ladylike ... and reported the results of their aerial reconnaissance in detail.

"This great cliff is an island, as the lad said, 'bout three by five miles 'round, I judge, and two hundred feet high. Flat at the top. It stands just off the mainland to the west and southwest. Mainland's heavily wooded. Maybe ten miles away."

"Abandon *Bedstead*, then?" considered the Otter, snagging the last of the tiny fish which they'd found tasty, if oily and salty. "Our Prince, here, can fly us to the mainland, I'd think."

"The best plan," Ben agreed. "Soon as I finish breaking my fast."

Lorianne nodded. "The *only* plan, unless we plan to live on top of these cliffs and eat gull's eggs and nibble stewed kelp."

"So be it!" cried Marbleheart. "If you see no trouble carrying us that distance, old boy?"

"I can do it," Ben assured him stoutly. "Whenever you're ready. Wish we'd saved some water, however. The fishes've made me terribly thirsty!"

"That's why you've a Wizard's Familiar along on your Questing," Marbleheart reminded him. "Forgot about water, did you! We Sea Otters *never* forget about water!"

He scrabbled about in the loose beach stones until he found one which centuries of waves rolling and grinding had formed into a shallow basin, cupped in the middle, enough to hold several pints.

"Otter magic coming up!" he announced, and by the time the other travelers had returned from inspecting the black stone wall at the top of the beach, he'd conjured enough water from Fairy Well at the High to fill the bowl and, from that, the empty water jugs from *Bedstead* which the flying fairy fetched.

"Heading for the High," called the Innkeeper's son Rolfe, reining in the Inn's piebald pony to greet Precious on his Jennifer, coming from the opposite direction. "Father sent me to tell the Wizards the Brightglade kids are with us at the inn, being fed and properly coddled."

"*Whew! That's* a relief!" sighed Precious gustily. "Well and unharmed, I hopes?"

"Nothing wrong with 'em Ma's scrambled eggs on toast won't cure. Shall I ride on to the High, d'you think? I imagine their folks are worried about 'em."

The orchardman allowed Jennifer to move shoulder to shoulder with the inn's young pony, whom the Innkeeper's lad called Prissy, while he thought.

"*One* of us should ride to the High to tell Myrn and Douglas, o' course. And as 'tis on my way home, I shall do it."

"And I'll return and tell my folks that I met you on the road. Is that right?" asked the boy, a bit disappointed not to get to visit the exciting and mysterious Wizards' High. "Well, so be it!"

"It's best," agreed the orchardman, reining Jennifer around in the path. "Ask your folks to keep 'em safe for a few hours longer, until I see what Myrn decides. There's a rough bunch of men up at the High, you see, and she'd sent the children off for safety."

"I'm for home, then," sighed Rolfe. "We'll feed and bed the young-uns safe 'til we hear from you or the Brightglades!"

The two rode in opposite directions, pleased with the outcome of their meeting on the way.

Chapter Twelve

Up the River

A pair of spindly-legged sandpipers, happily turning over small, flat stones in search of an early lunch, trotted up to say hello.

"This coast is sometimes called The Main," chattered the lady bird, cocking her head to the left. "Nobody much lives here in the way of Menfolk. Lots of shore and land birds, wild pigs, tree and ground squirrels, a few snakes . . . none poisonous that I've ever met . . . and a few fearsome jaguars. Occasionally wild oxen and elephants, but we haven't seen any of those for some years."

"Home Port lies a goodly ways south . . . I *think*," put in her mate, sampling a bit of scrambled egg left over from Marbleheart's breakfast. "Never been so far from home, myself, but . . . well, word gets around, you know."

"We'll head south, then," Marbleheart decided. "Thank you, sandpipers! We needed some local directions."

"Easier to fly than swim or walk," considered the hen, cocking her head to the right. "Forest's pretty thick hereabouts. No roads that I know of. And there's a great, wide river runs down into Sea a few hour's flight south of here, I know. Alligators and hippopotami there, they tell me . . . but I've never been there myself.''

" 'They' being our old folks . . . who never wanted us wandering off that way,'' explained her mate. "Good commons, friends! Thank you!''

"Don't mention it,'' Lorianne said with a pleased laugh.

When the tiny birds had skittered off among the boulders in search of something less exotic to complete their morning meal, the Seacaptain said to her companions, "Well, if there's heavy jungle and a large river, perhaps we should float *Bedstead* again and travel by water.''

"Worth the try,'' agreed the Otter, nodding. "Save flying for scouting and such important things.''

Ben ferried them back to the reef where *Bedstead* was stuck, high and dry. They examined her situation carefully for a long minute.

"Tide's turned,'' Marbleheart observed. "She'll be almost afloat in a few hours.''

"But then she'll most likely wash out to Sea with the next ebb. Give 'er a push here and a shove there, now,'' Ben figured, "and she'll be in the lagoon instead. Smoother for sailing, I expect.''

It wasn't as easy as all that.

With all three pushing and lifting and struggling in the swirling wash across slippery rocks, they only managed to move *Bedstead* at last when a pair of neighborly eared seals, attracted by all the commotion, came by and lent their strength, pulling on a line.

Thanking the seals, the travelers wearily boarded their bedraggled craft and hoisted her single sail, catching the first of an offshore breeze.

"Starboard tack, now,'' decided Lorianne. "If I can manage it, that is. Run across the wind, down the coast. And we'll need a rudder, too. What to use?''

She showed them how to angle the narrow sail between opposite legs of the bed to catch the light land breeze at an angle.

Then she bundled several light blankets together, tied with pieces of cordage, and dangled the bundle over the stern, in such a way that it would serve as a sort of rudder.

Once *Bedstead* was moving smoothly ... well, *fairly* smoothly ... southward, parallel to the heavily wooded coast, the weary sailors settled down to mopping water from the bottom, turning the soggy mattress, wringing out the bedclothes, and hanging them over the headboard and footboard, the better to dry in the mid-morning's hot sun.

"Won't need a Drying Spell," decided Marbleheart. "If this wind holds, we should be able to ..."

"*Shhh*," whispered Lorianne. "Prince's asleep!"

Sure enough, Ben had made himself a nest among damp, salt-stiff sheets and blankets and fallen fast asleep.

"Come a ways since he left his mother's fairy castle, I believe," Marbleheart chuckled fondly.

"I'll take the helm," Lorianne decided. "I'll call for help if things change. Get some rest, Otter!"

"No sooner said than done," agreed Marbleheart with a wide yawn.

In less than three minutes he, too, was asleep.

Lorianne expertly tied off the tiller-ropes, keeping *Bedstead* headed slightly inshore so she was carried, slowly but steadily, southward following the distant line to starboard of thick greenery.

The afternoon air had turned quite sultry, and the pungent smell of jungle flowers and trees wafted across the intervening two miles of water along with the sounds of the forest, the singing of a half-million birds, and the occasional call or bark of a forest beast.

"Glad we decided to get you off that old reef," the girl said, patting *Bedstead*'s high side fondly. "Heard tales of hungry and ferocious beasts in these thick forests, when I was a child. *Ho! Hum! ...*"

An old hand at long, tedious watches, she began to sing to herself, stopping only to call out friendly greetings to birds wheeling low overhead in the strengthening wind.

"Watch yourself!" a curlew called, dropping low to be-speak her. "River's delta starts about here. Currents can be pretty tricky. Long, low sandbars and occasionally reefs of rock, barely awash at low tide. Good fishing grounds but not so good for sailing, Seacaptain!"

"Thank you, matey!" Lorianne called back.

She hauled at the sheet to swing the luff of the single sail wider and pointed the leading edge of *Bedstead* . . . you could hardly call it her prow . . . out to Sea, intending to give the turbulent waters off the river's mouth a wider berth.

"Keep the shore in sight?" she muttered to herself after a wide yawn. "*Ah! Oh, me!* I wonder how far it is to home?"

The new course took *Bedstead* further and faster away from land. After a while Lorianne decided a strong set of the current was carrying them too far to the east.

"Hard to tell," Lorianne explained to Marbleheart when she'd touched his shoulder with her foot to rouse him. "I think our heading is true, but it must be a really big river! I've lost sight of shore in the distance altogether."

"Well, well! Can we tack closer to the wind, I wonder?" yawned the Otter. "Head more westerly?"

"I'll try! Wake the boy and give us a paw with these braces."

All three pulled and tugged until the sail shivered and shook and *Bedstead* lay over on her port rail, all but dumping them into the water.

"Not very handy, is she?" Lorianne gasped, hauling the tiller rope back sharply, trying to correct the list. Her action headed *Bedstead* out to Sea more than ever, gathering momentum as the wind increased.

"Worst luck is . . . we don't have an anchor!" Marble-heart realized.

"Anchor? Plenty of line, however." Lorianne paused to consider. "Here! Hold her steady for a while. I think we might rig something. I saw it done a few times.''

She caught up a heavy, square patchwork quilt from the foot of the bed and quickly lashed eight-foot lines to each corner, bringing them together in the middle.

''Hand me that line *there*,'' she ordered Ben and, when he'd obliged, she fastened the heavier line to the quilt's harness. With the fairy's help, she dumped the whole arrangement over the stern and let it play out astern. When it had gone to the limit of her line's length, she snubbed it securely. The quilt opened like an umbrella just beneath the surface, held in place by the water.

''Sea anchor!'' Marbleheart exclaimed. ''Never thought of that!''

''It *should* slow our drift somewhat,'' puffed Lorianne.

Bedstead jerked twice, hard, as the anchor line reached its full tension, and abruptly slowed, swinging uneasily from side to side as the wind continued to push against her tiny sail and headboard.

The lady Seacaptain called to the Prince of Faerie, ''We've got to lower this blasted bedsheet!''

Lowering and furling the light sail proved a worrisome matter for the girl and the lad, but at last they managed to fold it and stow it in the bottom without tipping the bed over.

''Just hang on and ride 'er out,'' Lorianne advised the crew.

''Heavy weather coming!'' said Ben, who'd been keeping an eye to the west.

''Hang on!'' Marbleheart echoed, reaching out a paw for Lorianne and with the other clutching the tiller ropes.

In an ordinary boat the wind would hardly have caused them a worry. Ungainly *Bedstead*, however, had a perverse mind of her own, determined to capsize or change directions at unexpected moments, tugging at the taut anchor cable one minute and the next minute swinging wide to port or around to starboard.

''Anchor line might give way!'' Lorianne said. They

were all three clinging to the tiller ropes, fighting the con-
flicting lunges as best they could. "If it does . . ."

"We'll end up back in mid-Sea!" agreed Ben. "Or on
the bottom!"

All sight of land had disappeared. Darkness was falling,
and visibility was made even worse by sudden bursts of
rain. *Bedstead* tugged at her sea anchor, slacked off, then
jerked again in a new direction.

Marbleheart cried aloud in dismay, and Lorianne nearly
lost her footing among the sopping bedclothes. Together
they forced the bed's head around once more, easing the
tension on the anchor's cable a bit.

"Keep it up!" called Ben.

He flew strongly, pushing urgently at the port gunnel to
steady the bed-boat and slow her violent overswings.

"Carefully, Marbleheart!" he called. "Time to use a
spell, I wonder?"

"Spell?" Marbleheart gasped. "*Which* spell, would you
say?"

Not waiting to explain, the fairy boy hooked his left knee
over the footboard to free his hands, and began to gesture
and murmur a string of arcane words. Marbleheart and the
girl watched, waiting for the result with more than a bit of
trepidation.

Who knew what the young fairy would attempt?

"Over the side!" Ben pointed to port, shouting above
the rush of Sea and whistle of the wind.

"Huh?" Marbleheart chuffed, leaning over the bedside.

A huge, smooth, deep green, wide-set face with huge
golden eyes grinned up at him.

"Hello, Sea Otter! Fine evening for a little surfing, but
I fail to understand why you choose to do it in so strange
a craft," called Thornwood from the Sea Tortoise's back.
"There must be better ways!"

"*Oval? Thornwood!*" shouted Marbleheart. "Well met,
ancient amphibian and young Duke! What in World are *you*
doing here?"

"Someone hoisted a distress signal," explained the Great Sea Tortoise.

She bumped against the bed-boat's side with the forward edge of her heavy carapace so that Thornwood could clamber aboard.

"To tell you the plainest truth," he admitted, "I decided to follow you, Marbleheart. I thought you and the boy might be in danger!"

"A matter of interpretation . . . as Flarman is so fond of saying." The Otter shrugged. "We've had some rough times . . . and this is certainly one of them!"

"So, what's the problem?"

"We can't keep the wind from carrying us back out to Sea," the Otter explained hastily. "Sea anchor's barely holding. Could you manage to tow us ashore, Oval, my dear? We haven't the handiest sort of craft here, I'm afraid!"

"No task too great for an old friend," replied the Sea Tortoise calmly, and in less time than it would take to describe, she'd positioned herself at the headboard and began to churn the water into foam, shoving the bed-boat backward, against the breeze.

Thornwood and the Seacaptain retrieved the sea anchor. *Bedstead* stopped her wild jinking and wallowing and began easily to breast the offshore wind and choppy waves, headed for the out-of-sight delta.

"A tortoise could have advised you," said Oval, once *Bedstead* was well ashelter in one of the river's wide channels . . . largest of its many mouths.

"We'd no choice," Marbleheart explained: "It was swim or sail the bed, you see, when Lorianne's sloop broke up in the storm!"

"I feared that'd happened," sighed Thornwood. "But you overcame adversity quite well without me, I see."

"Not really," the Otter assured him. "Although I suppose we'd have survived. We were just not going toward

our destination when you came to answer the lad's distress
call, Thornwood. And Oval, of course!''

"Do you have an immediate destination in mind, Sea
Otter?'' the Tortoise asked. "We're in brackish water here,
and getting fresher by the yard.''

"No . . . look for a dry spot to land and we'll take time
to look to our course ashore,'' Marbleheart decided. "Go
on up this channel for a way.''

Oval steadily pushed on against the sluggish river current
until, as night fell, they moved between low, heavily
wooded shores where great trees almost overarched the
stream.

Bedstead behaved admirably under the Sea Tortoise's
firm control, keeping to the deeper parts of the channel and
avoiding the frequent sand bars and snags of half-sunken
tree trunks and forest debris.

"This looks like higher ground,'' the Tortoise called at
last, slowing her pace. "Unless you want to continue into
darkness, friends?''

"Take a rest, anyway,'' decided Marbleheart, glancing
to his companions for their comments. "A fire to dry us
out, some supper, and time to rest and talk. Run us ashore
over there, please, Mistress Oval! See that bit of beach?''

Oval expertly swung the bedstead from center stream and
shoved *Bedstead* well out of the flow, until her forelegs
embedded themselves in the narrow strip of sand.

"*Wow!*'' Ben puffed. "We fairies of Faerie are land
creatures, Mistress Oval, and it feels good to touch dry soil
again!''

"I, myself, prefer safe, open Sea . . . but then, I'm considerably heavier than you, Prince of Faerie. No tides here,
so your bed should be safe until you need it again. Unless
it rains hard, upstream. If you don't mind, folks, I'll go off
and see if there's anything fit to eat along this reach.''

She slid silently back into the river and disappeared in
the darkness.

Marbleheart and Ben erected three tents from their handkerchiefs . . . actually, they were mere shelter roofs, for the air here was humid and warm. Lorianne and Thornwood, chatting together about sailing and ships they had known, first gathered armfuls of dry marsh grass for kindling, and then driftwood. They soon had a cheery blaze going.

"Nothing to eat, however," sighed the Seacaptain.

"Now we're on solid land, maybe I can remedy the empty larder, Marbleheart said. "Oh, dear Blue Teakettle!" He made a complicated pass with his forepaws. "What's for dinner, old pot? *Ah-ha!*"

Before them appeared a linen tablecloth, followed in turn by a tureen of steaming corn chowder, loaves of hot, fresh rye bread, and a fresh garden salad topped with tuna-fish chunks, just as the Sea Otter best liked it.

"Come and eat," Marbleheart called to Thornwood and Ben, who were off a ways exploring the island on which Oval had beached them.

"It *is* an island," Ben reported. "The river flows on either side."

"Safer that way, if there be wild beasts hereabouts," the Duke assured Lorianne. "Have some butter, young Ben, and pass me the dish when you're finished!"

After they'd finished a very satisfying supper . . . their first good meal in days, in fact . . . Lorianne retired to her tent but the Otter, the Duke of Dukedom, and the Fairy Prince sat before the embers, telling of their adventures, and fighting sleep for a while longer.

As the flames died to coals they were startled to see, on the edge of the island, at the top of the bank above the beach, several pairs of yellow eyes reflecting the firelight. The eyes blinked, moved, disappeared, and reappeared again.

Shading his eyes from the firelight, Marbleheart could just make out several long, tapered, low forms moving toward them.

"*Ho!*" he called sharply. "Who goes there?"

A rumble and a snuffle were his only answers, and for a while the dark figures were still.

"Alligators!" whispered Ben, whose fairy eyes were almost as sharp as the Otter's. "Thinking of us as supper!"

"Alligators or crocodiles," observed Thornwood gravely. "Interested in only three things . . . swimming, eating, and sleeping. They do all three extremely well, I've heard. Not terribly bright, however. I suggest we make no sudden moves."

For a long while there was no further advance by the river swimmers. As their eyes became more accustomed to the gloom away from the dying fire, the travelers could see six full-grown alligators, with a couple of younger ones trailing behind.

"I must advise you, strangers," Marbleheart said in his best and deepest Familiar's rumble, "that we do *not* intend to be your dinners. Come in peace and we'll see you're well fed otherwise."

Thornwood added, "Come for trouble . . . and you'll find more than you might like!"

The nearest and largest pair of shining eyes blinked slowly, and the beast's harsh voice, sounding like someone talking through a long hollow log, answered.

"Supper's our concern. And otter meat suits us best, with human meat not far behind!"

"Otter meat's the world's very best, I agree," snorted Marbleheart, "but I've better use for it than you. I offer you other delicacies . . ."

"Chops of otter and ham of grown Man might serve as an appetizer, yes," countered the alligator, grinning ferociously. "And I smell tender young maiden in yon shelter, too."

"Not too fast!" cried Ben, drawing his knife. "You might get stung by a sharp fairy blade!"

"Oh, we really *are* frightened! Yes, we really *are*!" sneered several of the great saurians, grinning and clicking their wickedly sharp teeth. "With tough hides like ours, little boy, you'll need more than that darning needle to make us flee!''

"If it's food you seek," Marbleheart insisted, quite reasonably, "we can offer enough for even such vast diners as you!"

He waved his right forepaw, and between them silently appeared another tablecloth, blue-and-white checked, spread with trays of steaming fish-fry, slabs of savory cornbread, bowls of tartar sauce, heaps of smoking barbecued ribs, and a large tureen of Seafood chowder.

"Just as you like it best, I guarantee you, alligators!" the Otter called proudly. "Come to table! We'll talk a while, after you've dined."

For the first five minutes the scene was one of loud snorts, ugly snarls, and angry struggle as the 'gators fought for places around the picnic. When they at last realized the food was both very good and more than enough for all, they fell to eating in a more orderly manner, pausing only to belch, grin apologetically, and smack their sharp, white teeth in appreciation.

At last their leader looked up from the scattered remains of the meal, grinned in a somewhat more friendly manner, and began picking his teeth with a long, sharp foreclaw.

"Very good, Magician Otter!" he grunted. "I seem to have neglected to introduce myself. I am known as Major Scales, Chief of the Lower Atamazon River Alligators. These are members of my clan."

He introduced each of the adults by name and relationship, ending with a negligent wave of a claw at the youngsters.

"If you're still hungry, there's plenty more," Marbleheart told him evenly. "Just ask and I'll provide."

"No, no! Thank you! We Lower River Alligators appreciate a good meal and really are, at heart, peaceful critters, enjoying nothing so much as good conversation and a sunny mud bank on which to rest all day . . . once we're fed. Did I say thank you? Well, we do thank you! Call me Major.''

Marbleheart introduced himself, carefully stressing his Familiarity to a certain powerful Fire Wizard, and then Prince Flowerbender of Faerie, and the Duke of Dukedom, each by their full names and titles.

He decided to leave the Seacaptain to her slumber.

By now most of the Lower River 'gator clan was either asleep or very drowsy, lying in a semicircle in the damp sand, half in and half out of the water. Only Major Scales seemed awake and alert.

''We'll leave you alone. At least until we're hungry again,'' he said to Marbleheart. ''Especially in view of your connections with certain powerful persons. I wouldn't linger here in the bayou if I were your sorts, however. A hungry 'gator is an awesome and terrible sight.''

''So's an aroused Sea Otter! Tell me . . . is it your plan to spend the rest of the night here on our sand spit? Or do you have homes to go to?''

The huge 'gator chieftain rumbled a laugh and shook his head. ''We're but resting up for a night's carouse in the open channel downstream. We'll leave you to your rest, shortly. We feel obligated to return a favor for the very good dinner, however. What can we do for you, while our better natures prevail?''

Marbleheart glanced quickly at Ben and Thornwood, but the two shook their heads slightly.

''Leave us to our sleep until we wake in the morning,'' Otter said. ''Do you plan to spend much time down in the mouth?''

''Just 'til first light. We'll probably be hungry again and come seeking some breakfast. If you're still here . . .''

''You'll find a good, hearty breakfast waiting for you,'' Marbleheart promised. ''But you won't find *us*.''

''Wise Sea Otter,'' rumbled the lead alligator, nodding his head slowly. ''I'll even give you a word of warning. Watch out for a gang of fierce hippos, upstream. Frightening, terrible, ravening monsters! Pink, if you can believe that! Not at all trustworthy nor even very bright, either. Danger by the ton!''

"Appreciate your warning, Major," replied Thornwood. "We'll keep a few eyes out for them, even if they never eat meat, as others do."

"Don't let those vegetarians fool you, Lord Duke," sniffed the 'gator. "They're dangerous! Ugly! Sneaky! Wicked! Ponderous! Trample you flat at the drop of a palmetto frond!''

He yawned mightily and, without further ado, whipped fully about and slid into the dark stream behind him with a great splash.

His entire clan, suddenly awake, followed him, churning the water into grayish froth. In a trice the 'gators had disappeared.

Oval, who had returned silently during the fireside chat with the 'gators, decided to stay out of sight but keep her eyes open, a silent guard over her friends as they slept.

She emerged from the water only at the first sign of dawn and daytime life in the bayou under the great, grey, moss-hung oaks and bald cypresses, bringing with her a mess of fresh-caught catfish, ready for grilling.

"Alligators won't be back for a while, yet," she told Marbleheart. "Let's eat, then prepare to leave."

"Alligators?" asked Lorianne in surprise. "Did I miss something?''

"Not much. Just some night visitors," Thornwood assured her. "They went their way. If they come back they won't find us, as the Otter says, for we're going upstream, seeking higher ground."

"I thought we intended to sail down the coast on the bed-boat," Lorianne said in surprise.

"We'll be better off on dry land, after all, what with the contrary winds and currents . . . and all these 'gators," Marbleheart told his companions. "*Bedstead* will carry us at least as far as the uplands beyond the delta, maybe. I don't

want to have to watch my backwater for starving suitcases.
Enough worry about herds of crazed hippos, anyway!''

The idea of sailing *Bedstead* upstream was defeated by
the morning's land breeze, quite strong, and the fact that
the current of the fairly shallow delta waterway was against
them. The channel was too narrow for beating upwind, even
if they could manage it.

''I could tow her, but I must warn you that the river
quickly becomes much too shallow for both me *and* your
bed,'' Oval advised. ''Better to abandon the poor thing and
let me carry you as far upstream as a Great Sea Tortoise
can swim. Some miles, I should think.''

They adopted the Sea Tortoise's suggestion and, selecting the driest and sturdiest of the bedclothes for use as
cushions, folded and tied with line and loaded on Oval's
broad, flat carapace, they abandoned the faithful bed-boat
to its fate on the midchannel sandbar.

Before they shoved off, Marbleheart remembered to
leave behind an enormous breakfast of hard-boiled eggs,
buttered toast, kippers, bacon, and strong coffee in an urn.
Lower Atamazon River Alligator Clan would have no cause
to complain of their leaving without saying good-bye.

After a longish day of cruising . . . the Tortoise's speed
was surprisingly good and her back quite dry and comfortable . . . the rising ground on either hand showed they'd
passed above the low-lying delta at last.

That evening they camped on a grassy bank under
spreading tree ferns and enjoyed Blue Teakettle's wonderful dinner, along with some deliciously tart wild oranges
Ben discovered not far inland.

''I'll be leaving you in the morning,'' Oval sighed with
real regret, for she'd enjoyed their company. ''Overland
travel is far too difficult for me. The river is now entirely
fresh and is getting too shallow for my depth of keel.''

''We understand, dear Oval! We really do,'' cried Lorianne, who had come to love the gentle giant early in their short acquaintance. "I wish you could go along with us to Home Port. What a sight for the children! Scare the waders off some of my uncle's shipmates, too!"

"I try not to scare people any more than they deserve," Oval chuckled ponderously. "I'll call at Home Port one day, mistress Seacaptain. Now I must head east for Warm Sea and my own home waters. I've duties to attend to, and a family to grandmother, although my grandchildren are all full grown by now. Still, I feel it my duty to be fairly close for them, in case they need me. I greatly enjoyed our excursion, youngsters!"

She turned downstream, toward Sea, glad to head for salt water again, if truth be known.

"Send me word of what you see and do, here in Southwest," she called back as she glided off.

"I'll come and visit you, I promise, and tell you everything!" shouted Ben. "Thanks again for the lift!"

"Wonderful old lady!" Thornwood said to Lorianne. "Salt of the Sea, that one!"

Chapter Thirteen

Meanwhile . . .

AFTER dinner Douglas and Myrn had sat talking to the much-subdued Bladder, until darkness had fallen.

"I imagine you're quite tired," Myrn suggested, giving a tiny magical flick of her forefinger as she said it, to make quite sure. "Douglas will show you to a comfortable bed aloft. We retire early here at the High. Much work to do on the morrow!"

Bladder caught himself yawning vastly, and rubbed sudden grains of sleepiness from his eyes.

"Perhaps it'd be best," he said to Douglas, "if I sort of . . . disappeared? Leave you to your important work?"

"Nonsense!" cried the Fire Wizard. "Sleep well tonight, and after breakfast I'll give you a letter of introduction and directions to friends of mine on the east coast. The Fairstranders will appreciate gaining a strong and skillful mechanic, and won't question you too closely about your origins and history."

"Well . . . *yeow!* . . ." Bladder yawned again, even wider and louder. "If you say so, Douglas. Much obliged, I'm sure! Your servant, ever, ma'am! If you ever need an honest, skilled blacksmith . . . I'm that sorry to miss meeting your young-uns. Good night, everybody!''

He waved to the ranks and rows of Dishes and Plates, Pots and Pans, Tools and Utensils, and the rest of the kitchen staff on their shelves and in their bins and cupboards. Silverware rattled, clicked, thumped, and banged softly, calling sleepily, ''Good night, Mr. Smith!''

Douglas showed the sleepy blacksmith-to-be to a pleasant guest room on the second floor of the High cottage and, before he left him, assured Bladder he would be safe and sound for the night.

''Eunicet'll stay well mazed under Workshop, warehouses, stables, coops, cots, and all, for as long as I wish him to be so,'' Douglas explained. ''When I'm ready, I'll let him find his way out. Which reminds me . . . what do you think should be done about your crewmen? Are they professional criminals, actually, or just down-out-of-luck Seamen who followed Eunicet to get regular eating?''

''The latter, I should say. Not very good pirates. Worse as soldiers, I always told old Eunie. It was his ill will kept us getting deeper and deeper into piracy, rather than settling down somewhere once we got back to civilized places.''

The young Pyromancer stood in the doorway for a moment, thinking of what his guest had just said.

''I'll expect them all to return their booty as soon as they can, of course. I'll talk to you about that later, in Fairstrand. I suppose Eunicet hid it away somewhere?''

''Eunicet was looking for cash. The worst we did was capture a few cargoes. He couldn't be bothered with rope and sailcloth or barrels of tar and such.''

He yawned yet again and shook his head.

''We had no time to bury what loot we took . . . treasure, as *he* calls it. It's still hidden aboard the ketch.''

''Someone'll have to track her down,'' Douglas sighed. ''Well and well, as Flarman says. Thornwood and his men, perhaps. Now, there's hot water in the ewer and a bar of

Trunkety Store's best clover-scented soap. Good for shaving, too, I find.''

"I long ago lost my razor . . .'' Bladder began, fingering his unkempt black beard.

"There's a razor, sharp as you could ever desire, on the washstand. Good idea to scrape your beard off. Its been so long since anyone saw you clean-shaved even Eunicet'll never recognize you!''

"I'll take your hint,'' chuckled the former pirate, soldier, roisterer, and scapegrace. "And say my thanks to your goodwife, again, Master Douglas. I'll leave before dawn, so as not to (*yawn*) be underfoot.''

"No, no! Stay for breakfast, and receive my note to Mayor Beckett of Fairstrand. I must write a note to Bryarmote, also, or he may discover your presence on his borders and take strong action.''

"I remember Prince Bryarmote, and a note to him is a *very* good idea,'' agreed the smith. "Good night, good Wizard! I'll earn your trust, believe me!''

"I've no doubts of that at all,'' replied the Pyromancer, and he left, closing the door on the man already stripping off his tattered, filthy clothes before bathing, and yawning mightily.

"Do you think he'll *really* reform?'' Myrn asked as she prepared to fly off to Trunkety to fetch their children. Precious had just come up to the front door to tell them the twins were to be found at the Oak 'n' Bucket.

"Odds are in our favor,'' said her husband, busily penning his notes to the Dwarf Prince and to the Mayor of Fairstrand. "If nobody else, Grammar Maryam'll keep him in straight line!''

"Trust Grammar Maryam for such a task, yes!'' Myrn laughed at the memory of the elderly lady who was mother, aunt, cousin, sister, or grandmother to just about every fisherman on the east coast. "Well! I'm off to the Oak 'n' Bucket.''

"Spend tonight at the inn; go on to Perthside tomorrow, then hurry back! Take my love and devotion to my mother and father."

"See you day after tomorrow," said his wife, leaning over his shoulder to place a kiss on his cheek.

She nodded her head twice, whispered a certain rhymed spell while touching a strand of pearls about her neck, and blinked out like a blown candle.

Bronze Owl slipped through the front door, flew down the hall to the darkened, still-warm kitchen, and there found Douglas sipping a glass of milk and eating chocolate-frosted cookies by the light of the low, late coals in the Dwarf-built fireplace.

"Not abed yet?" Owl asked, shaking his head with a soft creak of metal feathers. "'Tis well past midnight! Thornwood's fleet will be at anchor in Farango Water tomorrow. What's going on here?"

"Pirates in the cellar," Douglas explained. "And they're just fine; sound asleep now. I'll be the same, very shortly. Myrn's gone off to take the babies to my mother's home for safekeeping."

"Pirates, eh? Tell me the story!"

Douglas related the appearance of Eunicet and the outcome of his invasion of the High cottage.

"I don't envy his men in his evil company. A bad night with Eunicet is a night that lasts forever and forever, I'd say." Bronze Owl chuckled wickedly at the thought.

"Still," he added in a more sober tone, "I imagine they must be getting pretty hungry, by now. I know a man can go for days and days without food, but I'm told it's not the most comfortable feeling in World."

"Blue Teakettle'll send them down a hearty breakfast when they wake. By the time they finish, I'll be ready to distribute the crewmen where their skills will earn them a proper, honest living. Maybe a little Forgetfulness Spell? They'll make no more trouble."

"But . . . Eunicet? A born troublemaker, or I miss my highly educated guess . . . which I seldom do, being a wise old metallic owl."

"What's to do about Eunicet? He's never had any real skills at magic, so *that's* no great danger. He's tried to accomplish his heart's desires by being wicked, intolerant, bullying, biased, bad-tempered, pigheaded, stubborn, churlish, mean, foul-mouthed, cruel . . ."

"Good description of the man, far as it goes," agreed Bronze Owl. "Have you considered . . . destruction?"

"A very serious and completely final solution," Douglas murmured, shaking his head in doubt. "It's tempting . . ."

"Save your pity!" scoffed the metal bird, who tended to be hard-hearted in such matters. "You've tried putting Eunicet away where he couldn't do any further harm . . ."

"Yes, but the middle of Warm Sea was not far enough! He's a tough old bird . . . sorry, Owl, I didn't mean to insult birds."

"No offense taken. Now, then . . . how about leaving him and his men where they are under the High? From what Bryarmote claims, they could stay lost there forever, and then some."

"We could . . . but it'd spoil an otherwise pleasant home, to hear Eunicet snarling and grumping and seething under our feet . . . and especially at night when we want to sleep!"

"Rather disconcerting, I agree. Even for Flarman, who has even more reason to dislike and distrust the man."

For a while the old friends sat watching the embers in the fireplace glowing and popping on occasion, casting longer and longer shadows on the far side of the darkened kitchen.

"Well . . . let me sleep on it." Douglas decided not to decide, at last.

Rising, he took a glass-bowled oil lamp from the mantel and lighted it with his left forefinger, Pyromancer-fashion. "Maybe something'll come to me. But I hope total and

final destruction will not be the final solution. Not even for
Eunicet, although goodness knows he deserves it for what
he did to old Duke Thorowood, to name just one of many.''

As the young Wizard started up the stairs to bed, Owl
flew to the front door and found his favorite nail, to watch
out the rest of the night.

Pyromancer Flarman Flowerstalk balanced a burning,
foot-long splinter of fat-wood on the tip of his left index
finger, allowing it to turn slowly, like a compass needle on
its pivot.

As the spinning splinter came to rest, the end ember
flared and gave off an acrid purple smoke which rose in
the still air in a flat corkscrew.

The Fire Wizard held his breath as long as he possibly
could, but at last he had to gasp, blowing the smoke away.

''No luck!'' he called across the towertop room to the
Water Adept. ''We'll have to try something else.''

''I will resolutely refuse,'' sneezed Augurian, ''to say 'I
told you so!' ''

For several long minutes Flarman sat staring out the
tower window at a piling-up mass of black thunderclouds
on the western horizon.

A flash of distant lightning brought him from his reverie.

''How about you, Waterboy? You've been examining
something for hours and hours!''

Augurian sat back in his chair and rubbed weary eyes,
shaking his head at the same time.

''Maybe a bit of lunch would rejuvenate the investigative
juices,'' suggested the Pyromancer. ''You're trying *too*
hard!''

''There's no way I can try *too* hard,'' objected the Water
Adept, rising. ''But your idea of lunch is inspired! What
time is it, anyway?''

Flarman pulled a gold watch from his waistband and
opened the case. A tiny mechanical bird popped out of a

hatch above the ornate numeral XII and cocked his jeweled head to the right.

"Time for lunch!" it sang out. "A quarter-hour after one in the afternoon, Waterand Island Time, Pyromancer! And it's going to rain!"

"It always rains at two in the afternoon, here," grumped Flarman. "One hardly needs a mechanical cuckoo to tell one the weather!"

The tiny bird shrugged its shoulders and retreated into the watch, slamming the hatch with a loud *click*.

Flarman grunted and returned the watch to his pocket. "Tell me something I don't already know!"

"Your temper seems a bit frayed, which surprises me. All you've done all morning is play with your fire-sticks, Smoky," chuckled Augurian, gesturing his friend away from the work table. "Lunch, did you say? Come along!"

Flarman followed him down the winding stair, shaking his head as he went.

"I think we should talk to Lithold," Augurian suggested. "The lens is evidently made of quartz, not Man-made glass as we at first supposed."

"Yes, I think it's time to call in our stone expert," agreed his companion. "You call the lady Geomancer. I'll give Douglas and Myrn a peep. Lithold will want to see the lens, and Douglas still has it, of course. What's for lunch?"

"Shrimp salad, I see," replied the Water Adept. "Ship's hardtack. Cocktail sauce hot enough even for a Fire Wizard!"

He lifted the covers from the dishes laid out on a table on the shaded terrace by a trio of pretty island girls in grass skirts. "Iced tea? Ah, yes! Sit ye down, Flarman, so the ladies can serve."

The Fire Wizard plunked gloomily into his chair and tucked his linen napkin under his third chin.

"Probably all's quiet, over to home," he muttered, passing a basket of ship's bread as one of the young ladies began to ladle steaming clam chowder into his bowl. "*Too* quiet, I would guess. What of Thornwood, eh? How about those pirates?"

"You're distracted by things the youngsters undoubtedly have well in hand. Have some salad and stop clouding matters."

After a bowl of chowder and a healthy helping of the salad, Flarman was obviously in better spirits, despite the afternoon rain shower now beginning to fall. The maids expertly unfurled a bright-striped awning to keep off the pelting raindrops.

"You're right, of course, Waterboy. The lens, quartz or glass or clear diamond, whatever it is, demands attention. Do we dare try fire on it?"

"I don't think it would melt or crack . . . if we're careful," Augurian decided after a moment's thought. "Yes!"

"Douglas can heat it carefully in the Workshop kiln, I should think. Your excellent cook has made delicious passion fruit tarts. There's but one left! Will you claim it . . . or shall I demolish it for you?"

Augurian waved a negligent hand, and Flarman ate the last tart.

Chapter Fourteen

The Horrendous Hippos

WEST of the wet, tangled, steamy delta the land rose slowly into verdant savannas clad with sweet-smelling grasses half as tall as a Man, with scattered hummocks on which grew luxuriant, leafy trees bearing ripening fruits and spicy-smelling flowers.

On the western horizon they saw a jagged edge of mountain peaks over which afternoon clouds built into towering thunderheads.

"*Ugh!*" Lorianne wiped her neck and brow with a soggy handkerchief. "Don't you think we could find some shade? I'm about to stew!"

"You don't even have a fur coat to put up with," growled Marbleheart, softening his retort with a wry grin.

"Actually, fur is better than getting sunburned . . . like the rest of us," Thornwood told him. He'd shed his velvet cloak and carried it now over his left shoulder, so it would not hamper his right arm, should he need to draw his sword.

Ben, who was fanning himself with his lacy wings, stuck a pink bit of tongue out at the Otter.

"Sunburn's not one of a fairy's problems, nor is heat,"

the boy said. "Try to think of yourself as a cool cucumber, or a dish of ice cream."

"If you can manage that, you're lucky as can be," Lorianne sighed, tucking her wet handkerchief under her belt so that it could dry a bit before she used it again.

"Sunlight here is painful, however," the lad continued, frowning fiercely. "In fact, it's more than that; it's almost unbearable!"

"The dark fur on my face cuts the glare," Marbleheart claimed, "so sunlight doesn't bother me. However, let's find some shade. And if our clever Prince of Faerie should wish to practice his magic by producing a cake of good, old Briny Deep pack ice . . . *that* would bring comfort and ease to us all!"

"Never thought of ice," admitted Ben, and he began to weave a spell softly to himself as they hiked along.

"Not here, child!" cried Marbleheart. "Let's find shade and a soft place to sit. I think I can manage a pitcher of lemonade . . ."

He led them to a pleasant hummock grove of five or six wide-spreading, lacy-leafed trees which cast cool shadows under their boughs.

"Let's stop for lunch," Lorianne suggested.

"Not a moment too soon!" gasped Marbleheart, pretending to be weak with hunger.

Once under the trees Ben carefully materialized four huge blocks of clear, blue ice as big as easy chairs, while Otter ordered lunch and lots of lemonade in a frosted pitcher. Lorianne poured them each a tall glassful, garnished with cool, green mint leaves plucked from the Wizards' High herb garden just a few minutes before.

"Whoever complained of the hardships of travel?" chuckled Thornwood, downing half his drink at a single long gulp.

"Even so . . . the business of being afloat on Sea in wind and rain was no picnic," Ben observed. "I feel sorry for mortals and such, Men and people like that, who must endure such things!"

"Mortality hath its compensations, however," insisted the Otter, curled up on his block of ice. "More lemonade, my dear, please! Thank you!"

The afternoon sun slid with increasing speed toward the western mountains. The companions sat in comfortable silence for a long time, waiting for an afternoon breeze to make their trek more bearable.

"*Ho!*" cried Ben, who was braiding a necklace of bright blue wild grass-flowers for Lorianne. "What was *that*?"

"Didn't see a thing," mumbled Marbleheart sleepily.

"Something moved in the taller grass over to the right," Ben insisted, standing on his block of ice and shading his eyes. "Something big!"

Lorianne, Thornwood, and the Otter followed suit and shortly, from the river's swampy margin, they saw a herd of huge, pinkish grey beasts lumbering in their direction at a ponderous trot. Now the ground shook with their weight.

"Hippos!" guessed Thornwood, although he'd never seen one of the fabled river-horses before. "Should we retreat, d'you think?"

"No!" whispered Ben. "*Never* run from an animal, if you can help it. Besides, there's no sign they're angry or hungry, is there?"

"I've heard of hippopotamuses," Lorianne said bravely . . . but she pressed close to Thornwood for safety. "Men who tell the tales say they're often extremely dangerous. But they're grass-eaters, so that's no problem . . . perhaps."

" 'Perhaps' is not much comfort," Thornwood told his fair companion. "I think we'd better stand our ground here among the trees."

"Here they come!" yipped Marbleheart, more excited than afraid.

The herd of huge riverine monsters rumbled up at about the speed of a trotting horse, heads held low and tails held high. Ten yards short of the waiting travelers on the rapidly melting blocks of ice, the foremost hippo suddenly slid to a halt and stood peering at them nearsightedly.

"You're supposed to *bolt*!" he bellowed, snorting a bit from the cloud of dust raised by his own heavy hooves. "Most people, even those nasty tidewater 'gators, dash off rather than face our fearsome charge!"

"We choose to stand and talk," Marbleheart replied. "We're doing no harm that we know of, sir, and have nothing to fear."

The hippo shook his vast head, seeming bewildered.

"Usually . . ." he began.

"Oh, go on!" cried a pinker and smaller . . . barely smaller . . . she-hippo just behind him. "Trample them and stomp them into the mud, Bluster! Get rid of this hot distraction and let's get back to the river! This sun's awful!"

"Now, Selaney!" said the leader. "They say they're doing no harm!"

"Will you please tell me what this is all about?" Lorianne asked, somewhat angrily. "We were just sitting here on our nice, cool ice, enjoying the shade and a bit of lunch. We'd have been on our way, shortly, if you great things hadn't hove up in such a terrible rush."

"Ah, well . . . I, well . . . *er* . . ." muttered the hesitant hippo leader, turning a deeper shade of pink. "Well, we all had a meeting, some years ago, you know, and agreed it was safer to *chase* intruders off than to . . ."

". . . to take a chance they might harm *us*," finished the female hippo Bluster had called Selaney. "We used to be really quite cordial to strangers. Showed them the deepest pools and the best fishing holes, even the softest grasses for bedding. But time and again they stole our fodder from our mouths and frightened our children. A time or two they even tried to *ride* us, shouting, 'Giddy-up, you River Horse!' Can you *imagine*!"

"Yes, she's absolutely right," said several of the other hippos.

When these intruders had refused to run from their

charge, they'd huddled nervously behind their leader and began shuffling about uncomfortably.

"Oh!" Marbleheart said into the following silence. "Well, anyway, you have the right to chase people off your land, if you choose, I suppose. It has, however, given you a pretty bad reputation in the eyes of certain 'gators . . ."

"Those awful, sneaky, slinking, bad-smelling, long-tailed, meat-eating mobsters!" shrieked Selaney angrily. "You shouldn't pay any attention to them! I'm surprised they didn't try to eat *you!*"

"Well, they did have that in mind," Marbleheart admitted. "Just as you hippos had trampling us into the mud in mind, just now. But we managed to turn the 'gators' wrath . . . and their hunger . . . aside."

"*Ah-ha!* You must be *magicians!*" cried Bluster, jerking his head up at the thought. "Maybe 'tis *we* should run away, fellow Hippos!"

"Oh, now . . ." said Lorianne hastily. "We're nothing of the sort! Just a Seacaptain, a Duke, a Fairy Prince, and a Sea Otter, on our way to my home in Home Port."

"An Otter who happens to be Familiar to a famous Fire Wizard, however!" Marbleheart added hastily. "Not to be trifled with! Peaceful when not riled, I assure you."

The huge pink animals glanced at each other uneasily, but the herd was content to let their leaders decide how to react to these pronouncements.

"Just passing through, then, are you?" Bluster asked at last.

"Just passing up the river until we can reach the shade of the upland forest," agreed the Otter with a nod. "Then we'll head south to this lady's Home Port, as she said."

"Well, we really aren't all that ferocious," the leader of the hippos admitted. "It's just that . . . well, we've had bad experiences with Men and alligators in the past."

"There are wicked and thoughtless Men just as there are probably wicked and thoughtless hippos," Lorianne pointed out. "We came in peace, Master Hippo. And we'll go the same way, if allowed."

"But a Wizard's Familiar . . ." put in Selaney.

". . . can be downright dangerous, if aroused," finished Ben. "And a fairy, especially a Prince of Faerie like me, can be a formidable opponent, too, if an enemy gives him reason."

"*Humph*," snorted Selaney, pushing Bluster on the rump with her left shoulder. "An impasse! Let's go home and leave these folks to resume their journey, I vote. Good day, Seacaptain, Duke, Familiar, and Prince of Faerie!"

She began to move backward into the taller grass, pushing the rest of the hippo band backward also.

"Now, just wait a minute!" shouted Bluster. "*I* didn't give an order to withdraw! These people are here in peace, and I, for one, wish to assure them the River Horse Clan will give them no further trouble."

"No, no trouble, because we can be on the other side of the river in no time at all," snapped the pink female testily. "Are you going to lead, or are you going to follow, buddy? Make up your mind!"

The vast male regarded her with his tiny but sharp right eye.

"*I* am elected leader here," he said evenly. "If you're going to take the responsibility for the clan, my dear, just say so . . . and I'll let you try your hand, especially when the 'gators come upstream looking for tender young colts next birthing time!"

Selaney dropped her head and averted her eyes.

"Well, then . . . let's be courteous to these strangers. Come on, fellows! You don't often get to meet a fairy, a Seacaptain, a Duke, and a Familiar all in the same afternoon."

Slowly the hippos returned to stand facing the travelers, just within the shade of the acacias.

"I apologize," Bluster said. "We . . . rather, I . . . had

decided to chase the 'gators and other dangerous strangers
away when they came again.''

"Case of good idea misapplied, I suppose. No harm,
Master Bluster," Marbleheart said with an understanding
nod. "I'm glad *that's* straightened out. It's much too hot,
anyway, to fight.''

"My sentiments exactly!" the head hippo grinned. "Tell
me, Familiar, is there anything we might help with? We
must return to the river shortly as this sun burns our tender
skin very badly, especially this time of day.''

Marbleheart considered. "You could advise us on the
best trail south.''

"We advise you, then, to head off that way. The ground
rises slowly, but there are several streams of fresh water on
the way. Eventually, I understand, although I've never been
there myself, you'll come under the edge of the forest.''

"Another jungle?" asked Lorianne, thinking of the delta
they'd passed through.

"No, not a jungle," said Selaney, shaking her head.
"Upland hardwood forest, rather. I'd advise you to look up
a porcupine named Toothpick. He knows more about the
forest than most plains animals hereabouts.''

"Now, that's what I call good advice, Mistress Selaney," Ben said warmly. "We'll certainly look for this
Toothpick person. Lives in the forest nearby, does he?''

"That's my . . . our . . . understanding," agreed Bluster.
"Now we must bid you farewell, good travelers. Being out
of water too long causes hippos all sorts of skin troubles.
Safe journey!''

"And you . . . a peaceful summer," replied Marbleheart
courteously.

The herd moved off, disappearing into the tall cane along
the bank of the river.

"Not much help, were they?" Ben sighed, once the hippos were out of earshot.

"On the contrary," Marbleheart said. "They've given

us, at least, guidance to a guide for the way ahead. All we must do is find this Toothpick person.''

''I've met a few porcupines in my day,'' Lorianne said, sounding not too pleased with the idea of meeting another. ''But if he can point the way . . .''

''Pointing is what porcupines do quite well. I hear they're pretty sharp!'' Thornwood said this seriously enough. Lorianne and Ben thought his puns were very funny.

The tree line seemed very little closer when Marbleheart, seeing the girl and the young Duke were foot-weary, suggested they find a place for the night. The lowering sun was close to touching the serrated horizon, throwing bare peaks into stark relief. A cool breeze had at last sprung up, bringing, at first, welcome relief but later a touch of chill after the heat of day.

''Over there,'' suggested Ben, pointing at an isolated grove off to one side. ''Water there, I 'spect. And we can put up the tents and build a good fire against the chill.''

The travelers found to their delight that the trees bore a variety of fruit. They plucked hard, shiny, round, purplish globes that proved, when split, to contain juicy sweet red pulp that tasted like a cross between oranges and peaches.

A tiny spring bubbled out of the ground, cool, clean, and tasty, to slake their thirst and bathe their dusty bodies. Once the sun had dropped behind the mountains, the fruit and a dinner of roasted pork chops and sauerkraut from the High kitchen consumed, they were ready to retire.

''We'd better take turns at watching,'' Thornwood suggested.

''I'll take my turn at guard,'' Lorianne said quickly. ''You Menfolk must stop treating me like a dainty bit of fluff. I've stood many a lonely midnight watch, in port and under weigh.''

''Draw straws for the order, then,'' suggested the yawning Otter.

He was pleased to draw the morning watch, with the girl drawing the first watch of the night and Thornwood coming on duty at midnight, followed by the boy at eight bells of the morning watch . . . four a.m., Lorianne explained to Ben.

The grove murmured to them in the evening breeze and the smell of grasses and tiny flowers, the sounds of late birds and evening animals in the distance calling back and forth, as well, soon put them in their beds and deep slumber.

Marbleheart wakened for a moment at midnight when Lorianne came to waken Thornwood for his tour of duty. A thin new moon was sailing high by then, lighting the broad, empty-seeming savanna and throwing the edge of the forest into sharp, dark shadow.

Otter awoke again just at dawn to a strange sound like a bundle of dry sticks, rattling together. He popped his head from his tent and blinked out at a strange and rather frightening sight a few inches before his nose.

All he could think of was a brown, old haystack with bright yellow eyes, sharp buck teeth, and a pink button nose.

"*Oh!*" Marbleheart snorted, at a loss for brave words. "*Ah?*"

The beast, who appeared to be almost the size of one of the smaller hippos, grinned toothily and nodded.

"Master Sea Otter, I presume? Familiar to the famous Pyromancer Douglas Brightglade of Wizards' High?"

Encouraged that the rather intimidating animal knew his name, Marbleheart managed to nod. "What can I do for you, sir?"

"It's *I* who came to help *you*," replied the beast, grinning even more broadly. "I am called Toothpick . . . although that's just my nickname, not my full name at all. The hippos sent a mutual friend, a tick-bird, around last evening to tell me you were looking for me."

"Oh!" cried Marbleheart, sliding out of the tent, rising on his hind feet, and bowing politely to the enormous porcupine. "Pleased to meet you! Should we call you Toothpick, too? It doesn't seem fitting. Well . . . maybe it does, at that. I know a Toothpick Dispenser, whom you do resemble more than a little, in the kitchen at Wizards' High."

" 'Dispenser?' " questioned the animal, sinking back on his haunches.

Seen with fully wakened eyes, he was not really as big as a hippopotamus, after all, but still quite bulky. "A pleasant-sounding word! I don't know what it might mean."

"Oh, a dispenser is . . . a little, round glass ball with lots of little holes in it . . . in which we keep small, wooden sticks sharpened at both ends. We use them to get at stray bits of meat and seeds that're stuck between our teeth, you see."

"I understand 'toothpick,' and now 'dispenser' makes some sense, Marbleheart Sea Otter," the porcupine said. "I'm here to help you."

"Quick to get to the point, I see!" chuckled the Otter. "Come meet the rest."

He led the prickly animal—most of his seeming bulk was, the Otter realized, the thick, rattling coat of stiff, extremely sharp, hollow spines that grew all over his neck, shoulders and back, and down his short, thick tail—across to the other tents, where the Otter rattled the flaps and cleared his throat.

"May I present Seacaptain Lorianne of Home Port," he told the porcupine when the lady emerged. "The gentleman over there is Thornwood Duke of Dukedom, across Sea."

"Very pleased to meet you, there's no doubt about it," said Lorianne, who didn't seem at all surprised by the porcupine's strange appearance.

Thornwood nodded politely to the newcomer. Marbleheart looked about, expecting to see the Prince of Faerie.

"Where's the boy? Seen him about? He never called me for my watch at eight!"

"I just awoke, myself," yawned the Duke. "Pleased to meet you, Master Porcupine . . ."

"Please! Call me Toothpick," urged the prickly one. "It's safe to shake my forepaw, but if you're the kind which likes to hug, I'd advise extreme caution."

"I can see why," laughed the Lady Seacaptain.

She and Thornwood shook the proffered paw warmly, but carefully.

"You outrank your companions, Sir Duke," Toothpick murmured, "although I admit I'm a bit rusty on ranks and titles."

"Marbleheart's the leader of our expedition. I'm just a follower. However, if you're interested, I think we can persuade Marbleheart to stop sniffing all about the campground and provide some breakfast."

"Trying to locate that dratted boy. He's disappeared!" explained Marbleheart, sounding more than a bit worried. "Not like Ben to wander off . . . yet his scent indicates he went off toward the forest. Hours ago."

"I smell his footsteps, also," the porcupine said, nodding slowly. "Is your young friend lost?"

"No, no! The lad's a Fairy Prince, the son of Queen Marget of Faerie and her consort, Prince Aedh. No, I don't *think* any harm could befall him," Marbleheart insisted, but he was frowning deeply.

Through the pleasant business of calling breakfast from the kitchen back at the High, Marbleheart was distracted, and kept glancing off toward the distant trees as if expecting the boy to emerge from the greenery at any moment.

"He knows better than to wander off alone," he said for the fourth time.

"He's just a boy, after all," soothed Lorianne.

"There's danger in the forest for soft, young things who're careless or unwary," the porcupine agreed gravely. He was nibbling daintily on a pancake, piping hot, soaked in maple syrup, and topped with a generous handful of pecans. "Should I go off and look for him, do you think?"

"We'll all go," Marbleheart decided. "I'm responsible for the lad. Be just a short minute while we break camp."

While he quickly reduced the tents to pocket-size, and sent the china back to the High with a practiced flip of forepaw, Thornwood doused the fire and saw that all their gear was carefully packed.

Lorianne and the porcupine waited and chatted, the girl describing their adventures at Sea and with the alligators and the hippos.

The porcupine was most interested in the girl's description of the Great Sea Tortoise.

"Never been close to Sea, I'm afraid," he sighed. "I really must go look at it, some day. I wander all over this land, being a footloose sort. Thanks to my even disposition and sharp quills, not even lions nor even 'gators care to trouble me."

"Lions?" The girl jumped in surprise. "Of all the beasts of the forest, I fear lions most!"

"No need! They're usually polite and rather lazy, to tell you the truth. Many of them are my good friends," the prickly Toothpick claimed amiably. "All set to go, Familiar? Follow me, friends."

And he waddled off in the direction Ben had taken some time before dawn.

At first the forest was tangled, thick with vines and clogged with heavy, often thorny underbrush, which made for very slow going. The porcupine's pace was leisurely, however, and despite the growing humidity and mid-morning heat, the party had no trouble keeping pace.

"I suggest a short stop to catch a breath," Marbleheart said after two hours of tramping. "Look about a bit?"

"Certainly," agreed Toothpick. "However, a hundred thirty-four paces ahead we'll be at a Wanderer's campsite. It would seem to me that the boy was headed there. You see?"

He led them into a large clearing. A spring burbled merrily under the roots of a huge tree. The party splashed water to cool their faces and hands while Marbleheart sniffed about.

"Some Men camped here last night," he reported. "Here are signs of Ben, too. Fairies don't leave much trace, but I catch his scent. Did he arrive before the campers departed? Did he join them? Or was he captured?"

"Not the easiest thing in World to do, capturing a fairy," observed Thornwood.

"No, but it seems your boy deliberately left signs for us to find," the porcupine commented.

Marbleheart threw himself full length on the ground by the trickle of spring.

"Anyone around to see what went on here, do you think?" he asked Toothpick.

"Plenty of birds. Flighty things, at best, but . . . I'll ask."

He waddled slowly to the far edge of the clearing and returned in a moment with a large, brown rodent of some sort.

"I be Paca," the furry animal told them by way of introduction. "The porcupine says you're searching for them Wanderers?"

"We believe they may have captured one of our party and carried him off," Marbleheart explained. He offered the ratlike animal some bacon left over from breakfast.

"Good! My thanks! Yes, I imagine I saw your friend, for what that's worth. Fairy, is he? I should have guessed."

"What *did* you see?" Lorianne urged. "We fear he was carried off a captive!"

"Possible explanation," agreed their furry informant. "However, it seemed to me he went willingly enough."

"I don't think any fairy could be captured and held against his will," Thornwood said. "Did Ben join them willingly, do you think?"

"Perhaps to protect the rest of us?" Lorianne guessed. "There're tales of fierce armed men in these parts. Tales told to make children behave and stay close to home.''

"Be that as it may,'' Paca the rat said, accepting a second bit of bacon, "I saw him talking with these Wanderers, as I've heard 'em called. Their leader, General *he's* called, immediately gave orders to pack up, tents, stewpots, and all! Took the lad by the hand and led him and all his men off into the forest. Did the fairy go willingly? No way to tell! It's all I saw, you understand.''

"Strange doings,'' murmured Lorianne.

"Not to fuss, my dear,'' said Thornwood, patting her shoulder. "Fairies . . . and especially Fairy Princes . . . are born with the power to protect themselves.''

"Still,'' Marbleheart worried, "his mother'd have some serious things to say about my guardianship of her Princeling.''

Paca could add no more. He pointed out the way the Wanderers had gone when they broke camp . . . a bit south of west . . . and scurried off into the trees looking for any family or friends who might be able to tell them more.

The porcupine said to Marbleheart, "Well, you've found your fairy. I can't help you more than that, I'm afraid. I would, if I could. Too slow. Rather too large to conceal.''

"Slow-paced, I'd agree,'' Marbleheart said, adding, "although I imagine few predators, Men or beasts, ever bother you for long, Toothpick.''

"True . . . but I'd slow you down, and you'll need some speed to catch up these Wanderers. Isn't it so, Sea Otter?''

Reluctantly Marbleheart agreed, and after they'd eaten lunch—ice cream was the most welcome part, next to the iced tea—and were preparing to follow the trail, they said farewell to the porcupine.

"I wish you would come, even so,'' said Lorianne. "In a short time I've learned to appreciate your strength, your sharp wits, your quiet self-assurance!''

"Most flattered, mistress,'' Toothpick answered shyly. "I'll be off! You'll want to be on your own way. Wish I could tell you more about these Wanderers . . . but, there it is! We plains creatures seldom go far from home.''

''We Sea Otters are famous world travelers,'' Marbleheart claimed, ''but even we appreciate home.''

Lorianne patted the great beast under his chin . . . about
the only spot where there were no quills . . . and they all
said farewell, promising to look the porcupine up the next
time they were in the neighborhood.

''Now!'' cried Marbleheart after the porcupine had
slowly shuffled off. ''*Now!* Let's go find these kidnapping
Wanderers and rescue our fairy lad.''

''Do you really think he's being held against his will?''
Thornwood asked as they set off. ''Perhaps by threat to
us?''

''No telling, but I don't think Ben'd have deserted us on
a whim.''

The Duke admitted the truth of the Otter's words. ''Oh,
well . . . I trust your instincts and the boy's good sense, too.
How far do you think it might be to your Home Port, lassie?''

''I'd guess . . . forty leagues? A bit of a walk, yet,'' answered Lorianne, slipping her hand under the young man's
arm. ''But I don't think we're in any real hurry.''

''Only to rescue Flowerbender, Prince of Faerie,''
Thornwood reminded her. ''I imagine, as the Otter says, a
Fairy Prince can take pretty good care of himself. Even in
very tight places.''

''I don't want to risk it,'' said the Lady Seacaptain.
''He's so delicate and so young and so inexperienced.''

''Experience is what his Venturing is all about,'' Marbleheart called back from the lead position. ''At least the
underbrush here has less tangle to it. And the air's somewhat cooler, too.''

Chapter Fifteen

The Wanderers

WHEN he'd taken over the watch from Thornwood at four a.m., Ben first stirred the embers and added a stick or two to keep the fire burning until sunrise.

Then he'd circled the camp twice, listening and peering with night-sharp fairy-eyes into and beyond the deep shadows.

Standing on a low hillock, he scanned the distant forest edge. He at once caught a faint glimmer of light . . . a campfire? . . . beyond the first line of trees.

"Wake the others?" he debated with himself. "No, it's needful they get their rest. I'll just flit over that way and see who our neighbors might be. Only Men and Dwarfs light fires at night. Good idea to learn which they might be."

Even a very young fairy moves quicker than a light breeze and more silent than the flight of a night owl. In a few minutes Ben paused on the edge of a fire-lit clearing.

"Men, they certainly are, not Dwarfs," he said to himself. "Wandering wilderness aboriginals, perhaps . . . but they have steel swords. Steel-tipped arrows too! Some steel armor . . . badly dented and rusty, but serviceable.''

A pair of guards moved about the fire before a ragged, sagging canvas tent and among the blanket-wrapped forms of men sleeping on the ground. The guards spoke only when they passed near one another. The fairy estimated a hundred or more Men, altogether.

How many in the tent? No more than one or two, considering its size.

As he watched, three new guards were roused by the men on duty. The new watch rose, stretching and yawning. One doused his head with water from a leather bucket, and the other two wolfed leftover bits of meat and bread near the fire.

''Change of guard,'' Ben guessed.

The retiring soldiers stripped off their helmets and unbuckled their breast-plates, all the while chaffing and joking quietly with the new watch. Ben drifted forward to better hear their words.

''General means to march again at dawn,'' one of the new men grumbled. ''He'll be up and about shortly.''

''Snatch a few minutes in the sack before he rouses the bugler,'' yawned one of the off-going watchmen.

They bid each other a good-night.

''Something curious about . . .'' the lad murmured half aloud.

''No more curious than a spy in the bushes!'' rumbled a deep voice at his shoulder, and a heavy hand closed on his neck, lifting him to his feet.

''Hold still and come out into the firelight where we can look at you, laddy,'' growled the voice.

Ben felt himself being propelled forward. His captor called softly to the guards, who came running.

''Found *this* sneaking about in the underbrush! Spying on us,'' explained Ben's captor, giving the boy a shake to show him he was still firmly in charge.

There were, perhaps, eight or nine spells which came immediately to Ben's mind in the seconds after he was grabbed . . . any one of which would have instantly gained him freedom with varying degrees of mayhem to the strangers.

But something stopped him before the necessary spellwords could be uttered. He allowed himself to be shoved into the circle of firelight where the other guardsmen stared at him, open-mouthed.

"Just a boy!" one said.

"More'n that, Arbuttle!" grunted Ben's captor. "Notice these?"

He turned Ben about so the others could see his back. Folded against the cloth of his shirt was his pair of crystalline, blue-tinted wings glinting in the firelight.

"A *fairy*, by Grummist!" swore one guard.

"Hang to 'im fast, there, Marty! Watch 'im! He'll cast a spell! Don't let 'im speak!" advised another.

Ben's captor quickly placed his horny, not-too-clean, left hand over the boy's mouth, holding him fast, on the quite sound theory that a spell had to be uttered to be cast.

Ben struggled for a moment, then stood calmly while the six soldiers consulted on what should be done.

"Damned *flitter-fliers*!" one of the older guardsmen rumbled angrily. "I vowed to destroy any I ever found. They left us to die there, in Last Battle!"

" 'Twas two hundred years ago!" objected a younger man. "Best we waken the Old Man."

"Quite young, I say," said another, "compared to those Faerie Riders we once knew."

"Knew . . . feared . . . and hated!" growled the man who'd first found Ben in the forest. "*Beware*, says I! Wake General. *He'll* know what to do."

One of the guards ran to the tent, shook the flap, and entered, reappearing a moment later to gesture to Ben's captors to bring their captive. Keeping his left hand clamped firmly over the boy's mouth to prevent fearful spells from slipping out, the soldier picked him up bodily and carried him into the tent.

A lantern was lighted. The tent had but one occupant, a small, rather bent, wrinkled old man in underdrawers and bare feet, sitting on the edge of a folding cot.

"A fairy spy?" the old man said in a sour, sleepy tone. "Let's see him. Bring him into the light more, Sergeant Skittle. *Ah!* For once, you're right as rain, Skittle! A young fairy. Remove his weapons, fool! He may be light and small, but his weapons'll bite sharp, you should remember."

Sergeant Skittle set Ben on his feet and deftly removed the boy's knife, belt, unstrung bow, and quiver of arrows, dumping the weapons behind him on the canvas floor covering.

"This here's General," he said gruffly to his captive. "Stand quiet and be still. Answer questions when asked. Any sign of spelling or such fairy nonsense out of you, laddy, and I'll lay you out on the ground with a blow to the head."

"No fear," Ben sniffed. "I'll listen."

The old man struggled to his feet and walked slowly about the sergeant and his captive, examining Ben carefully.

"Would appear to be of Faerie," he muttered. "Notice his violet eyes? And the belt and sheath are the kind Faerie Riders wore when we knew them, before they ran from Last Battle and left us to die!"

"We *didn't* run!" exclaimed Ben angrily, drawing himself up. "There was just a . . . a . . . mixup in orders! So it was told to me."

"Whoever told you that, boy, either was lying," snapped the old man, "or had his facts twisted. Ran from the Bloody Brook killing ground, I swear! I was there!"

"I told you to keep silent unless bespoken!" growled the sergeant, giving the boy a sharp shake.

"At ease, Skittle!" the General ordered. "Boy . . . I'll do the asking and you do the answering. Understood?"

"Yes, sir!" muttered Ben, casting his eyes down to hide the fury he knew was in them.

"That's better," the General said with a humorless smile. "I'm not going to argue Last Battle with you. I want to know, however, why you're here. Are you from the Queen of Faerie? What rank does your daddy have, boy?"

"Which question first, may I ask?" Ben said softly.

"Take 'em in order!" snapped the grim sergeant.

Ben paused to consider. "I came here in company with Marbleheart Sea Otter . . ."

"A Sea Otter!" cried the General in surprise.

"A Sea Otter who's Familiar to a Pyromancer . . ." Ben continued.

"That'll be good old Flarman Firemaster, the Wizard," cried the General. "Does he yet live?"

"Alive and well, last I saw of him, sir," Ben replied, deciding not to confuse the issue by mentioning Douglas and the other Wizards just yet.

"Well, then! This Sea Otter's his pet, eh? Who else in your party? More than just a waterlogged mackerel-trapper, I suspect?"

"There's the Duke of Dukedom. Thornwood is his name."

"Thornwood? Don't know that one," muttered the General, turning to sit on his cot. "I heard of a Duke with a similar name, however. Thorowood, as I recall."

"His father, long since gone."

"And that's all, is it?" demanded the old man.

"A Seacaptain. A lady Seacaptain, I mean."

"And her name? From where does she hail and sail, this lady Seacaptain?"

"Of Home Port, I understand, General. Her name is Lorianne . . ."

"Lor . . . !" coughed the General. "*Eh? Lorianne?*"

He jumped to his feet and began to pace, frowning deeply, muttering to himself half aloud, pulling his short, white beard nervously. For a while no one spoke. The ser-

geant stood stolidly by, watching his prisoner, alert for any
false moves or words.

Outside a bugler sounded a lively wake-up call and there
were sounds of men stirring, talking, coughing, gargling,
splashing water, and gathering about the fire.

"We'll put some distance between this Thornwood and
us, at any rate. And the Familiar-thing, too. Need time to
think," the General growled at last. "Orders! Men to eat
whatever's cold and ready! Pack up at once! I want us in
the thickest part of the forest before the sun's an hour old!"

"Yes, sir!" cried the sergeant, half turning away. "*Er*
. . . what of the boy, sir?"

"Leave him to me."

The General reached out and grasped the boy's left wrist
with a thin but surprisingly strong hand. Ben shrunk away
from his touch and took a breath, perhaps to utter one of
his nine escape spells.

"No you won't!" snapped the General. "I realize who
and what you are, now. Look just like your dad, I bet."

"My father is Aedh of Faerie," said Ben, more stoutly
than he felt. "As good a soldier and as good a fighter as
any being ever in World!"

The General grunted with a sour grimace, but made no
comment on Ben's claim.

He stood in thought for a moment. "I require you to stay
here with me, young Aedhsson! I know enough of your
kind's spelling to avoid or avert whatever you'd care to
attempt, if you try me. I didn't survive Last Battle on blind
luck alone! Behave and be quiet, boy, or I'll be forced to
bind, gag, and blindfold you!"

Ben thought about his predicament for a moment. He had
no real fear of his captors. A fairy, even one so young, had
great powers upon which to call, if he needed. These men
knew his father. Ben was intrigued and gave little thought
to his companions, left behind on the edge of the forest.

He decided it would be better to submit. Besides . . . the
Bewildered Band intrigued him.

"I hear and obey, grandfather!"

"Smart laddy!" the General clucked. "You *may* come safely away from all this, after all."

"*Where in Blue Blazes has my Familiar Otter gotten to?*" Douglas demanded of the dancing flames in the Workshop forge.

A single Blue Blaze leaped high and bright, then dimmed, swirled rapidly clockwise, then reversed to counterclockwise. It finally drew together, exploded in a silent puff of actinic glare ... and died down to two small, red coals, glowing like angry eyes in the bottom of the fire-pot, slowly fading.

"I can hardly make it out," Myrn whispered anxiously, leaning over her husband's shoulder to stare into the forge hearth. "That's a sign for ... what?"

"Far as I can tell, Blue Blaze says something like: "*All's well! Ring the bell! Hard to tell! Oh, well...*""

"Is your Blue Blaze always so *cryptic*?" cried Myrn in exasperation. "Augurian's Waterglass is *much* clearer, I vow!"

"Maybe I asked the wrong sort of question," muttered Douglas, shaking his head. "Unless all really *is* well."

"Nonsense! Marbleheart and little Ben are lost at Sea! All is *very* wrong! Let me try Augurian's Waterglass."

"Calmly, however," Douglas advised, giving her his seat on Flarman's favorite three-legged stool. "Lack of concentration confuses the best spelling."

Myrn sat perfectly still for a long moment, eyes closed, breathing deeply and evenly.

She said at last, "Pass me yonder ewer, please."

Douglas had to admit she appeared much calmer and more businesslike than he'd felt when invoking Blue Blazes. She carefully poured an exact quarter-inch of Old Fairy Well water into a shallow glass dish and waited patiently, barely breathing, until the ripples subsided.

She spoke a series of spell-words Augurian had insisted,

years before, that she memorize until she knew them backward and forward . . . which is how she pronounced them now: "*Sissinli dormited—detimrod ilnissis! Firailite yen callinisa. Etiliarif! Ney asinillac? Banitorof.*" The words sounded like rushing wavelets over rippled sand.

The water shivered, as if a soft breeze had sighed across its surface. The water glowed for a moment. Its surface then darkened, and reflected a rapid succession of scenes, some familiar to the young Wizards, some quite strange.

At one point Douglas saw Marbleheart, an unknown auburn-haired young woman, rather pretty, and Thornwood, walking in single file through a thick forest.

Before he could comment, the scene changed and they caught a flashing view of Pyromancer Flarman Flowerstalk just climbing out of his bed in Augurian's palace, far to the east.

"*Damnation!*" the usually very proper Lady Aquamancer swore. "Nothing we can use here! Did *you* see anything, sweetheart?"

"Afraid not! Shall we try again?"

"No. A second attempt too soon would be worthless. Wait several hours. Did we learn *anything* from all this folderol?"

"If there was information there, I failed to see it. Maybe we should seek help. Flarman could probably handle the matter more wisely, or Augurian."

Bronze Owl, attracted by the stirrings in the Workshop in the middle of a quiet night, arrived with a soft cymbal-clash of bronze feathers.

"Call *both* older Wizards, of course," he advised, perching on the top of a tall cupboard. "Bright, clear minds and still spirits are necessary . . ."

"I *know* that, Owl!" snapped Myrn. "But where is our Sea Otter? And the little Prince?"

"Good questions," Douglas admitted glumly.

"Send for *both* Wizards!" Owl insisted. "If there were no responses to your Seeking Spell . . ."

"There *seemed* to be none," Douglas admitted. "Just veiled hints!"

"... then send off to Waterand, at once," the Owl repeated. "The fastest way ..."

"... is to send Deka the Wraith," Myrn nodded in agreement.

Douglas spoke Deka's special calling, and the Wraith began to materialize in the darkest corner of the Workshop, swirling and whirling until she formed in the shape of a pale, rather wistful, lovely young maiden ... one who happened to be among the oldest of all beings in World.

Chapter Sixteen

≋

Huddle at the High

FLARMAN, still dressed in a short summer nightshirt, and Augurian, wearing a navy blue robe and slippers and wiping shaving soap from his lean cheeks, popped out of emptiness into midnight in the High courtyard.

"You called?" murmured the Aquamancer, stooping to kiss his former Apprentice on her worried brow. "Deka said . . . something about the Otter and Prince Flowerbender being lost, strayed, or stolen?"

"Lost, stolen, or shipwrecked?" the older Pyromancer asked, giving Douglas a slap on the shoulder and Myrn a reassuring hug. "We came 'as is,' you can see. Time for me to find a pair of trousers? Or should we confer in the buff, do y' think?"

"I'll fetch you something, Magister," Bronze Owl volunteered, and he flapped noisily through an open second-story window.

"Break our fast?" suggested Flarman, turning to lead them all into the big kitchen. "And hand the damp Aquamancer a dry towel, somebody."

They seated themselves at one end of the kitchen table.

Blue Teakettle and her helpers at once brought hot oatmeal in bowls, with brown and white sugar from old Sugar Caster and fresh cream from Cow Creamer.

The older Wizards listened and ate in silence while Douglas told of the invasion by Eunicet and his pirates, Myrn adding a professional opinion here and there.

"Well, now . . ." began Flarman with a side glance at Augurian, who was just finishing his second cup of coffee. "You've tried . . . which spells, young Pyromancer?"

"The usual. Then Blue Blaze. It gave me a poem which said, basically, 'All's well!' "

"And my Waterglass showed a mixed bunch of scenes we don't really understand, including one of Marbleheart, Thornwood, and a pretty young lady. In an unknown forest. Somewhere."

"That would be Far Southwest, I suspect," Augurian mused. "Last time I checked, Marbleheart and Ben were sailing on a ship hailing from there. They were later joined by Thornwood, I presume. They were accompanying the lady Seacaptain to a place called Home Port."

"Home Port? Never heard of it," Flarman mused.

"It is, I believe, to the west and north of Choin," the Aquamancer told him.

He drew a musty old atlas, faded, water-spotted, finger-smudged, and dog-eared from much use, from his left sleeve and began thumbing through it. "Here 'tis! Home Port. Homeland. Home Shore . . . yes, an old Man-given name for the Seacoast of Far Southwest. Also known as Parambit . . ."

"Names *I've* never heard," Douglas exclaimed.

"Nor I," Myrn added with a nod.

"I've never been there, but this Parambit sent a sizable contingent of soldiers to Last Battle, as I recall," Flarman said. "Don't remember much else about Parambit, however. What was their monarch's name, Augurian? Do y' recall?"

The Water Adept closed his eyes, searching his mental archives for the name.

"I can see him . . ." he said slowly. "Auburn hair. Tall chap. Oh, dear me . . . slain on the first day of Last Battle! By a Darkness's poison quarrel. I'm sorry to say I never knew him, poor chap. There were so many kings and knights and such, War-Captains and Generals . . ."

"And his soldiers?" Douglas wondered. "What became of them?"

"I've no recollection. It was a badly muddled time. Do you remember aught of the poor King of Parambit, Flarman?"

"Wait . . . I remember his name!" exclaimed Flarman, screwing up his face for intense thought. "*Ho!* Parambitis? No! *Parambonus*, 'twas, I think!"

"*Paradone*, rather! Yes! I remember him in council a few times," Augurian agreed. "He and his soldiers were assigned to the Forward Right, next the Faerie Ride under Aedh. Terribly knocked about, they were, when Aedh was drawn off in the wrong direction by a ruse. Allowed The Darkness to rampage into the Right Center. You remember, Firemaster? Awful slaughter on both sides, early the second day!"

The two war veterans silently considered their memories of that terrible fight for a long moment while the others allowed them their awful remembrance.

"Well . . . why do we need to know?" demanded Flarman, jerking himself back to the present. "Oh, yes . . . the Parambiters! I think I'll have to do some looking-up before I can tell you anything more. You know that Marbleheart is there . . . in the Far Southwest?"

"Last *I* heard," Douglas shook his head, "Marbleheart and Ben were on Farango Water."

"They took ship there, but the recent storm at Sea blew them pretty badly off course," Flarman told them. "You caught that glimpse in Myrn's water mirror of where they

now are ... somewhere in the Piedmont Forest of Southwest.''

"But I didn't see Prince Flowerbender with them!''
Myrn objected.

"We'll try some Descrying Spells I know, shall we?''
Augurian asked. "Where's my Petrel? Ah, there you are,
my boy! May we use your Workshop, Flarman, while you
hit the books to fill in the gaps?''

"Of course!'' The elder Pyromancer rose from his seat.
"Send the rest of my breakfast up to the library, Blue! I'll
need your help, Douglas. We mustn't waste a moment!''

"The children are safe with Glorianna? That's very
good,'' said Augurian as he led Myrn toward the underhill
Workshop. "*Ho!* What's the noise I hear below?''

"Pirates in the cellar,'' Myrn laughed. "Nothing to
worry over!''

Flarman and Douglas climbed to the second-floor study.
They were followed by Black Flame. Tea Cart rumbled and
thumped up the stairs after them, piled high with steaming-
hot pancakes, maple syrup, butter, steaming Coffee Carafe,
and Jampot filled with wild strawberry preserves.

"Some progress, perhaps,'' Augurian reported when
they gathered once more at lunchtime. "It concerns the
mysterious crystal disk Tet's man found, Flarman.''

"So!'' cried Flarman. "What do *you* make of it? For
Douglas and I are stumped. Everything we find suggests
the Ice King's magical intervention and purposeful clouding.''

"Smacks of old Frigeon, all right!'' Douglas agreed.
"But it could be much older ...''

"No, I think Flarman's correct. The disk is made of a
sort of crystal found only in the far west,'' Myrn said excitedly. "The words are Ancient Krine ... a dwarfish language nobody speaks or writes anymore. Except Frigeon!
He used it for certain spellings.''

"Just so!'' said the senior Water Adept, patting her hand.

"Frigeon used it as a secret language in his earlier spells. They are, as a result, among the most obscure I've ever encountered!"

"Go on!" insisted both Pyromancers at the same time. "What does the disk say?"

"You had it almost right," Myrn told her husband. "Here's what it *really* says, we're now quite sure . . ." and she read from a notebook she'd brought to the table.

"*Good advice*," she read aloud, "*is to look closely in a far country, over the left shoulder of the south wind in the darkest part of a day to find a slain King's daughter and restore to her his Crown!*"

"Well, *almost* the same," considered Douglas.

"Not quite!" Augurian said, firmly. "Key meanings are slightly altered, my boy."

"Don't you see?" Myrn nudged her husband in the ribs, fondly. "It actually says '*in* a far country,' as opposed to '. . . *from* a far country . . .' Also, as I remember it, you said, '*to see where a Princess-daughter must go a-seeking her King-father's Crown*,' as opposed to: '*to reveal a King's daughter and restore to her his Crown . . .*'"

Douglas thought about the corrected wording in silence for a few seconds, then nodded agreement. "Yes, I can see where I made my mistakes."

"Don't worry about your wording being a bit off," Augurian advised. "Not many Wizards could have done nearly as well. Not myself nor Flarman at your age!"

"But," Bronze Owl put in a puzzled question, "what do the words *mean*? And where is the left shoulder of the south wind?"

"We'll have to work on it a bit more, of course," admitted the elder Aquamancer. "Everyone is welcome to have a stab at it."

"Which still leaves us mystified about Marbleheart and little Ben," Douglas pointed out.

"Yes, well, so it does," Flarman sighed. "Our books haven't been any more help. And nothing seems to explain why the Seeking Spells we've been trying just won't work.''

"What's to do, then?'' wondered Myrn, sighing.

"Pursue the matter of the enchanted Princess of Parambit and her crown, I think. It might reveal where we've lost the Prince of Faerie,'' Augurian insisted. "Someone must take the lens to Marbleheart and Thornwood, for they're in that vicinity.''

"Yes, Marbleheart and Thornwood will help find the missing Princess,'' Douglas agreed. "I'll go, for he's my Familiar . . .''

"And I'll go, too,'' Myrn said flatly.

"And I'll stay here . . . with my fellow Wizard, the Water Adept,'' announced Flarman, "and we'll keep trying and trying to locate the missing Prince *and* the Princess, too, along other lines.''

Myrn jumped to her feet. "When can we leave, Douglas? Sooner the better!''

"Sooner the better! At once,'' Douglas agreed.

And, after a hurried preparation, the husband and wife Wizards joined hands and shot off into the afternoon sky at tremendous speed, propelled by the magic of the Feather Pin.

Weary Bewildered Bandsmen filed between the thick boles of enormously tall ironwood trees, moving in deep gloom under the thick leafy canopy, although it was midday. The air was thick with the oily scent of the great hardwoods and felt heavy on the marchers' shoulders.

There might have been birds and small animals in the treetops, far above, but here on the forest floor only the occasional soft scurry and squeak of a startled lizard broke the silence.

Ben, looking about him at his captors, was impressed with their generally positive attitude. Falling back behind Sergeant Skittle, who led the way, the fairy lad found his neighbors eager to chat . . . when the path was wide enough to allow it.

"We're heading for Camptown," explained a young man carrying a ten-foot pike . . . a rather unwieldy weapon in the forest, Ben thought. "Maybe another twenty miles. We'll never make it before the rain comes."

"Rain? How can you tell?" Ben wondered. "Can't see the sky at all!"

"Rains every afternoon, regular as clocks," insisted the young soldier, whose name was Friday because, he explained, he'd been born on that day of the week.

"Are your families at this Camptown?"

"The women and old men and youngsters stay there, yes," replied Friday, hitching the heavy pike to his other shoulder. "I'm not married and my Da and Ma are my family. Most here are married."

"How do you live, though?" Ben asked another soldier when the Band paused to catch its breath beside a tea-dark pool.

"Women and children do planting and gathering. Menfolk hunt, you see," explained the bowman. "General takes us out every few weeks for a bit of field exercise. Keep us on our toes and fit . . . so says he."

Ben noted the faint hint of dissatisfaction in his tone.

"The gals do just fine. 'Course, we miss their company," the unmarried soldier said wistfully.

From the head of the line, the General ordered the march to resume.

"Through the Gap before it rains, Sergeant!" he called to Skittle in the van. "Onward! Supper by our own hearths tomorrow night, lads! Onward!"

"I can't figure out this General person at all," Ben said to Friday, who had fallen in again beside him.

"Hard to figure. Old as the hills, is General. Been leader since . . . well, long as *I* can remember."

"All of you men go back to Last Battle?" Ben asked.

"Many of us! Except for the youngest. Not me! Da

served on Bloody Brook, however. Lost his right eye. General tells us when and where to march, summer or winter. Not that winters are much different here from summers,'' the young man said, a bit sadly. ''Rains a bit more in wintertime.''

''Do *you* remember real winter weather? Up north, I mean?'' the fairy lad asked one of the older hands.

''Oh, very well! I have memories of cold winter! Much prefer the warmth hereabouts. Ah, well . . . it's really not for me to say.''

Ben slowly gathered a picture of the Bewildered Band's life. Some of the older men remembered the days before Last Battle and then the fearsome fight against The Darkness on Battle Plain, two centuries back . . . before the Band fled south.

Under some sort of spell, Ben decided.

''Oh, aye!'' said Friday when Ben asked him about it.

He wasn't much interested, if the truth be known.

''But will you go on being ever the same . . . living the same kind of life, never changing your course?'' Ben cried softly in exasperation.

''Oh, aye . . . I s'pose,'' repeated the pikeman. ''Until someone tells me I must change, I s'pose.''

Ben thought his attitude rather strange, especially for one who seemed quite bright, but by that time the Band had reached a line of bluffs running north to south, towering over the forest. He realized that the whole Band shared Friday's unusual lack of interest in their past . . . and future.

''Definitely some sort of enchantment,'' he thought. ''Well, I know my own strength, and it isn't enough to unravel this kind of magicking!''

Just as the Band climbed single-file through a narrow gap between two steep bluffs, rain began to fall, blurring the scene but doing little to make the air cooler, for the rain was warm, almost steamy.

At the last moment before entering the narrow way, Ben

dropped his pheasant-feathered cap beside the path. He went on, not looking down nor back.

"A certain sharp-eyed Otter I know might read that sign," he thought.

The soldiers passed through the Gap. Nobody noticed the cap draped limply over a longthorn bush, matching its grey to the bush's rough bark and thick, grey-green leaves.

Traveling long distances swiftly is one of the most difficult things a Wizard could accomplish.

The Feather Pin, therefore, was a marvelous help, and Myrn's Traveling Pearls almost as remarkable. Both charms allowed their owners to fly at as great a speed as they could withstand, limited only by the fierce winds of passage.

With the Feather Pin, for example, Douglas could go from the High to New Land in six hours. Or from Dukedom to Samarca, on the far eastern littoral of Sea, in a little over twenty hours.

Instant travel was possible only with extremely strenuous, almost debilitating, magical exertion. When the powerful Geomancer Lithold had shot herself from the Atacomba Desert across Sea to the frozen valley of the Stone Warriors, even she had been forced to break her journey for rest and recovery at Wizards' High.

Flying southwest over Sea by the Feather Pin, Douglas and Myrn kept their speed to a fairly moderate pace. Much faster would have been very tiring, breath would have been hard to catch, and their eyes would have watered so badly neither of them could see dangers, if any approached.

"Our best pace," Myrn had agreed, "is to stay below the level of discomfiture."

"'Discomfort,'" her husband corrected her mildly.

"Isn't that the same thing?" Myrn asked. "Discomfiture . . . discomfort?"

Douglas reached into his left sleeve and withdrew a leather-bound book of considerable size and very fine print.

"Let's see what Bronze Owl's *Pronouncing Dictionary*

says," he suggested, flipping though the tissue-thin pages, flapping and fluttering in the wind of their passage. "Ah! Here 'tis . . ."

"What's it say?"

"*Discomfiture*: the act of being foiled, or thwarted, or frustrated," her husband read, shading his eyes from the late afternoon sun glinting off Sea. "*Discomfort* is something that annoys, pains, or harms you."

"Well, when I'm frustrated, I'm also annoyed," Myrn insisted. "Too fine a distinction, darling!"

Amiably arguing the point helped them pass the time. Late in the long afternoon Douglas tilted their flight path in a steep descent toward a group of wave-washed, palm-shaded islets.

"Halfway Islands, according to Flarman's Map of Sea," he told his wife. "We'll camp here and go on in the morning. Too many things can happen to fliers by night."

"If you say so, my own true love," Myrn yawned.

Douglas gave a great, wide, gaping yawn, also, and within a few minutes of touching ground among the graceful palms, having eagerly devoured a light supper, the pair stretched out on a blanket laid on grass and tiny pink flowers and fell at once into deep slumber.

Chapter Seventeen

≈≈≈

Sudden Departure

BEN watched with interest as the Band, who called themselves Parambit soldiers, made night-camp in a grove of wide, flat-crowned trees, a species he didn't recognize.

Ropes were fastened between low limbs, and tarpaulins were stretched over the ropes, making wide, flat roofs under which, in turn, the General's tent was pitched and campfires laid and lighted.

Sergeant Skittle inspected the work with satisfaction. "Stay under the tarp, I advise, young Ben. Weather is usually dry here, but there will be heavy dewfall by morning."

Ben thanked the man and, as no one ordered him otherwise, he selected a bed of soft, grey-green moss beneath the edge of the tarpaulin not far from the communal cook-fires to leeward and there spread his tattered cloak. Supper was being prepared and, confident he'd be fed in due course, the lad flung himself on the moss, clasped his hands behind his head, and watched the activity about the camp.

Hunters had been dispatched into the forest, and others were told to take fishing lines down to the shallow, swiftly flowing stream nearby. Shortly the fishermen returned with a goodly catch.

The hunters took somewhat longer but returned before full dark with several wild pigs and a dozen or two large hares, skinned and cleaned, ready to spit and roast.

"We'll eat in an hour or so," the General announced, coming up to Ben's bed of moss. "Short march home to-morrow! Time to talk, boy."

Ben made room on the moss for the old man who, with a grunt and several painful groans, lowered himself to a seat.

"Now!" the General exclaimed. "Tit for tat! You tell me what I want to know . . . and I'll answer any questions you may have. Agreed?"

"Agreed," replied Ben. "Who goes first?"

"As elder, I claim the right to lead off."

He leaned his elbows on his skinny thighs and began to fill a long-stemmed clay pipe with coarse-cut tobacco which, even to Ben, smelled comfortable and spicy in the still, warm air.

"Who exactly *are* you, youngster? You're no ordinary, everyday fairy. Your weapons and your clothing bespeak high rank, even though they're rather the worse for wear."

"I am who I've said I am . . . Prince Justin Flowerbender Aedhsson," Ben said with a touch of pride. "Son of Queen Marget of Faerie."

"Ah, yes . . . Aedh! The runaway war-leader," snorted the General. "I know of *him*!"

"I'm sorry you've bad memories of Last Battle, sir," Ben said evenly. "It was quite some time ago. Long before I was born! I've only heard my father's side of that tragic history . . . he and my mother told me of it as I began study-ing the History of Faerie."

"Well, what would you expect?" asked the old man with a shrug.

"I expected the truth. History's not a story to be twisted nor revised at will or whim. So I was taught."

"By Prince Aedh?"

"Yes, by my father, who's an honorable and truthful fairy, sir!" the prince said, a bit piqued by the other's stubborn doubt. "And others, including my mother, the Queen."

"So *you* say, Princeling!" scoffed the General. "Who else?"

"I'm quite young and little-traveled, it's true, but I've spoken with powerful Wizards and others who were actually at Last Battle. They tell me an honest mistake was made in the heat of conflict. Such things do happen in war, to everybody's regret, sir!"

"*Which* Wizards?" the General demanded, interested in spite of his doubts.

"I spoke not long ago to Pyromancer Flarman Flowerstalk . . . you'll remember him as Flarman Firemaster."

"Aye, I remember Firemaster. If anything good came of Last Battle, laddy, it was thanks to Flarman."

"He understood the terrible misfortune of the Faerie Ride's withdrawal in the midst of the fight. My mother and my father and Flarman are the closest of friends now. I've supped and slept under Flarman's roof as recently as a fortnight ago."

The General mulled over his words for a long, silent while, puffing his pipe and blowing clouds into the still air. Ben watched the preparations for supper and for the night.

"Well, I've no reason to doubt the Firemaster," the General sighed deeply at last. "It makes no difference, anyway. My people were badly mauled by The Darkness, as your friend Flarman could have told you . . ."

"He had no occasion to speak of you, for that matter. I don't even know who you are . . . or who you were . . . way back then."

"I'm not surprised. There are so many loose ends, too long unraveled."

The old man rose and gestured for the lad to follow him to the fire, where blankets had been laid out and loaded with smoking pork roasts and broiled fish, fresh salads, and hot biscuits.

"Eat now. I intend no harm to you, son of Marget."

"What *do* you intend with me?" Ben asked, helping himself to a leg of roasted bird of some forest sort.

"In a word . . . ransom!"

And he would say no more at that time.

When the meal had been consumed and the evening watch paraded and set to their posts, the General beckoned to Ben and led him to his tent, where a lantern was burning and his cot set up with the covers turned back. Opposite the bed, under the lamp, were a rough campaign desk and several folding canvas stools.

"Sit ye down, lad," the General invited. A good supper and time to think had made his words and his attitude considerably more mellow. "We need to talk."

Ben wordlessly selected a stool.

"Now!" said the old soldier. "I said 'ransom,' and I intend to collect it to the benefit of my people, I assure you. We've been wandering naked and lost in these forests, plains, deserts, and mountains for over two centuries, seeking our way home. Many of us have grown quite old in the search! It's time we Parambit had a safe and sound homeland, once again."

"Parambit?" Ben asked. "A name new to me, sir."

"The name of my people and our kingdom, ages before our soldiers marched north under King Paradone, poor soul! . . . to help the Forces of Light against the terrible invaders. Now my men call themselves 'Bewildered Band.' Well, we've been be-wildered much, much too long . . . and your powerful Queen must help us regain our land and our heritage!"

"Mother wouldn't for a single minute refuse to help you, Sir, if you asked her help."

The old man considered his words for a moment, then shook his head.

"No! We are still proud Men and will not beg! What we want is ours by right and we will *demand* it."

"What can my . . . the Queen of Faerie . . . do for you, do you believe?" Ben asked calmly.

"I'll demand of Queen Marget, as ransom for her son, magic powerful enough to find our native lands, pastures, groves, and the wealth and power to hold them safe in future. As simple as that!"

Ben made no comment. There was, he thought, a burning fire of some sort . . . a flicker of insanity, perhaps? . . . in the man's old grey eyes.

General coughed sharply. "I'm about to write a letter to your Queen-mother telling her I hold you captive and detailing my . . . *our* . . . demands. And you will countersign it, to show her I tell the plain truth!"

He scrabbled in a battered war chest at the foot of his cot and drew out a packet of old, yellowed paper and a folded kit containing pens and tablets of dried ink. Placing the paper on the desk, he put water in a battered metal cup to which he added half of one of the ink tablets.

After sharpening and slitting a fresh quill-end with a pen-knife, he dipped the nib in the ink and began to write, speaking his words slowly as he wrote.

" 'To Her Royal Majesty Marget, Queen Regnant of the Land of Faerie: Greetings!' " he dictated to himself. " 'Be it known by these presents and attested to by the under-signed, who is well known to you, I am . . .' "

He wrote slowly in an uneven, rather old-fashioned script replete with formal curlicues and much heavy underlining. His demands were as he'd already told Ben. Magic spell-ings and devices to disenchant and restore the lost Parambit homeland. Wealth to protect it, thereafter. A treasure with which to buy supplies, building materials, clothing, arms, and to support a standing army of at least a thousand men.

"A thousand!" cried Ben in surprise. "You haven't more than two hundred here with you, Sir!"

"Never you mind! A thousand men will be kept under

arms, once I regain Parambit! And a trained militia of ten times that many. Oh, Parambit will grow to the proper number . . . and to spare! . . . once our homeland is released from whatever wicked spells were placed on it.''

The fairy nodded his understanding, and the General continued to draw his letters, pouring out onto the yellowed foolscap all the hurt, disillusionment, discontent, weariness, fear, and bitterness of two lost centuries.

He paused, dusted the last closely written sheet with fine sand from a leather pouch, and silently reread the document, grunting when he thought he'd made a particularly valid point.

Ben sat on his camp stool, listening and watching.

''There!'' the General said once again. ''You will countersign this!''

Ben took the quill, the cup of black ink, and the paper, and began to read it to himself.

'' ' . . . in payment of . . . demands . . . requirement . . . spells and amulets to save and protect . . . their ancestral homeland . . . given this day under my authority as General of the Army of Parambit, as decreed and commissioned by His Majesty Paradone the Sixth, late Monarch of Parambit.' And so on and so forth. I see! Is it permitted to ask a few questions, Sir?''

''Ask away,'' yawned the old man, pushing back his stool and flexing his fingers to restore circulation. ''But don't think to delay overlong your signature. It's but to convince your mother and father that I do, in fact, hold you, awaiting their compliance. There are other, less pleasant, ways to do that!''

''You speak here of the Kingdom of Parambit. You have mentioned . . . a King . . . Paradone, I see it written. Where *is* your King?''

The General sniffed twice and wiped his nose on his sleeve.

''Paradone was foully slain by a Darkness Warrior on

the first day of Last Battle. I thought you knew that.''

''You derive your powers, then, from a long-dead monarch?''

''Aye! Until such time as a new monarch be found for Parambit. Paradone gave orders, just before Last Battle, that I was to lead and rule in his stead, if he were captured or slain. I've followed his dictum, as have my men and their women, ever since. Who could doubt it?''

''There's no heir to the throne of Parambit, then?'' the boy asked, twiddling the quill pen.

''None! Well . . . there *was* a girl-child, as I remember. A pretty little Princess. Long since lost and never seen or heard of again. If she's still alive and can be found . . . and if she's capable of ruling, of course . . . I would step aside in her favor.''

''I see. If I may make a suggestion, sir? You should ask my mother to assist you in regaining not just your kingdom, but your Queen as well.''

''Don't think I haven't thought about her, the baby Princess in her cradle! No, I'm obligated to lead and protect and make well and happy *all* her people. If she can be found, I reserve the right to step down or refuse, as I see fit!''

Ben opened his mouth to object, but just then an orderly stuck his head into the tent, saluted, and reported the midnight watch well and carefully posted. The call to sleep had been blown by the bugler long since.

''Carry on!'' the General said to the orderly, waving his hand. ''Now, Sir Prince! Will you sign? It will make it much easier for both of us. Your mother will realize that you really are captive. And I . . . we . . . will treat you as befits your rank and race. Otherwise . . .''

He left the rest of his sentence dangling ominously.

The Prince of Faerie reread the long and wordy document and observed aloud that it was rather difficult to read, thanks to the many mistakes and corrections.

"Shouldn't you have this recopied? 'Tis hardly fit to be read by the Queen of Faerie!"

"Just put your mark or sign your name, there," the old man insisted.

Ben dipped the pen and wrote:

"Dear Mother—I am truly being held prisoner against your fulfillment of the above demands." He underlined the word "demands." "Please consider them kindly, for this General's sake and those of his poor, lost people."

He carefully signed his full name, *Justin Flowerbender Prince of Faerie*, with a suitable flourish.

"Tell me," he said while the General sanded his inked words dry. "How do you intend to get this to my . . . to the Queen?"

"By the old way we were given for communicating with the Faerie Ride. It should still work quite well," muttered the military man. "It will be delivered within the hour!"

"In that case, I think I'll retire to my bed of moss," Ben yawned. "Let me know if there's anything else I can do for you and your people, General. Good night!"

And he left, dropping the tent flap behind him as he went.

"Blue!" called Flarman bursting through the courtyard doorway. "Lunchtime, old girl! I . . ."

He stepped to the kitchen table. It had already been set for the noon meal.

". . . think I'd like pork chops with your splendid sage dressing. It's been a long morning since breakfast."

Blue Teakettle shot a sharp jet of teasing steam from her spout and waved the Pyromancer to his usual seat next to Augurian, already seated. Platter arrived, seeming a bit out of breath for he was giving off puffs of savory steam, laden with tender chops and a golden mound of cornbread dressing. Gravy Boat sailed close behind, being very careful not to spill a single drop. Last came a great bowl of apple sauce sprinkled with red-brown cinnamon.

"As I was saying . . . pork chops and cornbread dressing," muttered Flarman.

Even he was amazed that Blue Teakettle always seemed to know exactly what he wanted to eat even before he knew himself.

As the older Wizards sat eating, chatting with Bronze Owl, there came a loud knock on the front door, followed by the chime of the doorbell, vigorously rung. Owl excused himself and flew off at once to answer the call.

A moment later he ushered into the kitchen the beautiful Queen of Faerie and her consort, the tall, handsome Prince Aedh.

Flarman and Augurian jumped to their feet.

"Now, Wizards! Sit ye down!" Marget began without preamble. "Here! Can you tell me anything about this? *Demand*, indeed!"

Prince Aedh was beside her, handing Flarman pages of cheap, yellowed foolscap inscribed in a messy, minuscule script with at least a score of strike-throughs and a dozen inky blots and fingerprints.

"Let me see," murmured Flarman, plucking his reading spectacles from his left sleeve while waving his visitors into chairs. "Be seated, my dears. Hello, Aedh, old chap! Try the chops. Tender as a fairy mother's love, I vow. Good enough for the Queen of Faerie! Welcome, by the way . . ."

"*Read!*" ordered the Queen angrily, plopping in a most un-Queenly manner into the chair offered. "Oh, I'm sorry, Flarman! I'm so upset . . . as you can see! I'll have a bit of tea with cream and sugar, if you please, Teakettle! There's a dear! What do you think of that, Flarman! I'm terribly flustered! He is holding my son! My beautiful baby boy! Oh . . . !"

"Not at all like you to be so upset, Marget," rumbled Augurian, sending Platter to the newcomers and signaling to tall, dignified Teapot to fill their waiting cups.

"I've heard nothing so wicked . . . so *depraved* . . . since

The Darkness fled north,'' the Queen snarled, pounding the tabletop with both fists.

"*Ah! Um?*" Flarman muttered into his beard, still reading the General's rambling, rancorous, ransom note. "This is, I take it, your son's true signature?"

"It is," Aedh, who seemed rather calmer than his wife, confirmed with a nod.

Marget waved away Platter, who was offering her meat and potatoes, and contented herself with a sip of hot tea.

"*Oh?* Er!" Flarman continued, reading the note once again, this time aloud so Augurian and Bronze Owl could hear. "Is this possible? I mean, I wouldn't think even as young a fairy as young Ben could be held captive."

"Of course you're right," sighed Marget.

"He wouldn't stay captive a minute, if he *wanted* to escape," agreed her consort. "Ben knows a half-dozen spells good for quick escapes. Fire escapes? Clock escapements? Unless he's held by *very* powerful magic."

"Now, I don't think any magic could have forced him to write this addendum," Flarman pointed out. "He's perfectly in control of his pen and his person, and probably the situation, too."

"Which means, I should say," added Augurian, "that your boy was fully aware of his situation and that he wishes our help *for his captors,* not for himself."

"I'll help the wretch!" snorted Marget, angry again. "Faerie'll make real trouble for this General, whoever *he* is."

"I remember the Parambit quite well," Prince Aedh said. "And it's just about what you'd expect a tough, old soldier like their General to do. He was brave to a fault, hearty, and bluff . . . but a bit pigheaded, too, at Last Battle."

The Queen of Faerie snorted in a most unladylike manner. "I remember now! Appears he's not yet forgiven us, Aedh, for our terrible error during Last Battle. Oh, *dear!* His Men were very badly cut up, I recall. Many killed! And then to see the famous Faerie Ride pulled from the line by a filthy, underhanded Darkness trick! Oh, *dear*!''

"King Paradone was, early that morning, slain by a hidden archer,'' Augurian commented sadly, taking the letter from Flarman's fingers and studying it carefully. "I've made a study of handwriting. Handy to know, in the Aquamancer business. Let me study this for a moment. Please go ahead and eat, dear friends.''

He pushed his chair back from the table and strode over to a window to hold the paper in the noontime sunlight reflected from the courtyard.

Flarman and his guests finished lunch and sat at table, talking of past and present events, attempting to tie them together into a coherent story.

"Let's see, then,'' Aedh said, "you say Douglas's Familiar and my son left here twelve days ago with the intention of taking ship at Farango Water for New Land and perhaps Nearer East?''

"That's the idea,'' agreed Flarman, lighting his ancient briar pipe with a blazing forefinger. "They boarded a schooner named ... er ... *Peachpit*, I'm told. They must have been blown way off course by last week's storm.''

"And, when last I looked, were somewhere on the Far Southwest coast,'' Marget said thoughtfully. "On my little Ben's very first Questing!''

"After they left here,'' Owl added, "that wicked old reprobate Eunicet and his band of pirates tried to capture this very house. Eunicet's still wandering about in the cellars beneath the Workshop. If you listen carefully, you can hear him rumbling and ranting. Douglas and Myrn intended to turn him over to Duke Thornwood for trial and punishment ... except that Thornwood is somewhere at Sea, himself, looking for Marbleheart and the little Prince!''

"Eunicet!'' Flarman exclaimed. "I wondered about that fussing from below stairs. Has he had lunch yet, Blue ?''

On the front of Range, Teakettle shook her spout emphatically with a sniff of steamy disapproval.

"Um, yes, he *might* learn a lesson from going hungry.

But that would be unkind . . . and we're never intentionally unkind, if we can help it,'' Flarman reproved her.

Blue Teakettle made an impolite sound, and returned to managing the washing-up.

Marget, much calmer now, picked up her empty teacup and gazed intently into the wet leaves in the bottom.

''There're more than enough signs of furors and dangers. All rather confused and unspecified!'' she complained after a moment.

''Let Augurian look at the tea leavings. He's the expert,'' Flarman advised. ''Are you finished with the ransom note, Waterman?''

Augurian came back to the table and laid the message beside his own teacup.

''Written in anger, angst, and anxiety, it's quite obvious,'' he reported. ''The writer, this General, seems rather vindictive . . . but desperate, too. See his botched spelling . . . ?''

''What of my son, Water Adept?'' sniffed the Queen.

''*His* writing is calm and purposeful,'' Augurian assured her. ''He's not afraid, and truly hopes we'll help the poor people of Parambit.''

''Parambit? Parambit!'' mused Flarman aloud. ''I should know exactly where that is . . . or was. But I can't quite recall. I remember the name. I remember its slain King Paradone, too. Now, why can't I remember where his country was?''

''There were so many places and peoples lost . . . and it was a longish time ago,'' Aedh sighed. ''I can't recall Paradone at all, myself.''

''*I* remember!'' his wife said, sitting up straighter. ''They came from the south of Old Kingdom, northwest of the Choin Empire. The Parambit called it Homeland.''

''Fairy memory is less affected by whatever spells addled the Parambit's progress, I suspect,'' Augurian said. ''It makes sense. It was to that part of World your son and the Sea Otter were blown by the storm.''

"And to which Douglas and Myrn have flown, hoping to rescue them, in case they need rescuing," added Bronze Owl. "They should be there by now."

"I'd say," Flarman began slowly, "that with two full Wizards on the scene we needn't worry too much about what this General is trying to accomplish by kidnapping little Ben. Don't you agree, Water Adept?"

Augurian nodded.

"Oh, I know," sighed the Queen of Faerie. "Our young Wizards are fully capable of straightening things out and allowing my baby boy to finish his Questing. I should not be such a silly ninny, Flarman! But it's hard, being the mother of a growing boy."

"I know! *I* know," sighed Flarman, then chuckling sympathetically and patting Marget's hand. "I worried a great deal about young Douglas when he was a lad. Still do, at times! But, other than keeping an eye on what's happening ... just in case, you know ... I think we can depend on him and Myrn to handle this General and his Parambiters. Parambites? Parambulators?"

Despite their worry, Ben's mother and father laughed at Flarman's words ... which is exactly what he'd intended ... and the party fell to discussing the nature and strength of the enchantments that held the long-lost subjects of Parambit in thrall.

"There was a child, wasn't there?" Queen Marget asked as she and Flarman walked over to the Workshop to run some diagnostic tests. "And whatever happened to the Queen of Parambit, I wonder?"

"We'll have to look into some very old books and raise some ancient shades, I think," replied the Fire Wizard.

"Let's get to work, then! I'll send a message to my own advisors."

Flarman cleared a tangle of stoneware, copper and silver wires, glass tubing, retorts, alembics, trays, ceramic and glass dishes, spring clamps, and three-legged stands from his worktop, muttering to himself all the while about having to do his own housekeeping chores.

The flight across westernmost Sea seemed quite slow. There were few islands . . . nothing but blue waves with white trim from horizon to horizon.

As dusk approached Douglas accelerated, hoping to reach the mainland before complete darkness fell.

"We'll have to land soon," his wife said, yawning for the third time in as many minutes. "I wonder . . . what would happen if we both fell asleep while traveling by Feather Pin?"

"Have to ask Finesgold," Douglas shrugged. "She knows the pin better than anyone . . . except the Cloud Fairies who made it in the first place, and perhaps Flarman, who altered its enchantment at one time for the Dowager Princess of Dwelmland."

The moon rising behind them lighted their way, and now they could see the dark, tangled coast with its winding silvery ribbon of river reaching inland toward distant mountains.

"Marbleheart is somewhat to the south of our line," he heard Myrn murmur. "Can you sense him?"

"Enough to find him, if we must go on in darkness."

"He and the lady Seacaptain are already in the forest, I see," Myrn continued. She was consulting a Farsight Spell Augurian had taught her while she was still in her earliest training. "Thornwood has joined them! That's good! Ben is not with them, however. As in the scene we conjured. I wonder why."

She yawned yet again, even more mightily, her need for sleep belying her willingness to continue into the night.

"There's an island of sorts there, in the middle of the delta," Douglas said, pointing down. "Safe place to get supper and a little sleep, perhaps?"

"Whatever you say," agreed his sleepy Wizard-wife. "Down we go!"

■   ▦   ▩

"Down you go!" growled the midnight visitor.

Myrn woke with a start and a soft scream, catching close sight of twin rows of wickedly sharp teeth gleaming in the moonlight. Without sitting upright she gestured toward the apparition.

"*Umph!*" grunted the 'gator, finding his gaping maw filled suddenly with a cake of vapor-streaming ice. "*Ung! Mmmf?*"

Douglas, wakened by the fuss, sprang to his feet, ready to do battle, but the enemy was . . . enemies were . . . already in retreat.

"*Ugh!*" Myrn grunted, sitting up. "Some sort of awful dragon or monster!"

"Alligators, I suspect," Douglas agreed. "*Ho!* You beasts! Come back here and talk."

In the inky water just offshore he heard a stirring and a churning. At last a huge alligator slithered slowly out of the water and lay, half in and half out of the river, regarding the Wizards balefully.

"We Alligators consider just about *anything* on our river . . . or near it . . . as fair game," the beast growled, smiling wickedly. "I didn't appreciate the tooth-aching stuff you fed me!"

"I prefer not to be a meal, thank you!" said Myrn tartly, brushing sand from her skirt and feeling about for her sandals. "Sorry about the ice, but I didn't intend to be gobbled in my sleep."

"My mistake, then." The alligator laughed uneasily. "Major Scales, Chief of the Lower Atamazon River Alligators, at your service, Mistress! Forgive my intrusion and the misunderstanding!"

Douglas helped Myrn to her feet and stood regarding the long-tailed reptile for a moment. Then he introduced himself and his wife to the 'gator chieftain, adding, "If hunger's your problem, we can solve it in better ways."

"Alligators are *always* hungry," rumbled the Major.

"More or less. It's been three nights since we last had a really good dinner! Right here on this very sand-spit, actually. Which is why we came this way tonight. In case there were more vittles available."

"Tell your friends I see them trying to circle behind us," Douglas warned. "Maybe they'd like a mouthful of Eternal Ice, too? It can be arranged!"

"Come off it, fellas!" the Major roared to his followers. "The nice young Wizard says he can provide better food . . . at least a dinner which'll not chill our teeth and shiver our timbers."

"Come out where we can see you all clearly," directed the Pyromancer. "We'll lay out some goodies you'll like, up here on the grass."

The five great alligators and two smaller, half-grown offspring as well lined up, chomping and slurping industriously at the fish chowder Blue Teakettle had provided on very short notice.

Myrn and her husband sat on a grassy tuffet, watching the reptiles dine . . . not a lesson in polite table manners. In a few minutes the contents of Teakettle's wicker basket were gone and the 'gators had settled down to digest their midnight snack. The youngsters and several of the adult 'gators closed their eyes and appeared to sleep.

"Who provided your last meal here, if I may ask?" Douglas asked Major Scales.

"An interesting, rather tasty-looking quartet it was," replied the monster. "They were led by a Sea Otter named . . . what was it? . . . Granitequarry? Slatetummy?"

"Marbleheart, I suspect," laughed Myrn.

"Right!" chuckled the alligator. "Accompanied by a lad . . . a fairy, if I don't miss my guess. Called Ben?"

"Ben we know," agreed Douglas. "Who else?"

"A young lady. Red-haired. Willowy, one might describe her."

"That would be the lady Seacaptain," Douglas said to Myrn.

"And a Man, too. Said he was Duke of Dukedom, whatever and wherever that might be," finished Scales.

"Thornwood! I didn't know he was on young Ben's Questing, too. Last I heard," Douglas said, "Thornwood was leading his fleet to Sea to chase Eunicet's pirates."

"We'll have to catch up to them to hear the whole tale, I guess," sighed Myrn. "What do you plan to do now, Major? My husband and I would like to get a few more hours of sleep before we move on."

"Oh, we'll doze over there on the north bank, if we may, and at dawn I plan to lead my troop upriver to catch grunion when they start to run. Go back to sleep, Wizards Brightglade. We're quiet sleepers . . . and we'll guard your refuge from further interruptions, too, if you like."

"Wake us before you leave, then," Douglas suggested. "We'll see if we can scramble up some eggs for breakfast."

Major Scales nodded his head ponderously, yawned cavernously, and blinked his eyes, then slithered across the wet mud to the water's edge.

"Do you think," Myrn murmured to Douglas, "that it'll be safe to sleep with these creepy things almost at our doorstep?"

"Perfectly safe . . . as long as we feed them in the morning," her husband said. "I'll set a Warding Spell to warn us if they come close again."

"I don't think I could close an eye," Myrn insisted. "*Ugh!*"

Douglas wove a minor Warding Spell to discourage mosquitoes, tiny midges, and wakeful alligators from approaching their campsite.

Two minutes later both Wizards were sound asleep again.

After breakfast and the departure of the alligators, well fed, Douglas sat cross-legged before the fire and hummed a Calling Spell he often used to contact his Familiar.

"Here I am," said Marbleheart's voice at once, sounding a bit muffled with sleep. "Where are you, Master?"

"Near as I can tell, forty or fifty miles northeast of you. On the ait in the Atamazon Delta you stopped on when you first arrived here, according to some alligators we met last night."

"Don't trust 'em further'n you can spit," Otter warned. "Keep 'em well fed and logy, is my advice."

"Figured that out already! What are you about?"

Marbleheart explained about the capture of the fairy by the large band of armed Men, as closely as his instincts and investigations could tell. He planned to follow them that day, he said, and attempt to rescue Ben in the dark of night.

"But I'm surprised Ben hasn't escaped on his own hook," he added. "Any ideas?"

Douglas thought for a moment before he spoke.

"I agree. Even a very young fairy should know how to escape from mere Men. Do you sense any powerful magic about these people? Anything that would nullify Ben's fairyness?"

"No, nothing like that. What does it mean?"

"That Ben remains captive because he *wants* to remain captive."

Marbleheart thought this over, then said, "It may be that he's agreed to behave . . . against some threat to us. To Thornwood, here, and Lorianne. And me, of course."

"A possibility . . . but I'd think the lad would have sense enough to flee his captivity and come to warn you."

"The way to solve this is to ask Ben," Marbleheart decided. "You and Myrn are an hour's flight away? What do you recommend we do when you catch us up?"

"Keep an eye on those nomad warriors," Douglas decided. "We'll follow them and see what Ben wants us to do."

"Good to have you along," the Otter Familiar told his Master. "Shared adventure is always the best."

"You're doing extremely well on your own. You, the

fairy boy, and Thornwood. And the lady Seacaptain!"
Myrn put in. "See you directly, Marblefoot!"

The Otter groaned dramatically over the nickname she
gave him. Douglas cut off the spell and said to his wife,
"Let's get out of this damp and dismal place!"

"I'd have been gone long since if I hadn't had to wait
for my sleepyhead husband!" Myrn snapped, but she
grinned playfully to show she was just teasing.

Chapter Eighteen

Reunion

THE Sea Otter woke Thornwood and Lorianne to tell them the news.

"One of us ought to keep a close eye on Ben's captors, in case they move on," the Duke advised. "The rest should stay put, to show Douglas and Myrn the way."

"I'm better suited to close following," declared Marble-heart. "Let's have some breakfast. Then I'll slink off after them bandits while you two wait here."

"Bandits?" Lorianne asked. "Do you consider them criminals, then, Otter?"

"Honest men don't hold a little boy hostage!" Marble-heart said, poking at their tiny fire with a stick. "Let's see . . . how about eggs and bacon or ham? Whole wheat toast with cream cheese? Lilac makes a wonderful cream cheese spread with chopped walnuts and diced apples. Most tasty!"

He wolfed down his own meal as soon as it arrived and left his companions sitting in the shade of a great, gnarled, old live oak to eat at a more leisurely pace. He plunged directly into the thickest of the underbrush, following his nose and his excellent sense of direction as silently as any shadow.

"Good morning!" Marbleheart called to a hummingbird who was hovering before a glorious clump of dainty red-and-yellow trumpet-flowers. "Can you tell me . . . ?"

"Hold on a moment!" buzzed the tiny bird. He darted up into the air, then zoomed down again. "Be right with you."

The tiny hummer . . . a male with brilliant metallic blue and shiny green plumage on his back, breast, and wings . . . performed a dazzling aerobatics show, darting here and there, hither and yon, for a full minute before he returned to where the Otter waited, bobbed to a full stop before Marbleheart's nose, and cocked his head to the left.

"You were saying?" he hummed pleasantly. "I'm sorry to have made you wait, but I was signaling my crew about the most likely locations of the best, freshest flower nectar in this honeysuckle."

"Is that what it's called? A most delicious perfume! I envy you, ah . . . what's your name? I'm Marbleheart Sea Otter of Wizards' High and Briny Deep, way east and north."

"I'll take your word for it," hummed the bird. "I know there's a lot of blue water east of here, but the nectar business keeps me close to home, most of the time. My name is Berlios. Pleased to meet you!"

"Likewise," responded the Sea Otter. "I just wanted to ask you about the Men who camped near here last night. Do you know who they were?"

"They camp here several times every year, that I *do* know," answered the hummingbird, finally alighting on a honeysuckle vine and folding his short, tapered wings. "Call themselves Bewildered Band. Their leader is an old Man named General."

"General who?"

"Never heard him called anything but just General," admitted Berlios. "Say, do you mind if I start gathering nectar from this branch as we talk? It takes most of the morning, as it is, to gather enough to keep pinions fluttering and tail feathers fanning.''

"Go right ahead! I won't keep you. You don't know anything else about these Men, do you?''

The hummingbird darted a short way off and began sliding his long, sharp bill into the throats of the yellow flowers, humming happily.

"Sorry!'' he said, coming up for air. "You really should talk to the ravens, I think. They pay closer attention to Men than we do. Ravens make a living scavenging at their camps. There's one over there . . . you see? On the long palmetto frond? Big, slow-winged, black thing? Gaudy orange bill?''

"Yes, thank you! I see him,'' Marbleheart called after the tiny bird.

He trotted over to the palmetto thicket and nodded politely to the large, black raven who watched him approach with a bright, beady eye.

"Good morning!'' the bird greeted the Otter at once. "Going to be a hot day. Stay under the forest canopy or in the creek, I advise.''

The Sea Otter introduced himself, not forgetting his official standing with a certain famous Wizard.

"What can you tell me about the band of Men who recently passed this way?'' he asked, once the amenities were out of the way.

"Oh, the Parambites? They've been coming here for years and years,'' the raven said, hopping closer along the palmetto frond. "I almost know them all by name, they've been coming this way so long.''

"Who do they say they are? I only ask because I believe a friend of mine has been captured by them. I hope to rescue him. He's just a lad.''

"Ah, that will be the fairy child!'' cried the raven, whose name was Forrest. "Saw him quite clearly last evening and again this morning. Interesting folk, the fairies! You don't see many this far south, these days. Time was . . ."

"He's being treated well?"

"Seemed so." Forrest nodded his head several times.
"Dined well. Talked in the tent for several hours late last
evening. Rumors about the campfires were he is, indeed, a
captive. General sent off a ransom note to his mum, they
said. She's the Queen of Faerie."

"Just so! Know her well; Marget of Faerie," Marbleheart confirmed. "Ransom, is it? Dangerous doings, med-
dling with the wee folk like that."

"I was pretty surprised, myself, but I've a notion the
plight of the Bewildered Band is desperate. They've been
wandering around and around these parts for as long as
anyone cares to remember."

"I wonder why?"

"No one knows, least of all the Bandsmen, themselves.
By the way, the troop you're looking for are only a part of
a whole flock . . . if that's the right word."

"Where're the rest, then?"

"Somewhere to the west, over the mountains. They
come along every other month, you see. Doesn't make
much sense. Never go anywhere different. Just hike down
to the river, spend a couple of days, then hike back home."

"Interesting!" Marbleheart murmured. " 'Bewildered,'
is it?"

"So they call themselves and so they seem to be," answered Forrest, shaking his head in sympathy. "So, you'll
rescue your fairy friend from them, eh?"

"I intend to. I'm responsible to his parents."

"Maybe I can help," the raven suggested. "Sounds like
an Adventure, and Adventures don't come along too often!
May I help?"

"Very likely! Come along, then. Not much pay, but the
food's pretty good. I'm going to trail them today and, if
possible, speak to the boy when they stop for the night."

"Lead the way, then, friend!" agreed the raven. "I'll

follow you overhead, at least until we're out of this grove. Sort of an aerial reconnaissance?''

The odd pair set out, the Otter *gallumping* along at a surprising clip and the raven flapping from plane tree to widespread oak to dark mahogany, as they followed the faint signs of the marching Band, which now tended southward, paralleling the line of rugged, blue mountains.

Once every quarter-mile or so Marbleheart paused to knot a clump of dry grasses together, twisted to indicate the direction they were going. When the grass petered out, he built small cairns of stones as indicators instead.

"How long did Marbleheart think it would be before your friends show up?'' said the lady Seacaptain.

"Any moment,'' Thornwood replied. "They're coming by air . . .''

"A nice, clean, cool way to travel,'' Lorianne sighed. "There's a stream making a deep pool, off there a short way. Did you notice? Do you think it'd be safe to bathe in? I don't know about you, Thornwood, but I feel as if I haven't had a clean patch of skin on me for about a year!''

"Go ahead. Take your time,'' Thornwood laughed. "When you've finished, I'll follow suit, for I'm just as filthy as you after slogging about in the delta mud. I wouldn't dare to peek.''

"Oh, well . . . all right, then!'' Lorianne grinned. "Here I go! I'll call to you when I've finished. You don't happen to have any soap in your kit, do you?''

Thornwood searched his pockets and shook his head.

"There's something called a soap-bush in these parts,'' Lorianne remembered, brightening once more.

"I'll take a look, shall I?'' Thornwood volunteered. "I'll call out to you if I find one.''

"Wonderful!''

She walked away toward the hidden pool.

Thornwood watched her go until he saw her begin to untie the strip of sailcloth binding her auburn hair, aflame in the bright sunlight. He turned resolutely away, beginning a methodical search for a soap-plant.

"I should recognize it when I see it," he muttered to himself, bending low to inspect each bush in his path. "Flarman showed it to me in a picture, one time, long ago. No, not that one!"

He wandered in widening half-circles about the campsite, keeping track of Lorianne's location by the sound of splashing and her sailor's "make and mend" chantey.

The forest was much less dense here. Bright-colored birds were chirping happily in the trees, chasing each other and searching for luncheon bugs or seeds, depending on their tastes.

"Do you ever use a soap-bush?" Thornwood asked a white-and-brown-feathered ring-necked pheasant hen leading a line of recently hatched chicks down to the stream.

"Use it all the time!" chattered the pheasant hen. "Oh, yes! Mother's Friend, we calls it . . . don't we, children?"

"Bath! Bath!" the chicks peeped, staring fearlessly up at the Man.

"Gather leaves fresh every morning," the hen went on. "They suds up best after a night of cool rest, I find. Now, let me see . . . there *was* one around here, somewhere. Scatter, children, and help us look!"

A moment later one of her scurrying chicks found a soap-bush and called to his mother to come that way. Thornwood followed.

"Here we are!" cried the mother pheasant. "Very good, Philip! A good, healthy one, too. I find it best to pull the older leaves from the base of the stalks. Take too many leaves and it harms the poor plant. It might even die! No, no, Flutteron! It's not to *eat*, even though it has a wonderful smell. It's for the young Man's bath."

"Thank you most kindly, ma'am," Thornwood said, bowing politely. "I'll try not to hurt your soap-bush, you can be sure. *My!* It does have a very pleasant aroma."

"Yes, doesn't it," the mother twittered. "Come along

now, children! I know a place where we can get our morning dip without disturbing the handsome young man. Good morrow, Sir!''

The seven chicks all bobbed politely and scurried off toward the stream in a single line, following their mother.

Thornwood carefully stuffed his jacket pocket with fragrant leaves, feeling their soapy-oily texture on his fingers, and walked back toward the campfire.

"Miss Lorianne!" he called aloud. "Miss . . ."

"Yes, M'Lord?"

"I found a soap-bush. I can bring some to you, if you wish."

"Yes, if you will, bring them, please! Save some for your own use."

Blushing furiously, the Duke walked toward the sound of her voice and that of running water. Passing between two tall, thin candle cedars, he came upon the pool. At first he couldn't see the girl, but she suddenly surfaced at the near bank, gasping, hair streaming water.

"You're so very nice!" she called. "I can smell the leaves from here. Delicious!"

"I'll just lay them here, shall I?"

"No, bring them here to me, M'Lord," Lorianne laughed. "I won't bite you! There! Leave half under that smooth rock for yourself. Oh, how delightful!"

"And how delightful *you* are, too . . . if you don't think me too bold when I say it," gasped Thornwood, coloring even more brightly. "I . . ."

Lorianne pushed her wet hair out of her eyes.

"You've not much experience of girls . . . of ladies, I should say?" she teased.

"Hardly any at all," the young Duke admitted. "I don't wish to hasten or bother you, Miss Lorianne, but . . ."

"Let me bathe, then," said Lorianne, laughing and breathless for some reason. "I won't be long. I'll call out when I'm dry and dressed and then you can bathe, also. Then we'll sit together and wait for the Brightglades."

"My great pleasure!"

He returned to the fire, which he fed dry twigs so it wouldn't die before lunchtime. Without the Otter there to order a meal from the High kitchen, he didn't know what they could find to eat.

Although it was already well past mid-morning, he didn't feel a bit hungry.

There was a rustle in the grass and Lorianne, looking radiantly clean and fresh, stepped between the candle cedars.

"Your turn," she said softly. "I'll find something for us to eat."

"You can find food here in this wilderness?" asked the Duke, turning to go.

"There's plenty to find, if you know what to look for, M'Lord. Not just Wizards and Familiars know how to get a meal in the woods."

Thornwood stopped before he stepped out of sight between the dark cedars, turning back to her.

"A favor, if you will?"

"I will, if I can," answered Lorianne, matching his suddenly serious tone.

"My name? I'm Thornwood. Titles don't mean much to me, especially here."

"I'll call you . . . Thornwood," she promised shyly. "And I am Lorianne. Not a Duchess nor even a Seacaptain, since my schooner's lost . . ."

"But a lady, all the same," he assured her solemnly.

After a lunch of fresh fruit and hard-boiled eggs . . . a bit lacking in savor, as they had no salt . . . and a salad of tender young greens that tasted faintly of onion, the pair sat side by side in the deep shade of the overhanging live oak, talking of their childhoods and youthful adventures, and listening to the shrill, sweet singing of weaver birds high above them.

"I hardly remember my Papa and my Mama," Lorianne

said sadly. "Uncle Braiser and Aunty Philadestra tell me they were very fine folk. But nobody could tell me what happened to them. Lost at Sea, I always thought, as sometimes happens to fisherfolk. So I've had to imagine them."

"And how do you imagine them?" Thornwood asked, watching her expertly braid a chain of white-and-gold daisies to wear in her flaming hair.

"Tall. Handsome. Brave in adversity. Gentle in love."

"I'm sure they were just as you've imagined," Thornwood told her. "For that's just as I see *you*, Lorianne."

The girl blushed with pleasure.

"And your own parents?" she asked.

"My mother, of course, is my closest advisor. Her name is Marigold . . ."

"What a beautiful name!"

"You'd like her. You *will* like her, I mean, for I insist you come to meet her, as soon as we rescue the fairy boy and decide what's to be done about his captors."

"Is it difficult to talk of your father? You at least remember him, do you not?"

"I was just a child. A foul man named Eunicet did away with him and took his place as Duke of Dukedom."

" 'Did away with him'? You mean . . . had him slain? I'm sorry, Thornwood. Perhaps I shouldn't speak to you of such things."

"No, no! Perfectly all right. My mother's told me I could always be proud of my father. Thorowood was a good man, a wonderful husband, and, for too short a time, a very loving and proud father. As for what happened to him . . . I really don't know! He may have been killed outright or he may have been imprisoned somewhere, or maybe enchanted. I once tried to learn what happened to him from the wicked usurper Eunicet, before the Court Martial banished him to a deserted island in Warm Sea. Either he *wouldn't* or he *couldn't* tell me."

"You should try to find out what happened to him. I know how *I* feel about my father and mother. It wouldn't be nearly so awful if I *knew* they were dead. But the thought of them imprisoned, somewhere, or enslaved by some wicked master! I try to believe that they drowned in a shipwreck, as my uncle believes. But somehow I didn't . . . don't want to believe.''

Thornwood took her hand.

''When we've rescued Ben and punished the Men who stole him away, I'll go with you to Home Port and we'll find what happened to your mother and father!''

''Oh, my dear,'' whispered Lorianne. ''It's one of my oldest and fondest dreams.''

She looked so forlorn and sorrowful at the thought that Thornwood took her other hand and held them both between his own strong, capable, and yet gentle hands.

''*One* of your dreams?'' he asked, huskily. ''And the others?''

Lorianne opened her lips to speak when they heard a sudden strong wind blowing, tossing the treetops. Old leaves and bits of twig and bark fell like snow about them.

''Here we are,'' called Douglas Brightglade, stepping from the vortex, steadying his lovely wife with one hand and waving with the other. ''Hello, Thornwood! Introduce us to your lady friend!''

Seated in the shade of the ancient oak, Douglas described the pirate's raid on Wizards' High. Lorianne told of the shipwreck and Thornwood in turn told of his setting out with the Great Sea Tortoise in search of Marbleheart and Ben, and about the fairy boy's disappearance.

Myrn and Lorianne went aside to order an early supper, chattering like old friends and exchanging recipes, while Douglas and Thornwood gathered dried cedar boughs to feed the fire against the coming night.

''Here's my strayed Familiar, at last!'' called Douglas as he and the Duke laid down their armfuls of wood. ''Ahoy, Marbleheart! Have you found Ben? Is he safe?''

''I wouldn't be here if he weren't! What's for supper,

ladies? I see you've already been introduced. Let me introduce my own newfound friend Forrest. He's a raven, as
you can easily see.''

"Blue Teakettle's sent us roast duck and fried rice," said
Myrn after everyone had welcomed Forrest and made him
feel at home in their midst. "She seems to think we're in
Choin. Do you like barbecued ribs, Forrest?''

"I never ate a meal I didn't like," Forrest replied, dropping wearily to the ground near the fire. "*Woof!* What a
day! The Otter leads a merry chase.''

"You can start telling us about it now," Myrn told Marbleheart, setting before him a platter of fried noodles topped
with green peppercorns and strips of tender beefsteak
broiled in sesame oil.

"Which story first, then?'' Douglas wondered. "Best to
start with the earliest and go through to the latest, Familiar.
I'll start off with Eunicet, and you tell of your shipwreck-
ing?''

"Fire away," Marbleheart agreed, stuffing rice and steak
into his mouth. "I'm much too busy to talk, anyway. And
almost too tired, as well.''

"Poor old Familiar!'' His Master laughed. "Well . . .''

Night had fallen, and the sky was magnificently spangled
with bright and steady stars before the Otter finished picking barbecued pork from his teeth and took the floor to tell
of his doings that long day.

"This Bewildered Band moves rather slowly, I found.
Marches at best ten miles in a day! Only as fast as the
slowest of their people, some of whom are pretty long in
the tooth, as Frenstil says of his horses.

"Forrest and I followed their trail south along the mountain flanks. After noon they turned west and climbed up
through a narrow gap between two peaks. They've camped
in a spot on the other side where a wakeful guard could
see us coming, miles off. We decided to return for you.''

Douglas sat very still and silent for several seconds, his

eyes focused on the fire. Pyromancers do such things, at times.

"Well, Ben's not in danger, we can be pretty sure," he said at last.

"You're able to see him?" asked Lorianne in surprise.

"Outlines and circumstances . . . and they can change at the turn of a minute, of course."

"I really know very little about such matters, Wizard Brightglade . . ."

"Douglas, only," cried the Pyromancer with an embarrassed laugh. "And my wife is Myrn and prefers that to any kind of titling."

"Time to rescue Ben, however," Myrn said softly.

"I do agree," her husband nodded.

"Let's go! Time to stop pussyfooting around in the hills!" cried Marbleheart, jumping to his feet.

"At first light, and we'll go by way of the Feather Pin, instead of on foot," decided Douglas. "To go at night'd only leave us at the disadvantage of not being able to see very well, even those of us who are night-visioned Otters."

"First light, then," yawned the Sea Otter, flopping back down on his tummy. "Shall we set a watch? We're pretty safe from intruders here."

"A good idea, anyway, to have someone alert. I'll take first watch until midnight."

"And I'll take the midnight watch," Thornwood volunteered.

"I'll wake you all in the middle of the morning watch, then," promised the Otter. "Time for bed, folks!'

He made himself comfortable on a pile of dried grass, once having dug out any acorns which littered the ground under the oak.

Forrest flew to a high branch and fell at once asleep, snoring softly.

Myrn composed herself for sleep on a mattress of fragrant grasses, ferns, and flowers, and surprised herself by falling into deep sleep almost at once.

Thornwood thoughtfully prepared two beds near each other for himself and Lorianne, but the pair sat long awake, holding hands, and whispering to each other.

"Up that draw," called Marbleheart.

He was at the far forward end of the Feather Pin line with Douglas in the middle and Myrn at the rear.

They were a strange sight for the huge birds (vultures or condors, Myrn guessed) perched on rocky pinnacles far above them, waiting for the first updrafts of morning to carry them aloft for a day's soaring and hunting.

Beyond the range of sharply upthrust mountains, a broad valley opened to view. Down its center dashed a fast-running, foaming river, falling from pool to pool over low falls or dashing down ragged rapids. The loud voices of the wild water reached up to them as they dropped toward it.

The Otter yelped, pointing an eager foreclaw. "Here's our raven come to report!"

Forrest climbed from the riverbank, flapping his long wings as rapidly as he could manage. He was aware of the eyes not only of the Wizards' party on him, but those of the great birds of prey high above.

"Most strange," he cawed as he approached the flyers supported by Finesgold's pin. "*Most* strange!"

Chapter Nineteen

River Chase

THE Pyromancer hovered a hundred feet above the stream and the ragged tarpaulins stretched between eucalyptus trees growing on its verge.

"Camp," Marbleheart said, dangling at the extreme end of the line, swinging slowly in the breeze. "Camp, but no campers!"

"Take us down," Myrn called to her husband. "There's nobody there!"

The travelers were deposited on trampled grass beside the tarpaulin, under which stood the General's tent. A mound of ashes showed where a fire had burned itself out during the night.

"Where'd they get to?" Thornwood wondered.

He knelt beside the cold fireplace. "Personal equipment everywhere! Someone left a perfectly good belt knife, and someone else left his spoon and a soiled but empty bowl. For whatever reason, a sudden departure . . ."

The Brightglades walked slowly around the deserted campsite in opposite directions, studying the ground, the trees, and the sky. Marbleheart poked his head into the empty tent, sniffing at the smells of old sweat and stale tobacco smoke. Lorianne and Thornwood examined the equipment and clothing scattered about.

Bluebottle flies buzzed nervously about the scene, and a flock of brown wrens watched from a nearby almond tree.

"They left suddenly, I'd say," Douglas said, nodding to the papa wren courteously. "Did you see them go?"

"Not really," the small bird admitted. "We found things just as you see, young sir. If you like, we'll ask around. But it probably happened very early, just at dawn, when most of us were still roosting."

"Please ask anyway," Douglas requested.

The wrens fluttered away, chirping excitedly.

"They'd started breaking their fast. Few had even done up their bedrolls," Marbleheart told Douglas. "So it would have been just at first light. Not many minutes before dawn."

"No signs of struggle," the young Duke reported. "In fact, much of their armor and weapons are still stacked about. Wherever this Bewildered Band went, they went suddenly."

"Over there, on the riverbank," Lorianne said, pointing. "There's an acre or so of open sand and a great many footprints. All heading downriver."

Douglas, Thornwood, and Marbleheart went to see for themselves, while Myrn and Lorianne poked about the deserted campsite, looking for further clues.

"Ben slept here," Myrn exclaimed, bending down. "That's his cloak. I recognize his mother's fine fairy handiwork. Notice the lining of spider's silk?"

"The Queen of Faerie makes her son's clothing?" Lorianne asked in surprise.

"Marget says her boy deserved only the very best and, as she's by far the best seamstress in all Faerie, she makes all his clothes. I'm not that fond of sewing, myself."

"Again I fail to understand why the boy just went along with what happened," Douglas muttered to Marbleheart and Thornwood. "Someone or something came upon them, and led or drove them away?"

"Ben may feel some responsibility for the . . . what did you call them? The Parambit?" said Thornwood. "I can understand that."

"Strange and stranger," muttered Myrn when the men-folk rejoined the ladies in front of the empty tent. "They left *everything* . . . clothing, bedrolls, even their tin plates!"

"This calls for a bit of Wizardry," decided Douglas. "With your permission, my dear?"

"Go ahead! I'll add my water-power, if you need a boost."

"Sit down and be quiet, everybody!" Douglas called out. "Myrn, maybe something cold to drink would help."

Myrn nodded and set about placing an order to Blue Teakettle. By the time everyone, including the raven Forrest, had a tall glass of iced tea in hand, claw, or paw, the Pyromancer had kindled a tiny fire in the cold ashes and dropped a bit of Summoning Spell mixture, with the proper incantation, into the flames.

"I heard your call, Wizard!" said a tiny voice from his shoulder. "You wished something?"

"Yes, if you please," Douglas answered, turning to gaze at a tiny red ant who'd crawled up his sleeve. "Do you live nearby?"

"Along with thirty thousand others of my nest," replied the insect, nodding. "Our hill is over yonder, under that grassy bank. Has been, for long as I can remember."

"Then perhaps you saw what happened here early this morning?" Douglas asked, allowing the ant to trot onto his left forefinger. "Don't let these other big folks frighten you, by the by. They're all friends of mine."

"I'll take your word for that, Fire Wizard," said the red ant, looking about the circle of faces bent over Douglas's hand. "Although I'm not sure about the raven. Is he safe?"

"His name is Forrest," Marbleheart said. "And I don't think he's much interested in eating fire ants."

"Not at all!" croaked the raven, shaking his head. "Be at ease, won't you please!"

"A sip of icy tea'd be nice," suggested the insect, waving his foremost pair of legs at Douglas's cup.

Douglas poured a dollop of the iced liquid into an acorn cap he found on the ground and everybody waited while the ant sipped at it, tentatively.

"Delicious!" he pronounced. "Now, how may I help you?"

"What happened here? Do you fire ants know?" Douglas asked. "There were two hundred or so Men and a fairy youngster sleeping here last night . . . and now they're gone with hardly a trace."

"Of course I was sound asleep underground, as were all of us fire ants," declared the insect. "However, there's a band of gypsy moths camped in a birch tree, nearby. They're fly-by-night insects, you know, and must have been still fluttering about at dawn."

"Can you introduce us to them? We'd appreciate it."

"My pleasure! Anything to help a Pyromancer. We're great admirers of your craft, sir."

"Fire ants!" coughed Marbleheart as the tiny ant dashed off into the trampled grass. "They aren't exactly harmless bugs, Master!"

"The ordinary sort of ant wouldn't have been as quick-witted, however."

"Yes, well . . . I always said most ants are a pretty dull lot, always herding their aphid cattle, moving about in great columns, and things like that."

Shortly a somewhat unsteady greyish moth appeared from the direction of the river, fluttering along uneasily as if the bright daylight pained his great compound eyes. He came more or less straight to Douglas's hand.

The fire ant rode on the moth's furry back.

"His name's Softly. He can tell you about the doings here," the ant said. "I wish I had time for another sip of

your delicious tea, but I must be on my own way, Master
Pyromancer. Unless you need me further?''

"No, you've done very well. Thank you, fire ant!''
Douglas said gravely.

The red insect waved at the circle of faces and scurried
off into the grass once more.

"Now, Master Softly,'' Douglas addressed the moth,
cupping his left hand over the insect to shield him from the
bright sunlight. "Did the fire ant explain what we wish to
know?''

"Ho . . . *hum*, yes! Glad to be of help!'' yawned Softly
sleepily. "Sorry! Been up all night! I saw it all, yessir.
Beginning to end!''

"Tell us then, please,'' the Wizard urged gently. "Can
I offer you a bit of this iced tea first?''

"No, no, no, thank you! Well, on second thought . . . a
drop or two, to wet the old thorax.''

He sipped a bit of tea and then began:

"Men came late yesterday afternoon, built a nice big fire
. . . which attracted us at once, of course. Nothing more
enticing than a campfire! Wasn't long before the lot of us
were flying round and round, enjoying the warmth and
brightness.''

"Kind of dangerous, wasn't that?'' Marbleheart asked.

"Fool youngsters sometimes get singed, yes,'' the moth
agreed. "But any sensible gypsy moth knows getting too
close to a flame can be . . . well . . . dangerous, as you say.''

"Please go on,'' Douglas prompted.

"Men slept until just before dawn, being night sleepers,
I gather, when their leader, a wrinkled little person with
white hair and tiny eyes, came out of the cocoon, there,
and called them all to gather round.''

"That would be their leader, I imagine,'' said Marbleheart. "I saw him when I got close to their camp late
yesterday.''

"They call him 'General,' '' the moth went on. "Or-

dered them to get into lines and follow him. They all
dashed off down the river.''

"None of you followed?" Myrn asked.

"No, ma'am! We're," Softly yawned again, ". . . sorry!
. . . not really interested in Men. Their fire died down to
ashes so we went off to bed ourselves."

"I can imagine," murmured the Aquamancer. "But what
I can't imagine is why this General, or whatever his name
is, rushed his men off into the brush like that."

"Enchantment?" Marbleheart suggested.

"I somehow don't think so," Douglas said. He shook
his head in bewilderment. "We'll follow their tracks and
see where they went," he decided, glancing about to see if
the others objected.

"We can follow faster'n they can march, even without
all their baggage," Thornwood agreed. "Were they called
away by someone or something? I guess the best way to
find out is to follow them and ask."

"My thinking exactly," agreed Douglas, taking Myrn by
the hand. "Ben's Questing is getting rather complicated!"

"Fly high," cawed Forrest, the only one of them who
didn't join the Feather Pin line. "I'll go low. Keep us hot
on the trail!"

"Good thinking," agreed the Pyromancer. "*Now!* Here
we go! Oh, and thank you, Master Softly!"

The moth bobbed sleepily and returned to his swarm,
settled away from the bright sun deep under a nice damp,
dark, riverside rock.

The river in the valley between the mountain ranges now
slowed, wandered back and forth, split, looped, formed
shallow pools, rejoined, then ran down shallow stairstep
rapids for a mile or so. The valley itself gradually widened
until the ranges on east and west melted into the horizons.

Forrest at last hovered until the fliers caught up with him
and thankfully settled on Douglas's shoulder.

"Track goes on and on!" he panted. "I need a drink. Can we stop for a bit?"

"Yes, and get some lunch, I think," the Pyromancer said with a nod.

The travelers sank gracefully and gratefully to the river . . . now much wider and only inches deep. They found a spot of shade and shortly they were eating cold chicken sandwiches and potato salad, and drinking Blue Teakettle's tangy orange punch.

"I'm amazed how fast the Band is moving," Myrn said after finishing her first sandwich and reaching for another. "They didn't cover this much mileage all day yesterday!"

"Well, they were then in rugged country, crossing the mountain pass," Thornwood pointed out, "and heavily laden with weapons and baggage. Still, I agree with you, Myrn. They're going a pretty good clip, even moving on the level and unencumbered."

Marbleheart and the raven returned, dusty and hot, from a ground inspection.

"They can't keep up this pace without resting," Otter insisted after he'd drained a glass of orangeade and reached for the last sandwich. "They're just short of trotting, and in this heat, too!"

"Where *could* they be going?" Douglas asked the raven. "Do you know the country ahead?"

"Been here and further south a few times," admitted Forrest. "Not much to tell, Wizard. Eventually the river flows into a lake. It's there the Band makes its home. That must be where they're going—the north shore of the salt lake."

Lorianne asked, "You're sure it's not Sea? Rivers usually end only in Sea."

"This one ends in a great shallow, bitter lake, however, Mistress," Forrest insisted. "Shallow and very briny!"

"Unusual," Douglas said thoughtfully. "You're the Aquamancer, Myrn. How does it strike you?"

"I've read of lakes without outlets. They're usually quite

barren of life and filled with salts and chemicals which can't be carried off when the water evaporates. I don't remember ever hearing of one here in Far Southwest, but even Augurian hasn't explored this far!''

"All I can tell you is,'' piped Forrest, ''the land ahead gets barrener and barrener! Awful place!''

"Are the Parambit hiding from danger?'' Douglas asked. ''I can think of no other reason to settle in such a harsh wilderness.''

His wife snorted. ''Why else live in an empty desert beside a lifeless sea? Water must be a serious problem.''

"It's not unknown for Men to hide in such out-of-the-way places,'' Thornwood considered. ''Have you ever asked yourself why Frigeon chose to live on Eternal Ice? He could've chosen a pleasanter place, Myrn.''

"You're right, but it must take a powerful fear for anyone to *choose* to live either on Eternal Ice . . . or beside a barren salt lake.''

"Animals have adapted to such places,'' Marbleheart pointed out.

"On Eternal Ice,'' Douglas nodded, ''there are birds with furry feet called ptarmigans. Right at home on ice and snow. And polar bears, too, further north. Marbleheart, you once spoke of them on the ice pack north of Briny Deep.''

"I never thought of polar bears as fugitives from anything,'' Marbleheart scoffed. ''But . . . you may be right. Not much bothers the white bears of the empty Northland. They're pretty much loners.''

"All of which is instructive,'' said Thornwood, ''but doesn't suggest a reason why this General's Band rushed home, leaving baggage and weapons behind!''

"I'm stumped, I admit,'' said Douglas, shaking his head.

"We must push on,'' said Marbleheart. ''I owe it to young Ben!''

"Well, so do we all,'' agreed Myrn, beginning to pick up and send back to the High all their plates and tumblers. ''Can't we make some shade?''

"You're the Aquamancer," said her husband, helping her and the Seacaptain clear luncheon things away. "Got any useful Cloudy Spells handy?"

"Let me think about that. Yes, I think I can cover that necessity. No use being a Water Wizard, folks, if you can't whiz up a bit of cloudiness, now and then, to the good of all!"

When they joined hands again and popped aloft, the upper air had already turned cooler, thanks to Myrn's magic. Thick clouds hung low over their heads like a great grey umbrella.

Myrn laughed. "Or, more properly, a parasol."

Chapter Twenty

Permanent Camp

ALL that day Ben had skipped along, easily keeping abreast of the hurrying Bandsmen . . . although they now seemed more worried and frightened than bewildered.

His guards of the days before now ignored him and he could have, if he'd wished, dropped behind, or simply disappeared, and never be missed. Something very serious had happened, told to the General in the early hours that morning, that had sent him dashing off down the stream.

When they reached the still, lime-green waters of the Great Salted Lake, however, the General was forced to call a halt. Many of his older warriors were unable to keep up the killing pace longer. No one had eaten or rested since dawn.

"Fall in!" shouted the General after a brief rest. "Who will go on with me . . . stand to the right. Who can't march further . . . fall in to the left and stay here until you can come after us."

"Is this necessary?" Ben asked. "Surely 'twould be better to rest until dark, to move more sensibly in night's cool?"

"No! As many of us as can put one foot before the other, *must*!" hissed the General . . . but quietly, as if he feared his soldiers would hear the lad's sensible suggestion and side with common sense. "It's a matter of *utmost* urgency we reach Permanent Camp *as soon as possible,* and in as large a number as can stay the course!"

"Perhaps so," Ben murmured. "I've no idea why we're rushing off across this desert of dried salt, beside brackish water, through coarse sand, without spare clothing, without spears, swords, bows, and pikes. Without proper rest! Perhaps someone would take the time to explain?"

"None of your business, fairy sprat!" the General spat. "Stay out and away!"

Then he softened. "I'm sorry, my boy! This *is* none of your problem, and you'll be forgiven if you go your own way, now, and leave us to our own troubles."

He started to turn away, accepting a cup of water from an aide.

Ben shook his head.

"No!" he shouted after the old man. "I want to know what's going on, Sir, and why're we rushing off, it seems, without proper thought or plan."

The General dropped wearily onto a flat rock at the edge of the lake, shaking his head and then gesturing the boy to sit beside him.

"Carefully. Stone's hot!"

Ben perched, sitting on the edge of his short tunic to keep the blistering stone from touching his bare thighs. The General drank deeply from the cup, held it out to be refilled, then offered it to the boy.

"Our women and children, the very young and the elderly, too young or old or too weak to march, live down the shore a few miles. Permanent Camp."

"I understand, Grandfather."

"Grand . . . ? Well, yes, so I am, a grandfather, lad! I take that as a title of respect."

"So intended, Sir," the boy told him, sipping gingerly

at the cup of blood-warm water with the sharp metallic tang of dissolved minerals. "Why *are* we rushing homeward, then?"

"There's been a revolt! Some of my people are seeking to displace me as Parambit's leader. We rush to rescue my people from their own folly! I, and I alone, was chosen by Paradone to lead his people until . . . until . . ."

"Yes? Until? Until what?" Ben murmured. "Until your people find another leader? What have *you* done for the Parambit for more than two hundred years, Grandfather? Marched them up to the south bank of the Atamazon every other month, as I've heard? And then marched them home again! In time, I think, it got pretty monotonous. Pretty boring. Unrewarding!"

The General flushed angry red and caught his breath to make a sharp retort, but held his peace. For a while this strangely assorted pair, the young fairy and the wrinkled old soldier, sat side by side, staring out across the lake.

"Who leads this revolt?" Ben asked at last.

"Someone left behind," growled the General. "Are we ready to march again, Sergeant Skittle?"

"No, wait a minute or two," begged Ben. "You're keeping me in the darkness and I can't tell which way I should think! *Who's* decided to end your rule? Decided to take over the Band?"

The General looked at him for a long moment without replying. Sergeant Skittle limped painfully up, saluted, and reported, "Ready to resume march, Sir! But twenty of us must rest for a day or so, and will follow you later."

"So be it!" sighed the elderly leader, rising stiffly.

He helped Ben rise, also, looking at the lad steadily,.

"The mutiny is led by a *woman*," he said in a whisper. "A *woman*! Can you believe that?"

"I've no trouble believing that," said Ben. "So?"

"She's my very own granddaughter, young Garran!" the old man sobbed, deep hurt as well as anger behind his tears.

"A twig sprouted from the tough, old trunk, then," said

Ben, smiling. "What can you expect, sir? She drank your courage and habits of command with her mother's milk!"

"Perhaps . . ." the other said in sour surprise. "Hadn't thought of it in those terms. But I was *chosen* . . ."

"By good King Whatever-his-name-was, the one slain at Last Battle? That was two centuries a-back! Things change! Doesn't everyone, even a fairy, grow older and change over time?"

"But . . . but . . . !"

"And what will you do, when you get home? Confront your granddaughter? Accuse her of treason? Hang her from a gallows . . . providing you can find a tree tall enough for gallows in this waste? A girl . . . and your own kith and kin, at that!"

"How can I do otherwise?" the General choked. "Duty is duty! She has mutinied against authority. Authority direct from the King!"

"Came from your King, perhaps, but gone nowhere at all ever since," said Ben stoutly, but still so softly the nearby men could not hear.

The General angrily drew himself up straight, threw out his thin, old chest, and balled his fists.

"If you were of our Band, sirrah, I'd have *you* put in irons for insubordination! Treasonous utterances!"

But he, also, kept his voice low.

"Now, boy, if you're going with me, fall in line and march. Or go back to your Queen-mother and Prince-father! This is Man's work and I intend to do it! I have decided!"

"I'll go along. Maybe I can talk some sense into you, Grandfather!" Ben retorted, showing a bit of anger himself. "Stubborn old mule! Lead on!"

"They stopped awhile here," Marbleheart announced after scouting along the shore at the mouth of the river.

"Marched west along the shore, I see," agreed Thornwood.

"Hello! Who's that?" Myrn cried out, pointing.

A bedraggled group, a score of men, some with grey beards, some very young, and some supporting their blistered, ravaged feet by leaning heavily on each other's shoulders, straggled from behind a large, flat rock down the shore a bit. They limped forward, painfully and slowly, waving a white rag tied to a pike-shaft.

"Mercy! Mercy, powerful Wizards!" they cried piteously as they came.

"Poor things!" wailed Myrn, dashing forward. "You're all but done in by your morning's dash! Douglas . . . *Douglas*! Come help me tend these poor unfortunates! They've bleeding blisters and black bruises and sadly weary legs and running eyes!"

She quickly gathered the stragglers under the shade of her cloudlet and began selecting those who were hurt worst for immediate washing, bandaging, and giving of fresh cool water, and sound Wizardly advice.

Douglas, Lorianne, and Thornwood, and even Otter and the raven, rushed to help.

"Get 'em out of the sun," recommended Marbleheart, for without Myrn's attention, the cloud overhead began to disperse. "Here! I'll do it!"

He plucked a handkerchief from Douglas's hip pocket and spread it on the ground. As the others moved among the weary soldiers, the Otter muttered Flarman's good old Tenting Spell and the handkerchief grew, spread wide, and was hoisted on sturdy silver poles, forming a wide and airy pavilion under which they all could gather.

"A breezy shower, perhaps?" Marbleheart suggested to the busy Water Adept. "I . . . I . . . never learned any Windcalls, dear Aquamancer. Help me out?"

Myrn paused, made a quick beckoning gesture with her left hand, and spoke a rushing string of soft spelling words.

At once a cool and steady breeze rippled the waters of the salt lake and fluttered the edges of the handkerchief-pavilion cheerfully. Cool rain began to fall.

Myrn returned to bandaging a grey-haired old soldier

whose feet were badly bruised and torn. "Take a drink, sir, and we all would like to bathe in clean water, shortly, wouldn't we?"

"You be a kindly, merciful sprite!" wheezed the soldier. "Much better already, mistress! Thankee! Thankee!"

And he began to weep softly, so exhausted was he . . . and many of his fellow Bandsmen wept, also, in weariness and in gratitude.

Sergeant Skittle, who'd developed painful blisters on both heels and one big toe, had been able to go on no longer, much as he hated deserting his General, and so elected himself spokesman of the stragglers.

"We offer complete surrender to you, Wizards," he said, after his poor feet had been bathed and bandaged and his body made comfortable in the shade of the pavilion. "We could go no single step further!"

"Surrender, my dear sir?" cried Douglas cheerily. "We're friends and rescuers! When you all are ready to walk again, maybe as early as tomorrow morning, we'll go on after your General and see what's going on, up ahead. Meanwhile, rest and allow your heels to heal. A bit of my Myrn's magic'll help your recovery, I assure you. Rest a bit!"

"What were you rushing off to, anyway?" asked Marbleheart, handing the sergeant a cup of clear, cold water transported from the Old Fairy Well at home. "Left your gear and ran off into such a dreary, dry, fearsome place!"

"I'll try to explain," said Skittle, sniffing mightily.

And he told the rescuers of the word about revolt the General had received early that morning.

"Now listen to me, all!" shouted Douglas, waving his hands for silence.

The Bandsmen had settled down in the relative comfort of the wide pavilion and showed themselves prepared to listen to the young Pyromancer.

"I plan to go on to Permanent Camp, as you call it . . . but my goodwife will stay with you here. Shortly there'll be a good supper for all, and you're to rest easy until you can walk the rest of the way home, tomorrow morning. Understand?"

"We understand, Fire Wizard!" many replied.

"Marbleheart, go with me. Myrn, my dear, I must leave you in charge of these unfortunates."

"I'll go with you, Douglas," volunteered Thornwood.

"I shall stay with Myrn and help," decided Lorianne.

The raven Forrest added, "It gets very cold here when the sun goes down. Some of these men are very ill. Cold night airs can prove as fatal as midday heat, if they're left unattended, I fear. I'll stay with Mistress Myrn."

"Good bird," Douglas said with a firm nod. "How far then, Sergeant?"

"A short walk, if one could walk," said Skittle pointing to the west. "An hour's march . . . maybe two. I'll come with you, sir Wizard . . ."

"No, come tomorrow when your blisters've healed," Douglas told the sergeant. "This will be work for a Wizard and his Familiar, not weary, sick soldiers, no matter how well intended."

"We'll follow them as soon as we can," Myrn promised. "Be careful, Douglas! The Band may be deeply divided between General and his granddaughter who's revolted, Master Skittle says."

"I'll be careful, never fear, my very dearest!" Douglas gave her a firm hug and encouraging kiss. "Hurry to catch up, when your charges are able to walk. Come on, Marbleheart! Thornwood! We must try to make this march before full darkness."

"Not much hope there," Marbleheart grunted. "Darkness comes fast in such a place as this. Only an hour hence, at most. We'd better fly, Master!"

"I think we'd better walk, for now. Others may have

fallen by the wayside and need our help. Best to get started, Thornwood! Rain's easing off, at least.''

The companions followed the wide trace left by Bewildered Band which, they found, wisely followed the firmer wet sand at the waterline, where walking was easiest.

A half-hour after they'd started out, Marbleheart found a huddle of a dozen exhausted, thirsty, hurting, and sunblasted Bandsmen crowded in the narrow bit of shade beneath a low sand dune.

Douglas plucked canteens of water from the thin air, and gave them kindly words of instruction to wait until dark and then move back to the pavilion at the mouth of the river.

"There'll be supper, medicines, and fresh bandages there for you,'' he told them.

"Thankee, sir! Thank you, Fire Wizard! Your water bottles are life-savers!'' they called as Douglas's party moved off again, westward along the shore.

"How many Parambit, do you figure, altogether?'' Thornwood wondered aloud as they trudged along. Marbleheart tried to swim in the lake, but pronounced its waters too bitter of taste and too harsh on his tender skin.

"Hard to say. There were two hundred Men and a dozen or so officers in Bewildered Band, night before last. I counted 'em several times,'' replied the Otter.

"At least three or four times that many at this Permanent Camp,'' Douglas guessed, "since there are women and children too.''

"But where did their womenfolk come from, I wonder?'' the Otter asked. "I thought only men fought Last Battle.''

"Not so!'' cried Thornwood. "Queen Marget led a troop of Faerie Ride bowmen herself. Slew her share of Darkness followers with her terrible longbow, I've heard! Not a few of the old armies brought their women along to cook, and tend their sick and injured also.''

"So these people have been lost, wandering about here

for over two hundred years, looking for their homeland?''
Marbleheart asked.

"So it would seem. We'll find out shortly," the Pyromancer told him. "See . . . smoke rising in the air over that
tall dune! We're close!"

Night fell suddenly after a brief twilight. Otter took the
lead, for his eyes were far more night-sharp than those of
the two Men. All fell silent and walked softly in single file.

"I would think," whispered Marbleheart, pausing to let
the others catch up to him under a thorny desert bush,
"that, being experienced soldiers, they'd post guards?"

"Keep an eye out for their outposts, then," advised
Thornwood, nodding.

Marbleheart *gallumped* ahead again, moving as silently
as the little thatchmouse lad raiding the High's pantry.
Shortly he indicated with gestures that he'd located a darkened outpost ahead on the side of the great dune. He led
them in a wide circle to avoid being challenged, although
it seemed unmanned.

"If we're spotted, or when we come at last to the camp,
let *me* do the talking, fellows!" Douglas murmured.

"You're welcome to the task," whispered the Duke.

"Granddaughter!" snarled the General. "At risk to discipline and good order, I offer you amnesty for this wicked,
wretched, perverse mutiny. Step aside and let me do my
assigned tasks, young lady, and nothing more will be said
of it."

"No, Grandpapa!" cried the pleasant-looking young
woman across the fire. "*Someone* needs to put us on a
sensible course and stop this marching forever in circles!
It's me who will do it, or die trying, Sir!"

"Granddaughter!" repeated the General, gesturing in
supplication. "Garran! Don't make me do what's dictated
by our law. Treason! Insubordination, at the very least!"

"Oh, poor, dear Grandpapa! Wake from your long round

of bad dreams, I beg you! Consider the facts! For two hundred years and more . . ."

"Don't try to teach your grandsire history, girl! I was given charge of Parambit by our late Lord King Paradone. I am General! I . . ."

"You miss the real point, old fool," cried a large, rather florid woman in the forefront of the crowd. "To lead you have to have followers! You've no longer got any to follow you! We'll follow only our newly elected leader—Garran!"

"Oh, is that so?" shouted the General. "*Here!* You soldiers! Forward and arrest the leaders of this . . . this . . . conspiracy! *Now!*"

"But, Sir!" objected his second-in-command, a middle-years colonel named Briale. "Which are revolting and who remain loyal?"

"Arrest them *all*, dammit!" shrilled the General. "Sort 'em out later."

"Now, but . . . *Sir*," whispered Briale. "That's my very own wife, just spoke up to you! She's angry and standing beside your Garran! Arrest my own wife? *Sir!*"

"Take this mewing rabbit under close arrest, Sergeant Skittle!" snapped the General, forgetting his faithful sergeant had been left behind. "And the rest of you . . . follow me! Mothers, wives, or granddaughters, they all be mutineers and deserve . . . deserve . . ."

"Deserve a fair trial, as we always have done for anyone accused of any sort of crime," insisted Garran stoutly, refusing to give ground. "Come ahead, Bandsmen! Arrest us and find a fair jury to *hear*, let alone *convict* us of treason!"

The General gave a wild cry and rushed around the fire, reaching for Garran with outstretched hands.

An older woman stepped between them.

"Hold up, there, Papa!" she screamed in a piercing voice. "Lay a violent hand on our daughter and I'll . . . I'll . . . !"

"Moira!" choked the General, stopping his rush just

short of his own daughter, Garran's mother. "Blast it, Moira! Step aside! The girl's in revolt! I'm duty-bound to arrest her, set her in irons, and bring her to trial . . ."

"Then arrest me also, Papa!" cried Moira defiantly. "For I am in revolt, too, and just as guilty of treason as she . . . and everyone here, young or old!"

The General stared at his daughter and granddaughter, stricken, unable to speak or move.

A youthful corporal, one of the few soldiers who'd thought to bring his sword, stepped up beside the General and laid his hand on the old man's forearm.

"Sir!" he said. "Sir?"

"What is it, child?"

"Sir, if this thing you order is to be done without hurt . . . hurt to brothers and sisters and parents . . . we must do it calmly and properly!"

The General took several deep breaths, unspeaking but furiously thinking.

"Your name, Corporal?" he asked. "Oh, yes . . . Dontal, grandson of old Skittle. I remember you. Good soldier, as is your grandfather. Where is he, I wonder? I gave him an order!"

"He stayed with the wounded at the river's mouth, you'll please recall, General. Bloody blisters, and scratches and cuts and . . ."

"I remember! Well, I hereby promote you to Master Sergeant, young Dontal, in your grandfather's place. Take a squad and round up these women who are in defiance of the king's law."

Dontal shook his head and whispered hoarsely, "Sir! We're *outnumbered*, when it comes to that. And many of our men may refuse to seize the mutineers. Who can blame them? Could *you* bind fast your own mother, or your sister?"

A new voice interrupted before the General could reply.

"Consider, dear General, that not just the *womenfolk* stand accused of mutiny! We men and boys agree with

Mistress Garran. She was freely chosen as our spokesman
in this matter. Look around you, sir! Everyone here agrees
that we must stop our unending, senseless marching about.
We need to find, elect, select a ruler . . . other than a
soldier-boy carrying out the temporary orders of a long-
dead king.''

"You, too, Ballel!" General choked.

"Not just old Ballel, but all of us, here and behind you,
General. Arrest our leaders, including me, and bring us to
trial. We'll trust out fate to the knowledge and wisdom of
our fellows!"

He held out his wrists.

"Bind me! Bind us all! And let the trial begin!"

Thornwood and Douglas lay under the fringe of low, dry
scrub along the top of the great dune overlooking Permanent Camp.

Stretching a half-mile along the beach and almost as deep
inland on the coarse sand, Permanent Camp was neatly arranged, sun-bleached tents in rows and ranks, each with
perhaps a quarter-acre of land. Each family had made an
attempt to grow vegetables and even some flowers beside
their tent home.

It was obvious to Douglas that this had only been done
with a great deal of backbreaking labor, for the lake water
was much too saline. Fresh water would have to have been
carried by hand from the low hills to the north and west.

"Either that, or collect rainwater. Probably both," he
decided.

"It doesn't look like it rains around here much," the
Duke sniffed. "You'd think these people would've moved
to the northeast, where there's plenty of rain and a deep
river!"

Douglas nodded wordlessly. While the Duke watched
their rear, the Pyromancer strained his Wizardly senses to
hear what was being said below them in a large square in
the center of the tent city. A crowd had gathered to meet

the homecoming soldiers. From the dune-top they could hear the angry murmur.

Suddenly it became a louder uproar, men and women shouting and waving their arms about wildly.

"The girl, General's granddaughter, has surrendered to the soldiers," the Pyromancer relayed softly to his companion. "She's to be tried for mutiny or treason!"

"Surrendered! Only thing to do, under the circumstances, I suppose," muttered the young Duke. "What'll *we* do, Douglas? I don't think any of the outposts are manned, if that's any help."

"Nobody's going to get hurt, unless I'm completely wrong. Better if they can work it out for themselves!"

Thornwood wriggled about to face the village of tattered, bleached, patched tents and the fire built in the middle of the square. Several hundred people, men, women and children, soldiers and civilians, milled about the fire but left a wide empty space in front of the man known as General, his granddaughter, and another, a middle-aged man.

The young woman and the man had their hands bound before them . . . more symbolic than actual, Douglas realized, for the ropes were quite loose.

There came the soft sound of a sand-slithering Otter, and Marbleheart appeared under the cover of the low creosote bushes.

"They're quiet, now," he reported. "Cooler heads and all that. Did you hear, Master?"

"Most of it. How will this trial work, I wonder? I gather General will be judge?"

"That's as I understand it, from where I lay listening."

"And then all bloody fury will burst," growled Thornwood. "We've got to get in a word at this trial, Douglas, and keep things from falling completely apart."

The Pyromancer agreed with a slow nod.

"At the right time!"

■   ■   ■

"My soldiers haven't eaten since last evening," the General said. "And you people, especially the children, need supper and a good night's sleep. Court will convene after morning chores. You are prisoner, girl! You'll spend the night in your mother's care. Moira will be responsible for you. No arguments! I have decided! Ballel will be held in his own tent. Master Sergeant Dontal will post a guard on you both."

Dontal paled but said nothing other than "Yes, Sir!"

"Not necessary," said Ballel, shaking his head. "Let the Bandsmen get their rest. They're dead on their feet!"

"Let me worry about military details," snapped the General. "Post a trusted guard, Master Sergeant."

"Yes, Sir," the young man repeated, unhappily. "Come away, Master Ballel, Sir. Might as well get some rest!"

Dontal sent four very weary Bandsmen to reman the outpost on the eastern slope of the great dune They were met by Douglas and Thornwood. The young soldiers drew their short swords, cursed angrily, and rushed the intruders.

"Now, now, and now!" Douglas said, holding up both hands. "We've decided to hold your post this night, soldiers. You need your rest more than your General needs your watching."

He made an encircling gesture. The charging soldiers stopped in their tracks, lowering their blades.

"Some mistake, I guess," said the Corporal of the Guard, saluting Douglas and then the Duke of Dukedom. "Yes, we could use rest, I vow! Well, then . . . good watch! Call if there's trouble . . . but who would expect trouble here on the dune? Good night!"

And he and his three yawning, stumbling fellows slid down the west dune-side, headed for their homes, suppers, beds, and families.

"Marbleheart, go ask Myrn to bring the others up in the morning, if she can. Thornwood and I'll watch here," said

Douglas to his Familiar. "Might as well catch some sleep also."

Marbleheart nodded and disappeared in the gathering darkness.

"Good night, Sir Duke!" said the Pyromancer, wriggling his hips into the soft, dry sand to make a comfortable place to lie.

"Good night, Sir Wizard!" chuckled Thornwood.

In three minutes he was asleep, dreaming of the pretty Lorianne. In his dream they walked hand in hand on the pebbly Westongue strand. The sun was rising behind them, and Thornwood was calling out the names of the dozens of ships lying in the roadstead or moored at the long docks.

"There's one I don't know," he said, pointing at a schooner sailing away toward the horizon.

"I know her well," said his dream-Lorianne, sadly. "Her name is *Peachpit*."

"Strange name!" laughed the dream-Thornwood. "And that one? Tacking toward us? Who is *she*, pray tell?"

Lorianne frowned, shading her eyes with her free hand.

"I . . . I . . . d-d-d-don't know!" she said, and she began to weep.

Chapter Twenty-one

Trial and Error

THORNWOOD awoke. It was already full day and getting hot very quickly, especially as the early sun was shining directly into the guard post where he and Douglas had slept.

Beside him was a basket of hot sweet rolls, a carafe of strong, black coffee, a canister of sugar, a bottle of heavy cream, and a hastily scribbled note saying:

"We're at the top of the ridge, above. When you've broken your fast, come up and watch the trial!"

. . . signed with the Otter's smudged paw-mark.

Thornwood quickly ate the sweet rolls and drank the excellent coffee, then climbed to the top of the sand dune, where he found Douglas sitting in a shallow trench under a windblown eucalyptus tree, studying the tent city below through a pair of brass-bound binoculars. The Pyromancer snapped a second pair from thin air and handed them to his friend without looking up.

"We'll watch and listen," he said. "They've just

brought young Mistress Garran from her tent.''

Thornwood knelt beside Douglas and fiddled with the focus knob of the binoculars. He was more accustomed to a Seaman's simple spyglass, but then he found the Wizard's instrument not only brought him a closer, clearer view of the scene below, but perfect far-hearing as well.

''Where's the Otter?'' he asked, managing at last to bring the figure and face of the Parambit's prisoners into view.

''Went to have a closer look,'' Douglas answered. ''Otter can stroll through a pack of ravening wolves and not be noticed when it suits him!''

''I wanted to thank him for breakfast. Who's the older man with the girl? She's General's granddaughter, you say? And have you seen this General, himself, yet?''

''The middle-aged gent with his hands tied? Marbleheart says he's called Ballel. Accused, along with Mistress Garran, of high treason, I gather,'' Douglas replied. ''He'll stand trial with her. Soon as rascally General appears.''

''Interesting legal question,'' Thornwood muttered. ''Can you commit treason against your Kingdom if your King's been dead for two centuries?''

''Don't know,'' Douglas shrugged. ''We'll see now, for here's our General.''

The dour old warrior, attired in a neat red-and-tan military-style outfit and a tall, plumed helmet, marched slowly and with high dignity across the open square from his tent, looking neither left nor right. The solemn effect and the colors of pageantry were somewhat dimmed by lowering clouds and intermittent spits of rain.

There came a distant rumble of thunder.

The Parambit sat or stood silently about a great empty square surrounding the accused.

''Hear, now, all ye Parambit!'' a young officer shouted. ''Hear your General! A Court Martial of certain persons accused of high treason is hereby convened, pursuant to orders of General, here serving as Lord High Justice!

"Draw near and listen well, all ye Parambit, so all may speak to the justice of the proceeding!" he finished, bowing with a flourish to the crowd and then again to the General.

There followed a quarter-hour of solemn preliminaries, beginning with the bringing forth, by three soldiers of the Bewildered Band, of the formal Chair of Justice. There was a long pause while several women rushed to get dust cloths and damp rags to clean the ancient artifact. It was covered with thick, greasy dust, ugly smudges, and two centuries' accumulation of chicken feathers and mouse dung.

When the Chair was clean to the General's satisfaction, he took his place upon it, nodding to a drummer to beat a long, loud roll.

The trial began.

The accused were named and the charges against them were recited by the elderly sergeant at arms, who stumbled over the longer words but made it through to the end at last.

The General nodded, and spoke slowly and clearly to the accused.

"You understand the nature of your crime?"

"We understand the nature of the crime *of which we are accused*, yes," answered Ballel.

"And you, granddaughter? Do you understand the nature . . . ?"

"I understand!" said Garran firmly.

"And do you Ballel, and do you Garran, standing accused of this crime of treason against your monarch, plead, each or both, guilty? Or not guilty?"

Both prisoners stated clearly they were not guilty.

"Bailiff, remove their shackles," the old man ordered.

No one moved for a moment, but then the sergeant at arms shuffled forward and removed the loose ropes from the prisoners' wrists.

There followed the naming of nine adults . . . six men and three women . . . as jury. Looking unhappy and more than a bit confused, the jurors were led from the crowd to stand apart, beside the Chair of Justice.

"We will hear the testimony of witnesses, beginning with that of Moira, the mother of the accused Garran," announced the General. "Call Mistress Moira forward!"

A middle-aged woman came before him, bowed respectfully, and stood waiting to be sworn.

"Moira, daughter of General," recited the sergeant at arms quickly, "will you testify truly and completely to the events under examination, as you personally saw them and heard them, as regards to the accuseds' words and deeds in that they stand accused of the intention to displace the lawful government of Parambit, appointed by royal authority?"

"Interesting! General's daughter, eh?" murmured Douglas.

Moira swore the oath. The court asked her to describe the actions and discussions begun some days before, during a meeting of all citizens on this very spot.

"My daughter Garran . . ."

"*Prisoner* Garran," prompted the General.

"The *accused,* " Moira amended, "officially raised the matter at the beginning of the Common Assembly. It had long been discussed, as you probably know, but never in Assembly. Garran was elected by the citizens then present to confront you, her grandfather, to explain our concerns and desires, and request your resignation from office in favor of an *elected* civilian leader to carry out the duties which, it was our unanimous opinion and belief, you had ceased to fulfill satisfactorily."

The General leaned forward, grimacing as if in pain, and waited until the murmur of agreement from the crowd had died completely away.

"Moira, daughter! Did you agree with this rebellious action?"

"As a citizen of Parambit, I saw your inaction and pointless marching, Father! The necessity to replace you as *temporary* Head of State, Sir, is clear to all," the witness replied, loudly but less firmly. "As Moira, your loving and respectful daughter, I wept bitterly at the decision, but my tears do not make facts less true. We Parambit . . ."

"Enough!" barked the General harshly. "I call Frawl, son of Brawl."

Moira, openly weeping, backed from the arena.

The General examined three older men and two women about the meeting two days before his return from the north. Each testified gravely of what was said and decided. Some appeared angry. Others were saddened. One of the women began to weep uncontrollably and had to be excused.

Garran, whom all agreed was the prime mover in the decision to ask the General to resign, was called before the Chair of Justice. It was already past noon.

"Before I call for a recess for lunch, granddaughter, I wish you to have a chance to agree with or rebut the testimony of your fellow conspirators."

"Sir!" cried Ballel at that point, "I must respectfully remind the court that the fact, or not, of conspiracy has in no way been proved."

"I will, in courtesy to you, change my choice of words from 'fellow conspirators' to 'fellow accused,' " the General said softly. "Granddaughter? Will you speak?"

"I would rather wait until after lunch, Lord High Justice. My statement will take some time."

"I was hoping you would agree to that," her grandfather sighed wearily. "Court is therefore in recess until after lunch hour! Prisoners are to be re-bound and returned to their places of incarceration . . ."

"Lunch!" said Douglas, lowering his binoculars. "What do you think, Thornwood? How goes it for poor Mistress Garran?"

Thornwood rolled over on his back and closed his tired eyes.

"The whole matter rests, as I see it, on the legal interpretation of General's powers and from whence and whom they came."

"But no one has denied, or even asked if, they came from the King of Parambit shortly before he was slain," said Marbleheart, who had arrived atop the dune to see if there was any lunch forthcoming.

"True! Did Paradone appoint him Leader of the Parambit *forever*? Or just temporarily, as the man Ballel implied, in expectation of the uncertainties of battle?"

"If I were speaking for the defense," Marbleheart considered, "I'd argue the second as true fact. How many times have we all heard Flarman say, 'Good Wizards make terrible Kings'? Good military officers are just as likely to be bad rulers, and General, I submit, ladies and gentlemen of the jury, has fully proved the theory over two centuries!"

"Bravo!" Thornwood cheered softly. "You agree, don't you, Douglas?"

"Oh, I agree . . ." Douglas nodded. "But we have other concerns for the moment. We are about to be captured by seven heavily armed soldiers."

Thornwood and the Sea Otter spun about and found seven sharp spears pointed at them from the lip of their dugout.

"Strangers!" said Master Sergeant Dontal between clenched teeth. "Spies!"

He gestured to the three companions to climb out of the sandy trench while his guard backed cautiously away, keeping spear-points trained.

"Spies?" Douglas said evenly. "Observers, rather, Master Sergeant! Not wishing to disturb the proceedings, of course."

"We'll go down and you can 'observe' from a much closer viewpoint . . . while awaiting your own trial for trespass," Dontal growled. "Walk before us slowly, strangers! Down the dune!"

"Shouldn't we bind them, Corporal?" asked one of his soldiers.

"No need!" Douglas said with a broad smile, clapping his hands together softly twice. "We are honorable people, a Master Pyromancer, a Lord Duke, and a Familiar Sea Otter. You can be at ease about us, can't you?"

"Well, I . . . suppose so," agreed the young Master Sergeant, blinking his eyes three times, fast. "But you must come down into camp with us, at any rate. Not so comfortable up here, and getting beastly hot and thundery!"

"Stay a bit and share our lunch, however," the Pyromancer invited. "There's plenty for all, and it would go to waste if you don't help us eat it!"

Marbleheart ushered the troopers into the dugout, which had the advantage of being somewhat shaded by the low trees and thus cooler, and began pulling sandwiches of sliced roast beef, fried chicken, and spicy sausage, on seeded rye, along with sliced tomatoes, lettuce still fresh with dew, red radishes, and spears of tangy dill pickles from Blue's latest picnic triumph.

He passed them out to the soldiers and to Douglas and Thornwood, saving a good-sized pile for himself. The Bandsmen stuck the butts of their spears into the soft sand and fell to with a will, chatting animatedly of the progress of the trial with their captives all the while.

By the time Dontal's guard escorted them down the face of the dune, slipping and sliding in the loose sand with much good-natured merriment, the atmosphere was very cordial.

"Nothing like a good free lunch and a few magical passes to turn suspicious enemies into firm friends," Marbleheart whispered quietly to the Duke.

"Wizards are past masters at transforming circumstances, I've always found," Thornwood agreed with a grin.

"I have to take you to my officers," worried Dontal as they entered the camp.

"Don't see why not. Can they get us good seats at the

trial, do you think?'' Douglas asked. ''Incidentally, you'd best send men back to the east side of the dune. The poor soldiers left behind at the river mouth yesterday are approaching and should be here in a few minutes. My goodwife is with them.''

Dontal gave orders for the stragglers to be met and then found his own officer who, in turn, spoke of their arrival with the General, just finishing lunch in his tent, accompanied only by Ben.

''Not time to antagonize powerful strangers,'' the General decided. ''Give them seats. Offer them food and drink. Tell them I'll speak to them this evening, after this trial business is finished.''

''*No!*'' cried Ben. ''It's Douglas and Thornwood, the Duke of Dukedom! Good friends and always welcome guests, Grandfather!''

''Still, our business is *our* business, and very, very serious. Tell them I greet them and will speak to them later, please, Prince of Faerie.''

And he would say nothing more but prepared to resume the Chair of Justice.

''Our argument,'' said Ballel, who spoke first for the defense, ''is that the people of Parambit met in legal Common Assembly and took certain decisions on matters concerning all the nation. No treasonous purpose was proposed nor implied, Honored Lord Justice! We agreed we needed a new course toward regaining our lost homeland. We believe new leadership is necessary, in view of your own efforts, which have proved unsuccessful, and in consideration of your age, which is considerable. A new, younger leader is the common desire, much as we love and respect our General.''

''The fact remains,'' said the old man in the Chair of Justice, ''that His Majesty King Paradone, himself, gave me the responsibility of leading Parambit, in the case of his death or capture in battle. His action was in keeping with traditions and laws long ago established by the Kings of Parambit. I was made Leader. I was then and am still your Leader! I was to lead until relieved by death or by decision of our sovereign!''

"I remind Your Worship that I was there, standing no further away from you than I am now, Sir. I heard our late King bestow on you the authority to lead us. I heard his words . . . and understood his intention!''

"I know you were there,'' the General said testily. "Which is why I can't understand why you oppose me in this matter!''

"Listen, then, to what our late King said on that, the last day of his life.''

The spectators, who had been hanging on every word since early morning, edged forward. The story was as familiar to each of them as their own names.

"You and the other officers of Parambit stood under an ancient magnolia tree on the bank of what came to be known as Bloody Brook. It was just dawn. We had eaten a light, cold repast, and were buckling on our armor and taking up our weapons,'' Ballel said slowly. "There are at least fifteen others remaining of the older men who were there, and they remember it well. All of us remember hearing our King's exact words and understood his intention.''

"I grant you all that, Ballel, but . . .''

"Listen!'' the other insisted. "King Paradone laid his left hand on your right shoulder. He said: 'If anything happens to me, good friends, I wish this man to carry on in my stead until this matter is finally decided between us and Darkness. He is your Leader after me! Do you all agree to serve him as you would serve me?' ''

Ballel paused and bowed his head, moved deeply by the memory. Many of his listeners were also so affected, including Douglas and his companions, seated near the Chair of Justice.

"He said, again, '*Lead in my place, until Darkness and*

Darkness's Minions are broken and driven from this land!'
Those were his very words.''

General was bowed double by the memory of that long-ago morning and that terrible day. Tears streaked his cheeks, and he could only nod at first.

Then he croaked, ''I recall his words. Ballel, old comrades, friends! I did not seek the honor nor the heavy duty! I've followed his orders, then and ever since!''

''I submit,'' said Ballel very quietly, ''his orders, given in such circumstances, included these words to you: *'If I die, and the Light yet wins this battle, lead my people back to our homeland, and see them safely there.'*''

''He did say that, word for word,'' admitted the General, with a deep sigh. ''But . . .''

''But you have never carried out the last part of his order. We Parambit have not been returned to our homeland!'' Ballel continued, almost in a whisper. ''I regret to say, old friend . . . you *have* failed our King! Failed us! The time has come to choose a new leader!''

The General slumped back in the Chair of Justice and raised his hands to his eyes, wiping away bitter tears.

''You're very old, my dear Sir. Less able, if no less willing, to lead us in battle or on long marches than you once were. As your lifelong friend . . . I greatly regret it . . . but you *must* step down and allow a new generation to assume the burdens. To find our homeland! You *must*!''

''I *cannot*! I . . . I . . . have done my best! In time, we *will* return to our homeland, friends. I promise you!''

There was a great, mournful silence, except for the sounds of soft sobbing. The rain, which had held off since dawn, began to fall as softly as tears, drumming on the tents and tapping insistently into the packed sand underfoot.

Into the stillness dropped a clear, new voice.

''May I approach the Chair of Justice as a friend of the court, Lord Chief Justice?''

''You are Douglas Brightglade, the younger Pyromancer

of Wizards' High in Dukedom, are you?'' the General asked sharply. ''Or so you claim.''

''I vouch for Douglas Brightglade!'' cried Ben, stepping forward. ''I've been a guest in his home and have met his goodwife, the Lady Aquamancer Myrn, and his teacher, the famous Flarman Flowerstalk. And Douglas is close friend to my parents, Queen Marget and Prince Aedh of Faerie! This *is* Pyromancer Douglas Brightglade, as he says he is!''

''I . . . I . . .'' stuttered the General. ''I cannot deny you, Prince Flowerbender! He is who he says he is!''

''Thank you, Sir General! How are you, Ben? Marbleheart is about, somewhere. And yonder, over the dune, come the Bandsmen left behind as too weary or too hurt to travel yesterday. They are accompanied by Aquamancer Myrn Manstar Brightglade, my beautiful and capable goodwife. Shall we wait until they join us?''

Over the southern shoulder of the great dune came the stragglers. The raven Forrest circled overhead, cawing excitedly, in the warm rain.

''Welcome all!'' cried the General, although he sounded very weary. ''Important guests! Welcome to the men of our Band, also.''

The Parambit rushed to embrace the stragglers and call them by name and pat them on their backs in relieved greeting, chattering a mile a minute about the morning's doings here at Permanent Camp.

Myrn and Lorianne came up smiling, despite the rain, to Douglas and Thornwood, giving them embraces and kisses before turning to be introduced to the General.

''Please take chairs, and as soon as this matter of high treason is decided, we'll go to my tent and dry ourselves.''

''The rain's just fine,'' laughed Myrn. ''However, if it bothers you, Sir, I can arrange for it to stop.''

And to everyone's delight and amazement it not only stopped drizzling at her signal, but the clouds parted, the sun shone through, and a cool, salt-smelling breeze began to blow from across the open lake.

In no time at all the standing water had disappeared into the sand underfoot and the Parambit, at the General's order, resumed their seats about the open square before the Chair.

"You say you know something of this matter, although I'm inclined to point out that this is . . . well . . . a private matter among us Parambit, my dear Wizard," said the General, sounding rather pompous while attempting to sound cordial.

"It occurs to me," said Douglas when all had fallen silent around him, "that you in your deliberations are not aware of a single very important fact."

"If this is so and it changes the matter materially," the General conceded. "we must hear it, of course."

Douglas stood and paced slowly to the center of the open space before the Chair.

"At the end of Last Battle in Old Kingdom," he began, "there was no organized, purposeful demobilization of the Forces of Light, of which you Parambit were a small but important part. I wasn't there, but I've learned of it from my Master, Flarman Firemaster, now called Flowerstalk, of Wizards' High. You've heard the stories . . . at least some of them, Thornwood Duke?"

"Many a time, at Sea and about my own hearth," Thornwood nodded. "Confusion was the watchword that day, I've been told, by those who *were* present."

"Confusion, certainly!" agreed the General, also nodding. "Terrible, horrifying, fearsome panic, with people running headlong from the field. But Darkness had, some shouted, retreated to the Far North, never to return!"

"So it's said," agreed the young Pyromancer. "I do warn you, however, that Darkness still exists, and ever must be guarded against! However, more to the point . . . virtually everyone in the Forces of Light, including you, General, and your soldiers, fled as far and as fast as possible, once the fighting was over and the dead buried in long, stark barrows on the edge of Battle Plain. I've been there, and seen them."

"I've seen those terrible mounds, also," barked Marbleheart, who'd appeared from his vantage place under a tent in time to hear Douglas's story. "Terrible, and yet beautiful, they are."

A shudder ran down his sleek back and he fell silent, remembering.

"So it was, and nobody should be ashamed, for the fight had been bloody in the extreme, the slaughter horrendous, and Light was never certain of victory," added Thornwood.

Douglas nodded.

"Flarman, who'd lived in the Olden Days on the wide western plains of Old Kingdom, fled east to Dukedom, where he hid and began to rebuild his exhausted powers and skills."

"And my Master Augurian fled to Waterand Island," Myrn remembered, "where he lives to this day, far across Warm Sea. And a lady Geomancer named Lithold Stonebreaker disappeared into the mountains in the middle of Serecomba Desert, south of Choin."

"And we Parambit fled in the direction of our homeland," said Ballel. "Following General. But *we never got there*! We've been wandering in circles, ever since!"

Douglas raised his hand to still the conversations that sprang up everywhere. "Other Light Forces found their way somewhere, to their homes or to safe havens. And they remembered and were remembered."

"But we . . ." began the General.

"But some became lost and never found their way to hearth and home," Douglas continued. "Some became mysteriously enchanted! I've devoted much of my life to finding these lost or enchanted persons, tribes, and nations. In fact, it's the prime purpose of the renewed Fellowship of Light. We Wizards seek to repair some of the damage brought on during the long aftermath . . ."

"This aftermath," said the General, leaning far forward, "was the result of Darkness's terrible spellings and enchantments!"

"Well, sir, as a matter of fact . . . no! Darkness was so badly hurt at Last Battle it was eager only to hide and lick its wounds!" Douglas said with a solemn nod. "The damage done to Parambit after Last Battle was *not* the result of Darkness hate and fear. It was the doing of one battle-crazed Wizard . . . an Aeromancer named Frigeon."

"I've never heard of that one . . . or have I?" gasped the General. "The name is strangely familiar!"

"You were magically forced to forget him," Myrn explained. "The difficult and important work the Fellowship of Light has undertaken has largely been as a result not of Darkness's evil, but that of Frigeon, the Ice King!"

"I seem to recall . . ." began the General, but he fell silent, sitting back and turning his attention inward on old half-memories.

"Recently a certain piece of crystal was found . . . a sort of lens. It was engraved about its edge with a strange Elvish rigamarole which we never quite understood. It refers to one of Frigeon's earliest and most wicked spellings."

He rummaged in his left sleeve and produced a cloth-wrapped packet. He unwound the soft, grey cloth and held up the mysterious lens.

"When any powerful spell is cast, the balance of magic requires an *anti-spell*. If I don't entirely miss my guess, this artifact is the key to stripping away the enchantment forced upon the Parambit!"

The crowd gasped and cried out in wonder and, it must be admitted, in some fear. The sun caught the lens, and it flashed like fire in the Pyromancer's hand.

"How does it work?" asked Marbleheart. "And what does the writing say, eh? A mystery to me, Douglas!"

The Pyromancer waited for the tumult to subside.

"The Old Elvish words engraved here say:

"My Power is to look closely from afar, over the left shoulder of the hill, in the darkest part of day, to find

*a Princess-daughter seeking her King-father's Crown
and to save her people.''*

"As the good Otter says," Thornwood was the first to
say, "it still makes no sense. What do *you* make of it,
Wizard?"

"The answer came to me last night as we lay, up there
on the dune," Douglas told him. "The great sand dune
slopes both to north and south, very much like shoulders.
You see? And when at dawn I looked over the left side . . .
the southern shoulder . . . through the glass, I saw the
Princess-daughter who was stolen from Parambit, shortly
after your King died in battle."

Uproar, followed by urgent *shushing*.

"The little Princess is just a tiny, newborn babe! Who
stole her?" a woman cried. "I was her nursemaïd, and one
morning her cradle was empty! The grief of her husband's
death had already weakened the Queen's will to live and
the loss of the child drove her to her death!"

"Where is she?" the General cried, leaving the Chair of
Justice to rush to Douglas's side. "If she yet lives, *she* is
the true monarch of Parambit, and I am relieved of my
duties! Where is she? *Did she survive?*"

Chapter Twenty-two

Lost Princess Found

"NO need to drag this out," said Douglas. "You have but to stand on the right shoulder of the dune, up above, just at sunset, the other 'darkest part of day.' And look through the lens. It'll show your missing Princess, at once."

He turned to the General.

"Will you truly step down for your Princess?" he asked softly. "Just as King Paradone wished, as I'm sure you'll agree."

"Of course!" cried the old soldier. "Of course! I'd prefer to turn Parambit over to Her Majesty in better shape. Don't you think she'll need my assistance? She's just a tiny baby, after all."

"We'll talk more of that, once her enchantment is broken," Douglas promised. "For now, everyone stay here with Myrn while General and I climb the dune to look through the lens as the sun goes down."

"Shouldn't we come along?" asked Thornwood, who'd forgotten to drop Lorianne's hand since her arrival.

"No, stay behind, please! Come and look with me, General. Marbleheart? I'll need your help. And let's ask the elder who was accused of treason to come, also, as witness. Ballel, isn't it? You can speak and see for all the citizens, I take it? Agreed!''

He slipped the lens back into his sleeve, took the General by the arm, and, followed by the Otter and Ballel, they passed through the encampment and began to climb the steep, slippery sand slope, angling toward the south, to the dune's shoulder.

The Parambit stood gazing after them, their faces cycling from fear, to excited anticipation, to wonder, to confusion, to sudden hope.

Almost an hour later, after complete darkness had fallen, the climbers returned, sliding down the face of the dune. Torches had been lit and raised on poles around the square where the Parambit waited.

Douglas raised his arms, and the crowd fell silent.

"We've begun the process, at least," Douglas announced. "It takes only one more act to complete the whole disenchantment, which proved to be rather extensive. Will you do the honors, General? You've served your late King well, despite enormous obstacles, and are worthy of your people's honor and gratitude!"

The General stood forward, his head bowed, and his face lined, and his fine uniform grey from the climb up and down the dune.

Then he looked up and smiled . . . something most Parambit hadn't seen for years and years.

"Gentle my people! It's been an inestimable honor to have served you these long, long years . . . and I hope my service has been, on the whole, good and well."

"We never dishonored you, Father," cried his daughter Moira. "What have you seen in the Wizard's glass?"

"We all four looked through the lens. We all saw who it showed. We saw . . ."

He might have paused for dramatic effect, or it might

have been because tears filled his eyes. He choked out his next words.

"We looked . . . and we saw . . . *this* young lady!"

He raised his right arm and pointed straight at the tall, pretty, auburn-haired Seacaptain standing nearby, arm in arm with Thornwood of Dukedom.

"Lady Queen!" gasped young Garran.

"The Princess-child grown to womanhood!" screamed the woman who had been the baby's nurse. "I . . . I . . . recognize her red hair! *Yes!* It *is* she, full grown!"

The General laughed aloud through tears, and nodded, and waited for the tumult to die down.

Beside the handsome Duke of Dukedom the lady Seacaptain stood, stunned and speechless, suntanned face turned as pale as a desert lily.

"Yes, 'tis so! I recognized her in the lens at once, despite her maturity," the General said at last. "In the name of Parambit, of all of us, I proclaim her Lorianne, Princess-daughter of King Paradone and Queen Grace! Our liege and legal monarch, returned to us at last! I say *hail! All hail!*"

The lady Seacaptain's face and neck glowed now bright crimson. She clutched Thornwood's arm and hid her face for a moment upon his broad chest.

"Speak, Majesty!" begged the General. "Your people have waited . . . I don't remember *how* many years . . . not that it matters! Do you remember? Do you accept your birthright?"

Lorianne drew Thornwood's arms tighter about her shoulders but turned slowly to face the laughing, crying, cheering throng.

And she broke into a brilliant smile.

"*Hail!*" shouted Ballel. "I vouch for the vision in the Wizard's lens! This is Laurel Anne, Princess Royal of Parambit! The lost is found!"

He fell to his knees, and the General followed suit, then all the others. Lorianne cried aloud and ran forward to raise them to their feet.

"No need for that, my very dear and faithful!" she sobbed. "How can I let you abase yourselves, when you're the greatest, finest, bravest of heroes! Rather, cheer and shout for General. He's long led and long cherished you so!"

She smiled even more broadly, kissed the old man on both wrinkled cheeks, then hugged and kissed Moira and Garran, and then Ballel, too, while the crowd cheered, shouted, and wept unashamed, and called out her name.

"I remember!" Moira said, speaking breathlessly to Myrn and Douglas. "Terrible mists have been blown away!"

"A very beautiful and sensible sort of ruler, I should say," said Myrn, wiping away her own tears. "You're most fortunate, Princess Lorianne! And the Parambit are most lucky, too!"

"When things settle down to a simple uproar," shrieked Marbleheart in Douglas's right ear, "I hope *someone'll* tell me what all this means. Lorianne . . . a *Queen*? The long-lost baby Princess? Most . . . well, *astounding* is the first word that occurs!"

"Astounding, it certainly is," agreed his Master. "And it was your Questing, Ben, and your Questioning that brought this about. Parambit'll all want to hear the whole story, I'm sure. Maybe we can sit down and have some supper and learn how all this came about."

"Don't you know . . . what happened, I mean?" asked the Otter.

"I can guess what I haven't already learned. And you, goodwife?"

"Let me cry a bit more and then I'll take time to show and tell," sniffed Myrn. "Ben! You and Marbleheart managed to save a *whole nation*! What a splendid Questing!"

She stooped to give the Sea Otter a loving hug, and then put her arms about the Prince of Faerie and kissed him, also. Then she hugged Douglas and Thornwood and Lorianne, and even the General, laughing and crying at the same time with them all.

"Now that we're all comparatively calm," Douglas said much later, "and we've cried and laughed and giggled and cheered to our heart's ease, I'm ready to answer questions."

The General, who had laid aside his dress uniform and donned a simple brown jerkin and trews, and a plain cloak of dun and dark green, rose slowly, to enthusiastic applause.

"I have a great burden of questions, Sir Pyromancer," he said, when he could be heard. "May I begin?"

"Of course, General. I'll try to answer them all!"

"First, however, I wish it to be known that, with appropriate ceremony, I shall resign my commission and become . . . whatever retired soldiers become when they lay down heavy responsibilities."

"Dearest General," cried Lorianne, who was sitting at the head of the great table that Myrn had conjured in the square so that all could sit and enjoy the rain-cooled evening air. "I really *do* wish you would delay your retirement for a bit. I may be good at reefing, tacking, and laying a true course, but as to ruling a kingdom . . . I'll need all the help I can get!"

"My whole being is at your service, Majesty," replied the old man. "I have only one thing to ask . . ."

"Ask it! It's yours!" cried the newfound Queen, beaming at him proudly.

"I wish to be known from now on by the name my dear mother and proud father gave me . . . the one I haven't used, or even *heard,* for over two hundred years . . ."

"Name?" asked Marbleheart in surprise. "I thought 'General' *was* your name!"

"No. Before the war . . . before Last Battle . . . I was known as Pillow. A good name, handed down from father to son in my family for many generations. We were simple farmers, fowlers, and orchardmen. I wish to be known, again, simply as Pillow, son of Pillow, son of Pillow . . . and so on.''

"Pillow it is, then!" cried Marbleheart, laughing and clapping his forepaws gleefully. "A much more comfortable name than General!"

"So I've always secretly thought," Pillow chuckled softly, bowing to the Sea Otter. "Now, as to my questions . . . ?"

"Ask!" Douglas invited.

"It's clearer every moment," Pillow said, stroking his short white beard thoughtfully. "I remember poor Paradone asking me to lead if he perished. I remember his death . . . it was terrible! Wickedly done! He was a great King, a good man, and a brave soldier, too. Some sort of monument should be built . . ."

"It shall be! Although I don't really remember him or my mother, poor, broken-hearted woman, I honor them both beyond words," Lorianne said sadly.

"We fought on Battle Plain that day and the next. It was, and still is, all rather confused and mixed. A courier came, near the end of the third day, from the Fellowship of Wizards. Youngish-old man named . . . what *was* his name? . . . Cribblon, was it?"

"Yes, Cribblon. Frigeon's apprentice," Douglas said with a nod. "Doing well and a Journeyman Aeromancer himself, these days, living in western Old Kingdom."

"This man Cribblon came to me where we lay exhausted from the bloodiest fighting in two days and a night of battle. We'd managed to cross Bloody Brook under cover of darkness that second night. Cribblon told me Darkness had fled the field and his Master . . . ?"

"Frigeon." Douglas supplied the name.

"The Apprentice said we'd nothing further to fear from the terrible foe, but that stray squads of its allies were still in the vicinity seeking revenge. He advised us to withdraw to the south. Weary as we all were, I had to agree."

He thought for a moment. Everyone in the fire-lit square waited in silence.

"We marched south that morning, heading for our Homeland. I remember that well. It was a cool and blustery day, with black thunderheads sweeping across Battle Plain; sharp rain washing away the blood on the grass.

"This Aeromancer, this Frigeon, came to me as I prepared to march with our rear guard. He asked where his Apprentice had gone. To tell you the truth; I'd no idea.

"Frigeon flew into a towering rage! What's the best way I can say it? Insane fury?"

"Not a bad guess, when it came to Frigeon in those days," agreed Thornwood. "Flarman has said Frigeon was driven out of his mind by his fear."

"I was in no mood to take such abuse as he heaped on my Parambit, you can imagine, Aeromancer or not! I'd lost a hundred . . . nay, *two* hundred . . . good, brave men, knights, archers, and pikemen. This furious Wizard *demanded* that we pursue and capture his runaway Apprentice! I refused! I'd promised my men, I told this crazy Air Wizard, I'd lead them home at once. For us the bloody war was over!

"He became blue with an awful, ice-cold fury. He demanded and demanded, but in the end I . . . laughed bitterly at him and told him to get out of our way.

"He puffed himself up and thundered, 'You'll *never* find your way home! *Never! Wander forever! I will* be revenged every day of your poor, confused, lost, forlorn lives. March forever around in circles!'

"And he shot off in a great burst of swirling mist. We never saw him again."

"I see," Myrn thought aloud. "He struck out at you and you were lost, from then on."

"We never could find our right path homeward, nor any memory of the way," Pillow nodded sadly. "We tried again and again and again!"

"He wished to deny the Parambit their rightful leadership, so he whisked you away, Lorianne," Douglas said to the young Queen. "He sent you to the fishermen at Home Port, thinking to lose you among them."

"It's all so strange! But I know it's true," Lorianne said, nodding slowly. "I know somehow I'm the lost Princess, now a Queen, but I still feel very much like Lorianne, my Uncle Braiser's little Lori, or Aunty Phil's baby Lorikins!"

"All of those *are* you," Marbleheart assured her. "You've had a good upbringing among honest, hard-working, loving folk!"

"We must see to it your uncle and aunt learn you're safe, immediately!" said Thornwood softly.

Lorianne nodded earnestly. "Perhaps I should go to them and bring them here to live? I must do something nice for the fisherfolk of Home Port. They were really very good to a little lost child."

Pillow described how the lost Parambit army found their wives, children, and old folk here on the barren shore of the vast salt lake. They named it Lake of Tears and camped there for lack of any place else to go.

"I was certain our beautiful Homeland was somewhere nearby. We looked *everywhere* for it. But every time we set out to look for it, every march ended at the Atamazon. At that point everybody began saying, 'Let's head back, please, General,' and I hadn't the heart to deny them."

"Part of Frigeon's spell, you see," Douglas explained. "It kept you running around in circles!"

"What's next, then?" asked Thornwood.

"Well, now that we've got these good people out of their doldrums, we must find their Homeland once more, so they can resume normal lives," Marbleheart said quickly. "Er . . . how do we do that, Douglas?"

"No great problem for a marvel-working, highly skilled, deeply educated, widely traveled, handsome, mature, sweet-tempered Master Pyromancer," Douglas chuckled.

"Who's that?" laughed Myrn, looking aslant at her husband. "*You?*"

"No! None other than the Fire Master of us all, beloved!"

And he pointed to the great bonfire in the center of the camp square.

"Hello! Nice weather you're having, now the rain has stopped," came Flarman Flowerstalk's cheery voice from the midst of the flames. "I persuaded this ancient Aquamancer to come along, too, you see."

He stepped out of the roaring flames, reaching back to help another figure, shrouded in hot, blue steam. "Hoy, Rainmaker! You forgot to spin the proper Fireproofing Spell. You're about to become a torch!"

The other man beat at his gown's hem where sparks had caught. When the fire threatened to get the better of his skirts, he gestured sharply.

Out of the star-filled night a small, very black cloud charged up, stopped over the Water Adept, and began to rain lustily on him until the blaze was completely drowned.

"Magisters!" cried Douglas and Myrn . . . and Marbleheart, also . . . and all three rushed to greet the newcomers. Someone pressed a dry towel into Augurian's hands, and someone else handed Flarman a plate of barbecued ribs and a brimming mug of beer.

"Welcome," called Lorianne. "I think I know you. You must be Flarman Flowerstalk. And you are Augurian, the famous Water Adept of Waterand Isle! Marbleheart has told me all about you during long nights at Sea. Welcome!"

"Your Majesty," murmured Flarman, bowing so deeply that his sleeves swept the ground and all sorts of foil-wrapped candies and sweetmeats tumbled out. A shouting cloud of Parambit children swooped down on the gifts. It'd been a long time since they'd seen candy!

"We've been watching things going on here," Flarman explained. "Most interesting, and smartly solved . . . so far . . . by the Sea Otter and our former Apprentices."

He was about to kiss the Queen's hand but changed his course in midstream and kissed her cheek instead.

"I feel as though I know you, my dear! Old friends, even though we've never met!"

"Let me introduce you to the Parambit . . . my good people who are standing about wondering who you are to be kissing their Queen. And whether to flee, fight, or dance!"

"Dance! Sing! Celebrate!" Flarman called out to the crowd. "Introduce us, of course, my dear. Hello, Thornwood! What brings you hither? No, tell us later! Prince Flowerbender, your mother's a bit worried about you, but I told her you were fully capable of taking good care of the Sea Otter. Keep him out of trouble!"

"Sleight-of-tongue artist," growled Augurian. Having embraced both Douglas and Myrn, he grinned fondly at Marbleheart and Ben and bowed gracefully to the young Queen and Thornwood Duke. "Be quiet a moment, Flarman, if you ever possibly can! Douglas was about to undo a rather complicated Aeromantic Spell."

"Nonsense," puffed Flarman, sitting down at the head of the table next to Lorianne. "I can do it with the wave of a hand . . . this very hand! Once you smell Frigeon in a spell, it's fairly easy to unravel his wickedness."

"Now that Douglas has done all the hard work," Augurian snorted. "And Myrn, too. I think maybe even you could clean up the odds and ends!"

"*Hah!*" Flarman snorted back, making a face at his best friend. "How about *this*!"

He jumped to his feet, raised both hands, all fingers splayed wide, and shouted.

"*Nona penta rio duo-quatro!* Old Frigeon was a bit of a nut for archaic numerical spellings, you know."

Before anyone could say a word, the sky was rent by a terrific bolt of blue and gold lightning. Ear-splitting thunder crashed and cracked again, causing everyone to jump to his feet or dive under the table.

Augurian, Marbleheart, Douglas, and Myrn, however, sat smiling through the tumult.

The salt lake steamed, boiled, and roiled.

The tall sand dune over the campsite glowed and coruscated with all colors of the rainbow. Then it slumped and slid, making a sound like a great, deep, relieved sigh.

Deep darkness came down in the wake of the lightning, for the campfire and the torches had been snuffed out by a sudden torrential rain that smelled of sulfur.

A dry wind sprang up from the east.

"Sorry, friends," came Flarman's calm voice in the inky blackness. "Just a temporary inconvenience! Can't make powerful magic without a bit of fireworks. Relax! Now . . . *there*! Here's a scene you almost all will recognize. Here's . . . Homeland! *Parambita!*"

They no longer stood in a dusty, sandy, sun-blasted desert camp of ragged, faded tents of old leather and bleached canvas.

Where the steep dune had overloomed the site now stood a graceful, white marble and bright copper palace, with soaring towers and wide domes reaching into the night sky where stars again twinkled and the moon was just rising over the lake.

"Parambita! Homeland!" someone sobbed, unutterable pleasure in her voice.

"Homeland!" echoed the beautiful Queen Lorianne. "Look! Oh! Look, Thornwood, beloved! Even I, stolen from here as a tiny baby, remember this beautiful place!"

"Well, now," sighed Flarman contentedly, wiping his face with a large, red handkerchief. Magic-unmaking is, despite what some people might think, a great deal of hard work. "You'll notice the orange trees are as good as ever? Pillow, here, will have oranges and grapefruits and lemons and such things to harvest, come next January."

"And all the ragged, ratty, old, sagging tents are now comfortable houses, lined neatly along straight, well-paved streets," Marbleheart cried in delight. "And there're all sorts and sizes of green parks, each with deep pools and high fountains! And just look at the beautiful pleasure-boats on the shore!''

He scurried up to Douglas and Myrn, standing with their arms wrapped about each other and laughing.

"The lake!" the Otter shouted. "That blessed old lake!"

"What about the lake, Familiar?" asked Augurian, smiling broadly, for he had sensed the change in the waters also.

"Fresh as a Valley spring rain!" shouted the Sea Otter, jumping up and down. "Not a pinch of salt left in her!"

Dozens of Parambit who heard him ran down to the sandy shore and began scooping up the lake waters in their hands and tasting it, wondering and exclaiming and splashing and even swimming about in it, fully clothed, laughing and giggling hilariously all the while.

"Really quite a pleasant, good-looking place," Douglas approved, giving Myrn another hug. "Fit for a Queen!"

"I think, however, that we'll see her in a less exotic setting, now and again," his goodwife whispered in his ear.

She pointed to where Lorianne was tripping gaily down the broad avenue from the palace foregate to the lakefront, intent on inspecting the wonderful fleet of boats and ships.

Leading a willing Duke of Dukedom by the hand.

"When Frigeon enchanted the Parambit," Flarman explained over a late supper on the terrace of the old-new palace, "he enchanted the lot . . . people, animals, homes, fields, orchards. Quite an undertaking, done on the spot as it was! Queen Lorianne, you'll find that you've several tens of thousands of subjects now, living in your city or farming the countryside, fishing, mining copper . . . all sorts of people, long enchanted as jungle beasts, birds, and even a few rhinos and 'gators!"

"It'll take you a while to get settled in," Myrn advised Lorianne. "But there'll be no more useful helpmeet than Thornwood!"

"He's my choice, it's true," laughed the auburn-haired

Queen, rather dreamily. ''Wonderful, splendid, thoughtful, sweet man!''

''You've decided you're to be married, already, have you?'' Douglas's Familiar asked, popping a hot, frosted almond cake into his mouth.

''It should be obvious, even to a dunderheaded Sea Otter pup from Briny Deep,'' Myrn teased.

''I do believe you're correct,'' yawned Flarman. ''About the 'dunderheaded' part, at least. We should be getting home, don't you think?''

''And sleep in our own bed, once again!'' sighed Myrn, catching his yawning. ''See and hug my children! Oh, my . . . !''

Before she could lift her hand to her mouth to politely cover the next yawn, the Wizards' High party . . . disappeared.

Chapter Twenty-three

≋

Where the Heart Is

IN as neat a bit of mass transport as ever a Wizard had spelled, Flarman distributed all to where they would be happiest and would do the most good.

Augurian, who was concerned about projects he'd sadly neglected of late, found himself standing beside his waterbed in his tower high atop Waterand Palace.

He stripped off his pointed hat, then his best blue robe studded with silver Seashells and Seastars, and kicked off his sandals. After drenching himself in hot, soapy water (a minor spell he used when he'd no time for a slow, luxurious tub), he popped into his bed and, chuckling sleepily to himself, fell at once asleep.

Myrn and Douglas, in the same Pyromantic flash, found themselves sitting on the stone curbing of Old Fairy Well.

"The babies!" Myrn cried, jumping to her feet.

"Nothing to worry about," her husband yawned. "Sound asleep. Flarman brought 'em from my mother's house, just now."

"They were happy and safe at Perthside, I'm sure, but

272

I'm delighted they're home with us!'' their mother exclaimed.

They walked, arms still warmly about each other, toward the wide, double front door of the Wizards' High cottage. Bronze Owl had just settled for the night on his familiar old nail in the center of the right-hand leaf.

''A Fire Wizard and a Water Adept should never have to worry about their children.'' Myrn gave a mother's sort of happy groan.

''Who was worried?''

''*I* was . . . and so were *you*!'' Myrn insisted. ''We'll look in on them, shall we? Just to check!''

''Let 'em sleep,'' Douglas advised. ''They'll be ready for new adventures in the morning.''

''As I suppose we will, also,'' their mother agreed.

''Something's . . . *missing*!''

''What?'' Myrn sighed. ''Everything's just fine, far as I can tell. And I'm enough of a Water Wizard to tell when the sailing's smooth as spider silk.''

''*Too* smooth, I think. Too quiet,'' Douglas insisted. ''What is it we *don't* hear?''

Myrn listened to the silence of the night.

''I don't hear a thing, fussbudget,'' she said, mystified.

''What I *don't* hear is Eunicet blustering about in the cellars. Must be asleep.''

''He should be! It's past two in the morning!''

''What's to do with such as you, wicked, lazy, old scalawag?'' Flarman asked the former, the renegade, the usurping Duke. ''A fully qualified Court of Justice deported you in hopes you wouldn't be able to harm anyone, not even yourself, for a long, long time! What do you do? Turn yourself into a fourth-rate pirate! Shame on you!''

Eunicet shrugged uneasily.

''There was nothing to do on that boring, nasty, little sandspit. Except fight with Bladder, yell at the Seagulls, eat sandy clams on the half-shell, and wonder how long it'd be before the whole place blew away in a hurricane, or was washed away by a tidal wave.''

"Our mistake was putting you alone, anywhere," Flarman considered. "Well, this time we'll not make *that* mistake.''

Eunicet raised his head to stare angrily at the Fire Wizard. "Leave me here to rot? Here! Under your precious High? If there's a way to get out, I'll find it!''

"No, you raise too much rumpus. Toss too many conniptions! I could do a bit of memory-erasing, I suppose. Goes against the grain," Flarman admitted, mostly to himself. "Even your bad, blusterous, bibulous Bladder has 'gone straight,' as old lags say. He's happily banging away at red-hot iron and bashing cold rivets by now.''

"*Ah*," sighed Eunicet wearily. "He was born to low and dirty work. He'll be very happy at blacksmithing, I suppose—as long as someone doesn't offer him an army to bully, a maiden to despoil, or shiny gold to steal.''

The senior Pyromancer threw back his head and laughed. "Don't *you* have any lowly skills to make yourself useful, Eunicet? Now that your false duke-ing and nasty pirating days are over for good and all? Anything at all?''

Eunicet considered the question for a silent moment.

"I can't think of a single thing I'd really want to do, unless it's to make trouble for people like you, Fire-blower. The idea eats at me. Revenge! And don't tell me how bitter revenge can be. Only if vengeance fails is it bitter, *I* say!''

"You're incorrigible!" Flarman snapped angrily. "The question before this meeting is, however, 'What's to do with this worthless, bad-tempered, unrepentant evildoer?' I don't wish to destroy you . . . that's what *you'd* probably do, were the circumstances reversed!''

The former Duke snorted softly, but made no comment.

"True, I *could* whip up some really nasty spells. I could wipe out your memory, as Frigeon did to the poor Parambiters, and make you forget your nasty, selfish, shifty, old ways!''

"Don't do to me what you did to Frigeon!" cried Eunicet, shaking his fist at the Fire Wizard. "You turned him into a . . . a . . . a *vegetable*! Locked him off in a boring wilderness! Made him a goody-goody *nonentity*!"

"Still . . ." Flarman considered.

"No! Kill me! Destroy me! I couldn't stand being anything else but what I've made of myself!"

"You deserve that fate," Flarman flared.

For a long moment the two old enemies glared at each other.

Neither blinked.

Flarman at last said, "*Right!* I'm going to inflict you on a certain very tough old gentleman, way over in Far Southwest. He'll be glad of some help digging out of the mess your friend Frigeon made of his life and of his country. I mean the man Pillow."

"Never heard of him!" snapped the prisoner "Pillow? Soft-headed and soft-hearted, I'll wager!"

"You won't get around this Pillow easily! Strict old bird, but firm and fair. And you might learn to like growing oranges, limes, grapefruit, and lemons. Might make a worthier man of you, after all!

"No, I won't take your memories away from you. I *want* you to remember everything, especially this: This is your *absolute* last chance, Eunicet! Backslide one more time and I know some Near Immortal keepers who'll watch you very closely, every minute of every day . . . and night, too. The Stone Warriors'll be pleased to keep you close prisoner for at least as long as they were imprisoned in their glacier!"

"I had nothing to do with that!"

"Granted . . . but the Stones owe the Fellowship a favor. And they are strong, hard, determined, honorable beings. Your choice! Oranges and lemons . . . or quarrying blue gabbro for building houses and paving roads forever, up in the frozen Northland?"

"Well . . . given the choice . . . I'll pick oranges," Eunicet muttered.

Before he could change his change his mind, Flarman snapped his
fingers three times and the deepest cellar under Wizards'
High was suddenly empty and silent.

"Ought to get Bryarmote to give me a tour of this
place," Flarman muttered to himself. "More extensive than
I ever imagined! Typical of a Dwarf, I guess. Digging and
tunneling is their greatest joy!"

He retraced his steps to the entrance to the labyrinth.
Stepping through a solid-seeming stone wall, he was in his
Workshop. The sun was just peering over Near (or Far,
depending on how you approached it) Ridge to the east.

Three thousand miles west, as a Wizard flies, Eunicet
awoke in a neat little bungalow on the brow of a low,
grassy hill overlooking a sparkling, blue lake, and sur-
rounded by acres and acres of twelve-foot-tall, glossy-
leafed trees in perfectly straight rows, liberally hung with
small, round, green fruits.

"Oranges?" Eunicet exclaimed.

"Fix yourself a hearty breakfast," said a voice from the
open door. "And I'll show you how to tend these trees so
the fruit'll be regular, firm, and sweet when we pick them
next winter. I am Pillow, by the way."

The retired General stepped into the room. He eyed the
false Duke of Dukedom carefully, head to one side.

"Work!" cried Eunicet. "Me? *Work?*"

"No, not if you want to forego eating," Pillow chuckled
good-naturedly. "Hot sun and good, sweet rain in season.
There's a great deal of pruning, spraying, and tending to
do."

Eunicet groaned aloud but, realizing he hadn't had a
thing to eat for three days, he rose, pulled on the coarse
work-smock and heavy sandals laid out beside his cot,
quickly ate his breakfast, and went out to learn how to
cultivate citrus trees.

■   ■   ■

"Why is it sailors don't like fish?" Thornwood complained as he baited a hook with a bit of chum.

"Sailors? Fishermen, too, for that matter." Queen Lorianne laughed, delighted. "But all sorts of good people love fish. Fishing is a noble occupation! To be a good Duke of Dukedom, M'Lord, you must never forget you were once a humble Seaman. And I must remember I was a fisherman's niece who can bait her own hooks."

"So do it! And we'll broil our catch over there on the grassy bank under that banyan . . . is that right? Banyan? And invite your uncle and aunt to dine with us. I learned enough cookery from an old friend of mine named Blue Teakettle."

"Great idea!" cried his fiancée. "An engagement banquet!"

Thornwood took a long moment to share a kiss with the lovely Queen of the Parambit. Then he had to turn his attention to his fishline, which was jerking frantically in his hands.

Marget led her son to a rustic bench under a rose tree in the garden of her palace in Faerie. She sat and waved for Ben to join her.

"My only *complaint*, my only *misgiving*, my darling, is that you chose to leave your father and me without notice. We could have helped you . . ."

"But don't you see, Mama?" Ben said quickly. "I didn't *want* help. I wanted to do it alone!"

"But, think, my beautiful son! Did you do it all alone?"

"Well . . . I did have help, of course."

"Then why deprive your parents of the pleasure of sharing your Venture? Oh, I admit I would have worried and fussed a bit. What's a mother supposed to do, anyway? But I'd have agreed, in the end. You had no need to go without our blessing."

Ben sat scuffing the toe of his left boot in the diamond dust of the pathway.

"The duty of a monarch," Marget continued after a moment, "is to make his concerns his people's concerns. That's all I say. You were remiss in not allowing your parents, whether Queen or common housewife, a part of your Questioning."

"Questing!" Ben said with a broad, brilliant smile.

"No, Bronze Owl was correct. The proper term is 'Questioning.' Next time . . . ?"

"I'll talk it over with you and Papa. Because I really want to!"

"Good Prince and son!" laughed the Queen-mother. "Now go and try on the new shoes I had made for you. Diamond buckles . . . in case you go off again and need the cash in hand."

Marbleheart shoved hard with his webbed hind toes and shot to the surface of Sea. His head broke water and he found the chill northern wind bracing, invigorating, and smelling of salt tang and Sea birds.

In fact, a large flock of grey-and-white northern Seagulls exploded into the air at the sight of the Sea Otter in their midst, crying raucously, "Thief! Thief! Robber! Egg-napper! 'Ware! 'Ware!"

"Oh, poof!" Marbleheart yelled after them. "Poof, woof, and piffle!"

But he had to admit that the thought of a few soft-boiled eggs and a filet or two of tender, tasty herring would serve well for breaking his long, wet fast. Boats and ships and bedsteads were all very well, but for the best of Seagoing, he thought, Otter-power was best. It saved trouble and time.

He swam smoothly and swiftly toward busy Perthside, then Trunkety Town . . . and then home to Wizards' High.

"*Always* time for a good yarn and a happy ending!" chuckled the Otter, waving to an outward-bound square-rigger under full ordinary sail, headed for . . . who knew where?